"VOWS ARE WHA

Brock caressed her shoulders with gentle hands. Seduced by his touch, Maddie leaned dangerously into the solid length of his body. "You are what I want, completely."

What if he meant that, even a little? It would not matter, she told herself. She would not belong to any man ever again, especially not a treacherous one.

"I'm here to be your mistress, Brock. Take me now, tomorrow and every other night for six months. During that time, I will be yours completely. But I will not marry you."

Brock's jaw tightened as he grasped her arms in a tight grip. Her heart beat faster yet at the feel of his warm, lean body—and full arousal—heavy against her.

"You will marry me, Maddie. I will come here every night to seduce you until you do. But I won't make love to you until you agree to be my wife."

The hard glitter of his green gaze told Maddie he was deadly determined. He was going to seduce her without making love to her? A dozen half-complete images flashed through her mind of Brock holding her, all wanton, making her yearn for his touch. She stared at him, inexplicably intrigued. And scared to death he could succeed. . . .

Books by Shelley Bradley

ONE WICKED NIGHT

"Brothers in Arms" Series
HIS LADY BRIDE
HIS STOLEN BRIDE
HIS REBEL BRIDE

A CHRISTMAS PROMISE
STRICTLY SEDUCTION
STRICTLY FORBIDDEN
(coming September 2002)

STRICTLY SEDUCTION

SHELLEY BRADLEY

ZEBRA BOOKS
Kensington Publishing Corp.
http://www.kensingtonbooks.com

ZEBRA BOOKS are published by

Kensington Publishing Corp.
850 Third Avenue
New York, NY 10022

All Kensington Titles, Imprints, and Distributed Lines are available at special quantity discounts for bulk purchases for sales promotion, premiums, fund-raising, educational or institutional use.

Special book excerpts or customized printings can also be created to fit specific needs. For details, write or phone the office of the Kensington Special Sales Manager: Kensington Publishing Corp., 850 Third Avenue, New York, NY 10022. Attn. Special Sales Department. Phone: 1-800-221-2647.

First Printing: April 2002
10 9 8 7 6 5 4 3 2 1

Printed in the United States of America

To my agent, Deidre Knight, for listening, encouraging, and believing.

And for the wonderful ladies of the Red River chapter of Romance Writers of America in Wichita Falls, Texas. I treasure your friendship, laughter, and unerring support.

ONE

London, March 1834

"My late husband's bills have been paid? D—did I hear you correctly?" Madeline Sedgewick stuttered.

"You did," Mr. Hockelspeck said, mouth thin with irritation.

Maddie stared at the gaunt, bald-pated tailor, blinking once, then again, in shock. Paid? Truly? By whom?

If it is true, do you care? a voice inside her whispered.

To assure herself that Hockelspeck hadn't engaged in some awful joke, Maddie opened her reticule with deceptive calm and withdrew a few bills—the bulk of her remaining funds. "I need not pay you this installment, then?"

The tailor sighed impatiently. "It's quite unnecessary."

Dear Lord, her debt *was* paid! Jubilant, she grabbed her daughter's small hand and squeezed. Though Aimee was too young to understand, Maddie wanted to share her joy.

For so long, she had hoped—prayed—for some miracle to save her from her late husband's obligations. With this fortunate turn of events, relief surged so powerfully within her, it nearly made her limp. True, the amount owed to the odious Hockelspeck was not the sum of her debt, but it was a start.

Her nightmare might soon end! Perhaps she could make

a few repairs to Ashdown Manor, buy Aimee new shoes—a million needs came to mind—

"Perhaps I should explain, my lady," Mr. Hockelspeck intoned, interrupting her daydreams. "You see, a man paid me. To be precise, he bought your debt."

Maddie frowned, turning the skeletal man's words over in her mind. The syllables tumbled about until comprehension exploded in a cold rush.

She still owed *someone* more money than she could possibly repay. But who would buy her debt? And why?

After two years of saving every farthing, of quietly letting servants go one by one, of selling her late mother's prized furnishings, of seeing her sweet daughter silently suffer the winter chills of fireless hearths so she might slowly pay off each of her late husband's demanding creditors, now some stranger had purchased her notes—without a word to her.

Who would do such a thing? And what would she do if her new creditor demanded immediate repayment in full?

Maddie frowned. The few remaining members of her family had refused to aid her when asked, her father having alienated them long before he died. Her late husband's relations had all departed, save his sister Roberta, who had never welcomed her into the family. None of her acquaintances knew of her dire financial situation. She had struggled to keep that secret, hiding in Hampstead Heath behind widow's weeds.

So who would buy her notes? Cold worry clawed at her, as well as fear of what the stranger would demand.

"Are you happy, Mama?" Aimee asked beside her.

Bending to her daughter, Maddie smothered her anxiety and smoothed the blond curls around the four-year-old's pink-cheeked face. "Of course, sweeting."

"Now, you must excuse me. I have *paying* customers . . ."

As the odious tailor turned away, Maddie stuttered, "Wa—wait. You're certain there is no mistake?"

He stiffened, clearly affronted. "None whatsoever."

Maddie pasted on her best smile to hide the desperation and fear tearing at her hard-won composure. She didn't like mysteries; good rarely came from them.

"Forgive me," she murmured. "It's simply that I cannot credit who would buy such a debt and not present his terms to me. Can you not give me his name?"

"Indeed, I cannot. He asked very particularly to remain anonymous. However, I feel certain he intends to present himself to you soon."

That ominous note did little to cool the scorch of Maddie's anxiety. This time when the haughty tailor turned away she made no protest, and left instead to visit her next creditor.

When each reported the same mysterious gentleman had bought her debts, the foreboding deep in Maddie's gut told her something was indeed frighteningly amiss.

Two weeks later, spring hovered a breath away. And Maddie still had no notion who or what to pay, and when. Desperation urged her to believe the gesture had been the benevolence of some nameless saint who expected no recompense. Fear told her differently.

In the interim, Maddie had purchased Aimee a new pair of much-needed shoes, and Aunt Edith had persuaded her to splurge on a chicken for stew to celebrate her freedom from Mr. Hockelspeck's incessant demands. Maddie didn't have the heart to worry her elderly aunt about the money she still owed and the enigmatic stranger to whom she owed it.

At a sudden knock on her door, she frowned and gazed at the mantel clock. Nine o'clock in the evening; a very late hour for visitors, especially in quiet Hampstead. Setting aside Aimee's frayed frock, which she had been mending, Maddie strode to the parlor door.

In the hall, Matheson's heels clicked across the floor, and Maddie's stomach twisted, decidedly unsettled. She cursed the fact she could not see her visitor 'round the corner. Though creditors had ceased hounding her, she still felt the shameful sting of owing with no ability to pay, worried her anonymous creditor would appear suddenly, demanding what she could not give.

After a low-voiced exchange, Matheson approached.

"Who is it?" she whispered, then bit her lip fretfully.

"A gentleman who wishes to remain anonymous."

As she had suspected. Fear rushed through her in a dousing chill. She drew in a deep, trembling breath, knowing the moment she had dreaded had unflinchingly arrived, and she must face it.

"Is he anyone I know?" she whispered to her butler.

"I'm afraid he is," drawled a deep voice beyond the parlor's portal.

It was a voice Maddie never, *ever* thought to hear again.

Mouth gaping open, she reached for the wall in a sudden, dizzy lurch. Shock invaded with another insidious chill as she peeked past Matheson, hoping her ears had deceived her.

They had not. Brock Taylor had returned to Ashdown Manor.

As bold as could be, here stood the cad who had broken her heart five years earlier, when he'd left her to seek his fortune. Through gossip and reputation, she knew he had indeed found it. Now refined and wealthy—and more handsome than ever—he stood in her foyer wearing a stylish green coat and a faintly wry smile.

"Brock." The whisper fell from Maddie's numb lips.

"How kind of you to remember me, *Lady Wolcott.*"

He pronounced her married title with contempt, matched by the disdain in his familiar, vivid eyes. She swallowed, losing the battle to curb her racing thoughts. Why was he here? What did he want? Had *he,* of all people, really bought her debt? She fought for her next breath and beat down the encroaching panic.

Brock turned to her butler. "Your name?"

"Mine? It is Matheson, sir."

Brock smiled, the urbane charm he'd refined to an art dominating his strong features. "Splendid. Matheson, fetch your mistress a spot of tea. She looks unwell."

Her butler sent her a measuring stare. "Indeed, sir."

Matheson quit the room before she could object, leaving her alone with the man she'd sworn to hate for the rest of her life.

"Why have you come?" she managed to force out.

She looked up a long way, past broader-than-ever shoulders and a wide mouth that bespoke sin, to search his face for clues. An enigmatic green stare met her gaze, giving away nothing.

"Have you no kind words for an old . . . friend?"

She gaped at him, still scarcely able to believe Brock Taylor stood in her parlor five years after betraying her. Of all the things she'd envisioned saying to him if she ever saw the cad again, not a single one came to mind.

"Friend?" she retorted sharply.

"May I sit?" He did so without waiting for her reply, dwarfing the ancient rosewood armchair. "Perhaps you should sit as well. You really do look pale."

Though Brock's voice had acquired a definite upper-crust clip, one of the few qualities that had not changed about the scoundrel was his smile. The wicked tilt of that wide mouth remained as potent and beguiling as ever. Once upon a time she had fallen prey to the charm of his grin—to her misfortune.

Reminding herself that she was no longer a green girl, Maddie pushed aside her foolish observations. Desperately, she sought calm as she faced Brock. "Matheson said you are the anonymous gentleman. Is that so?"

"Yes."

His inexorable reply hit her like a blow to the chest. Legs weak beneath her, she tread slowly to the sofa and sank down to its threadbare cushions. "Why? Eight thousand pounds is a great deal of money."

He shrugged. "Or not, depending."

Disliking the sound of that dismissive remark, Maddie fixed narrowed eyes upon him. "Depending upon what?"

"The repayment one receives."

"I knew I could count on you to demand repayment." *You opportunistic blackguard.*

The words were out before Maddie could stop them. But as she clenched her hands into angry fists, she refused to regret them. Damn him for buying her debt! Damn him twice for taking her heart and her innocence five years ago, then leaving her in his quest for wealth. Damn him to eternity for coming here with the notion of collecting more.

A faint apology tinged his melting smile. "I'm not running a charitable organization."

"I did not ask you to buy my late husband's debts."

With a slight nod, he acknowledged her truth. "But now that I have, you owe me."

Fury seethed inside her, like a beast fighting its chain. "And you want your precious money from me?"

He paused. "I want repayment."

How dare he make demands of her in light of his deplorable past deeds! He was no gentleman . . . but then, he never had been. She had learned that the hard way.

Stewing, Maddie stared at her unwanted visitor. Brock had always been clever, and she sensed she must play his game now to ascertain why he had bought her debt, confronted her, threatened her peace.

Matheson appeared suddenly with the tea. As Maddie poured, the scent of the brew tinged with milk drifted up to her, calming her to a manageable level. Taking a sip, she dismissed the servant, then clutched the warm cup in her cold hands.

"If I had eight thousand pounds," she bit out, "I would

have paid my creditors already. So you see, immediate repayment is impossible."

At her challenge, he crossed his arms over his wide chest and nodded. But the arrogant, presumptuous cad said nothing at all about the biggest shame of her life!

Or one of them, anyway.

"In fact," she continued, "I believe you owe me a thousand pounds to replace the funds you accepted from my father."

Raising a dark brow, he shot her a surprised look. "He told you about our . . . agreement?"

"Of course. He told me the very night you left that he had offered you money to abandon me." Her fists clenched in her lap, hating him still for that. "And that you quickly accepted it with a smile."

"Abandon?" He gave her a mocking laugh. "You didn't suffer long, Lady Wolcott." Again he spoke her married title with disdain. "It's of no consequence, anyway. I returned that money to your father three months later."

"That is untrue! Papa said he never saw a farthing of that money again."

"And naturally you believed everything your father told you." Brock's voice held a faint note of derision. He shrugged. "If you want your thousand pounds, I shall give it to you. I'll even grant you eight percent interest. You still owe"—he paused, his gaze cast absently to the ceiling—"six thousand, seven hundred eighty-three pounds and twenty pence."

Five years of choking resentment exploded with the force of a volcano. "What is it you want of me?"

"A choice, Maddie. A simple choice."

Simple? Nothing about Brock Taylor had ever been simple.

Anxiety made her belly churn. Or perhaps anger drove her. Uncertain, she met his gaze with a wary glare. "What sort of choice?"

He shrugged casually. But Maddie caught the tension latent in his neck, his shoulders. Definitely this decision would be anything but simple.

"If you cannot repay me in full . . ."

"You know I cannot," she said through clenched teeth.

Brock rose from the armchair, the muscles of his hard thighs flexing beneath chocolate-hued breeches. Maddie chastised herself for noticing as he paced closer, brushing the muslin of her gray skirt as he walked past. He turned, faced her. Their gazes locked.

"Then you must marry me."

Brock's stare penetrated her bravado, seeking to see into her soul. Maddie stared back, stunned beyond words. He must be jesting, surely. But his square, solemn face said quite the opposite. Her teacup fell from her hand to the carpet with a soft thud.

Fresh fury made her whole body tremble. How could he even suggest they wed—especially since he had abandoned her five years ago? She had no wish to wed anyone, but if she had to choose between Brock and a snake, she would hope the snake would be content to share her quiet country life.

Because of Brock, Maddie had suffered doubts about her moral character. She had worried her past choices would someday haunt her small but close family. She had learned heartache.

Most frightening now, the law gave a man complete power over a woman and her body. A husband could beat and belittle his wife without repercussion. Her late husband had plied his own form of torture mercilessly during their three-year union. She refused to place herself in that hell again, especially with a man who behaved as if he hated her, who had proven in myriad ways that he had never cared. . . .

She could not wed Brock Taylor. Ever.

"That terrible idea—that is my simple choice?" she spat. "And if I refuse?"

"You will be a debtor, and your options will be those of most debtors. Very unpleasant, indeed, if you ask me."

Unpleasant? What could be more unpleasant than owing the ruthless Brock Taylor nearly seven thousand pounds?

Debtor's prison.

"The Fleet?" she asked, incredulous.

Certainly even he wasn't that ruthless.

He shrugged, his face mildly apologetic. "It is a common fate, is it not?"

Apparently she had misjudged Brock again—a nasty habit for sure. He *was* that ruthless, God help her.

Maddie grappled for a retort—and a way to pull her chin off her chest—unable to believe he expected her to select either alternative in his devil's bargain. Fleet Prison would mean squalor, hunger, and indefinite internment. Marriage to Brock would mean loss of autonomy and a legal servitude she knew too well. The prospect made her shudder.

"You cannot mean it." She gritted her teeth to keep the pleading note from her voice.

Brock, looking every inch a wealthy man from the rich burgundy cravat of silk about his neck to the supple leather boots with their shiny toecaps, simply raised a brow. "I never say anything I do not mean."

Liar! Five years ago he'd uttered many untruths. Bitterness iced her anger to cold rage. He had promised to return and marry her. Instead, he had left an hour after taking her virginity. She had never heard from him again . . . until now.

Fury surged anew. "Marrying you . . . it—it's inconceivable."

"Since I conceived the idea, I must disagree."

His smooth voice chafed her like the coarsest wool, rousing her temper.

"You are enjoying my distress, aren't you?" she accused.

Brock only shot her an enigmatic half-smile in response.

Fists trembling at her sides, Maddie stared, refusing to give way. Her gaze found the familiar wave of his mahogany hair, as thick and sleek as ever. Bitterly she noted that his mocking green eyes perfectly matched the costly double-breasted coat that fit snugly across his broad chest.

Purposely, she raised her chin, glaring at him as if he were an insect. "Marry *you?*"

"Is it the idea of marrying your former stable hand you object to?"

"I object to the entire idea of marriage, but particularly to you. Why would you desire such a ridiculous end?"

"I doubt you find your other option more appealing."

He paced closer, over the threadbare carpet. She inhaled his spicy, musky scent with her next breath. It brought forth a surge of long-buried memories of kisses in the hay and racing hearts. The reminiscence mixed with anger in a potent rush. She could not deny that she'd loved him once . . . and she hated him all the more for it now.

"Of course, I could be wrong," he continued.

His tone mocked his words. A man that arrogant would never believe himself wrong. Brock was more confident than most, for he had always been more clever. And manipulative.

A mental picture of all she imagined Fleet Prison would be rose in her mind, almost too horrible to contemplate. Darkness. Dankness. Nowhere to sleep. Nothing to eat. No way out.

Blackness floated at the edge of her vision.

Stifling her fear, Maddie shot him a frosty glare, hoping it hid her anxiety. She knew him well enough to realize he would only feed on it. "Perhaps you *are* wrong."

Brock shrugged, as if conceding the point, then moved closer. With his nearness, her memory flashed another image of their stolen intimacies in the stable years before. Breathless kisses shared with urgent sighs, nurtured by the love and dreams in her heart, all of which he had trampled to pursue his burning ambition for fortune.

"The choice is completely yours," he said.

Since Maddie had no family with the means to pay her debts, she knew her incarceration might be long, stretching into years.

But marriage to Brock would last the rest of her life.

Clearly, he had honed his ruthless edge to razor sharpness in the last five years. Resisting the urge to rail, which she knew would only provoke the predator in him, she thrust her chin forward and confronted him. "You planned this."

"How? It is your misfortune your late husband liked drinking and gaming beyond his means. I had no hand in that."

"Except to buy up his debt," she tossed back, ire boiling like a water in a hot kettle. "How like you to take advantage of my misfortune."

His expression never changed. "A smart man takes advantage of every opportunity."

And Maddie knew well he saw opportunity everywhere, even under the skirts of an untried girl. A blast of resentment swept through her. The blackguard had nearly ruined her life when he had taken her innocence, along with her father's money, and left. She would not become his opportunity again.

"Stop these games. What do you truly want? I doubt you paid my creditors a staggering eight thousand pounds for my hand because you harbor any feeling for me."

"No?" He shrugged evasively. "Believe what you like."

She never knew what to believe where Brock was concerned. Not five years ago, not now. She had believed in him once, in his brilliant mind, in his strong hands, all to her detriment. That the passionately driven boy who had labored in her father's stables had beaten the odds and become a shrewd man of means only made him more frightening.

"I would find it easier to believe the truth, if I knew it. Blast you, what do you want from me?"

A thin smile turned up the corners of his mouth as he

approached her again with measured steps. "Now there is a dangerous question."

Maddie ignored the suggestive note in his velvet voice. Rooted in place by anxiety, she watched him pace a circle around her, his fingers brushing an aging side table next to her. She shivered.

Brock had a scheme in mind. He always did. Why was he torturing her before revealing his plan? For his own perverse pleasure, no doubt.

Suddenly, he stopped before her, lifting his green gaze to her face with stunning force. In his eyes, she saw scalding desire and the determination to have her. Maddie felt the power of that connection in her sudden lack of breath. His next words confirmed her fears.

"We were compatible lovers, Maddie-cake."

She hissed an intake of breath. "Do *not* call me that!"

Her memory retrieved more images of their spring together, the first time he'd nibbled her tingling neck and whispered that endearment. An ache she'd thought long dead flickered inside her.

"You used to like that name," he whispered. "And I liked saying it." His eyes burned with heat, with the remembrance of their brief time as lovers. "Your skin tasted sweet as a pastry. Hmm. I wonder, does it still?"

Maddie turned her back on Brock and drew in a calming breath. He was playing with her, as a cat does a mouse. He wanted her off balance. She must not give him the satisfaction of recalling anything about that night, particularly not the feel of his callused palms touching her everywhere. Focusing on his betrayal and abandonment would better serve her.

She whirled to face him, again fortified. "Certainly you do not expect me to believe you plotted to buy up all my debts and created some elaborate scheme of marriage simply for the purpose of taking me to your bed."

He raised a dark brow. "Why not?"

"That is not the way you think. It is not logical."

"I am a wealthy man now, Maddie. I can afford to be illogical, if I choose."

Maddie saw his hand coming, knew he intended to touch her, and couldn't move. Brock caressed her face with his fingers. Fire screamed across her skin. She flinched at the contact, but he did not let her go, damn him. Instead, he cupped her cheek.

Her heart beat like an anvil, kicking the wall of her chest as he traced a torturously slow line down her jaw. Sensation burst through her at his touch. She could not escape his gaze. Her mind told her that he merely played a game, one that would affect the rest of her life. She could not afford to be his toy.

Jerking her head away, Maddie broke the contact. "If it's a companion you seek, crawl back to wherever you came from and buy yourself a two-pence whore."

He raised a sharp brow. "Tsk, tsk, Maddie-cake. You must know that doesn't suit me anymore. I expect only the finest, and I expect it on my terms. Now"—he brushed her collarbone with the pad of his thumb—"I choose you."

Meeting his stare measure for measure, Maddie willed her racing heart to slow. Brock clearly had other ideas, his gaze suggesting they share the stolen intimacies of the past and much more. Her stomach clenched in what could only be fear. After all the hurt he had heaped upon her, she would never respond to him as a woman again.

Brock gripped her wrist in his hot palm, then slid his thumb over the pulse point, a slow journey that wound to the center of her tingling palm and back. As the beat quickened beneath his touch, he smiled. Maddie gasped for her next breath.

Blast it all! His touch could still elicit a response in her. She found that fact humiliating.

"Release me," she demanded, pulling on her wrist.

After a moment's resistance, he let go. "Once we're wed, Maddie, I will never release you."

"You have no reason to want this marriage!"

Brock crossed powerful arms over his chest and sent her a long stare, a hot stare, designed to rattle her. "Of course I do."

Maddie crossed her arms over her own chest, refusing to be intimidated. "I do not believe you're willing to bind yourself to me for the rest of your life to—well, simply for . . ."

"Sex?" he provided helpfully, voice low with mischief. "It will be interesting to learn if you still blush when I undress you."

Despite herself, Maddie's mouth fell open. She tried to sputter a reply, but the shock and an odd shiver sweeping through her held her tongue.

Brock laughed. "Somehow I think you will."

He looked pleased with himself. Maddie wanted to hit him—hard. "Stop dallying and tell me what the hell you want."

"My, my, my. What shocking language, Lady Wolcott. What would the ladies of the *ton* think?"

"That you deserved such a slur and more!" She clenched frustrated fists at her sides. "Now answer me."

"All right." Turning away, he paced again, passing an armchair, gazing into the empty hearth. Long moments passed before he spoke again.

"There is one thing money has not been able to buy me: entrée into society." He glanced at her before pacing again. "I count some of the wealthiest lords in England as my clients. I've helped them regain their fortunes with well-placed financial advice. They come to my office willing to pay me a hefty fee for my guidance, for connections to lucrative investments. Some have even begged." Brock ceased traveling the floor and faced her. "Those same men ignore me if they see me on the street. I rival their fortunes, sometimes exceed them, yet they will not recognize me."

Maddie was not surprised. Brock, a self-educated man born to the serving class, had little hope of that. The *ton* fraternized only with those who possessed the proper bloodlines.

"They never will," she said with smug triumph.

"Wrong. They *will* acknowledge me. They will invite me into their homes, to their balls."

"You cannot force people to like you," she pointed out.

"I hardly care if they do." A wicked grin curved his mouth. The challenge clearly invigorated him.

Did he see her as a challenge too?

"Let them loathe me," he went on. "But I want them to accept my wealth, to realize I made each farthing using my instinct and skill. That will enhance my business. To gain their initial notice socially, I need you."

Brock's plan suddenly became clear to Maddie. The realization that it might indeed work sapped her of any hope that he had been trifling with her for the sport of it.

"So by wedding me, you think to change their opinion?" She fought the quiver in her voice.

"Not precisely. But with a well-born wife, say . . . an earl's daughter, the *ton* could not ignore me quite so easily. The doors of my clients—and their friends—would be open to me."

Anger burst through her. *No!* She would not sacrifice her independence for his ambition. Nor could she conceive of placing her body legally in his possession. Instinct told her he was not the same man who had taken her in a sweet but hurried loving once upon a time. From everything gossip said, this man was feral, noted for his ruthlessness to his enemies. She did not expect he would be any different with her. And after what she'd endured with Colin—the vicious taunts, his vigilant stalking, to that final assault—Brock might even be worse than anything she had encountered in marriage.

Maddie refused to let him use her again, to coerce her

back into the legal hell of matrimony. The fact he would even suggest it sent her temper careening.

"So you seek to buy a well-born wife." She let contempt roll off her tongue, which she followed with a shrill laugh. "Tongues will wag about our reasons for wedding."

"Let them. That will not change the fact we're married."

"I will not marry you."

In a handful of long strides, he was across the room, his hot green stare drilling into her from a scant few inches away. "Are you certain? Think very carefully."

Fleet was a terrible place, Maddie acknowledged, squeezing her eyes shut. It was infested with vermin and lice. She would be made to exist on one tiny bowl of flour-based slop each day.

Maddie pushed aside the vision and the fear it created, knowing he only sought to frighten her.

"Besides," he continued, coming closer again, "you have more than yourself to consider. What of your daughter?"

Maddie felt her eyes widen, her face drain of blood. A buzzing roared in her head as the blackness returned to her vision. Dear God, when had he learned of Aimee? How?

"And though your late husband was stupid, I doubt he ever intended a debtor's fate for his only child."

Oh, God. Aimee would go to prison with her, or be transported to a workhouse where children were forced to labor under cruel conditions—sometimes to death. But wedding Brock would not ensure Aimee's welfare either. Certainly a man ruthless enough to seduce an innocent young woman for financial gain would think nothing of destroying a child's life.

Fighting tears, she drew in a shaky breath. Hatred pounded fiercely in her every muscle, every bone. "Of course not. I love my daughter."

A fleeting smile softened his features for the merest of moments. "I never doubted you would be a wonderful mother. I will require your answer in a week."

With that, Brock turned away. Maddie watched his long strides eat up the room until he reached the door. She wanted to call him back. She wanted to ask if he would truly subject her and Aimee to the horrors of either prison or marriage.

But she already knew he would, gladly. Somehow she had to stop him.

The clock hanging in the hall chimed midnight when Brock returned home. Dismissing the butler, he jerked off his gloves before slapping them down on a convenient hall table.

He stalked into his study, only to find his father waiting there. Jack had never been long on patience. Brock supposed it was too much to hope that the man would leave him in peace after tonight's debacle with Maddie.

"Well?" his father prompted. "What happened?"

Sighing, Brock sank into his chair, wondering when this day would end. "I think it's safe to say she hates me completely."

Jack's disapproval of the plan had never been more apparent than in the scowl he currently wore. "What did you expect?"

Good question. Brock supposed he'd hoped she would be pleased to see him, or perhaps beg his forgiveness for marrying Viscount Wolcott so soon after pledging her love to him. Something other than staring at him like a pile of refuse she wished to God she'd never shared her innocence with.

Lowering his aching head into his hands, he gave a bitter grunt. "Naturally, she resisted the idea of wedded bliss."

"You've backed her into a corner," Jack, ever the voice of reason, pointed out.

"She had the nerve to say I abandoned her. What was I to do, stand around like a lovesick swain while she gloated over her marriage to the socially superior Colin Sedgewick?

Damn it, I nearly broke my back to be worthy of that woman."

Jack shrugged. "Did you correct her misconception?"

"Why should I? That explanation would only make me look more the fool. She doesn't want to marry me any more now than she did then."

Not that he wanted to marry her for the same reasons. Five years ago, he had believed she loved him, perhaps as much as he had adored her. Today, she was simply business—with a little revenge mixed in for pleasure.

Still, her sudden marriage to Colin Sedgewick five years ago had proven she felt nothing for him. She had only seen him as an unworthy admirer, foolishly in love. Trusting and naïve, he had believed that a young lady of quality who gave a man her body had also given her heart. After more than one liaison with women of Maddie's station, he knew better.

"You can't make Lady Wolcott love you, son."

Stiffly, Brock rose. "You mistake the matter. I have no interest in her love. Whatever I once felt for Maddie died the day she married Sedgewick. But she owes me."

"Does she?" Jack raised a graying brow.

"Stop trying to convince me that she was young and indecisive, or easily swayed by her father. She amused herself with me, likely plotting to marry Sedgewick all the while. Tonight, she even insisted I again repay the thousand pounds her father gave me!"

Jack chuckled.

Brock frowned at his father. "You would find that funny, you wretch."

"The girl always had spirit."

"Girl?" Not anymore, he thought with a long sigh.

Reluctant desire washed over him. Girl was the very last description Brock would give of Madeline Sedgewick. Part of him had hoped in the last five years that she'd lost the bloom of her beauty. Instead, she'd improved with age. At three and twenty, she no longer held a hint of girlishness.

From the soft curve of her breasts and the ripe swell of her hips to the determination in those amazing gray eyes, she was a stunning woman. He'd almost hated her for arousing him in the first twenty seconds of their meeting.

"Her papa must have told Lady Madeline about the money," his father guessed.

"Yes, old Avesbury did. So much for our secret gentlemen's agreement."

"I suspect he never considered you much of a gentleman," Jack said. "Besides, accepting the payment was a mistake."

"I considered it a loan, and it gave me my start. I took it with an eye to my future." The future he had planned to share with Maddie until she had married a titled popinjay.

"It wouldn't surprise me if old Avesbury convinced his daughter you took the money for its intended purpose."

Brock frowned. "She believes exactly that. But I had so little choice. No man in his right mind would have turned down that money. With it, I would have returned to marry Maddie in a matter of months, not years, if she hadn't leg-shackled herself to Sedgewick."

"So what now?" his father asked.

Brock shrugged. "I gave her a week to decide her fate."

The money she owed wasn't important. Nearly seven thousand pounds was more than cheese parings and candle ends, but he could afford it. For her deception, however, she owed him her status.

"No doubt she appreciates her options," Jack said wryly.

Brock knew Maddie had appreciated nothing about his visit. Worse, he had been unable to dismiss her fear-filled eyes from his mind since.

"Piss off," Brock shot back glumly.

"Charming as ever," Jack taunted, laughing. "Oh, before I forget, Mr. Stephenson popped in while you were out."

Brock rubbed his hands together, relishing the topic of business. It engendered no anger or guilt or other misplaced sentiment. "Did our fine engineer have good news?"

"Indeed. He said he has extended the frames of the engine rearward and added a trailing axle behind a much larger firebox. He said you would be well pleased because rail travel will be safer and smoother. Cargo haul will be much faster."

Brock smiled in triumph at the realization that they would beat their competition in every way. "He is a brilliant engineer!"

"Because you pay him to be." Jack chuckled. "So, have you given more thought to whom you'll approach about investing in the railroad, now that you have this wonderful engine?"

The proposed T & S Railroad was his life these days, the passion that would take him from merely wealthy to sinfully rich. Recently, however, it had also become a sticky situation. Besides the fact he'd sunk nearly every farthing he had ever made into this venture, he needed Maddie—or, more exactly, her land. Hence, the largest reason for his offer of marriage now, after five years apart.

In researching the idea of a passenger railroad between London and Birmingham, he had mapped out all the necessary land, particularly areas that would shut down competing canals and avoid his competitor's lands. To his shock, Maddie owned a parcel in Warwickshire. However, her father had left it to her in retainer, in the event she took another husband. It suited Brock's purpose well that she couldn't legally sell it herself. Because she would be good for his business, his rising social placement, and the railroad, he planned to be her husband.

Marrying her had nothing to do with love. Nothing at all.

But he would see to it that she wanted him in her bed, and he would give her what she wanted until they were both well sated.

"Brock?" Jack prompted, snapping his fingers. "Investors?"

With a sheepish grimace, Brock returned to the discussion. "I've given the matter a great deal of thought, actually. I've decided to pursue Cropthorne."

Jack's green eyes, a mirror of his own, nearly popped from their sockets. "The Duke of Cropthorne? Now I know you've gone mad. The man won't speak to you."

Brock rolled a pen across his desk, the challenge of the prey igniting his fire for the hunt again. "Come now, where is your faith in me? Have I been wrong yet?"

Jack scowled. "You are too cocksure by half."

"Not without reason. I've researched this thoroughly. One of his mines collapsed recently. He was forced to shut them all down."

"The man must have other income."

"Certainly," Brock conceded. "But he also has a doting aunt, a poor clergyman cousin, and two young sisters to support, all of whom adore everything the finest. I heard their modiste's bill last month alone was over a thousand pounds."

Jack nearly choked. "Can women really wear that much clothing?"

Brock shrugged. "The Season is about to begin, and appearances must be maintained."

"What about Lord Belwick? He's a strong competitor for this project. Perhaps he's already approached Cropthorne."

"Not according to my sources," said Brock.

"Even if Belwick hasn't come forward yet, will Cropthorne acknowledge you? He's the upper part of the crust, son."

He flashed his father a grin. "He's roughly my age, so he may be more modern in his thinking about social status than the late duke. He's also said to have a firm head for business and a mind of his own, but none of his papa's nasty scandals."

"Why choose an investor low on his blunt?"

Brock grinned, truly enjoying his work. "For three reasons. First, he doesn't yet feel the pinch, but if he doesn't invest well soon, he will. I think he is wise enough to know that. Second, he's well liked among his peers, despite the family scandals. If I gain his approval, he can open many doors for me. Last, he is a relation of Maddie's. Though Lord Avesbury fell out of favor with the late Cropthorne, I have no reason to suspect the current duke would cut Maddie altogether. Nor, as her husband, would he cut me."

Jack shrugged. "Still, all your work on this railroad will be for naught unless Maddie Sedgewick marries you."

"She will agree to marry me by next week." Brock tossed the pen aside with a confident nod. "She has no choice."

TWO

Maddie could not marry Brock Taylor. Not for any reason. Not now. Not ever.

Yet with so much at stake, how could she afford to refuse?

She clutched her temples, which still throbbed from her sleepless, tension-fraught night, and wandered into the sunny breakfast room. When she entered, she nearly groaned. There, despite the late hour, sat her chatty Aunt Edith, sipping tea with her Indian companion, Vema.

The elderly Edith, ever round and jovial, had adorned herself in vivid pinks and another frivolous hat, a sharp contrast to Vema's muted blue sari and quiet ways. A sedate bun held the Punjabi woman's glossy black hair secure at her nape, the perfect foil for skin the color of well-creamed coffee. The two women had been fast friends since Edith had lived with her cousin's family in Delhi some ten years past.

Though she loved them both, Maddie was in little mood for gossip this morning, the usual accompaniment to the meager breakfast fare at Ashdown Manor. As Maddie tried to tiptoe out of the room, Edith looked up.

"Dear child, do come and join us."

"No, I merely—" Maddie began.

"Nonsense," insisted Edith. "You must come in and sit this moment."

Escape was impossible now. Knowing her aching head

would have to suffer Aunt Edith's well-meaning chatter and Vema's sage sayings, Maddie ambled into the room and sat at the table with a repressed sigh. Vema flashed her a mysterious smile.

"I hear you had a gentleman caller last eve. Gads, not a new creditor, I hope!" said Edith, adjusting upon her head just so an old straw hat decorated with flowers and bees in flight.

Despite the seriousness of the topic and her headache, Maddie suppressed a rueful smile at her aunt's peculiar garb.

"You naughty girl! Do you laugh at my charming hat?"

Maddie cleared her throat and searched for a diplomatic response. "Not at all, dear aunt. Merely thinking how such adornment suits you."

Edith primped the graying hair beneath her unique bonnet. "Indeed, I've had it for some years and still find it just the thing." Her softly lined face turned serious again. "But enough of that. You must tell us of your caller."

Knowing the woman would simply ask questions until she pried the truth from her, Maddie confessed, "He is a creditor, in a sense."

"Whatever do you mean, dear?"

She sighed. "It was Brock Taylor."

Aunt Edith was speechless for fully thirty seconds, an unparalleled feat. "Brock Taylor? *Your* Brock—"

"The very one," Maddie broke in before Edith could finish the distasteful thought that somehow Brock belonged to her. "He bought the remainder of Colin's debt and says he will forgive it—if I agree to wed him."

"Shocking!" Edith exclaimed, her smirk not altogether appalled. "When is the wedding, dear?"

Incredulity swept through Maddie like a brisk winter wind. "Aunt Edith, I cannot marry him. You are no stranger to my past with him, and now the beast wants me for some manner of prized mare he can parade about the *ton*. It is not to be borne."

"And if you refuse him . . . ?"

Reaching for a cup, Maddie pretended interest in pouring tea. She hated confessing her situation to Edith and Verna and despised Brock for putting her in the position of explaining why she would refuse the logical but outlandish proposal.

"If I refuse, he's threatened to see me in debtor's prison, but—"

"Scandalous!" Edith looked well and truly shocked.

"But," Maddie continued through gritted teeth, "I am determined to find another way to repay him. I will not endure the parson's trap with so ruthless a cad."

Colin had been trying enough—the cajoling, followed by cold silences, absurd accusations, and ugly slurs. Frigid, he had called her, along with less polite names that shamed and incensed her at once. Finally, his rage had culminated in one night of violence. Sometimes she swore she could still feel the horror of his grasp and the pain of his fists.

Maddie had felt brutalized and betrayed by him. He had married her knowing she did not love him, knowing her past. Colin had vowed he would be content in their marriage. Naïvely, she had believed they could achieve a respectful, comfortable union. Two terrible years and one horrific night had shown her otherwise. Her husband's death a week after his attack on her had brought only guilty relief that her ordeal had ended.

Through her disastrous union, she'd learned that marrying meant a complete legal surrender of both possessions and body, even her daughter. It was too steep a price to pay to clear her debts. Wedding Brock, a man who had already proven himself without scruples, would be an unthinkable mistake. And if he were to learn the truth about Aimee . . .

God help her then.

"Dear girl, where will you find the means to repay him? They are not within our reach. I fear you must wed him."

Maddie absorbed her aunt's declaration like a kick to her

middle. "You're advising me to marry the man who left me during my most pressing time of need after taking money from my father and making promises he had no intent to keep? His abandonment is the reason I wed the despicable Colin, if you recall."

Edith patted her hand. "Mr. Taylor is offering marriage now. You must take it. He has the funds to keep you well and the ability to keep such funds coming."

Puzzled, Maddie frowned, unable to understand her aunt's uncharacteristic reaction. Pragmatism from the woman who epitomized frivolity?

"Besides," Edith went on, "Aimee is his daughter."

Maddie sucked in an alarmed breath. "A fact he must never discover."

She could only imagine the fury of his response should she tell him the truth now. Although he had taken money to abandon her and used it to seek further fortune, Maddie feared the Brock she had encountered last night would be angry indeed that she had not found him and told him of his daughter.

Besides, Maddie would not give Brock additional leverage to use against her in his ridiculous quest for her hand. Given his financial power, Brock might be able to convince a court that, as Aimee's father, he possessed absolute right to custody of his daughter. He might attempt to remove Aimee from her life completely, scandal be damned. And he would probably succeed; the courts had ignored the rights of mothers for years.

Panic gripped Maddie like a white-knuckled fist about her throat. Having her daughter ripped from her by a rake who didn't love the little girl, who was ruthless enough to force a choice between prison and marriage, would crush her.

Maddie glanced at her aunt and found mischief sparkling in her eyes. Unease prickled along her spine.

"He cannot know about Aimee." Maddie stared pointedly

at Edith. "Ever. Colin and I went to great lengths to record Aimee's birth as being a full six weeks after she was born. We wanted no hint of scandal attached to her."

"There is a Hindu saying," began Vema in her soft singsong voice, " 'All things we desire but do not have are found when we enter that space within the heart; for there abide all desires that are true, though covered by what is false.' "

Maddie stared at the Indian woman, confused at first, then incredulous as comprehension dawned. "You believe I secretly love this man but have convinced myself I do not?"

"If not, why have you never shown interest in another man, even your own husband?" countered Edith.

"Because I learned my lesson the first time."

Edith's expression chastised her. "Come now; you are far too young to put yourself on the shelf. Admit that you have always cared for Mr. Taylor."

Her headache now beating with a vengeance, Maddie stood. "The both of you have gone mad. Truly, truly mad. Too much tea, I am certain." She crossed her arms over her chest. "If I wanted another husband, which I do not, I would certainly look for a man other than Brock Taylor."

"Perhaps." Edith eyed her shrewdly. "But in my long life, I've discovered that the more one protests, the more she desires what she denounces."

Desire Brock? Maddie held a palm to her aching head. She had wanted the terrible man at one time, true. After he had left her five years earlier, it had seemed forever before she could think of anything or anyone but him, much to Colin's irritation. Though Brock had broken her young heart and left her, for some months, perhaps even a year, she had yearned for his return.

Today, she wanted him gone. Forever.

Maddie glared at the two women, a suspicion taking root in her mind. There was one thing this duo loved even more than gossip, and she would not stand for it.

Thrusting her hands on her hips, she stared at them both.

"Save your matchmaking schemes for someone who wants them. I cannot and will not marry that man!"

Edith merely stared at her, her blue eyes deceptively innocent. "As you say, dear."

Afternoon cast the brightest of spring rays through Maddie's parlor window when she slammed her account book shut. If throwing the slim volume against the wall would have netted her different sums, she would have cheerfully succumbed to the temptation, perhaps more than once.

Wearily, she rose from her chair, stretching her neck to ease hours spent hunched over her dwindling accounts. Aimee needed new dresses, and though she was hard on her clothes, Maddie couldn't bring herself to chastise the girl. Aimee deserved childhood innocence, and as much freedom from the cold reality of their finances as Maddie could provide.

Edith's small stipend of fifty pounds a year from her late husband, Mr. Bickham, helped a bit. That, along with the two hundred pounds per year provided by the farm lands her father had left her in Warwickshire, barely kept them in life's necessities.

Biting her lip mercilessly, Maddie felt anxiety grip her. Brock's offer would solve many problems—but create more permanent, dismaying ones.

At a knock on the door, Maddie called out, "Yes?"

"Matheson, my lady," came the servant's crisp voice through the door. "Mr. Taylor has come to call."

Apprehension and anger, along with something fluttery and nervous she didn't want to put a name to, raced through her. How dearly she would love to have Matheson tell the audacious Mr. Taylor that she was not at home. But practicality insisted she do something to bring about compromise in the hope he would settle her debts without marriage.

She sighed, her headache returning. "Show him in and leave us."

"Very good, my lady."

Drawing in a deep breath, Maddie clutched her whirling stomach. Brock Taylor must be made to understand that, no matter what he had grown accustomed to, no matter how ruthless his reputation, she would not succumb to his demands.

The quiet click of the door moments later unnerved her. She glanced up to find her nemesis hovering just inside the room, his gaze focused intently on her.

For a heartbeat, Maddie could not breathe. The room and its tattered drapes faded away until only Brock remained, as if illuminated in a black void. The low buzz in her ears only intensified the hum of awareness swirling through her.

It wasn't the clothing that made him, though the superior cut of his dark blue coat enhanced his aura of power. Nor was it the sheen of his well-trimmed mahogany hair, gleaming with faint brown-red highlights. The potent stare of those green eyes. They captured her. Held her. Made her remember his kisses, the touch of his hands, his fervent whispers of ardor as he joined their bodies fully those five years before.

Drawing in a shaky breath, she let her gaze travel his strong Roman nose, firm, square chin, the skin that was no longer berry-brown but would never be pale enough to please the *ton*. Before she could dwell on the breadth of his chest or the warmth of his hands, she admonished herself and looked away.

"Why have you come?" she blurted.

A wry smile curled the ends of his mouth. "I see you're pleased by my call."

Maddie nibbled at her lip in an effort to hold back biting words. Of course she wasn't pleased. Nothing would bring about that effect except his forgiveness of her debts, followed closely by his exit. However, she must tread cautiously in order to bring about compromise.

"I am pleased, actually. Do sit down."

Gesturing Brock toward the Louis XIV sofa, Maddie seated herself on the farthest armchair, wondering how best to proceed.

"Mr. Taylor," she began, praying he could not hear the quiver in her voice, "in light of our . . . awkward past and our differing lives, I wonder if we might come to some other mutually advantageous arrangement."

"By the awkward past I assume you mean the fact that we were lovers. But, I confess, the differing lives part confounds me. Are you referring to our differences in social standing?"

She was, but the razor edge in his voice warned her that admitting that would be tantamount to inciting his ire.

"Perhaps I could repay you over a period of time," she suggested, dodging his question. "As a gesture of good faith, I can give you thirty pounds now."

Not for anything would she tell him that sum was nearly every penny she had left, save that necessary for food. The rest of the money would come from somewhere. Later, she would figure out where that might be.

"I don't want you to call me Mr. Taylor, Maddie. Nor do I want your thirty pounds."

"But—"

"Even if you repaid me the six thousand, seven hundred eight-three pounds and twenty pence we established you owe me, and you paid it over five years at five percent interest, you would need to pay me"— he paused, clearly calculating—"one hundred twenty-eight pounds a month, give or take a pence."

Maddie felt her eyes widen as icy shock paralyzed her. One hundred twenty-eight pounds? Half of her annual income would be due Brock every month? She, Aimee, Edith, and Vema had lived on little more than that all of last year. How would she ever produce such an enormous sum each month?

Brock spoke, drawing her attention. "Keep your thirty pounds." He cast a pointed look at the faded lavender morning dress she wore. "Visit your modiste."

Feeling the sting of poverty, she lashed back. "I have no intention of marrying you, so you should take my thirty pounds. It will afford you some satisfaction."

Brock leaned back against the sofa, looking all too comfortable with his confident smile. "Not really. Your company affords me satisfaction. Indeed, far more than you know."

His steady gaze rested on her face, seeming to focus on her mouth. Ignoring the awareness of their solitude and her racing heart, Maddie pierced him with a glare. "I've no intention of satisfying you any way but monetarily."

He merely smiled, a warm, enticing curl of his beautiful mouth. "Since you still have six days to consider my proposal of marriage, you must allow me a proper chance to court you."

Court her? With Brock's charm, that could be ominous indeed. Lord knew what charming manner of lies the man would be capable of.

Though he'd proposed marriage, citing business as his primary reason, she felt sure he had very personal feelings about making this match. Something about the banked fire in his eyes, the carefully chosen words he spoke, told her that he had other motives. He acted almost . . . angry. Why? He had abandoned her, not the other way around. Not that she would remind him of that. She'd rather slit her throat than admit his rejection had crushed her. Moreover, any discussion of the past could easily lead them directly to the subject of Aimee.

Knowing she must act with caution, Maddie rose. "I would prefer to give you my thirty pounds."

The faintly sexual smile curving his lips fell, replaced by an expression of false regret. "I'm afraid I shall have to insist on the full one hundred twenty-eight pounds, if you wish to decline my . . . invitation."

"Now?"

At his nod, she scowled, hating these games. Hating him. "You know I cannot pay you right this moment."

Brock merely shrugged, his expression a blank veneer hiding his thoughts. "In that case, I shall pick you up tomorrow evening. I have a box at the Adelphi Theater."

He rose and approached on silent steps. Maddie resisted the urge to back away. Colin had taught her that fear was vulnerability. Brock took her hand in his, his skin communicating warmth and strength as he lifted her fingers to his mouth. He pressed those firm, full lips to her fingertips, his green gaze, full of mischief, never leaving her face.

Awareness shot from her arm to her heart, where it spread through the rest of her with alarming speed. She tore her hand away.

"I shall anticipate tomorrow night."

His silken voice slid over her senses, inciting response, despite her best intentions. She placed a hand to her throat, disconcerted at the feel of her racing pulse beneath her fingers.

"Good day, Mr. Taylor."

There, she'd dismissed him, as she should have long ago. She only hoped her voice didn't sound as breathy as it felt.

"Until tomorrow, Maddie-cake."

Maddie felt his soft endearment caress her senses as Brock crossed the room and opened the door.

A tiny blond tornado hit him with the force of a gale. With one hand, she held a stick adorned with yarn steady between her chubby legs. She carried a paper sword with the other. Sporting two swinging braids and gray eyes just like Maddie's, he knew this could only be her daughter.

"Aimee!" Maddie called out. Her gaze darted between the child and himself. She settled on the child again. "You should be upstairs sleeping."

"Only babies nap. I'm a knightess," the child said proudly.

Intrigued by the exchange, Brock bent to the child. "A knightess? That does sound important."

"I am Aimee. Who are you?"

The girl had already mastered haughty. He laughed. "I am Brock Taylor."

He extended his hand for the girl to shake. Instead, she grimaced, nose scrunched, and backed away.

"I will rid this house of you, Bad Knight."

"Bad, am I?"

She nodded her little blond head with conviction. "You made Mama mad."

Brock heard Maddie's embarrassed gasp over his own chuckle.

"Aimee," Maddie said, "we do not insult strangers. Apologize, please."

"So it's no faux pas for you to think me bad since you know me?" Brock teased, and was rewarded with a pink splash of color upon Maddie's cheeks.

"I challenge you to a joust," the girl declared to Brock.

"And should I win, will you stop calling me the Bad Knight?"

"Aye," answered Aimee, chin raised.

"If I should lose?"

"To the dungeon!"

"Aimee," Maddie cut in, tone warning. "Leave Mr. Taylor alone."

"But I can defeat this bl—black . . . What did you call him, Mama?"

"Blackguard?" Brock supplied helpfully.

"That's it," Aimee pronounced, prancing on her makeshift stick pony.

Brock cast his glance at Maddie, only to find her shielding herself from embarrassment with a palm over her face. He laughed again. Very interesting, indeed.

"Well," he addressed Aimee, "we can't have anyone

thinking me a blackguard. How shall we joust? Outside with swords?"

"No. It's cold and unsafe." She shook her head like a chastising parent, as if he ought to know better.

"You do have a point," he agreed.

"I hide and you find me," she explained, a little fist on a little hip.

"Aimee, now is not an appropriate time for this game." She shot Brock a glare. "Mr. Taylor was just leaving."

Brock watched Maddie. She looked distinctly uneasy. Why, he was not certain. Clearly she wanted him gone. He smiled. Perhaps remaining and playing this game would provide him clues.

He ignored Maddie and focused on the girl. "And if I cannot find you I lose?"

She nodded. "Close your eyes."

Maddie cleared her throat and approached the child. "Mr. Taylor is quite busy and does not wish to play right—"

"On the contrary," Brock broke in, gratified by the increase of her discomfort. "I would never turn down a delightful game with two such lovely ladies."

"See, Mama?" the child said, then turned to him. "Now close your eyes and count to ten."

"Brock, you don't have to—"

"It's no bother, really," he interrupted Maddie, flashing her his best smile. Clearly annoyed, she looked away.

"Start counting," demanded Aimee.

Closing his eyes, Brock began, "One, two, three . . ."

As the counting continued, Brock heard something fall to the floor, presumably her stick horse, followed by shuffling and giggling. He found his grin widening.

"Ten," he finished and opened his eyes.

Maddie stood mere feet from him, her gaze focused on his face. Her expression reflected the most interesting blend of antagonism and intrigue. That he would explore at length tomorrow night.

"I want you to leave," she whispered.

"And disappoint your daughter?" He smiled. "Never."

Strolling away from Maddie, he glanced behind the fireplace screen, behind the worn blue sofa, under an upholstered armchair that had seen better days.

The house needed updating, most likely from top to bottom. If the receiving rooms looked this shabby, Brock could only imagine the condition of the family's rooms. He would see to their renovation immediately after the marriage—new furniture, gardeners to prune the yard of weeds, new drapes, perhaps some paint.

And the rooms he would share with Maddie—those would receive special attention, particularly the room that held their bed. Definitely *their* bed. He would not have those oh-so-civilized separate bedrooms. He had been deprived of her sweet body for five years and had no intention of suffering the same fate night after night. Their bedroom would have the best. Fine fabrics to slide against the softness of her skin while he possessed her body. A wide, thick mattress so they would have plenty of room to enjoy every intimacy marriage afforded. Plush chairs and carpets, in case the bed seemed too far away.

Blood stirring, Brock sighed, his thoughts bringing a wide smile to his face.

The sound of little-girl giggling brought him back to the present. Aimee had hidden on the far side of the room, from the sound of it. Slowly, he sauntered in that direction.

She was an interesting child. Full of personality no one had yet forced her to repress. Possessed of Maddie's eyes, he wondered from whom Aimee had inherited her blond hair and faint olive complexion. Sedgewick had sported brown hair and very pale skin. Likely some distant relative, he decided.

Brock bent before a cabinet and heard a gasp. A moment later, he opened the door to find the child crouching inside.

She jumped out with a shriek, her braids flying behind her as she sought her stick horse.

"Am I still the Bad Knight?" he called after her.

"I guess not. Again!" she demanded.

"Aimee . . ." Maddie broke in. "That is enough."

The firmness in her voice told Brock the game was over—at least for now.

"Mama!" Aimee complained.

"Another time," Brock promised, and watched her little pink lips perk up with a smile.

"Promise?" she prompted.

"Aimee, leave Mr. Taylor be," Maddie chided.

Brock knelt down to the girl and tapped the end of her pert nose. "I promise."

"When will you come back?" the child asked.

At that question, Brock rose to his full height before Maddie and gazed down into the mysterious gray of her stormy eyes. He couldn't resist the grin sliding across his face. "Soon, Aimee. From now on, I plan to be with your mama very, very often."

Riding the old nag she could scarcely afford to keep, Maddie made her way through the spring chill toward the section of London known as the City. She clutched the address of Colin's solicitor in her palm. Desperation clawed at her throat. If the man had any answer to her dilemma, she must know it now. Though her father had discouraged discussion with the solicitor and society frowned upon it, she no longer had a choice. With the sureness of a master hunter, Brock was closing his trap around her.

Maddie had no trouble deciphering his ploys. In a mere two days, he had tightened the noose about her neck monetarily. With his invitation to the theater tonight, Maddie feared that, in his courting, he intended to set a silkier, more deadly trap for her emotions.

That realization frightened her beyond sleeping, eating. Aunt Edith had remarked just that morning at her preoccupied frown, while wearing her own impish smile. Though Maddie was hardly addle-brained enough to fall in love with the same cad twice, she could not deny that he made her nervous. Whenever he came near, she felt fidgety and excitable. She didn't like her fast breathing, racing heart, or that hum of awareness. She wanted to end the stray thoughts that recalled the flavor of his kiss and the feel of his love-making. It must stop.

Dismounting, Maddie secured the nag in the afternoon fog and entered the Palladian-style building. Her palms sweating inside her gloves, she made her way to the solicitor's door.

A plump, bespectacled young man opened the door, his face reflecting curiosity. "Yes?"

"I am Lady Wolcott. I must speak with Mr. Henry regarding my late husband's estate." Her voice shook.

Rejection flittered across the clerk's ruddy face. Desperate, Maddie grabbed the man's arm.

"Please," she whispered. "I truly *must* see Mr. Henry."

"What's this?" boomed a voice from behind the door.

The clerk cleared his throat. "Lady Wolcott to see you, sir."

Opening the door wide, Maddie glimpsed the portly Mr. Henry. He was at least fifty, if his graying hair and whiskers were any indication. The curiosity in his expression also said he was unaccustomed to seeing women in his domain.

"Come in, my lady."

He ushered her through the door, then into a smaller room, and shut the door behind them. A sturdy wooden desk, a book shelf, and two chairs ate up all the space in the tiny office.

"How may I help you?" he asked, gesturing for her to sit in one of the chairs.

Maddie did, then began wringing her hands in her lap.

"As you may remember, my late husband, Lord Wolcott, died nearly three years past." At the man's nod, she continued. "He did not leave me well off."

"I do recall that."

She swallowed her embarrassment, wishing she were anywhere but here. "I came to inquire if, perhaps, you remembered anything at all pertaining to his estate that had value."

"Hmm." The man frowned, bushy brows slashing downward. "I do seem to recall something unusual . . ." He turned about and searched the shelves behind him. Maddie felt her stomach lurch to her throat. After interminable minutes slid by, Mr. Henry retrieved a document.

Scanning the papers, his frown deepened.

"What is it?" she asked with concern, with hope.

After a long sigh, he set the papers aside. Lacing his fingers across his protruding stomach, he regarded her through shrewd eyes. "Your husband had no male heirs or relatives."

"That is correct." She clasped tense hands in her lap.

"Your father oversaw the disbursement of his estate."

"Yes." Maddie nodded, impatient.

"Your husband did own a cottage," said Mr. Henry with reluctance. "In St. John's Wood." He rattled off an unfamiliar address.

Maddie absorbed the man's words like a blow to the stomach. For years, men of consequence had kept such dwellings purely for cavorting with their mistresses. Despite her sheltered upbringing, she knew that. The heat of anger and shame suffused her all at once.

So Colin had kept a cottage for the purpose of bedding women he did not find frigid. Better that than bearing the brunt of his lust herself. Still, resentment reared its head. She could hardly help it if Colin's touch left her cold. She had not loved him, no matter how he had demanded it.

"I said nothing of it sooner, Lady Wolcott, because your father asked me not to. He feared you would find such knowledge . . . uncomfortable."

Uncomfortable, indeed! Clamping down on her anger, Maddie reminded herself of necessity. This might well be her way out of poverty. She must seize it.

"Not at all," she lied. "I should simply like to sell it, if such is possible."

"We can try," Mr. Henry said without enthusiasm. "I believe, however, you will have an easier time letting it if you are in need of quick funds. Perhaps it could fetch a hundred pounds a year."

Not nearly enough! "Did my husband leave anything else? Anything at all?"

He grimaced an apology. "I fear not, my lady."

Maddie closed her eyes, fighting off a wave of frustration. Letting the cottage would bring in money, yes, but not enough to repay Brock. And still she would be expected to see to its upkeep and pay taxes. She needed help, not another burden.

Maddie rose. "Please, make whatever arrangements you can and notify me," she murmured before she left.

Exhaustion claimed her body; despair seized her heart. As Maddie found her horse outside, she fought back tears. She must find a way to fend off Brock's proposal. Neither Fleet nor marriage were viable options. But the dread and anxiety deep within her told her that her chances of evading Brock Taylor and his unthinkable ultimatum were dwindling by the hour.

THREE

When Maddie arrived home, she found a pleasant surprise from an unpleasant source.

Spread out across her bed was a gown, a beautiful confection of pale, creamy green. Unlike anything she had ever possessed, it was made of a thick moiré, dazzling her with the revelation of all its subtle hues as the light caressed the fabric. Tiny ivory flowers had been embroidered with painstaking care on the bodice and the epaulets layered over large puffed sleeves.

Maddie lifted the garment against herself in delight and fingered the edge of the off-the-shoulder bodice, touched the embroidered belt. Superior craftsmanship showed in every stitch. An eye for cuts and colors was evident in the design. A lilt of excitement lifted her grim mood.

The dress made her giddy. How had it come to be on her bed? As soon as the thought drifted through Maddie's mind, she realized who must have sent it. In fact, had no doubt.

She caught a glimpse of an ivory-colored card bearing the name of an expensive London modiste resting on the bed, beside the spot the dress had once occupied. She lifted the card, the vellum thick between her fingers. Dread beating like a drum in her stomach, she turned the card over. *Se Souvenir de Moi Souvent*, it read. *Remember me often*. Naturally, Brock had signed it, adding how beautiful she would look at the theater on his arm, in this dress. Frowning, she wondered when Brock had learned French.

Heaving a sigh, Maddie resisted the urge to reject the card—and the dress. Then she espied a pair of drop earrings in stunning, flawless pearls and a matching necklace. With a gasp, she fingered the smooth surface of the pale orbs. When had she last seen anything so pretty—or so high-priced?

The audacious cad had known she had nothing suitable to wear to the theater and had provided it. He refused to forgive her debts but bought her costly clothing and matching jewelry? He definitely plotted something, and the idea filled her with an anxious flutter that thoroughly annoyed her. Plus, he had given her a spectacular dress in one of her favorite colors. That he had remembered her preferences irritated her for the excitement she suddenly felt.

She shouldn't wear it. Besides being too personal a gift, allowing him to send her clothing would be all but admitting she would wed him. It was worse than charity. Maddie wasn't beneath accepting what she might one day have to from friends. She could not bear it from Brock.

"My lady?" Matheson called on the other side of her door.

Before she could reply, Aimee burst through the door.

"Mama," the girl called, skipping around her in a circle. "Mr. Taylor is here. Where are you going?"

He was here already?

Maddie knelt to Aimee and held her warm little hand. "The theater, dear. I promise not to be gone long."

Dashing for her wardrobe, Maddie opened the doors, finding only serviceable garments. Brown and gray jumped out at her, worn fabrics with patches over patches. Even the respectable day dresses she had preserved and updated as possible were hopelessly casual for a night out.

Maddie hadn't cared for the state of her wardrobe before now. Most of the *ton* thought her hiding here in Hampstead, still deep in mourning. Her lack of funds with which to dress had hardly been an issue until tonight. Until Brock.

If Maddie could have worn one of her own dresses without embarrassing herself she would have. But looking at her meager selection, she knew that was impossible.

With another sigh, she shouted down the hall for Vema, who had been kind enough to act as her lady's maid since finances had forced Maddie to let her own go. Then she turned to the willow green dress. She really had no choice. The tingles of excitement hardly meant she wished to attend the theater. Mingling among the *ton* had always been exciting, but she was beyond such frivolity now. Becoming a mother and impoverished widow had changed all of that.

Moments later, Vema entered the room with a cryptic smile. "So he is here, and you wish to look well?"

Maddie harrumphed. "Presentable, and nothing more. Please help me into this dress so I can end this farce."

"As you wish," came the Indian woman's soft, smiling reply.

Gnashing her teeth, Maddie ignored the trickle of laughter she heard in Vema's quiet words.

Finally, Vema closed the last fastening. Maddie turned to stare at herself in the mirror, stunned by her own reflection. The muted green brought out the peaches in her complexion, giving her a flawless look that flat brown never did. And her eyes, always gray, took on the sparkle of the dress, appearing a unique shade somewhere between the two colors. As she stood mutely, Vema braided her hair, lingering over each strand. The Punjabi woman twisted the braids upon Maddie's head, leaving curling auburn tendrils to stray about her neck. Golden light from the candlewicks made her hair shine a deep red.

Finally as Maddie attached the eardrops, Vema fastened the pearls about her throat, the orbs luminescent against her skin.

"I am finished," Vema said in her accented tone.

"Mama, you look like a princess!" Aimee exclaimed.

Brushing a quick kiss across her daughter's cheek, Maddie pondered her daughter's observation. Odd, but she felt like a princess, like Cinderella on her way to a magical ball where anything was possible. In this case, that was not true. She must remember that Brock Taylor, no matter how intriguing, was no Prince Charming.

Brock stood in Ashdown Manor's drawing room, in the same room he and Maddie had occupied only the day before.

Glancing at the empty doorway, he cursed and turned his top hat over in his hands.

Ten minutes ago the butler had gone to fetch Maddie, and still no sign of her. Damn, she'd best appear. After he had nearly broken his back earning the wealth to keep her in style and she had eagerly wed Lord Wolcott in spite of his efforts, she owed him conversation—and more.

He intended to make certain she repaid him in full.

The sound of soft footfalls brought his gaze back to the door. Maddie stood mutely in the portal, chin raised, looking every inch a delectable challenge in the pale green finery and pearls he'd sent. With her fiery hair piled atop her head and curls dangling at her temples, her flawless face stood out like some painter's masterpiece, almost too beautiful to be believed.

In that instant, Brock ached to touch her again, the force of his desire as subtle as an explosion. He prayed his demeanor didn't show this unwelcome vulnerability.

Adopting a smile, he approached her as she entered the room. "You look lovely, Maddie. Do you like the dress?"

"Mr. Taylor—"

"Brock," he corrected with a raised brow. "I think we . . . know each other well enough to warrant first names."

Maddie raised her chin. The swell of her flushed bosom

drew his gaze above the dress's straight, low neckline. "This outing is ridiculous. There is no purpose—"

"You have an answer to my proposal, then?"

Her jaw tightened. "No. I intend to consider this matter thoroughly first."

"Your choices are only two," he reminded. "You won't find me nearly as confining as your other options, I assure you."

"Your assurances are of little comfort." Her stormy eyes flashed with fury. "If I alone would suffer in refusing you, be assured I would do so this instant!"

Though Brock had known her sentiments since proposing marriage, her words still knifed him in the chest. Five years ago she had thought him beneath her. Nothing had changed.

"I am not a man who likes to be gainsaid."

Fear and resistance flickered in her eyes. Yes, she knew he deserved his ruthless reputation. Whose story had she heard? That of the banker who had tried to steal from him and found himself trapped within Newgate's walls for the effort? Or mayhap she had heard of the factory manager who had substituted substandard materials and kept the profit for himself, earning him a lifelong trip to Australia. No matter, he thought, smiling. She knew enough.

He traced his finger along a hall table at his side. "Is refusing me in your best interest? In Aimee's?"

Maddie tensed, looking ready to scratch his eyes out. For a moment, he envied Aimee that kind of maternal love. His own mother had died bringing him into the world.

"You know nothing of my daughter's best interest!"

In truth, once they were wed, he would provide for Aimee. He had no intention of neglecting the child's needs. It was hardly Aimee's fault that he hated her father, a man he had seen only from a distance.

Suppressing his anger, he stepped closer. Anxiety crossed Maddie's face as he stopped within inches of her. Good;

disquieting her, keeping her off balance—all would play in his favor.

"That is one of your qualities I always admired, Maddie-cake, that passion you were never afraid to show."

The passion he suspected had only grown over the past five years. Before, she had possessed a girl's ardor. Now, she had a woman's needs. Though Sedgewick had received Maddie's favors before his death, Brock planned to kindle the spark of her desire for him into an uncontrollable inferno. He would bury himself so hot and so deep within her that she would never remember Sedgewick's touch again.

"I have no need for the kind of fleshy passion you hint at in so unseemly a fashion," she fired back.

With satisfaction, Brock watched Maddie swallow nervously—then he inhaled. The scents of jasmine and vanilla lingered on Maddie's skin, rousing the slumber of his senses. That perfume took him back five years, when he'd held her, his heart bursting with fierce need and hope for the future.

Desire erupted in a sharp blast. He retreated a fraction to draw in a steadying breath.

"Then I shall have to create such a need, Maddie-cake. And very soon." He leaned forward to whisper in her ear, "You have the most delicious scent. I could breathe you in all night."

At his words, shock stilled her. Maddie's anxious gaze snapped to his face. "You will not, Mr. Taylor, ever."

She turned her back on him, presenting him with a small waist, slim shoulders, and a graceful neck made more tantalizing by honey-cream skin. Gritting his teeth against her rebuff, Brock cursed his urge to touch her, to press his lips against that slender column. He forced himself to look away. Life and business had taught him never to show his enemies his weaknesses. It would not do for Lady Walcott to know how dangerously deep his desire for her ran.

* * *

An hour later, Maddie sat in Brock's theater box, clutching a lace handkerchief in her gloved hand. Beside her, he brushed a speck of lint that could only exist in his imagination from his immaculate ebony evening coat. His hand brushed her arm for the third time in ten minutes.

A tingly flash danced up her arm. She folded her hands in her lap, fingers pressed tightly together. *The feeling means nothing,* she told herself. *Ignore him.*

He placed an arm behind her chair. His thumb brushed the back of her neck before his hand settled so close to her exposed skin, she could feel his heat.

Though she refused to look at him, warmth curled through her.

Squirming away from him as far as the seat allowed, she clutched her fluttering stomach. It was not Brock. He did not affect her. She had learned about love too harshly at his hands once to actually desire the manipulative rogue again.

Beside her, Brock wore a touch of a smile at the corners of his full mouth, as if he knew he made her very nervous and enjoyed that fact. He looked devastating in full evening black, his appearance serving only to further fluster her. The man was entirely too confident. And infuriating.

She drew in a deep breath to calm her nerves, the scent of ale clogging the air as pot boys dispensed refreshments to the thickening crowd. Maddie stared blankly at the green baize curtain, ignoring the curious stares of the *ton*.

Their curiosity would soon die down, as her time with Brock was limited. She would find some way out of her predicament, concoct a plan to avoid the hells of both prison and matrimony.

"This is one of my favorite plays," Brock whispered suddenly, his mouth mere inches from her ear. The deep tones of his velvet voice vibrated within her. She repressed a shiver by gritting her teeth.

Refusing to be affected, she leaned away. "What play?"

"You liked Shakespeare in the past, so when I heard of this rendition, I thought it perfect."

Reluctant to admit that she hadn't noticed the play's title before entering the theater, she glanced down at the program in his hand.

The Taming of the Shrew.

Her eyes narrowed with animosity. Though Colin had taught her that keeping a tight rein on her emotions left her less vulnerable, the thought didn't enter Maddie's mind. She snapped her gaze back to his sinfully masculine face and hissed, "If I'm a shrew, you bounder, why wed me? Pick another impoverished widow, one who does not despise you."

"Ah, but then I would not have you to tame."

His smile widened. She felt the impact of that slow, suggestive grin like a flutter in her belly.

Maddie knew she ought to smack that magnetic smile from his mouth—immediately after she found a way to restrain her own wayward thoughts. How could Brock have this effect on her? Make her think of deep kisses shared, damp bodies locked in desire, covered by nothing more than sweet spring air?

"You will not tame me," she vowed in a low voice, pulling her mind back to the present. "Marriage would only make me hate you more."

He leaned closer. Her stomach tightened, quivered, blast him. That green stare of his, teasing, inviting, daring, ate mercilessly at her resistance. "Don't challenge me, Maddie. You know I will always accept."

Drat if he wasn't right. She must think more clearly before she spoke, but he'd always made her somewhat impulsive.

"I merely point out the impracticality of wedding someone you dislike," she moderated.

His gaze touched her face before dropping to caress the swells of her breasts exposed by her dress. "You have other qualities that make up for the impracticalities."

Maddie felt a shiver cut through her as her skin heated under his watchful gaze. Brock toyed with her, she knew. But he wanted her. She saw it in his eyes as clearly as the full moon on a starless night. Some long-buried chord answered with a resounding chime inside her. Calling herself every kind of fool, she forced her gaze away from Brock, to the stage.

At that moment, the curtain rose and the actors trouped out to perform. Act One passed quickly, Maddie's thoughts racing. At intermission, he inquired whether she would like something to drink. At her refusal, he rose, not returning when the play resumed.

Though she was loathe to admit it, his abandonment, however brief, stung. She caught a glimpse of him in another box, speaking with a wealthy baron. Catching her eye, he raised a brow at her. Miffed, Maddie looked away.

Why did she watch him, stare even? She hated him for the pain he had once caused her in pursuit of his fortune, for the manner in which he was even now trying to force her to the altar to fatten his accounts further.

But Brock had always held fascination for her. In the past five years, he had only grown more complex, more enigmatic. And like a fool, she was allowing him to intrigue her, despite her hatred for him.

Suddenly, Brock reappeared. A faint tinge of sandalwood, citrus, and man combined to wound her good reason.

"That mysterious expression is intriguing, Maddie-cake. Care to share your thoughts?" He handed her a glass of wine, eyes burning as if he could indeed read her thoughts.

She pasted on a falsely sweet smile. "Pleasant visions of you in boiling oil, impaled by sharp knives."

He laughed, a rich, mirthful sound that resonated deep within her. She turned away in frustration. Could the man not even take an insult?

"You wound me," he bantered with a mock pout.

She shot him a tart glare. "That was the idea."

Again, that vibrant laugh of his cascaded over her senses. "And here I thought it was my irresistible charm making your eyes sparkle."

He settled into the chair beside her. His thigh brushed hers. Even through the layers of her clothing, she felt him. Her skin tingled, seem to come alive, anticipate what might come next. Cursing him beneath her breath, Maddie drew her leg clear of his and sipped her wine while pretending deep interest in the performance.

Brock whispered in her ear, " 'Hearing thy mildness praised in every town, Thy virtues spoke of and thy beauty sounded, Yet not so deeply as to thee belongs,—Myself am moved to woo thee for my wife.' "

Maddie turned to Brock, utterly stunned. He had memorized Shakespeare?

She countered, " 'Moved! In good time: let him that moved you hither Remove you hence.' " After imbibing a sip of her sweet wine, she glared at him. "Petruchio you are not."

The teasing light left Brock's green eyes, replaced by something almost solemn. "You are fairer than his Kate."

She felt caught in his gaze, captive of his silken disclosure. Maddie could do little but stare. Just when she found a way to express her anger, his clever mind discovered how to turn her ire into the kind of passion he sought from her. How could he make her notice the strong planes of his golden face when she should be giving him the tongue-lashing he so richly deserved? How could he divert her attention to his firm, capable hands, and have her wondering what they might feel like upon her?

"That look of yours might melt me, love," he whispered.

Tearing her gaze away, Maddie gulped the last sip of her wine. He courted her with a fine dress and jewels, sweet wine, and now, pretty words. If he merely wanted to coerce her into marriage, why? Maddie dared not consider an answer, for she would not ever make the mistake of believing herself important to him again, except in his quest for wealth.

To believe otherwise, particularly in light of the foolish awareness growing within her, would be supremely dangerous.

Brock tucked away his notes on a diamond mine in South America—a bad investment in his estimation—knowing the only gem to occupy his thoughts again this afternoon—as with the past four—was Maddie.

He wanted to see her thick auburn tresses spread across the white of his sheets, ached to feel her naked breast in his mouth, tip hard against his tongue. Sighing, he closed his eyes, imagining her eyes stormy with desire for him, her voice trembling as she bade him to touch her.

But if her passion had matured these past five years, so had her determination. As a girl, Maddie had been eager to please, particularly her curmudgeon of a father. She had always worn a smile, spoken a friendly greeting, displayed eternal optimism. Today, she was both guarded and stubborn—and resolved to have no part of him.

No doubt he had earned her ire by presuming to again enter her life in very nearly the state he had left it, as her fiancé and lover. Clearly, she had banished thoughts of him to hell, along with her reckless youth. Still, he sensed she was not indifferent to him. That, along with her poverty, played directly into his hands.

Depending on what she thought of his note.

"Have you heard from her yet?" Jack asked, appearing in the doorway of Brock's office.

"Nary a word."

His father nodded. "She's going to be furious, you know."

Brock shrugged, pretending he did not care, feigning a confidence he did not feel. "She can't afford to refuse me."

Jack's taunting smile made his eyes dance. "As you say."

Irritation pricked him. "I do, old man. Now leave me be."

"Will you fetch her if she doesn't come 'round today?"

Annoyed with Jack's probing, Brock asserted, "She will come."

In the next instant, Brock's secretary poked his head into the room. "Mr. Taylor, I believe you were expecting Lady Wolcott. Shall I show her in?"

Flashing his father a triumphant grin that hid his relief, Brock answered, "Indeed."

A moment later, Maddie stood in the portal, hopelessly windblown, wearing another drab frock that had seen better days, long ago. Cheeks flushed from the cold—or her anger—she clutched a reticule with white fingers, looking angry enough to tear the skin from his body with her bare hands.

Jack backed out of the room's side door with a mirthful grin.

"What is the meaning of this missive, you snake?" she hissed. "Do not dare to presume you can, at your convenience, demand my answer to your ridiculous proposal."

Brock fought off disappointment and bitterness. She would rather go to prison than marry one of his class? Than to wed him?

"Your week is up. I merely meant to remind you that I require your decision today. And since you deem my proposal ridiculous, I assume you choose the debtor's option."

"I did not say that—"

Hope swelled. "So you choose me?"

"Blast you, I've chosen nothing! It is a ridiculous ultimatum, one you cannot possibly expect me to abide by."

"I fear I must. I think it is a fair trade, really. Your connections for my wealth. Security for your aunt in her dotage, all the finest for your daughter, even a generous dowry, if you wish it."

"That, sir, is very nearly blackmail," she choked.

He shrugged. "Perhaps, but I can offer you something else if you wed me."

Approaching her silently on the thick carpet of his office, Brock reached behind her to lock the door, closing them off from the rest of the world. He stood purposely close. So close, he could see the threads stretched thin at the bodice of her old dress. So close, he could detect the fluttering pulse at her throat, her spicy-floral scent teasing him mercilessly.

"You can offer me nothing I want but the forgiveness of my debt," she said with a proud toss of her head.

"I can offer you ecstasy," he whispered slowly, feeling the sting of arousal hardening him. "I can fill every cell of your beautiful body with breathtaking pleasure."

Silence hung thick. Maddie hesitated, stared, swallowed. A flush crept up her neck to her cheeks.

"Your modesty overwhelms," Maddie said finally, eyeing him with disdain he did not quite believe. "I am without interest."

"Hmm. So you are refusing my proposal?"

"I am refusing to be handled like a trollop."

She turned away and grabbed the door's latch. Brock seized her arm and spun her to face him again, putting her back against the door. With her breathless, moist lips parted inches below his own and her body flush against him, reason melted under the sizzle of desire.

"I've no intention of handling you like a trollop," he ground out. "But I will touch you as a woman should be touched."

Called by the defiant challenge on her face, he lifted his hand to her and curled his fingers around her nape.

For a suspended moment, Maddie stared at him, her eyes darkening to the shade of a rain-drenched cloud.

He kissed her before she could utter a word, covering her lips with one stroke. He took advantage of her gasp by sliding his tongue into her mouth to taste her. She stiffened and held herself tense.

Again, Brock claimed her mouth. And slowly she began to soften, lips turning pliant, her shy tongue grazing his. Finer than rare, sweet wine, her flavor seeped into him, blinding him to reason. His blood heated until it scalded his veins. Instant need clawed at his gut. His hands caressed the length of her back, down to her hips, pulling her femininity against the granite of his erection.

After five years of believing he would never hold Maddie again, Brock felt his self-control shatter. He could not find the sanity to care. The taste of her had never left his memory. He needed this kiss beyond reason, needed to know she was not indifferent to him, to the hunger between them.

He pressed his lips to the soft skin of her throat. "Sweet Maddie."

She made a mewling sound in answer.

Brock plunged deep into her mouth again, stroking, exploring. Maddie's moist lips beneath his opened wider to accept the untamed kiss quickly spinning out of control. Her hands upon his chest, once meant as a barricade, now slid about his neck to grasp handfuls of his hair. Another little moan from deep in her throat only made him ache to carry her to his desk, lift her skirts, and ride her until satiation claimed them both.

He drew in a breath, then rasped against her lips, "I want to touch every part of you, possess you, mind, body, and soul."

With a sharp, indrawn breath, Maddie stiffened and tore herself out of his arms. Backing away from him, she clapped her palm over her swollen, red-berry mouth and shook her head. Brock gasped to catch his breath as she stared, eyes wide with a mixture of accusation, fear, and want. Knowing that she could not deny the explosive desire between them only made him harder.

"Maddie . . ." He reached for her again.

Grasping her reticule to her heaving chest, she turned the latch and fled through the door before he could stop her.

* * *

The next night, Maddie paced the floor of Colin's empty, unlet St. John's Wood cottage, watching her shadow on the wall from the room's few candles. Would Brock answer her summons? Slowly, she nodded. Promised repayment, he would come.

Now, Maddie prayed she had the fortitude to repay him.

She had not mistaken that blistering kiss yesterday, nor the look in his eyes afterward. He had been affected, judging from his heavy-lidded gaze and stiff shaft. He had desired her, had admitted wanting to possess her.

She had felt a tight and tingly, lingering emotion for him. Desire? Blast him, yes. Still, she could restrain herself in the future. Brock had simply taken her by surprise yesterday—something she would not allow to happen again. She was a woman grown, in control, and could elude the sexual web in which he sought to ensnare her. Besides, Colin had called her frigid. Eventually, Brock would find her thus, too.

But something more had plagued her, something that brought fitful dreams of Brock's warm hands stroking her flushed skin. That something had felt suspiciously like yearning.

Impossible. She was too mature, had learned too much at his hands to be fool enough to want him again. This time, she would remain in control. And bring Brock to his knees.

Maddie smiled, rather liking that image. So many pleasurable associations . . . Brock would sacrifice his ambitions this time, for she refused to be his pawn. She liked the idea so well, she could almost forget her scandalous intentions, and the fact she had no notion how to go about them.

She sobered. This daring plan was her last option. She had no other choice except a surrender she refused to yield.

Beyond the candlelight, Maddie heard the cottage's front door squeak open. She saw only the outline of his body, tall, taut, broad-shouldered—definitely all man. Fear and awareness curled in Maddie's belly. Then she admonished herself. She must have faith, be firm. She would find the strength to carry out her brazen plan. She had too much to lose to do anything else.

Behind him, Brock shut the door softly; then his measured steps brought him across the tiled floor, slowly, slowly, until the candlelight illuminated his strong, expressionless features.

"Why did you write and ask me to meet you here? I am through negotiating, Maddie. I'm interested only in payment in full or your hand in marriage."

His words were hardly encouraging. She paused. Maybe this idea was a mistake; maybe he didn't want her . . . Then she saw his gaze surreptitiously touch her, linger on her breasts, measuring the span of her waist, her hips. No mistake. Only her own fears, her own insecurities, gave her pause.

"I think we have another possibility to consider, Brock." Maddie purposely let his first name roll off her tongue. His hot stare snapped to her face. His body grew visibly tense.

She smiled, hoping it looked real, and sidled closer.

The firelight licked his dusky face, lit his dark hair a deep, gleaming chestnut. His green eyes, so focused on her, held anger, yes. But they also glowed with desire.

Very good, indeed. She placed a shaking hand on his chest—and did her best to ignore his firm, oh-so-warm flesh beneath her hand, the thump-thump of his heart under her fingers.

"What possibility is that?" He stared pointedly at her hand upon him, his jaw clenched.

Refusing to back down, Maddie swallowed her lack of confidence, the resonance of Colin's taunts clear in her memory. Instead, she curled her hand around the hard width of his shoulder.

"I could be your mistress for tonight, Brock. All night.

Come morning, we could consider this little matter behind us."

Surprise flashed across his face. Then his eyes blazed with green fire . . . for a moment. Quickly, he doused desire with scorn. "Over six thousand pounds for a night's tumble?"

His voice sounded sharp as a razor's edge. Where was his lust, the unbridled acceptance she had imagined?

Maddie drew in a calming breath. Clearly, Brock would walk away if she did not sweeten her offer. As much as she was loathe to commit any more time to him, it would, no doubt, be better than legally enslaving herself to him for years to come.

"A month, then?" she countered.

He paused, his expression cynical. "Even if I found the time and inclination to bed you on each of thirty days, that amounts to over two hundred twenty-five pounds per day. I daresay no one makes that kind of money for that kind of . . . effort. Really, I should need at least a year to get the proper value out of such an arrangement."

Clenching her fists, Maddie restrained the urge to slap him. The swine was deliberately baiting her. "Six months." She contrived a pretty pout. "That seems fair."

As he shrugged, his face revealed no reaction. "And once this six months is over, what do you ask for your future?"

At least he hadn't refused her. Hopeful, she wound her free hand about his neck and leaned in, ignoring her tight-bellied anxiety. "I ask only for a chance to please you now."

Brock gazed down at the sight her closeness afforded him, a perfect view of her cleavage. He lifted a brow of disdain. "Not a clever plan, Maddie. Your reputation will be ruined."

"No. It will be clandestine, our secret. I shall come in disguise—"

"Even so, there might be other consequences to such an arrangement."

She had little doubt he spoke of conception. It was Maddie's turn to smile. Brock could not know that, after birthing

Aimee, the midwife had informed her that she had suffered too much damage to conceive again. The consequences he referred to would present no problem at all.

"Put your mind at ease." Her enticing whisper was hushed like the rustle of bed sheets.

He responded with a questioning glance. "And after our six months, how long before you have need of funds again? How long before you find yourself on your back, legs open for someone else to take his pleasure?"

Maddie flinched at his crudity. Suppressing a jolt of fury, she sauntered behind him and pressed her breasts to his wide back. Hadn't Colin mentioned such an act when he'd complained she knew nothing of enticing a man?

"Let me worry about that." She smoothed a light brush of her hand over the plane of his back. "Simply consider me your mistress, here to please you, for the next six months."

Brock turned, catching her off guard. Before she could stumble backward, he caught her arms in a tense-fingered grip. "Perhaps I have no need of a mistress currently."

Maddie flashed her gaze to his mocking face and panicked. She had not considered that he might already have his pleasures engaged, and most likely with someone who knew what she was about. And though she wanted to, Maddie could not deny the pang in her chest.

But she could not give up. Six months of sexual servitude to Brock was better than a lifetime . . . Colin had proven that.

"I can be better," she whispered, suppressing her uncertainty and fear of ineptitude. "And you want me."

Then she pressed her lips to his, fitting her body against his hard one until she felt each tense muscle, including his rigid manhood, against her. Celebration erupted within her. He did want her. Maybe this mad plot would work.

Suddenly, his hands were in her hair, strong fingers splayed against her scalp. He drove his mouth over hers and parted her lips with an insistent tongue to taste her everywhere, everywhere. Her awkwardness dissolved into yearning. Dear God, his kiss . . . hot, urgent, powerful. She felt utterly possessed—and the sensation didn't scare her. It merely made her want more.

That realization frightened her most of all.

Her legs melted beneath her. Her heart galloped. Maddie fought for control, trying to block the warm, encompassing feel of him. The manly musk of him spurred her deeper into the kiss, further under the spell of that conquering mouth.

Brock pulled away, eyes hard, hot, accusing.

Maddie gasped for breath. "See? I believe you could enjoy such an arrangement."

"Do you?" He covered her shoulder with his hand, his clasp firm, as if he wanted to be certain she felt it.

Brock was up to something. Feeling that as surely as her racing heart, Maddie tried not to panic, not to want. "Of course. That kiss . . . oh, my. That was only the beginning."

"If I take you as my mistress"—his palm left her shoulder to brush her collarbone—"be assured I will"—his hands inched down, down—"bed you until you can no longer breathe."

His words alone made Maddie feel faint. Then that burning green gaze of his fastened on her breasts, just as she felt his warm hand slide lower still, finally to cup her. He traced lazy circles with his thumb until her nipple tingled, swelled, stood glaringly erect.

She swallowed the sensations of embarrassment . . . and of pleasure. The urge to close her eyes, allow her knees to buckle, to melt into him, grew strong. Brock merely attempted to unnerve her. He assumed she would swat his hand away, chastise him so he could prove her offer was a sham. At the moment, Maddie wondered if she could have uttered anything more than a groan.

"Of course"—he leaned in to whisper in her ear, still fondling her aching flesh—"I can bed a wife as well."

As quickly as a flash of lightning, Brock dropped his hand, then turned for the door.

He was leaving? No! Her offer was supposed to entice him. Blast him, she had set aside her pride, her scruples, to protect her daughter and her independence from Brock's ruthless control.

On trembling legs, she darted after him, grabbing his wrist. "You cannot leave. Stay. Please! Consider my offer."

Fury etched itself into every hard line of his face. As if propelled by the force of it, Maddie stepped away.

"We have nothing further to discuss on this subject. Marry me or face the consequences."

He reached for the door's latch. Maddie grew desperate but dared not try to restrain him, not in his present mood.

"I shall be here," she blurted to his retreating form. "Each midnight, I will lie here and wait for you."

Brock shot her a narrow-eyed glance over his shoulder, a glance riddled with anger and contempt. "You're in for a damned long wait."

FOUR

Maddie paced the floor of her late husband's St. John's Wood cottage, the clay brick beneath her as cold as Brock's reaction to her idea of becoming his mistress.

It had been a week now. An entire week, and still he had not appeared to claim the passion she had been so certain he wanted. A week now she had been unable to erase the hot feel of his kiss from her lips. A week during which some long-buried part of her had again confronted the fact that the man who'd taken her innocence had never cared.

But Brock's rejection could not affect her. She mustn't consider him anything but an adversary to be defeated.

Pace, turn; pace, turn. She would not allow herself to become intrigued. Brock Taylor was a servant turned wealthy banker. That made him unusual, not irresistible.

With a sigh, Maddie released the bottom lip she'd been gnawing. Who was she fooling? Brock was, for some unfathomable reason, desirable in a forbidden sort of way. But rather than succumb to his charm as she once had, Maddie vowed to use him, as he had done to her. She would exploit his desire to end both her debt and his marriage threat. To wonder if the mastery he displayed in moneymaking would be equally unmistakable in his lovemaking was nothing short of reckless. The forbidden, Brock had taught her, was as dangerous as the man himself.

Dangerous enough to throw her and Aimee into the Fleet without a word? Yes; it was possible he might have her taken away at any moment. With Brock, anything was possible.

He must accept this mad offer of hers. He simply *must*.

She sighed and forced herself to sit on the green overstuffed sofa that dominated the cozy, firelit room. That clawing, panicked feeling of desperation in the pit of her stomach would not overtake her. The burn of anger consuming her heart, that was safer. That she could revel in.

Brock had charged into her life as if God had given him the divine right to do so and all but announced that she would marry him. He had rebuffed her attempts at compromise and refused her scandalous bargain. He risked nothing in accepting her proposition. Nothing at all. Oh, he might wish to expand his business, as he claimed, but why go to the trouble of coercing her to the altar to do so?

Because Brock was selfish and dastardly and arrogant.

And she would not fall prey to his schemes again.

Maddie rose as the hall clock struck one in the morning. Donning her cloak to leave, a renewed sense of purpose pervaded her. She would stop him from destroying her life.

She would have revenge for his abandonment.

That was what her soul had cried out for five years earlier, what she needed now to purge him from her life.

For the last three years, Maddie had relied on no one but herself. She alone had arranged to bury Colin and her father, taken on the mountainous debt, raised her daughter, made a home for her aunt, and kept Ashdown Manor running, despite the lack of servants and funds. She would not bow to Brock Taylor's ultimatum without a fight, without issuing her own reprisals. The cad would pay.

Exactly how she would accomplish this, Maddie did not know. But determination pounded like a hammer in her gut, and she vowed she would not rest until she had, and had freed herself from his matrimonial trap—and ruined him as well.

* * *

After making the trip to Hampstead again, Brock paused at Ashdown Manor's door. The thought of seeing Maddie once more had his palms sweating.

Each midnight, I will lie here and wait for you, he heard her sultry voice whisper over and over. Her words haunted him during the meetings necessary to secure parcels of the railroad's land, during important analyses of new securities that would earn more money and win new business, during sleepless nights when he craved the feel of her mouth beneath his. Damn! With one sentence, she had managed to revive his impassioned memories, erode his concentration, and threaten his future.

And it was that future—the quest for wealth and power he had yearned for all his poverty-stricken boyhood—that kept him from accepting Maddie's stunning offer in a mind-melting moment of desire. Sheer willpower had prevailed—so far. He could only hope it would last until he could get her to the altar.

Drawing in a deep breath of warm spring air, Brock knocked. Matheson answered moments later.

"Mr. Taylor," the old butler said by way of greeting.

"Good afternoon. Is Lady Wolcott at home?"

Matheson stepped aside to admit Brock. "Right this way, sir."

The butler took Brock's cloak and led him into Maddie's worn parlor, still somehow cold, despite the warm day. With a bow, Matheson left him alone with his thoughts.

Brock strolled around the room. April sun poured through the west windows, shedding its golden light on the dust motes slowly winding down to the faded carpet. A rag doll with a smudged face, blue button eyes, and a cupid's bow mouth sat in an old chair.

Regardless of the manor's shabby state, it held a comfortably elegant feel beneath the tall ceilings. Oh, Brock now had a fashionable town house. In Mayfair, no less, around the corner from Park Lane. But he liked the idea of being master in a house in which he'd once been servant. He could see himself living here with Maddie.

Shaking off his odd thoughts, Brock wondered if she would ask him for another delay. Perhaps offer him her paltry savings once more to postpone the inevitable? Or, dear God, would she offer herself again?

Each midnight, I will lie here and wait for you.

With a curse, Brock pushed the voice aside and sat on the worn sofa, feeling himself sweat. No matter when, where, or how often she lay in wait for him to claim her, he could not, not without marriage. He must have her connections and her land.

If investors chose to overlook his services because they believed them inferior or unbeneficial to their fortunes, he considered it their loss. If investors refused to visit his offices simply because they knew he had been born without connections or consequence, well . . . that kind of ignorance he objected to.

He knew he couldn't change the attitude of England's privileged class. Nor was he any kind of crusader. But to have another blueblood lacking the good sense God gave most mutts look down his thin, patrician nose at him was more than Brock could bear.

He needed Maddie to improve his lot. And she owed him for her defection, her perfidy. He was eager to extract a pound of flesh from Maddie, as long as it came with the silken caress of her hand wearing his wedding ring.

Each midnight, I will lie here and wait for you.

God, why couldn't he get her voice out of his head? Forget the temptation to claim her in a primitive taking?

Shifting uncomfortably to accommodate the front of his expanding breeches, Brock heard a hushed whisper at the parlor's portal. He stood, hoping his coat hid anything too telling, and faced the door as it inched open.

Instead of Maddie, little Aimee stood there, arm stretched out before her, ending in a fist. The late-day sun's brilliant rays streamed through the window, brightening the little girl's golden hair until it looked like a halo.

"Hello," she greeted with a smile, dimples showing.

She walked farther into the room, arm still outstretched but touching nothing. She smelled faintly of cherries.

"Hello, Aimee." He frowned as he watched her walk a circle around the couch. "What are you doing?"

"Walking my dog. See? I'm holding his leash."

Brock saw nothing. "What dog?"

"You can't see him," she whispered, as if letting him in on a secret. "He's invisible except to me."

A pretend dog? Straining to find the logic in such a game, Brock sat again. "And this dog is your pet?"

"Frog." She nodded.

He was really confused now. "Your dog is a frog?"

Aimee rolled her eyes and heaved a dramatic sigh. "No, you ninny. My dog is named Frog."

The girl's tone indicated that she thought the dog's name was perfectly obvious and logical. It was neither to him. "Why did you name your . . . dog Frog?"

She shrugged her little shoulders. "He likes to hop."

Brock frowned, trying to follow. "I've never seen a dog hop."

Aimee cast him a glance that was surprisingly disparaging for a four-year-old. "You've never seen Frog."

She had a point, though a very odd one. Resolved that he might never fully understand the rationale of her young mind, he simply nodded.

"I'm going to have a baby brother soon," she announced.

Shock bounced through Brock faster than he could make money multiply.

Maddie was pregnant? By whom?

Staggered, he stared at Aimee. Maddie was truly expecting? Was that why she wanted to become his mistress, to pin her pregnancy on him and make him . . . what? Marry her? He had already offered—insisted, actually—and she had refused.

He stared at Aimee with a jaundiced gaze. Or was this perhaps another of her games?

"A baby brother? You must be excited," he said carefully. "When?"

She shrugged. "I don't know."

"What did your mother say?"

After a little shake of her blond head, Aimee said, "She doesn't know."

Relief undulated through him in slow waves, until the illogical nature of Aimee's words hit him again. "Then how do you know you will have a baby brother?"

"God told me."

Brock wanted to ask her how she thought that was possible when her father was dead but realized that question would be lost on her innocent mind. Clearly, the girl wanted a sibling and was willing to invent a conversation with God to get one.

"God told you what?" Maddie asked suddenly.

With a glance to the portal, Brock saw her there. The doorway framed her, and he let his eyes feast on her like a man starved. She looked perfect, all creamy and regal despite her drab work dress. The auburn luxury of her hair was once again bound in a tight chignon he vowed to unwind the minute their vows were spoken. The cut of her coarse brown dress accentuated the lush curve of her breasts. He'd bet she wore just one petticoat. Lust started a slow burn in his belly and rippled through him without mercy.

"About my baby brother," came Aimee's weak reply. The soft tone was accompanied by a guilty grimace. Apparently, Maddie had heard this assertion before and disliked it.

"I'm sorry, sweeting, but there will be no brothers," Maddie said gently as she approached her daughter. She knelt to the girl and smoothed blond wisps from her little face. "We've talked about this. Remember?"

Glumly, Aimee nodded. "Yes, Mama."

"Good girl. Now go play upstairs. Auntie Verna wants to see your drawings."

"But Mr. Taylor—"

"Go on," Maddie ordered, her face becoming stern.

"But—"

"Go now, young lady."

Aimee's shoulders sagged visibly as she left the room. Brock found himself smiling at the girl.

"Good-bye, Aimee," he called.

" 'Bye," she muttered without turning to face him. She punctuated the dejected syllable with a halfhearted wave.

Brock wondered about Maddie's rapport with the child, but the mixture of guilt, exasperation, and fear on the determined oval of her face told him there was more to the mother-daughter exchange than any man could probably ever understand.

"She's really quite imaginative," Brock offered, somehow reluctant to allow Maddie's quiet mood to continue.

As if she remembered his presence, she turned to him with a stiff spine. Her unique scent, a mixture of vanilla and jasmine, pervaded his senses. He was too aware of her, the dewy texture of her skin, the sounds of her slightly agitated breaths, and that damned soft mouth he couldn't forget.

"I've waited for you at the cottage," she murmured.

He stared at her lips, ripe and tempting. A surge of yearning to feel them, taste their pliability with his own mouth, hit him hard.

Ruthlessly, he stifled the impulse. She had married Sedgewick, warmed his bed for two years, and borne him a child. Maddie had, no doubt in shame, buried her memories of her serving-class lover the moment he'd left Ashdown Manor. She had not wanted to face the fact that she had given her innocence to her stable hand, to a man with dirt beneath his fingernails.

Now, at her convenience, she wanted to use his desire for her to coerce him to forfeit his future, the railroad that would finally make him one of England's wealthiest men—and afford him the according power. Despite his burning to obliterate her memory of Sedgewick's touch, she didn't stand a bloody chance.

"I told you my answer, Maddie. No."

She walked to him, hips swaying with allure, with the ripe promise of pleasure so sharp.

Feeling sweat bead his brow, Brock swallowed against the temptation of her. "You owe me, Maddie. Think of this visit as a friendly reminder of that fact."

Maddie's seductive smile slipped. She glared at him for an unguarded moment before she righted her smoldering gaze. "Friendly reminder? I've no need for friendship."

"I think you do. I think you need it very badly."

With a flick of her tongue across her lush lips, Maddie sidled closer. "No, Brock. I need you to be my lover."

Her words punched him in the gut and challenged him to take her. Now. God help him, he wanted to do just that, claim her in a way so carnal, she could never forget him again.

Get hold of yourself, man. Clearly, Maddie wanted him to lose his head, do something rash. He refused to give her the satisfaction.

"Today, I came as a friend."

A flash of anger overtook Maddie's face. "If all friends threaten me as you have, God spare me such kindness."

Biting sarcasm, something she'd known nothing about five years ago. Touché.

Closing her eyes for a moment, Maddie composed herself. When she focused on him again, the practiced seductress was back. God, how he hated that. When he took her in their marriage bed, her passion would be damned real, he vowed.

"Maddie—"

"I don't need a friend. I only want you as a lover, Brock, in the terms we discussed. Come be my lover."

Someday he would be her lover, her husband, the father of her future children, in his time, on his terms. But not today.

Business had long ago taught him to attack when being attacked. He went on the offensive with Maddie.

"For argument's sake, say you considered me a friend. What would you expect me to do for you? Forget what you owe me?"

The implausibility of that suggestion rang in the thick air between them.

She hesitated. "No. I would merely ask for an extension or a compromise, both of which you have refused me so far."

"Because, as you say, I am not your friend. I seek a wife, not a mistress, not a debtor."

Maddie raised her gaze to him again, her stormy gray eyes locking with his, conveying her anger and some other tempestuous emotion with their darkening color.

"I made you an offer of repayment," she reminded him in a low voice reminiscent of honey and late-night whispers. It nearly undid him. "Repayment beyond your expectations."

He acknowledged her with a silent nod. She knew nothing of his expectations. Nor did he want to know what Sedgewick had taught Maddie about bed sport. Still, Brock knew he must distance himself from her—or she would drive him to reckless acts.

"I did not ask you to repay me with sex."

Brock expected her to flinch at his deliberately blunt statement. To his surprise, a smile played at the corners of her succulent mouth instead.

"And such a suggestion offends your delicate sensibilities?"

"No, just my financial ones," he said, repressing a grin.

"Then why are you here?" She scowled.

"So you do not forget what you owe me."

"You will never let me forget, I'm certain."

With a shrug, Brock made for the door. "Don't tarry too long, Maddie-cake. My patience is running thin."

"I can only threaten Maddie so much," Brock said to his father with a sigh as he entered the study in his town house.

"Not bending, is she?" Jack grinned.

Brock scowled as he removed his coat. "Not an inch. I don't remember that woman being quite so stubborn. She can't stand the sight of me. Hell, every time I'm in the same room with her daughter, Maddie sends the girl away, as if she's afraid I'm going to eat her for a snack."

Jack chuckled. "You really have made a good impression."

With a reproachful glance, Brock sat behind his desk. "Thank you. I needed your reminder that I've bumbled this." Brock raked a hand through his hair. "I have no idea what to do, how to make that woman marry me. My threats are losing their power."

"Would you really throw Maddie and her daughter in debtor's prison?" Jack asked over a glass of port.

"No." Though she had infuriated him by marrying Sedgewick, she hardly deserved that wretchedness.

"Maybe she knows your threats are hollow."

"I don't think so. I see terror on her face when I mention it." He sighed. "And she fears me, too. I see it in her eyes when I enter a room."

Jack rose and poured himself another glass of port. "That's your problem."

"What?" He frowned. "Maddie has to believe I mean business or I will never persuade her to marry me."

"All you've done with your threats, son, is put her back

to the wall. She's desperate and defensive. I don't think it was wise."

Bracing his elbows on his desk, Brock leaned forward. "Advice on women from the man who never remarried?"

Jack sent him a slow smile. "That hardly means I've spent all my time alone."

"Spare me the details." Brock held up his hand to ward off further conversation on that topic. "What would you have done, then? I could hardly kneel at the woman's feet and ask for her hand. That approach failed once. Five years ago she thought me beneath her. Her assessment has not changed one whit."

Bitterness surged like the tide in a storm, and Brock wondered why the hell Maddie's opinion mattered. It should not. She had made her opinion of him perfectly clear when she had refused to marry him—twice. This was not about his heart; it was about his future.

"And what have you accomplished with threats except to reaffirm her bad opinions?" asked Jack rhetorically.

Brock had no answer to that. "What are you suggesting?"

"Simply another approach. Since you can't go through her wall of defense, you must go underneath it."

Sighing, Brock stared at his father. "Translation, if you please."

"I've never known you to be so damned dense," Jack teased. "Seduce the girl, Brock. Ply her with wine, kisses, and compliments. Buy her clothes and jewels and nights on the town. Break down her resistance and she will accept."

"You've clearly gone mad," he muttered, then left the room.

But as the night grew later, Brock couldn't get his father's advice out of his head.

Each midnight, I will lie here and wait for you.

Brock lifted his glass of port to his mouth and consumed the contents in one long swallow, hoping to drive the echo of Maddie's voice from his head.

I need you to be my lover.

Wonderful; a new torment to add to his tortured mind and near-bursting body.

Gritting his teeth, Brock rose and opened the window in his bedroom, taking in huge draughts of the chilled night air, the soft scents of grass and impending rain, spring flowers . . . and Maddie.

Her voice rang inside him, the feel of her mouth beneath his like a drug, addicting him.

And his threats were losing their power—fast.

Drawing in another rush of sharp air, Brock pushed that fact aside and considered Jack's suggestion. It was ludicrous. How was he to seduce her without taking her as his mistress?

In the next moment, the answer came. Yes, he could do exactly that—and he knew precisely how. Turning from the window, he called for his cloak and his horse, purpose driving him, pounding in an impatient surge.

Outside, the crisp, dark night sharpened his senses. The moon's glow and mysterious fog heightened his fever.

He could reach St. John's Wood shortly after midnight, where Maddie would be, waiting just for him and his plans.

FIVE

Midnight chimed from the tiny clock beside her, startling Maddie. Dazed, she lay curled on the green sofa, a copy of a Fanny Burney novel belonging to Aunt Edith flat across her chest.

Brock wasn't coming. Maddie sighed, admitting the truth. He would not take her up on her offer. He would not be her lover to free her from debt. Defeat, disappointment, and fear together formed a solid stone in her stomach that weighed a ton.

What would she do now?

Maddie sat up and set the book aside. Prickly panic returned when she thought of facing either the Fleet or marriage. Rubbing cold hands together, she reconsidered her options. The Fleet could be deadly, a dark hell from which escape was impossible. Worse, Aimee might be taken from her, sent to a workhouse, where children endured terrible conditions and unspeakable cruelties.

Maddie would never let that happen—ever! Yet marriage could well be equally unthinkable.

Rising, she paced, nerves stretched taut and brittle.

Brock could make her life worse than hell if he chose. Colin had demonstrated with painful clarity that in marriage, a woman's body did not belong to her. She had endured his rough, inept couplings for years, along with his violent beating the week before his death—his answer to her lack of passion at his touch.

Though she felt desire for Brock—more than she thought possible after Colin's punishment—his actions bespoke an anger toward her, as if he somehow blamed her for marrying in the face of his abandonment. That, coupled with his ruthlessness, meant Brock could remove every ounce of autonomy, of life with peace, without violence, she had guarded zealously since Colin's death.

And if she married Brock, he could do far worse to Aimee.

Since she would become his child legally, he could mistreat Aimee simply because he believed the girl to be Colin's offspring. He could do anything he pleased to the child. Anything. Beat her, starve her. No one could stop him. He could even sell Aimee. He could send her baby away, where she might never see her daughter again. . . . Maddie would be powerless to prevent Brock from using Aimee to purge the anger he felt for her.

Even if he didn't harm Aimee, it would only be a matter of time before he discovered the fact that he was her father. He might take the girl from her, perhaps even poison Aimee against her mother for spite. Brock was persuasive enough— and wealthy enough—to do it. The courts would look the other way to anything he did.

Dear God, no. A tight fist of fear squeezed her insides as she worried, yet again, whether Brock saw any of himself in their daughter.

The Fleet or marriage—both options were completely unbearable. This plan, her only means of avoiding both, *must* work. Somehow, she would find a way to lure Brock to her bed.

Her mind whirled as she paced the stone floor restlessly. She must think of something else, some way to lure him here.

Behind her, a creak sounded, followed by the click of the door latch closing in near silence.

Maddie dashed to the foyer to find Brock in the cottage's doorway, winded, windblown, and silently imposing. He wore the hint of a smile, as if he hid a secret. Heat rolled off him in waves.

"You've come," she whispered, taking tentative, trembling steps in his direction.

"Yes." His gaze burned into her, pinning her in place as he removed his greatcoat and gloves. "I want to touch you, Maddie. I want to touch you in places you've never been touched before."

His bold confession sent heat bursting through her. Her head felt light. Her stomach clenched tight with desire. She swallowed against her fluttering pulse.

No. She had invited—encouraged—Brock's desire so he might fall prey to her wiles, not so she could succumb to his. She couldn't afford to lose her head, as she had with their last kiss, as she nearly had in response to his words.

Maddie drew in a deep breath. "That is why I'm here; to be your mistress, to please you—"

"I will not make love to you until we are wed, Maddie. But I want to touch you now."

Before Maddie could utter another word, Brock closed the distance between them in two long strides and took her face in his hot hands. He slanted his mouth over hers and took her lips in a melding of charged desire and shared breaths. She inhaled sharply in surprise, scenting something dark and strong and musky from Brock that sent her senses soaring. Mindlessly, she clutched his shoulders for support.

With bold insistence, he parted her lips and kissed her again. His tongue swept through her mouth possessively, as if it had every right to be there and always had. Her knees gave way beneath her, even as her mind screamed that she must think, must persuade him to become her lover—all without losing her self-control or another piece of her soul to this man.

Without warning, he lifted his mouth from her. Resting

his forehead against hers, his ragged breaths fell warm and erratic upon her lips. His chest heaved for air against her hands.

"Brock?" she whispered. "Make love to me now."

"Shhh." He stroked her face with a thumb across her cheek. "I gave in to temptation once before and shamed you. I will not do it again. I'll only have you as my wife."

Maddie cleared her throat against a sudden lump of emotion. Moisture stung her eyes. Angry at herself, she blinked it away. What a fool she was. Brock did not mean any of that beguiling speech. And even if he did, she did not believe in fairy tales of love or marriage anymore. Both made a woman too vulnerable in a man's world. But Brock's words . . . How sweet—and dangerous—to give in to the fantasy, for even a moment, that he cared for her, had always cared.

Practicality reminded her that she couldn't afford the price of fantasy.

She cleared her throat. "We are adults now, free to do as we please. We need not be bound by vows to enjoy each other."

"But vows are what I want, Maddie." He caressed her shoulders with gentle hands. Seduced by his touch, Maddie leaned dangerously into the solid length of his body. "You are what I want, completely."

Maddie felt her uneven breathing, her pulse accelerating at his words. What if he meant that, even a little? It would not matter, she told herself. She would not belong to any man ever again, especially not a treacherous one.

Her hands began to shake as she lifted them away from his chest and stepped back.

"I'm here to be your mistress, Brock. Take me now, tomorrow, and every other night for six months. During that time, I will be yours completely. But I will not marry you."

Brock's jaw tightened as he grasped her arms in a tight grip. He pulled her closer, under a raw stare that demanded her attention. Her heart beat faster yet at the feel of his warm, lean body—and full arousal—heavy against her.

"You will marry me, Maddie. I will come here every night to seduce you until you do. But I won't make love to you until you agree to be my wife."

The hard glitter of his green gaze told Maddie he was deadly determined. He was going to seduce her without making love to her? A dozen half-complete images flashed through her mind of Brock holding her, all wanton, making her yearn for his touch. Her skin flushed hot, a damp sheen of desire misting her all over. She stared at him, inexplicably intrigued, entranced. And scared to death he might succeed.

No. Forcing herself to look away, Maddie gathered her composure. Life, Colin, and Brock had all taught her hard lessons in the last five years, and primary among them was to never give over her self-control.

Maddie dug deep to find her bravado, deep from some store of boldness she hadn't even known she possessed until now.

Smiling in suggestion, she traced his mouth with her fingertip. "Let's not complicate our arrangement. Stay here and take pleasure in me."

Brock grabbed her hand, forcing her questing finger away from his mouth. "I won't do that, Maddie."

She sighed, confusion and frustration racking her. Couldn't he, for once, follow a path other than his own? Couldn't he take the offer she'd blatantly slid across the table to him?

"You can't mean to come here night after night to touch me yet not share my bed," she challenged.

"I'll do just that until you agree to my proposal."

Maddie stared at him, fighting a scowl. In her observation, men did not take waiting for physical intimacy well or happily. Surely Brock was no different. "I will have you in my bed soon."

Brow raised in question, intrigue transformed his square

face. Maddie wished suddenly that she could bite her assertion back. She'd bet her last farthing she had roused Brock's
unshakable competitive spirit.

"You're challenging me?" He laughed, his smile not at
all nice. "Yes, I like the idea of a wager. It would be very
interesting."

His implications horrified Maddie. "But—"

He went on as if she had not objected. "If I can . . . persuade you to agree to marriage prior to consummation, you
will be my wife. If, by chance, you are able to seduce me
into complete surrender, I will take you as my mistress and
forgive your debt."

Color flushed her face. Her heart rushed through her body.
Had he suggested what she thought he had? "Brock, I do
not—"

"And to win, you must seduce me into intercourse, Maddie. Anything else is merely . . . play."

Her body heated another fifty degrees. Anything else?
Did men have desires beyond the normal manner of congress? If so, she had little idea what they might be.

"Absolutely not! Private . . . matters like this should not
be fodder for games."

"Why not?" he asked. "We are at an impasse, otherwise."

"Touching me at all is like agreeing to make me your
mistress. I've let no one touch me since Colin died, so I'm
in no habit of taking lovers upon a whim."

His hands fell to her hips, fingers sinking into her flesh
as he pulled her closer to his hard body, his utter heat. The
blooming of warmth in her belly surprised her, and she bit
into her lip to hold a gasp inside.

"That argument doesn't follow, Maddie-cake. How many
men take a mistress without sharing her bed? And how can
you call me your lover if I don't make love to you?"

Maddie sighed in defeat, taking his point. Still, his wager
sounded too dangerous. They would grow close, very nearly
intimate, yet she would be no nearer to freeing herself of

debt unless he possessed her body completely. Could she take such a scandalous chance? Could she entice him to become her lover in every way when she knew so little about seduction?

She had more than a passing chance to succeed. Colin had roused only contempt with his touch, and despite the fact she had wanted Brock once, the desire had been in her heart, not her loins. Certainly she could resist him now.

The hells of marriage and the Fleet loomed large in her confused mind, pointing out that she had little choice.

"Agreed," she whispered finally.

Brock hesitated an instant before releasing her. A terrible return of vulnerability assailed her, dousing her body like icy water. She crossed her arms over her chest, as if that would save her from his searing gaze, which seemed to unravel her composure, layer by layer. He could never know how she feared the effect his nearness had on her self-control. He would have no hesitation in using it against her.

"Will you return here tomorrow night?" she asked, fighting to keep the tremor from her voice.

"Why wait?" he asked with a naughty grin.

With wide, wary eyes, she watched as he pulled out a Yorkshire bow back chair from behind the small breakfast table and sat. He bounced, as if testing its weight, before he raised his gaze to her, wearing a supremely satisfied grin.

"Come here," he said, crooking his finger to call her.

She didn't like his mood shift—from tender to challenging to serious to playful—any more than she liked his actions. Did he seek to have her on that chair? Her head spun. Her heart raced. Why could she not understand the man? Fend him off in the normal ways of logic?

Why did the thought of him taking her on the chair fill her with a sharp clench of forbidden need?

"No," she said automatically.

His generous mouth turned down in a mock pout that

somehow made Maddie ache to kiss him. "That's not the answer a good mistress would give."

"You said you did not seek a mistress."

"True." He shrugged. "But if that's what you seek to be, should you not act the part? You cannot seduce me into bedding you if I cannot get close enough to touch you."

He was right, she realized with panic. She was going to have to let him touch her, in any manner and in any place that he desired. The thought made her feel faint. Yes, she had always known he would touch her if he made her his mistress, but she had assumed that would be about creating his pleasure, not seducing her until she experienced her own.

"Come here," he repeated.

Maddie felt her body thrum at the mere sound of his voice, a voice that filled her with images of his hands on her aching flesh, his mouth clinging to her own. That self-reliant core in her resisted the idea of leading herself like a lamb to his slaughter. But she had no choice.

Her thighs trembled beneath her as she took slow steps toward him. Maddie drew in a deep breath for courage, feeling oddly like a soldier going to battle. Her pulse pounded in her ears with each step, closer, closer, until she stood inches away.

Without warning, he bent forward. His fingers brushed her ankles, her quaking calves and thighs as he lifted her skirts and snowy petticoats about her hips, nearly exposing her to his hungry gaze. Cool air and the heat of his stare hit her.

With seemingly little effort, Brock lifted her and slid her onto his lap, legs spread on either side of his hips. Maddie gasped. He did not pause until her skirts billowed around them, fabric rustling like a lover's whisper.

When he pressed her against him, she gasped in shock at the heat of him, the sensation of their contact. The crush of his steely shaft pressing through his breeches, against her feminine mound, flooded her with a sharp yearning. He smelled of night and insistence and musk as he clasped her hips and fitted her against him. Wriggling for freedom, she quickly discovered, only stunned her with a tighter ache, a more insistent need.

His steady green stare heated her face, touched her mouth, then focused on the swells of her breasts. Everywhere his gaze lingered turned hot; she was burning up from the inside.

"I told you I want you."

His husky quip held a smile. She responded to him like a flower, yearning to open for him, accept the pleasure his touch promised. Closing her eyes, she tried to remember all the reasons she must fight giving in to these sensations and still entice him into her bed.

His mouth closed over hers, a sizzle of insistence burning away at her ability to think, to breathe. She tasted him everywhere, inhaled him as she drew in her next sharp breath, felt him beneath her, around her. His hands rose to cup her face, guiding the blistering kiss as her passion rose a notch and his tongue entered her mouth with a demand that made her feel boneless. She clutched him, moaned into his mouth. Her tense fingers curled around the velvet stone of his shoulders when she felt his hands on her buttons, the dress yield to his efforts as he pushed it away from her torso, down her arms.

Seconds later, his hot hands cupped her breasts, pushed up by her corset. Jaw taut, eyes slitted like glittering shards of green, he lifted their weight, thumbs teasing their tight buds. That quickly, a relentless ache blazed through her body.

She had never felt like this—so wanton—in her life.

Her thin chemise served as the only barrier between them. Maddie arched toward his wondrous touch. She did not want to move, did not want to lose the pleasure.

Brock's fingers found the corset's strings. "You wear too many damn clothes, Maddie."

Her mind registered his breathy words as he removed the cinching garment, then yanked on the faded pink ribbon of her chemise. The thin garment fell down her shoulders to her upper arms, gaping open across her breasts. Before she could utter a word, he pushed the lawn garment aside with an impatient shove and lifted her flesh toward him. Then he fastened his hot mouth on her bare breast.

Ecstasy flooded her as he suckled hard, curling in her belly, winding around her thighs. Maddie grew moist.

He was heaven, filling her with the kind of need Colin never could. She gasped as her world tilted crazily, his tantalizing tongue swirling about her sensitive flesh to enslave her passion. Blindly, she reached out for support in her off-kilter world. Her tense fingers found the chair's curved back. She grabbed tight, the cool wood her anchor in a captivating domain of desire.

His teeth found her, abrading her aching nipples gently. Maddie cried out with need. By instinct, she tossed her head back, arching her breasts closer to his magical mouth.

Dear God, where had he learned to give such pleasure?

The tight clench in her belly moved lower, clasping mercilessly on the apex between her thighs. Hot want joined the fray there, creating a throb of pleasure that pulsed in rhythm with her heartbeat. She tried to wind her legs around him, but the back of the chair frustrated her efforts. Still, she pressed herself against the length of his erection, which had grown thicker, heavier. She rocked her body against his and called out his name on a throaty moan.

"What do you want, Maddie?" His normally smooth voice was as rough as gravel.

She could only moan again.

"You'll have to say it," he coaxed, then flicked his tongue across each sensitive bud of her nipples. "Tell me."

"You," she panted. "I want you."

He slid his hands beneath her green skirts, fingers trailing fire up her thighs, then reached for the opening of his breeches. He stopped. "Tell me what you want."

His tongue laved one tingling breast again as he cupped the other in his hand, rolling the tip between his fingers.

"Ask me," he urged, breath uneven.

Maddie swayed in his grip, arching toward his stiff arousal. He grasped her hips and rocked her against him.

The ache grew keen and demanding. "Make love to me."

Without waiting for his reply, she reached for the buttons of his shirt and ripped them open to run frantic hands against the taut planes of his chest. "Now."

Brock nipped her neck with his seeking mouth, then whispered, "Yes."

Their naked chests met, his unyielding, hers so responsive. Maddie moaned as she pressed her mouth to his steely shoulder, tasting the salty tang of his skin.

"I will make love to you constantly, repeatedly," he vowed, "once you agree to marry me."

"What?" she muttered, comprehending that he'd said something distasteful that she wasn't ready to face.

"Marry me and I will satisfy you every night of your life."

His whisper finally pierced Maddie's haze of lust. His words tempted her—all except the marriage part. Lord, how had she allowed herself to get so carried away in his arms?

Breathing harshly, she scrambled off his lap, struggling with her chemise and staring at him in accusation. "Marry? You should want to make love to me."

He stood. Maddie was horrified to see she'd torn away most of his shirt's buttons in her attempt to touch his skin. The slabs of his muscled chest lay exposed to her, his skin burnished like gold silk. Lower, she saw the thick proof of his desire through his breeches, rigid and irrefutable.

Her ache collided with anger and other, less easily defined emotions. She was horrified by her response to him, by her behavior. How had she lost control of herself so quickly? Furious tears pricked her eyes.

"You can see very well that I want you," Brock rasped.

He reached out, knuckles skimming the swollen tips of the breasts she had not been able to cover. Need screamed inside her again. She bit her lip against the pleasure.

"Answer the question, Maddie-cake. Will you marry me?"

Feeling betrayed by him, by her own body, she backed away farther, fumbling with the ties of her chemise. "No."

Anger thundered across Brock's face, but he did not look surprised. "Then you have the answer to your own question."

With that, he retrieved his coat and gloves, not bothering to don them, then left, disappearing into the night.

Brock felt Maddie's tense fingers graze his arm as he escorted her into Lord and Lady Moore's ballroom.

He'd been half certain Maddie would turn down the invitation from her mother's cousin, if she had received one at all. He'd been even more certain she would find a way to avoid accompanying him. He supposed his terse note yesterday hadn't been bad strategy, since she'd had little time to consider his demand. The fact that it accompanied a new and very expensive gown in exotic bronze that made her glow radiantly had not hurt his cause. But it was killing him to wonder if she'd worn the lacy undergarments he had sent with the dress.

Remembering the taste of her breast in his mouth and pondering the answer to that question, he almost wished they were back at that damned cottage . . . almost. Unfortunately, the restraint he had exercised three nights earlier had cost him lost sleep and erotic daydreams. He'd even had a difficult time focusing yesterday when he'd met with Mr. Stephenson, the railroad's brilliant engineer.

No doubt being alone with Maddie would likely lead his crumbling resistance to collapse. The gasping wonder of her response had fired his blood. Somehow she made him believe no other man had aroused her as thoroughly. The possibility made him ache.

Snorting cynically, he shoved the thought away before he embarrassed himself in polite company.

Besides, he could not mingle with the Duke of Cropthorne at Maddie's cottage. But here . . . here, he could socialize with the man, perhaps share drinks, a game of cards, and meaningful conversation about his favorite subject, money.

As they descended the stairs, the butler announced them. "The Viscountess of Wolcott and Mr. Brock Taylor."

Instantly, heads swerved in their direction. He heard a gasp or two. Maddie lifted her chin proudly, her mouth grim. Perversely, he pulled her closer. The *ton* needed to see them together, to get used to the idea that one of their own stood at his side, if they were to be man and wife.

Lady Moore rushed through the throng to greet Maddie, her complexion flushed. "Lady Wolcott, how wonderful to see you out and about again. I'd begun to think we would lose you to Hampstead forever."

Maddie turned on her smile, transforming her face into a stunning vision of burnished beauty, complete with a full ruby mouth. "I could not miss your affair. It seems an age since I've seen you. Do you know Mr. Taylor?"

"I do not," said Lady Moore crisply.

Maddie turned to him. "Mr. Taylor, meet Lady Moore."

Brock took the lady's hand and brought it to his lips for a proper greeting. "How pleasant to meet you, my lady."

"Mr. Taylor." She nodded and extracted her hand, clearly wishing him elsewhere.

Maddie resisted a smile. The snub served Brock right. He was naïve if he expected the *ton* to accept him easily. But if he wished to make a fool of himself, she certainly would not stop him.

Without another word to Brock, Lady Moore turned back to Maddie. "And Aimee—how is the little darling?"

"She's wonderful. Energetic and talkative, and wonderful."

"Splendid. Please refresh yourselves." She pointed to a room down the hall containing a full table of pastries and delectibles. "I must greet the rest of my guests."

With that, Lady Moore turned away and disappeared into the crowd again.

Brock smiled wryly. "Apparently I am not her favorite guest."

"Did you expect to be? People are stunned."

Indeed, Brock could see with a glance that most of the crowd in the ballroom stared. Ladies whispered behind fans and dance cards, while gentlemen merely cast him glances ranging from the disapproving to the curious.

He laughed. "You know what we must do, don't you?"

"Leave?" she supplied helpfully.

His grin widened as he winked. "No. We must dance."

Brock led her to the floor, nearly filled with couples lined up for a waltz, and spun her around to join the others. He ignored the crowd's stares and whispers.

His hands met Maddie's just as their gazes connected. He felt a throb of awareness, an instant urge to remove her dress and more fully explore all her musky secrets. Her scent of jasmine and vanilla clouded his senses. Lord, she could make him want her so easily.

"Where did you learn to dance?" Surprise lay evident on her ivory-skinned face.

Brock toyed with the idea of telling her that he, as a grown man, had hired people to teach him every social grace. Why remind her that he had not been born wealthy? Instead, he leaned in and whispered, "You look beautiful, Maddie."

Her gaze grew guarded at his compliment. "I truly think we should leave."

"Nonsense," he contradicted, pulling her closer. He drew his lips up in an amused smile. "I'm just settling in."

Later that evening, Brock approached the card table, his heart thundering. There sat the Duke of Cropthorne, playing cards with another gent. Quietly, Brock sat down beside the man whose help—and money—he needed for the railroad and waited for his opportunity.

At first, Cropthorne did not lift his head from his cards. His sleek black hair was cut to razor perfection. His equally black brows slashed over dark eyes that revealed no expression. Though fashionably dressed, the precision and severity of his garments conveyed his exacting standards. Cropthorne never engaged in any activity that might cause tongues to wag. Ever.

Perhaps the duke would not speak to him. To approach him, Brock would breach etiquette, which was bound to lift a brow or two.

"I'm done for the evening," Cropthorne said suddenly, pushing his cards across the table with a disgusted sigh. "Damnable luck."

The man at his side shot Cropthorne a happy smirk, then scooped up his winnings. "You do not have your father's luck with cards, your grace."

"Because I do not cheat."

With an awkward nod, the gentleman murmured a farewell and left.

"Perhaps I can improve your luck," Brock said into the thick silence.

Cropthorne turned his way. "Can you, Mr. Taylor?"

Surprise almost blinded Brock.

It must have shown, because Cropthorne laughed in a deep rumble. "Yes, I know who you are."

He stared at the man, wondering when and how Cropthorne had become acquainted with his name. No matter, he realized. Here was his opportunity.

"I'm confounded," he admitted finally.

"Don't be. Everyone wants to know someone who can make money multiply faster than rabbits. Drink?" He motioned to a servant.

"Indeed." Brock took champagne from the tray and sipped.

"How do you plan to change my luck?" Cropthorne asked without preamble.

"Railroads. London to Birmingham. I am looking for a partner."

Cropthorne said nothing, clearly mulling the thought over.

"The industrial possibilities are endless," Brock added. "First-class passenger service could be quite plush, with fares charged in accordance. We could provide second-class service that caters to the working class. The line could eventually be extended to the Scottish border, and perhaps into Edinburgh. We will line the route with profitable hotels. Within a year or two, we should be fully functional. I have consulted with some very shrewd people—engineers, experts on commerce. I've little doubt you would make your money back in three years or less."

"Getting started is an expensive proposition." There was no objection in Cropthorne's voice.

"With limitless gains to be had," Brock countered. "I've hired an engineer, Robert Stephenson. He has a brilliant engine design that far outclasses anything currently in use."

"Hmmm."

"The land is nearly secured, just awaiting funds." And Maddie's agreement to be his wife. "I've gained the Royal assent necessary, had the parcels surveyed and the track designed using the latest technology."

"Impressive," he said without sounding impressed at all.

Refusing to be put off, Brock continued, "Very. Rail travel

is happening now. People *will* make money, exponential returns on their investments, I believe. It is the future."

"Why me?"

Brock plunged ahead without hesitation. "After the unfortunate incident with the mines, I thought you might be looking for a lucrative investment."

A cynical smile curled the corners of Cropthorne's wide mouth. "How did you hear about that? I tried like the devil to keep it quiet."

Brock shrugged. It was his turn to smile. "Let's just say I make it my business to learn these things." It was one reason making money came more easily to him than it did to most.

"I'll think on it," Cropthorne said finally.

Holding in a sigh, Brock produced a card and handed it to the other man. He supposed any answer other than a flat refusal had promise. "Call on me when you decide, but it must be soon. We have competition. I want to start quickly."

Hopeful, Brock left the card table and the room to seek out Maddie. She wasn't hard to spot, dressed in such an unusual shade. Looking around, Brock noted with pride that she was the only woman in the room who could carry such a color. The rest had to settle for insipid pastels and pray the color didn't overpower them.

Beside Maddie stood a woman, tall with lush chestnut hair, wearing one of the aforementioned pale shades he disliked. The two women exchanged words—an argument from the looks of Maddie's profile. He edged closer, certain she had not yet spotted him.

"In under an hour, you have become the favored food for gossip," hissed the woman. "Everyone here is staring and whispering. Even worse, Lady Litchfield looked askance at me. You know if she cuts me, my season will be ruined. Ruined, I tell you!" the woman huffed, indignant. "Colin would be shuddering in his very grave if he could see this travesty."

Brock saw Maddie glare at the other woman. "Roberta, Lady Litchfield wounds people every season. You shall not be the last, I am sure. As for your brother, he has been gone for three years. You couldn't possibly believe his opinion— or yours—would sway anything I do now."

"I shouldn't expect so, given the fact you hardly cared for his good opinion while he lived. As his sister, I was often privy to the intimate details of his life. I know you never cared for him," the thin woman hurled in accusation.

Brock stood frozen in place. Was it possible Maddie had not loved Sedgewick? If so, why the hell had she married the fop instead of waiting for his own return? Position, he reminded himself. A title. *Blue blood,* his bitterness goaded.

"How much did you care for Wallace before his death, Roberta?" challenged Maddie.

"My late husband was twice my age and the match was arranged. Hardly the same thing at all. You only married Colin because you thought he had money, because you wanted to be a viscountess."

Maddie said nothing. The sinking stone of dread told Brock that Roberta's accusation held some truth.

Colin's sister looked ready to stamp her feet in frustration. "Why did you bring Mr. Taylor here? He is completely beneath the Sedgewick name, which you still bear."

"I came here tonight to see Lady Moore," responded Maddie, her voice on edge, "not that my actions are any of your affair."

"He is a *servant*. Your servant, at one time. This will reflect badly on the Sedgewick reputation, on me."

"You seem to think everything is about you, Roberta. You might be surprised to learn that isn't so."

On that stinging note, Maddie turned from the woman and nearly walked into Brock.

With a scowl, she grabbed his arm. "I want to leave."

Brock glanced at Maddie as he led her away from the whining Roberta. Maddie's pale complexion and tight lips only accentuated her heavy lids and the dark smudges beneath her pale gray eyes.

"You look exhausted."

She gave him a tired laugh. "Roberta has that effect on me."

Though he had questions, along with a healthy urge to verbally pound Lady Dudley into the highly polished dance floor, he refrained from either.

As they gathered their cloaks and departed, he wondered why he felt compelled to protect Maddie from the family she had abandoned him for and deemed good enough to marry into. Why did he care about her at all?

Kent Wainwright, Viscount Belwick, stared at Lady Dudley as she watched Brock Taylor and his lady leave the ball. Roberta's full-lipped pout more than hinted at her displeasure. He smiled as she tossed her head in agitation, sending thick strands of her glossy dark hair fluttering around her perfect profile. If anyone had ever looked ready to talk, it was Lady Dudley.

He inched back to approach her from behind, then leaned in to whisper, "Shocking, isn't it?"

Roberta whirled to face him. "Pardon me? Oh, Lord Belwick. I did not see you there."

"Not at all." He took her hand and brought it just short of his lips. "I said, isn't Brock Taylor's presence at a *ton* event like this shocking?"

"Exactly what I told my sister-in-law. But does she listen? Of course not! She hardly cares how I shall be talked about."

Ah, so Brock's lady was Madeline Sedgewick. Interesting, indeed. Rumor had it Taylor had once worked for the late Lord Avesbury, Lady Madeline's father, and that Taylor had been dismissed without reference. At the time, he had hardly paid attention, for he had never imagined a mere stable hand would ever be his competitor in opening England to railroads.

Thank God, he never forgot gossip entirely. One never knew when such tidbits would be useful. Or people, for that matter, he thought, staring at Roberta. Given her connection to Lady Wolcott, and by association Brock Taylor, he might do well to see just how much she knew. And since gossip had it that Lady Dudley had taken more than one lover in recent months, he saw no reason not to approach the widow.

"Lady Wolcott is indeed inconsiderate not to take your feelings into account."

Tears pooled in the woman's hazel eyes. "Completely!"

"Do not upset yourself," he crooned, producing a handkerchief.

Lady Dudley wiped her eyes and nose with the scrap of linen. When she would have handed it back to him with her thanks, Kent held a hand of protest aloft.

"Keep it, fair lady." He dropped his voice an octave. "You may return it to me when I call tomorrow. Perhaps we can talk more then?"

Roberta's gaze flashed across his face. Her inviting smile was indeed easy to read. Kent held in a sigh. Lady Dudley was an attractive, though tiresome, woman. Still, he could sacrifice a few nights in her bed for the potential to make a fortune. First, he had to eliminate the competition.

"Indeed, I shall look forward to talking with you tomorrow," came her reply.

Kent smiled and kissed her hand, lingering much too long for propriety. "Until then."

SIX

Brock entered the cottage the following midnight, wearing stunning evening black, his cravat askew and a gleam in his eye. Tonight, he seemed formidable, hungry. The impact of his presence made Maddie shiver.

Brock had always affected her, even five years earlier, when he had been a servant with daring ideas and big dreams of wealth.

He paused in the cottage's doorway. She watched silently, her heart beating in a heavy thud. The power of his reckless grins and drugging kisses should be illegal. She closed her eyes, praying for the strength to resist him. She must focus on the revenge she had promised herself for his abandonment. But wanting him came dangerously easy. She could hardly deny the heady anticipation that coursed through her when he closed the door with a quiet click and stepped into the flickering candlelight.

He looked ready with an easy smile, a wicked word . . . or more.

Drawing in an uneven breath, Maddie fought to find apathy. But from their last evening here, Maddie knew just how powerful an ache he could awaken within her. Gone was the ardent though awkward lover she had known in her father's stables. The bliss he had shown her that one stolen night in the hay had been of the heart, a joining of souls. The pleasure of flesh had been but a brief warmth. But dear God, what he had made her feel mere nights ago . . . She could scarcely find words to describe those hot, compelling sensations. She knew only one thing: when she next shared Brock's bed he would unleash a deluge of desire unlike anything she had ever dreamed. Few realizations had ever frightened her more.

Rising from her oversized chair on trembling legs, she greeted him with what she hoped was a seductive smile. "Hello, Brock. I'm glad you have come."

"Good evening, Maddie. Champagne?" he asked, lifting up a bottle she had not previously noticed for her inspection.

She frowned. "We have no society here."

"Must there be?" he asked, sauntering forward until the golden candlelight caressed his dexterous hands and tapered fingers as they worked at the cork.

"One usually drinks champagne at social events," she pointed out.

His reckless grin appeared with a flash of white teeth. "Why wait to enjoy the best?"

Why, indeed? Maddie had no real answer for that as the cork gave way with a resounding pop in the nearly silent room. "No reason, I suppose."

Foam bubbled over the neck of the bottle and splashed onto the breakfast table in a cool puddle. Brock laughed, a hearty sound that made her alarmingly aware of his mouth.

From his interior coat pockets, Brock withdrew two fine crystal glasses and filled them with the pale, potent brew, then handed her one. "What shall we drink to? Interesting wagers, perhaps?"

Maddie's fingers curled around the crystal, wondering if the man knew how to be anything but audacious. Here he was in the thick of the night, visiting his would-be mistress whom he had no intention of making love to. He sipped champagne without society and sported a too-attractive grin, while reducing the most important determinant in her life to a mere wager.

She had known he was different from the first time they had spoken. A week after he had come to work at Ashdown Manor, her father had informed her that she would have a season that year. With his shaking finger and stern countenance, he had made it clear that he expected her to marry well. Nervous and fearful, Maddie had sought refuge outdoors, on her mare's back. Unfortunately, thunder and twilight had proven too much for her skittish horse. The mare had reared at the sharp crack and sent her hurtling to the ground. Brock had been there first. He'd been so handsome and solicitous, setting her naïve heart to sighing. He had quickly ascertained that she was not hurt, made light of the fall, and used his words to put her embarrassment aside. For the next three months she had been love-struck.

Shaking away the bittersweet memory, she found Brock still awaiting a toast. Summoning every ounce of brazenness she possessed, she stepped closer, swaying her hips. She looked directly into his eyes, now the color of a summer forest. Placing her hand on the warm width of his firm chest, she whispered, "Why drink to wagers when you can toast pleasure?"

Without another word, Maddie lifted the glass to her lips and emptied it, her thigh pressed to his. She prayed it roused awareness in him, for the visceral contact did irrepressible things to her pulse.

The champagne tickled her nose, then sluiced down her throat in a tangy slide of effervesce. Moments later it warmed her belly. And the warmth spread to all parts of her body, most especially to their nuzzling thighs. Brock's heated gaze only served to make her aware of their seclusion. Apprehension squeezed its tight fist about her throat.

"Yes," he murmured, his gaze intent on her mouth. "I never refuse drinking to pleasure."

Brock threw his head back and gulped the liquid down.

Maddie watched the thick column of his throat working, surrounded by the loosened cravat of snowy white. The room felt much too warm as a flush of awareness came over her. Now that they had drunk to pleasure, would he take her to the bed upstairs and give her a night full of his touch?

"I'm in the mood for a good game, Maddie."

Mind racing, she pondered all the possible interpretations of that statement. A thousand tangled images of bare skin and openmouthed kisses leapt immediately to mind. She drew in a shuddering breath.

He produced a deck of cards. "Speculation, perhaps?"

Cards? Brock wanted to play cards? Maddie stared at the man who had become more of an enigma than she had ever imagined. Why would he not be interested in her as a mistress?

Purposely swaying against him and hoping she didn't appear awkward, Maddie curled her fingers about his shoulders. She ignored the small thrill being so close to him incited. "Cards are for dotty old ladies and stodgy gentlemen." She trailed a soft fingertip down the hard line of his jaw. "We are capable of far better . . . sport than cards, I'll wager."

Brock raised a contemplative brow. When his gaze left her face to glance down at her cleavage, visible above the green moiré dress he had given her, she tingled in anticipation. Would he touch her now? Maddie dropped her hands to her sides to afford him a better view of the swells of her breasts and waited for the sinful pleasure of his touch to come.

Instead, Brock stepped away and pulled out one of the Yorkshire bow-back chairs at the breakfast table.

Taking a seat, he waved her to one across the odious table. "But I find speculation so stimulating. Will you deal?"

Maddie stared at the deck as he slid the cards across the table. Apparently, he was serious. She could feel a damp ache building within her, and he wanted to play cards? With a sigh of frustration, she picked up the deck.

"Dealer wagers double, Maddie. Those are the rules."

Her gaze flew to him. "You know I have nothing to wager."

That brutally sexy grin returned. "Not true."

"You are fully aware I have no money," she reminded him in exasperation.

"You have words, Maddie. Answers. If you win, I will answer a question. If I win, you will answer two."

How like Brock to make up his own rules. His daring ideas, his unique view of life had always attracted her. Five years ago, she'd been suffering the pressures of preparing for a season that filled her with anxiety, the pressures of marrying very well, of exhibiting perfect behavior in polite society. All the while, he had talked of discovering what made her happy, of casting aside senseless convention.

Brock had listened to her dreams and feelings—and cared for them—in a way no one ever had, particularly her father. Certainly, the old man had never asked her what she sought from life, nor would he have cared for her answer. Her duty as his daughter had been to bring more fortune to the family through marriage. She had failed abysmally, and the rift between father and daughter had never healed.

Still, how wonderful Brock's bold ideas had seemed to her girlish heart then, the concept of doing nothing more than pleasing herself, marrying where she wanted—marrying Brock, even.

He had quickly shown her how foolish such dreams were.

"Two answers? That ante is unfair," she protested.

"I never claimed to be fair. Now deal."

Maddie thought briefly of refusing but knew it would not do to madden the irritating man. If he wanted to play his absurd game, she must play. As long as he was here and happy, she stood a chance of becoming his mistress and saving herself from the despised servitude of marriage or debtor's prison.

Without another word, Maddie dealt them each three cards, then the trump card faceup between them. Their play was swift. Maddie quickly discovered that Brock had a knack for cards, never forgetting what had been played and guessing all too accurately which cards she held. The game lasted less than five minutes.

"Now you must answer two questions," he reminded her, his smile that of a pirate.

Disliking his tone, she stared at Brock through eyes narrowed with suspicion. "What two questions?"

He looked at her, seeming to ponder his next words. Maddie gritted her teeth, for she had little doubt he already knew exactly what he intended to ask.

"Get on with it," she snapped.

"Always impatient." He laughed and reached across the table to brush a tender stroke across her lips with his thumb.

Maddie froze. The years between them peeled away as she recalled all the times he had touched her with that playful affection. Something inside her chest gave a quick pang.

She had missed that unforeseen way Brock had about him. Colin had always taken life so seriously. He had been self-indulgent and self-absorbed, and predictable for it. Brock had always been a mystery, a thrilling, heart-stopping puzzle. But that caress of her mouth . . . that had always been constant.

With a glance at Brock's face, she realized his smile had faded. He, too, remembered those days of love's exciting discovery, the belief that anything was possible between them.

He cleared his throat, his blatant gaze unwavering. "What are you wearing beneath that dress?"

Against her will, Maddie felt herself flush like a schoolgirl. "The sheer, lacy shift you sent, along with the matching garters and stockings."

Brock closed his eyes and groaned. "I dreamt of you wearing just those lacy underthings."

With the deep resonance of his confession, her attention belonged to him. Maddie could have no more turned away from the mesmerizing velvet of his voice and the curve of his rich mouth than she could have denied her next breath.

Brock opened those enthralling green eyes and stared at her, seeming to penetrate her mind, her soul. "I can't tell you how badly that dream made me want to kiss my way up your body, then bury myself deep, deep inside you."

His words nearly unraveled her sanity. Need flared through her like a midsummer skyrocket. Logic fled to God-knew-where. Why did her body want him so badly in return? Why was Brock, despite his betrayal, the only man she had ever responded to?

By the time she regained her reasoning and realized she should seduce him with an offer to show him those dainty underthings, he went on to his next question.

"How did you arrive here tonight?" He regarded her with thoughtful curiosity.

"My horse."

He scowled. "Did you ride into the City before dusk?"

"Heavens, no. I cooked for Aunt Edith and her companion, Vema, then we ate together. I read Aimee a bedtime story and tucked her safely away. After she fell asleep, I came here."

"You rode here by yourself, in the dark, across Hampstead Heath?"

The incredulity in his tone took her aback. "I've already answered three questions, sir. More than our ante demanded."

Brock leaned in, looking very unhappy indeed. "You did ride by yourself in the dark, and you've done it each night for the past two weeks. Do you have any concept at all how dangerous that is?"

Of course she did, Maddie thought with indignation. Still,

she could not seduce Brock from Ashdown Manor while he stayed in London. Necessity had forced her to sweep aside those realities.

"There are all manner of vagabonds and thieves, dastards awaiting a tempting morsel like you," he said, grabbing her hand.

Both annoyance and pleasure tugged at her. He had no right to judge her actions, yet he appeared to have genuine concern for her welfare. Why did the man confuse her so much?

She tugged her hand away. "I've nothing to give a thief. The vagabonds and dastards have thus far had no problem in resisting any temptation I might present."

His eyes narrowed. "And you leave here in the dark as well, I assume."

Maddie threw back her shoulders. "I like to be home when Aimee awakens and share breakfast with her."

Sweeping his gaze across her face, Brock seemed to take in every detail. "No wonder you look exhausted. How much sleep do you manage each night? Three or four hours?"

"That is another question and not within the ante."

"Forget the ante," he said as he rose and rounded the table to her side. "You cannot continue this way. You will either be attacked or become ill. I won't have either on my conscience."

Maddie watched with wide eyes as he knelt before her and took her fingers in his gentle grip. Concern shone from his eyes, despite his harsh words. She felt a wave of insidious emotion. How nice it was to be cared about instead of always caring for someone else. How like Brock to see through her facade of a seductress to find this weakness.

The Brock of old had been this way, too. Thoughtful, somehow understanding her needs before she understood them herself. She had missed that about him most after her dreadful marriage to the selfish Colin.

Gathering her scattered emotions, she murmured, "Should anything happen to me, I absolve you now——"

"You can't, Maddie."

"But I choose to come here——"

"For me," he said with a squeeze of her hand. "Stop this dangerous game and marry me."

The offer wrenched at her from somewhere deep inside. She stifled the feeling, reminding herself that Brock was good at weaving a dream where tradition was cast aside for desire, and all things were possible for the wanting. Colin, with his ugly words, degrading slurs, insinuations, and, finally, his brutal hands, had taught her reality.

No, she would not put herself in Brock's path permanently. He might seem to care now. Colin had, in the beginning. Caring had slowly turned to frustration, irritation, contempt, then hatred. Her days with Brock could likely end the same way. And Brock was likely to live longer than Colin's carousing ways had allowed. She would not gamble against logic.

"No," she said finally. "I will come here each night to warm your bed at your leisure, nothing more."

"Blast it, woman, do not be so stubborn! Marriage would solve so many problems for both of us."

"No."

Brock swore viciously. "Then I will find us a cottage nearby. In Paddington, perhaps. You will not leave Ashdown Manor until my carriage comes for you. It will return you home."

The biting finality in his tone very nearly made her flinch. She could not decide whether to shout or cry. Again, his brash care struck a cord within her, but anger felt safer.

"I do not have to do anything you say, you——"

"It will be my way or the wager is off. Then it's marriage or a debtor's consequence; the choice is yours, Maddie."

Which meant she would either be forced to wed him or find herself in the Fleet. She lunged out of the chair and tore her hands from his, letting a wide streak of anger charge through her. The wretch was high-handed, insistent on having things his own way. And he called her stubborn?

Still, having a trysting spot closer would solve many problems. She had often feared for her own safety, traversing the notorious Heath by herself so late at night. The extra sleep sounded heavenly to her weary body. And having Aimee a tad closer, just in case, would be something of a relief.

"Very well. I will accept the offer of a closer cottage," she said finally.

Brock released a sigh, as if he'd been holding his breath. "Good. I will look about tomorrow for some possibilities."

That settled, Brock turned away, abandoning the cards and the champagne, and headed for the door. Surprise washed over her mind as panic clawed at her stomach.

"Wait! You're leaving? We haven't . . ."

Maddie flushed as she groped for the appropriate words. Every term she knew—consummated, had intercourse, engaged in congress—sounded so awkward, so formal.

Brock watched her, a wisp of an amused smile curling up the corner of his wide mouth. Slow steps took him back to her side. She found herself holding her breath as his blatantly male face drew near. He stood so close, she felt the heat his strong body radiated, smelled his cologne and the elemental spice that clung to his skin alone. But he did not touch her.

"There's always tomorrow night, Maddie-cake. Tonight, go home and sleep." He turned and strode for the door.

Holding in a futile protest, Maddie watched Brock go, torn between fury at his imperious demands, the terrible tangle of desire he'd created, the worry that he no longer wanted her as badly as her body craved him—and a softness she wanted to deny.

At the peak of her feelings, however, was one that frightened her most of all: the trembling realization that some part of her wanted him to care.

* * *

As night fell in London two days later, Brock sat in the walnut-paneled study of Gavin William Alexander Daggett, the Duke of Cropthorne. Calling upon Cropthorne after receiving an invitation, the titled gentleman had promptly advised Brock to address him in any way except "your grace." Cropthorne didn't want a potential business partner addressing him with a formality nearly equaling the Pope. With a wry smile, Brock agreed, tried to slow his racing heart, and presented his proposal for the T & S Railroad.

Two hours later, firelit shadows slanted over the sketches, furious notes, and empty glasses of port that lay on the desk between them. Cropthorne's bottle-green superfine coat lay discarded on the back of the sofa.

With nothing more to say, Brock looked at Cropthorne expectantly. The solemn office, draped in subdued deep greens and browns, seemed to exacerbate the thick silence.

"You've put a great deal of thought into this venture," said the duke finally, as he raked a long-fingered hand through his black hair. "It is impressive, I confess."

"I believe we can make your fifty thousand pounds into two hundred in under five years," Brock assured him.

A burning resolve to make the railroad a reality scorched through his veins. The T & S would be the best in England, servicing passengers by the thousands every year, earning all her investors money beyond their expectations. His name would be one of the most venerable in London financial circles. Men would respect who he had become. His wealth alone would assure he would rarely—if ever—be snubbed by the *ton* again. His business would thrive beyond his every wild dream. The risk of his entire fortune would come back tenfold.

And Maddie would be his, for better, for worse. Forever. *Each midnight, I will lie here and wait for you.*

Brock bit back a sigh, wishing he could get that sultry

voice out of his head. He must focus on the business at hand.

"You sound confident of the returns," Cropthorne said.

"Indeed, I am," Brock answered, leaning forward on the plush burgundy velvet sofa. Bracing his elbows on his knees, he looked directly into Cropthorne's dark, astute eyes. "Businesses want to profit from cheaper transportation of their goods. The gentry want to travel more comfortably. The working man wishes to reach his job sooner. We can fulfill all these needs and make a fortune doing it."

"I believe you're right. And all the land is secured?"

I need you to be my lover.

Remembering Maddie's beguiling demand now was nothing short of foolish—and bad for his concentration, besides. Brock gave himself a mental shake. This discussion with his host represented the very reason he couldn't possess Maddie until after they had spoken wedding vows. Without Cropthorne, the railroad, and Maddie as his wife, all his dreams would be no more attainable than finding gold in a beggar's pocket.

Across the table, Cropthorne waited none too patiently for a reply. Brock knew he could never explain his strange marital wager with Maddie, yet neither did he wish to lie.

"I'm still working on one last parcel." *Working on it nearly every night, in fact.* "It should be ours quite soon."

"You'll keep me apprised."

Brock recognized the unflinching authority in the statement. Cropthorne was not accustomed to refusal.

"Naturally," Brock said smoothly.

Cropthorne stood, reaching two inches above Brock's own tall frame, then held out his hand. "You have a partner."

Brock clasped the man's hand. "You won't regret it, Cropthorne."

"See that I don't."

With that, he'd been dismissed. Brock left, drunk with elation. The feeling was far more potent than the finest brandy winding through his veins. His dream of utter wealth and respect, of having everything he had not been born with, lay one step closer to him.

After Brock left Cropthorne's, he enjoyed a first-rate supper of julienne soup, lobster rissoles, compote of cherries, and fine Madeira wine. Then he stopped by his office on Prince's Street, a stone's throw from the Bank of England, to follow up on his new ideas for the railroad.

Still, Maddie wouldn't leave his mind. The image of her skin, softer than crushed velvet in his hand as he lay atop her, inside her, finding heaven, reclaiming what should never have belonged to that wretch Sedgewick. Arousal peaked into an ache that seeped past his defenses, thicker and sweeter than honey on fresh bread. An urge to possess her threatened to drown all the logical arguments against taking her to his bed now, again and again and again. He pushed the thought away and let the noise, bustle, and scents of London in spring lead his mind elsewhere.

After an hour of wandering about in his phaeton, Brock looked up, shocked to find himself in his childhood borough.

Meanness still assaulted the senses in the odor of sewage, the acrid taste of starvation in the air, and the dark, pounding alleys winding to nowhere.

What the hell was he doing here on Finch Street? When he had left at sixteen, bound for a new life somewhere away from the mean streets of London, ready to take on the world, he'd vowed never to return.

But now that he was here, shouldn't he see what he'd left behind?

He urged his vehicle farther up the road, until he stood directly before the tenement house he had once called home. The streets were nearly deserted, save for a pair of young boys probably running gin. To his distant left stood an old woman selling herself, no doubt wishing for a bottle of said gin to ease the pain of her bleak life. Directly past him scampered a wide-eyed girl of six or so, hurrying home after a long day of selling scraps of candles. Would she find anything but a weary parent and an empty table for her trouble?

"Girl," he called down, surprising himself.

She stopped, wide brown eyes cast up at him. Clearly, the sight of a rich stranger terrified her. "I don't sell meself."

Dear God. That she should already have to know of such a reality bit into his gut. He'd forgotten just how terrible poverty was, especially to the young.

He forced himself to focus on her sad, smudged face and tattered clothes. "How much for the rest of your candles? All of them?"

The girl blinked rapidly as she peered up at him, as if not quite believing his question. "A crown."

It sounded more like a query than a statement. "Is that all?" he asked softly.

"Well . . . a crown 'n ten pence'll do." She pushed a limp strand of dark hair from her anxious face and into a kerchief knotted about her head.

Reaching into his waistcoat, he withdrew two sovereigns. The girl set the candles on the seat beside him with all haste and managed to have free hands by the time he handed the coins down to her. She peered at the shiny circles through the moonlight, then looked at him once more, this time with eyes full of surprise and delight.

Sadly, that was likely more money than she made in a month.

"Cor, sir. I ain't never seen so much blunt at once."

Something panged in his chest again as he forced himself to swallow poverty's bitter pill, evident in the child's eyes. "What is your name?"

Warily, she eyed him again. "Molly."

"You live here?" He pointed to the building he'd once occupied himself.

"Aye, sir." Suspicion tinged her voice. "But I still don't sell meself."

"Don't ever do that, Molly." Brock wanted to say so much more but felt choked by her reality, his past.

It was a past he hated to remember.

"Aye, sir."

Solemnity now ruled her luminous brown eyes. Somehow he knew her little face would haunt him for days, perhaps weeks.

Brock jerked the carriage west, toward the pristine villas and town houses lining the polished streets of Mayfair he now called home. He felt too restless to enter and find sleep. He ambled north and east, despite the stiff wind tugging at his coat, chilling his hands and feet.

Finally, he found himself on the doorstep of Maddie's St. John's Wood cottage. He checked his gleaming pocket watch. A few minutes past midnight.

The door opened easily beneath his hand, the creak of the old door greeting him as always.

Inside, the dwelling was small and quiet. The scent of damp thatch from the afternoon's rain and a good fire filled the small space. He sensed the woman he yearned for inside.

"Maddie?" he called from the little foyer.

"By the fire," she called from around the corner.

Though anxious to see her, he paused in the foyer to divest himself of his gloves. "Is the house I picked in Paddington acceptable?"

"We hardly require anything so lavish."

He grunted at that, wishing he could see her face. "Did my carriage come for you this evening?"

"At ten, yes."

He thought again of Molly and wondered if she would have a full tummy and a warm bed tonight, as all children should. "And Aimee. How is she?"

Maddie said nothing for ten seconds. Brock wondered if

she had even heard the question as he stripped off his great-coat. Finally, certain she hadn't, he started to ask her again.

"She is well. In bed, as every child her age should be."

Had poor Molly sought her bed, or was she busy doing chores after a long day on her little feet? Gritting his teeth, Brock pushed the picture aside. With a wry grin, he realized that thinking of Molly would certainly dampen the hunger he felt for Maddie's lush body.

Instead, this amiable, even comfortable conversation, their first in five years, warmed him. Not his loins, but all of him.

After laying his jacket on a nearby chair, Brock made his way across the short foyer, turned the corner just before the breakfast table, then headed toward the hissing fire.

Her pale shoes lay scattered on the threadbare carpet, her corset and petticoats draped over the sofa. What on earth . . . ?

Then Brock caught sight of his would-be mistress lying on the green sofa, and he knew nothing could keep his mind from the thought of Maddie beneath him, around him, on top of him . . .

Firelight caressed the ivory curves of her bare thighs, danced in the hollows of her abdomen and breasts—cloaked only by the lacy undergarments he had bought her, and accompanied by a bewitching smile of invitation.

He tried to swallow, but the air stuck in his throat. "Maddie?"

She eased up from her supine position until she sat with the light to her back, setting her unbound auburn hair ablaze and thinning her chemise's white into painful transparency.

His cock didn't just stir to life. It sprang with all the attention of an anxious soldier.

"You said I wore too much clothing," she offered so, so innocently.

Blast it, he wished he'd never said that. Yet when she stood, his eyes gorged on the visual feast, and he was damn glad he had uttered those careless words.

"You said you dreamed of seeing me in only this."

Had he? Yes, only he had been more explicit about it. Those images sprang to mind again, taunting, teasing.

He couldn't reach her fast enough.

Brock curled his fingers around her waist with a splintering desperation. As he lowered his mouth to hers, he could barely spare a moment of thrill when she met him halfway.

Maddie's mouth felt damp, pliable. He tasted something new on her tongue—cinnamon, perhaps—before she deepened the kiss, mating her mouth to his. The thought was gone, replaced by the need to touch her everywhere.

Groaning, he pulled her closer. Their thighs collided. The soft crush of her breasts, covered only by that frighteningly thin chemise, lay against his chest and spiked a furious need for more of her.

His splayed fingers found their way around her waist to her back. One hand he raised to cup her head, the other he lowered to cup her buttocks. He expected her to continue the kiss, moan for him at most. But Maddie had a delicious idea.

She plucked at the buttons of his shirt, baring the flesh beneath. The feel of her fingers on his heated skin, skimming over his nipples, the clench of his belly . . . Lord, where would he find the self-control to stop this, when what he really wanted to do was see what other delicious little surprises she had in store for him?

Her mouth followed her hands to his skin, skimming his neck, his shoulders.

He drew in a shuddering breath. "Maddie."

She lifted her mouth from him, and Brock heard her panting over the rapid *thump-thump* of his heart. His own breathing quickened further. He inhaled the scents of vanilla and jasmine, scents he always knew as hers. He wiped his thumb along his damp lower lip, praying for self-control. But he felt Maddie there in the tingle of his mouth. His tongue wet his lip again, and her taste lingered. Pounding urgency crept upon him again with all the subtlety of a sledgehammer.

"Yes?"

Her whisper cascaded over him like a warm waterfall, enticing, everywhere. Desire submerged him. He couldn't let go of her yet, just one more kiss, one more . . .

"Nothing," he said thickly.

Before she could say a word, he covered her mouth with his once more. That taste of cinnamon aroused his tongue, his senses again, lifting his lust higher. Her chemise beneath his hands seemed so thin, almost nonexistent. He swore he could feel her bare skin, so warm and vital, pulsing with life, with possibilities.

Brock felt her hands skimming his ribs suddenly, before they pulled the shirt from his breeches to dangle about his hips. He gave in to the craving to invade Maddie's mouth again.

Her palms encircled him then, scorching him like twin fires as they danced over his chest, to his waist, then across his back. Maddie pulled him so close, she could have little doubt just how much he wanted her.

Aching now, he snatched one of her hands from his back and held it to his rigid length. She hesitated for a painful moment before her fingers curled over his erection, through his breeches. She surprised him with her acceptance—and blasted his hunger for her to new heights.

His surprise became shock when she unbuttoned his breeches and drawers. He scarcely comprehended the goal of her fumbling fingers before she had freed him. Her scalding touch replaced cool air, questing the bare length of him with a firm grip.

Ecstatic torture, he thought, groaning. He could find no other way to describe her touch. Her fingers were by no means deft. They hardly had to be. Hell, she had sought him out, touched him now with willing hands. What more could a man want?

He took her mouth again, swirling his tongue around hers. Another groan erupted from his throat when her palm found its way down his length slowly, so slowly, then back up. He felt engorged, engaged, all too ready to lift that thin chemise around her waist, feel his way up the silky length of her stockinged thighs, then plunge within her.

But he couldn't.

That realization filled him with pain. Each of his tense muscles screamed to possess her now, before she got away again, before some other society simpleton lured her to the altar.

Sketches of the railroad flittered across his mind, followed by Cropthorne's thundering warning not to cause him regret over his investment. Then Molly's little face swam into view. He didn't know why.

Brock tore his mouth from the spicy haven of Maddie's. "Stop." The word came on a quick, hard breath.

Maddie's mouth found his jaw and placed soft kisses there before winding its way back to his lips. He jerked his head away. "Leave it, Maddie. Until we wed, I won't take ye."

Ye? Had he truly said that? Yes.

Humiliation smacked him. Horrified at the slip in the perfect speech he had sweated for years to attain, ice raced through him. He didn't know who to hate more for it, himself for the lapse in control or Maddie for exacerbating it.

"Love me now," she whispered, as if she'd heard nothing different. "Take me to your bed."

Maddie made it all sound so simple, as if giving in to her wouldn't mean giving up everything he'd sought all his life.

Extracting himself from her embrace, Brock stepped away and fastened his clothing with a curse. Dragging his fingers through his tousled hair, he regarded her with a strong mixture of lust, resentment, and something else that didn't have a name.

"That is enough for tonight," he said finally.

Maddie fought to catch her breath, drawing in one ragged

breath after another. She curled her arms about her waist in a self-conscious gesture. But when she looked up at him, anger flashed in her stormy eyes. "You'll be back."

Brock closed his eyes and cursed his weakness. He wanted her so badly he could scarcely breathe.

"You're undoubtedly right," he said honestly, then turned around to find his way out before he had no will left to do so.

SEVEN

Days after attending the Moores' ball, Maddie received an afternoon call from her very unwelcome sister-in-law.

Gritting her teeth, Maddie entered Ashdown Manor's parlor and found Roberta within, fluttering the embroidered folds of a stylish muslin pelisse about her legs in an absent, fussy gesture. Wondering what the witch wanted, Maddie held in a sigh and refused to consider her own fraying brown frock.

"Roberta, what a surprise."

With a lift of her pointed chin, Roberta regarded Maddie with icy blue eyes. "That is precious little by way of greeting. Am I not welcome?"

Maddie chose to ignore her question, finding her anger at the woman had not dissipated since their argument at the Moores'. "Your presence here after three years seems something of an . . . occasion, since I've not had the pleasure of a call following Colin's death. To what do I owe this honor?"

Hearing the sarcasm in her tone, Maddie couldn't find the inclination to care. Her encounter with Brock last night had made sleep impossible, despite her exhaustion. The passion of Brock's mouth on hers, the steely feel of him, rigid and thick in her hand, fired her imagination. She had yearned for him into the dark night, her breasts aching, her insides throbbing with the unsatisfied craving he had created in her with his drugging kisses and erotic hands.

"I've come to visit my niece," Roberta announced, patting a dark curl at the side of her immaculate coiffure.

Protective hackles sprang up within Maddie. Roberta had never cared a whit for Aimee. Not while Maddie had carried the babe Colin had told his family was his, not when her daughter had made her way into the world two weeks late, in a bloody birthing that had nearly been Maddie's death, not while Colin had lived and stared at Aimee with hate in his eyes.

"Aimee is sleeping," Maddie lied, and waved Roberta to the door. "Another time perhaps."

Roberta smiled but did not rise from her perch on the sofa. "As long as I've come this far, you might explain how you came to be at Lady Moore's with Brock Taylor."

"Why do you care? Has Lady Litchfield cut you from her guest list since that night?"

A cross look from Roberta let Maddie know she had not appreciated the jibe. "Not yet, thank goodness. But Colin—"

"Your brother is gone. My mourning is over." Maddie paced farther into the room and crossed her arms over her chest. "I may socialize with whom I choose."

Roberta set her face in a stiff pout. "Madeline, dear, I only mean to remind you that Brock Taylor is not good society. No one appreciates his presence at a gathering of quality."

"No, they only appreciate his Midas touch," she returned.

"Money interests everyone." She waved her hand in explanation. "But that hardly means they wish to see him among the *ton*."

"I will keep company with anyone I choose, Roberta."

She scowled. "Everyone thought it shocking that you should bring a man of such indiscriminate breeding to a gathering of his betters," her sister-in-law went on, as if her opinion mattered. "Still, I think I understand why you receive him. He is handsome, in a barbaric sort of way, and his wealth is massive. I suppose he might be . . . interesting. Do you agree?"

Maddie knew Roberta baited her and dared not comment. "I really have not given the matter much thought."

"Does he tell you of his latest ventures?" she asked.

The coy question annoyed her. Roberta could not possibly give two figs about Brock's business. Not that she had any information to give her sister-in-law. Maddie realized with surprise that Brock had never discussed the details of his business with her, only told her of his desire to mingle with the *ton* for his professional growth.

"I have no notion what Mr. Taylor's endeavors are, Roberta." *Except to conquer me with his kiss.* "I simply accompanied him to the Moores' at his request."

Based on Roberta's pinched mouth, the answer did not satisfy her curiosity. Maddie elected not to volunteer any more information.

The woman smoothed her mouth into a smile, too calculating by half. "Ah, so you welcome his suit. For the money, I presume? It cannot be for his breeding."

Though Roberta had no way of knowing about her past with Brock, warning instincts rose again. "Mr. Taylor is not courting me."

No, Mr. Taylor was simply intriguing and arousing her. With him, she never felt frigid, as Colin had accused. Instead, Brock made her long to feel his hot mouth laving her breast again, to see his impassioned green eyes staring straight into her soul as he seduced her with his scandalous words. He created a desire to allow her fingers the freedom of roaming his firm body at will. He had filled Colin's sordid little cottage nearly every night of late with his spellbinding presence and verve. No, he was not courting her.

He was trying to seduce her into marriage to further his own business and social plans.

And, heaven help her, she felt as if she were melting dangerously close to surrender.

"No?" Roberta asked, all innocence. "I felt certain Mr. Taylor had marriage on his mind when I saw you two dance. The manner in which he looked at you . . . well, it was rather marked."

Maddie refused to rise to the bait. "No one is courting me, nor am I interested in taking a new husband." *Thanks to your miserable brother and the financial magnate in question,* she thought with ire.

"I see." Roberta rose from the sofa.

Hoping Roberta could see nothing of consequence between herself and Brock, Maddie led the way to the drawing room's door.

"Are you going to a party?" Aimee asked as she sat at Maddie's feet four evenings later, clutching a rag doll.

Maddie bent to the little girl and tweaked one of her blond braids. "Yes, but I shall think of you while you have a cozy evening with Aunt Edith and Vema."

"Is Mr. Taylor taking you?" Aunt Edith asked, entering the room through the open door.

"Auntie!" Aimee jumped up and ran to the older woman, winding her arms about Edith's wide legs.

Edith bent and kissed the top of Aimee's head, then looked back to her niece with a shrewd stare.

"Yes," Maddie answered reluctantly. "Mr. Taylor asked me to accompany him to this gathering for business purposes."

"Business. Of course."

Edith sent her a benign smile Maddie knew too well to believe. The woman was likely running amok with matchmaking thoughts. Why? Could no one but she see how ill-suited they were?

Her aunt lifted her quizzing glass and peered at Maddie.

"And he sent you a new gown for the occasion, I see. It is exquisite."

In this, Aunt Edith was correct. A rich gray-blue color provided the background for a burnished tapestry of flowers. The flounced dress was trimmed in delicate ivory lace about the sleeves and neckline, which draped in a vee across her bosom. Only a small piece of lace preserved her modesty, shielding her cleavage from a stranger's eye. The wide sleeves clung to the edge of her shoulders, then belled out in a rich swirl of silk before curling tightly about her wrists once more.

Maddie certainly could not fault Brock for his taste in modistes. The colors, styles, and cuts were always superbly flattering. She could guess how he had managed to estimate her measurements so accurately and could only imagine the modiste must believe her to be Brock's mistress.

And if Maddie had her way, that would soon be true. Though she had had no luck in breaking Brock's self-control yet, she knew she must continue to dedicate her efforts to his seduction. Heat raced through her as she tried to picture what dedicating all her efforts to such a venture would entail.

Suddenly, Aunt Edith tittered. "That pretty flush on your cheeks makes you look even more luminous than the stunning dress Mr. Taylor sent. Have a smashing time tonight."

"It is purely business," Maddie repeated.

Edith winked in reply.

Maddie held in a sigh of temper. "Truly, I have no intention of marrying the man."

"You ought. I cannot remember when I've last seen you so passionate about anything. Come, Aimee; say good night to your mama."

"What's pass'nate?" asked Aimee.

"It's like having a fire in your belly." The elderly woman tickled the little girl's tummy. "Isn't it, Maddie?"

"It can be." Still, everything she felt was temporary. It had to be.

Knowing her denial would only fall on deaf ears, Maddie said nothing more. Instead, she held out her arms to Aimee, who ran to them with abandon.

Edith shrieked. "Do not wrinkle your mama's dress!"

Maddie held Aimee close, savoring her special smell. She would have known it anywhere. "I do not mind. Miss me?"

"I will, Mama."

"And I shall miss you. Be good for Aunt Edith and Vema." She kissed the top of Aimee's golden head.

The girl nodded, and Maddie had begun to shoo them out of her room when Matheson appeared.

"Mr. Taylor has arrived," he intoned.

Maddie swallowed. "Tell him I shall be right down."

In truth, she did not want to attend this party. But he had sent her a missive—and a new gown—demanding her accompaniment. As he had pointed out, she was hardly in a position to refuse. And in truth, if he wished to make a spectacle out of himself at *ton* gatherings, that was his affair.

She simply wished he did not feel the need to do so with her at his side.

Drawing in a deep breath, Maddie made her way down the creaky stairs, not unaware that the extravagance of her new gown looked distinctly out of place surrounded by crumbling plaster and faded blue carpet. She shook her head, refusing to dwell on what she could not change.

Left idle, her thoughts returned to Brock.

The cautious part of her knew that, if she had to spend time with Brock, doing so in public was far less dangerous than meeting him in Paddington. He could hardly seduce her in a crowd. But the fearful part of her knew that she had no chance of breaking Brock's will and persuading him to come to her bed during a friendly chat and a waltz.

Such conflicting feelings—wanting what she most feared, fearing she would lose herself in this want—distressed her.

At the threshold of her drawing room, Maddie found Brock within. She examined him as he stared out the window, elbow resting on the mantel. He was the kind of man made for evening black. The austerity of the color enhanced the silky coffee shade of his hair. The fine cut of his costly suit emphasized the breadth of his shoulders and back, along with the narrow span of his hips, the hard muscles of his legs.

From touching Brock, Maddie knew that, beneath his formal attire, he wore no padding. Indeed, he was all man. The thought did nothing to calm her senses.

Suddenly, Brock spun about. He displayed no surprise at her presence in the room. His gaze raked over her, the appraising stare blatant and appreciative.

"You look beautiful," he said simply, his voice raspy.

Resisting the urge to lift a self-conscious hand to her hair, Maddie enticed him with a low-voiced murmur. "Are you certain you wish to attend the party? Perhaps we should go to the cottage instead."

Brock's mouth curled into a mischievous smile as he crossed the room to her side. "You sorely tempt me, Maddie. But tonight is business. The Duke of Cropthorne is expecting us."

Without pause, Brock took her arm and led her out of the room, into the balmy London night.

"You know him?" she asked. She could not keep the surprise from her voice.

"Indeed."

"How? When did you have occasion to meet a man of . . ." Maddie hesitated, uncertain how to best point out the unlikelihood that a man of Brock's social standing should be invited to the home of a duke.

"His wealth? His rank?" Brock finished for her, his voice on edge. "As I said, it is business."

"Yet he invited you to his home for a social gathering?"

Brock smiled again. "Tonight they go together."

Glaring at him, Maddie quipped, "If you have Cropthorne's social backing, you do not need the consequence that wedding me would bring. He's far more powerful."

"He would not look nearly as lovely in your dress." He grinned.

Maddie was not fooled. She shot him a questioning stare, which he answered with a simple shrug. Her stare became a glare. Brock was many things—arrogant, demanding, ruthless—but never simple. He never did anything without a purpose. If Cropthorne was willing to invite him to gatherings, which gave him some social credence, then what role did she play in this game?

"I thought you were on a quest for acknowledgment, not beauty," she said carefully.

"Ah, but why not have both? Besides, I can hardly arrive at Cropthorne's without a proper female on my arm, can I?"

Not really, but the answer seemed almost too easy.

The puzzle taunted her during their brief journey to her distant cousin's house. She had not seen Cropthorne in some years, not since her boorish father had badgered his for money. Of course, the late duke's scandals had ensured that her father, though poor as a church mouse, could pass judgment and tell his audacious cousin exactly what he thought of such disgrace. The late Cropthorne had cared very little for anyone's opinion, especially that of someone with so little consequence. Accordingly, the old duke had not given her father a farthing.

Maddie and Brock arrived with the party in full swing. Upon their announcement, heads again turned. Furious whispering ensued behind fans. Gentlemen eyed her with frank consideration. She swallowed a curse.

She knew what they thought, that she was tart enough to sell her presence to Brock. True, some parents in need of money had begun to accept wealthy members of the merchant class as spouses for their titled sons or genteel daughters. But no one had welcomed such a suit without a parent's shove. The *ton* would expect a marriage between her and

Brock. And if none took place, they would imagine her to be his mistress.

Blast it, why had she not thought of that sooner?

Wishing the evening over, Maddie shot a furious glare at Brock. "You are creating their expectation of our marriage."

He smiled, something bright and cunning. "No one will be surprised when we exchange vows."

Maddie would have said more, but her cousin approached, escorting the venerable Lady Litchfield. Was Gavin courting the young widow? Maddie would hardly know, as she had not spoken to him since her debut. After his father's scandals, she supposed Gavin wanted everyone's good opinion. If so, he had to start with Lady Litchfield. As did everyone.

"Hello, Taylor," the duke greeted. "And dear Cousin Madeline," he said with a gracious bow, then placed a brief kiss on her hand. "It has been years since I've had the pleasure of your company. I was sorry to hear of your husband's death."

"Thank you," she murmured.

Around the room, every pair of eyes watched the exchange. Maddie felt their gazes—some curious, some disdainful—boring into her face, her back. As she felt the perspiration bead at her hairline, she stood even more stiff, more erect.

"I am pleased to see you both," Gavin said.

"Thank you for inviting us," Brock returned smoothly.

Her cousin turned to his companion. "Lady Litchfield, you must know my cousin, Lady Wolcott."

The pale beauty's smile was like ice, transparent and lacking warmth. "Indeed. How do you do?"

"I'm well, thank you. And you?"

Lady Litchfield merely manufactured her chilly smile again.

Maddie glanced about the sumptuous room. Liquor flowed, people waltzed, matrons chatted. And still, everyone watched.

"Mr. Taylor, may I present London's loveliest and most sought-after hostess, Lady Litchfield?" Gavin said. "My lady, this is Mr. Taylor, England's most clever financier."

Brock extended his hand to the pale widow, reaching for her gloved fingers. Lady Litchfield edged away and made a moue of distaste. Then she turned her back to Brock.

The party around them froze. The orchestra missed a note before blurring into quiet altogether. Utter silence descended before half the room issued a collective gasp.

Brock had been given the cut direct.

He stiffened, his smile fading. His jaw clenched so hard he looked as if he'd been carved from stone.

Red heat rushed to Maddie's face. She burned from the inside out, her entire body stinging with shame and anger. The haughty witch had been nothing but rude, rebuffing a fellow guest in front of their host, in front of the whole party! And Maddie knew that even now, the rest of the *ton* had taken note of the slight and knew that such behavior would be deemed acceptable.

All because he'd been born to lowly parents. As if he'd had any say in that matter!

And Brock—how must he feel? If she was embarrassed to be seen with a man who incited such rejection, the man himself must feel horrified by the slight of someone so socially important.

Maddie risked a glance toward him. Brock still stood in place, hand extended toward Lady Litchfield.

She burned with embarrassment all over again.

With a shrug, he adopted a rueful smile and dropped his hand to his side. "I knew I should have told my valet to put extra starch in my cravat. It's distasteful of me, I agree. I shall know better next time."

With a delicate little sniff, Lady Litchfield strode away from the group, making her opinion quite known. Brock watched, that wry smile still firmly in place.

As Maddie watched the self-important widow disappear

into the crowd, she could not remember when she had formed such an intense dislike for anyone so quickly. A glance at her cousin proved Gavin's chiseled features looked both tense and annoyed.

Despite the fact he must be suffering, Brock kept smiling.

Empathy for the enemy was both stupid and dangerous. But as she stood frozen in the shattered gathering, Maddie could not deny the feeling or its strength.

"I think your cravat looks all that is fine," she murmured.

"Of course it is," Gavin snapped, glaring in the direction of his retreating companion. "I'll introduce you to some of the others we discussed, Bathurst, Elvaston. They are here."

Brock nodded at her cousin, then turned to her. For the first time since his return to her life, Maddie saw clearly an emotion in his green eyes besides lust or anger; she saw appreciation, even a bit of warmth.

The look transformed his face into something warm and human. Something she remembered from that fateful summer five years before. "Thank you."

"You are welcome." Head held high, Maddie sent him a tentative smile in return as they walked into the crowd.

Drawing in a deep breath of the misty midnight air, Brock stared at the Paddington cottage's blue door. Tonight, he would meet Maddie here for the first time. She would be inside waiting, perhaps even pondering ways to break his self-control.

The memory of her warm hand stroking his shaft made him grit his teeth and sweat. Then into his mind thrust a memory of last night, when she had defended his cravat . . . and him to Lady Litchfield. He had appreciated her attempt to join his humor and diffuse the awkward situation. And she had surprised Brock. Hell, she had astounded him, for she'd always thought him beneath her. In that moment, however, she had taken his side against the ignobility of his birth. Why?

The smell of rain hung heavy in the spring air when he felt the first drop on his cheek, and he rushed to the door.

Brock reminded himself that he was the seducer. Though Maddie had been married to the despicable Sedgewick and shared his bed for two years, Brock had the advantage of wider experience on his side.

After Maddie's defection to her titled husband, Brock had hardly been a monk. Some of his lovers had been older, some younger—all experienced, knowing what they sought in bed. He had paid attention to their desires.

Tonight, he would use the knowledge to his advantage.

Still, he could not deny his own staggered breathing at the thought of holding her again. Nor could he lie about the wrenching of his heart at her mournful expression when he'd brushed her mouth with the pad of his thumb, as had been his habit all those years ago. He could almost believe she had loved him then and cared still . . . if she hadn't become Sedgewick's wife, if she wasn't so insistent on refusing his proposal now.

Yes, she had worked with him to smooth over Lady Litchfield's slight. That did not change the fact that Maddie was willing to take him as a lover but not a husband. His gut churned with resentment. She still looked down her pert nose at him, as she had five years ago. Too bad for her. She would not escape marrying him, by damn!

Maddie woke to the soft patter of rain upon the roof of the darkened cottage in Paddington—and the feeling that she was not alone. She sat up on the plush rose-colored velvet sofa, cursing herself for nodding off so near midnight, and wondered what had happened to the lamps she'd lit. Only two small candles flickered beside her now.

A vibrant warmth enveloped her shoulders, the back of

her neck. Anxious, she made to rise and turn. A strong hand clamped about her scantily clad shoulders kept her in place.

"Don't move," whispered a voice in her ear.

Brock. Not a stranger. Relief filled her.

Her relief was short-lived when she felt more than saw a soft silk scarf slide over her eyes, leaving her in the dark. Again, she made to struggle. Brock's soothing palm at the back of her bare neck stayed her.

Dear Lord, what did Brock plan to do to her with that scarf? Anxiety and anticipation mixed to form a surging uncertainty.

"I won't hurt you," he promised, as if reading her fears.

Crazily, she believed the low, hypnotic voice resonating in her ear, tingling down her spine. Yet she didn't trust his mood. "I intend to please you tonight. And I want you to think about your pleasure."

"But what . . . why—" she protested.

"Shhh. This is an adventure, an experiment, if you will." He knotted the scarf at the back of her head, rendering her temporarily blind.

"Experiment?" she squeaked. Though Maddie did not believe Brock would hurt her, being blindfolded left her with a terrifying feeling of vulnerability—along with a scintillating sense of the forbidden she would never have believed possible.

"Brock—"

"How else am I to know every inch of you, how you like to be touched, where you are most easily aroused? How else can I make you want to scream with pleasure?"

His voice was a deep undulation vibrating within her. Her silk-clad toes curled into the thick carpet as a dizzying, tingling disquiet washed over her in hot and cold waves. Maddie knew she should protest again but couldn't find her voice.

"I want to know what sets you on fire. And where your body needs special attention," he continued, stooped behind the sofa, his lips on the shell of her ear. "Shall you be best served if I use my hands or my mouth . . . or both?"

As Brock ran the tip of his tongue around her ear, uncertainty dissipated. A sharp pang of the arousal he'd taught her to feel took its place, tightening her stomach. How could she answer that question with a coherent reply? More important, would he really touch his tongue to her body anywhere he thought she needed it? The thought made her clutch the folds of her thin chemise—her only garment—in white-knuckled anticipation.

Why had she not worn something more substantial? *Would it have stopped him?* a voice within her asked. Having heard the determined seduction in his tone, Maddie knew he was driven to melt her into marriage.

God give her the strength to resist.

"Brock, please . . ."

She reached for the scarf about her head. Brock looped his warm fingers about her wrists, but she could not mistake the fact that his grip, no matter how gentle, meant to restrain her.

Tantalizing passion pervaded her every limb—her very mind—with insidious insistence. She should demand that he release her, she knew. But a growing ache wanted him to continue with this heady seduction.

When she felt his teeth nip the crook of her neck, Maddie tried to stiffen against the riot of sensations. He followed the playful bite with the soft temptation of his mouth tasting her skin, then a flick of his tongue over the sensitized flesh. Her response, a tight fist of fervor, plummeted to the pit of her stomach and lower. Though breathless in anticipation of his next touch, she managed to swallow the encouragement that lay on the tip of her tongue.

"Which do you like better, Maddie?" he breathed into her ear. "That, or this?"

His mouth inched up until his teeth nibbled on her lobe and his hot breath filled her ear. The resulting tingles raced through her body, again centering on her woman's flesh. She could not restrain her moan.

"Which one?" he prodded, his palms now skating down her bare arms.

That he cared for her preferences at all made her want him more. Colin had never cared, certainly. In truth, both of Brock's touches had affected her—more deeply than she would have believed—but his first act had started the fire.

And already she wanted to explore the sensations Brock had introduced her to, more than was wise.

"I prefer the latter," she lied, hoping to stave off the arousal climbing to new, loftier heights.

Brock laughed. Then he brushed his mouth over her neck again. Tingles screamed down her back, through her chest, setting her aflame. He'd known the truth, damn him. He had known all along!

Before she could gather her anger, his hands left her arms to stir across her stomach. Lazy fingers traced circles across her abdomen, up until they reached just below her breasts, then down until he toyed with the precipice of her female mound.

A fierce exhilaration, heavy with pounding pleasure winding through her body, had her nearly arching off the sofa. An arm about her waist brought her back to his mercilessly seeking mouth, the lips trailing down her shoulder, teeth lifting away the sleeve of her chemise.

When his hand rose from her stomach to the tie of her chemise and pulled, Maddie held her breath. With two excruciatingly gentle fingers, Brock swept the material aside. Cool night air caressed the breast he'd bared, tightening its tip. Tingling from the coolness, she felt unprepared when his hot hand closed over her, thumb teasing, toying with her crest.

A maelstrom of desire screeched inside her. She yearned for his mouth there now. The inviting moan she'd been holding back slipped out.

"I love the way you moan when I touch you," he whispered into her ear, tonguing the crease behind it.

She shivered. "Brock, I—" *Love it when you touch me, too.* Had she really thought that? Yes, and meant it, for he made her feel what Colin never had, a writhing desire she had never known possible. Lord help her.

"I can feel your excitement growing," he murmured.

Suddenly, he moved away. The departure of his warmth told her that. Then she felt him settle in front of her. Did he stand, kneel? Could he see her bared breast in the faint light? She swallowed thickly, her fingers biting into the sofa's thick cushions. The pleasure had to stop—before she lost herself to it.

When she groped to find the edges of her chemise to cover herself, Brock lifted her fingers again and laced them with his own. The gesture was tender and somehow reached within her to fire the ice around her heart.

"I want to look at you. Every nook, every inch, every shadow. I want to see all of you, Maddie."

Desire coiled tighter in the pit of her belly. She had never had the urge to bare her body to Colin. In fact, she'd always sought to hide beneath the covers and her nightrail. Now, the thought of revealing all to Brock's gaze excited her, unwise as it was. She wanted to pursue this vivid want pulsing within her, wanted it so much, she could feel the heart of her throbbing.

Maddie heard the rustle of clothing, then felt the brush of his sleeve against her outer thigh. She still could not see but guessed he knelt before her. He released her hand.

His hands skimmed her thighs, her hips, her waist, palming her breasts . . . Only when he yanked the chemise over her head did she realize that he'd been lifting it with his caress. And now she lay completely naked, save her silky stockings tied in place with their frilled bows. Maddie felt bare, exposed. She trembled with arousal, with apprehension.

From the feel of Brock's coat gently abrading her thighs as he held his arms around her, Maddie knew he remained fully clothed. It added to her arousal somehow.

"Beautiful Maddie." His voice shook.

Before she could utter a word, Brock's mouth claimed hers. He stole her breath of gasped air and took it for himself, robbing her of reason. His tongue engaged hers with an intimacy that shocked her. He demanded, yet gave her equal access to himself. And more to her shock, she took, demanded of him. He never backed away, but gave and gave, his mouth mating as he ensnared her in his web.

She moaned in protest when his lips left hers. Scarcely a moment later, she felt them on her bared breast, enveloping the sensitive crest. *Ah, heaven!*

With one hand, he lifted her flesh to the warm cavern of his mouth. The other hand drifted down the inside of her stockinged thigh, causing a shiver of sharp need. She held her breath when he skimmed her calf, then rested his fingers on her ankle. He lifted that foot to his mouth, kissed her silk-clad instep. Maddie found the gesture so tender, so unlike the blatant sexuality he'd been plying her with, her heart caught.

Brock set the first foot at his side and repeated the process with the other one. Boneless as hot wax, she leaned toward him, seeking support, seeking relief.

He eased her back against the sofa and shifted his mouth back to her breast, suckling. His linen shirt grazed between her knees. She realized she was utterly open and vulnerable to him. The thought terrified and thrilled her at once.

"Brock—"

"Shhh," he soothed. "You look beautiful lying there."

Then he brushed her mouth with his thumb again, a short, tender gesture. And for some reason, she trusted his words after that.

He fitted his palms around her hips and pulled her forward until she nearly reclined against the sofa. The smooth warmth of his shirt grazed her sensitive inner thighs.

Dear God, he'd wedged his shoulders between her legs!

"So perfect," he murmured, bending to rub his stubbled cheek against her thigh.

Maddie shivered. He couldn't possibly do what her wanton mind had conjured up, could he? Did people do that? She dug her fingers into his shoulders, trying to push him away, despite the shameless thrill that shot through her at the possibility.

She felt his hot exhalation low on her belly and held her breath.

"So edible," he whispered against her damp curls.

With a gentle nudge of his hands, he spread her knees wider. She felt him squarely between her thighs. Fingers touched her down low, where she most wanted him. With his thumbs, he spread her wide, open to his gaze . . . and anything else he wished. Her heartbeat stopped. Would he really . . . Oh, no—

Yes!

Brock's lips closed over her in a tangled half-gasp, half-groan. His tongue danced around the heart of her sensation, laving her in upward strokes that nearly made her mindless. Around, over, enveloping, his lips followed his tongue in the carnal worship. Maddie could hardly catch her breath. Her mind exploded with Brock's intimate kiss.

Rain fell hard, pounding on the roof in a roar—or was that her blood in her ears? She didn't care; the pleasure was too intense, too compelling to resist.

Brock never paused in his unsubtle pursuit of her pleasure as his tongue twirled over the top of her nub. Shafts of lightning need skittered down her legs, coiled in her belly. Before she could stop herself, Maddie cried out and grasped handfuls of his hair in her desperate fingers.

"You taste so sinfully sweet," he whispered against her. "I want to devour you."

Then she felt him again, with a new touch this time. His tongue lapped over her receptive bud side to side, in no apparent hurry, though he was driving her well and truly mad. She bit her lip to keep in a scream of pleasure.

"Would you like me to go slower? Faster? Softer?" he teased before flicking the tip of his tongue over her again.

She could not find the breath to answer.

As if sensing she was near the brink of some explosion, he inserted two fingers deep inside her, teasing her in a seemingly relentless quest for her reaction.

Maddie could no longer hold in the scream. The pleasure was rising to unbelievable heights. Surely she would soon explode or die from it. Her body could not withstand much more.

Then he enveloped her entire bud of pleasure with his mouth. And moaned long and low, deep in his chest.

At the vibration, Maddie bucked her hips against him, devastated by the razor edge of pleasure. She was so close . . . to something she did not understand. She chanted his name, an entreaty, desperate for him to ease the ache. Still, he held back just enough, ruthlessly stalked her rapture with his lips and tongue, yet held satisfaction at bay.

"Brock," she gasped. "Please."

Small, tight moans escaped her. He began to nip the insides of her thighs while his fingers remained buried deep inside her. She arched into his hand.

His body rose up over hers, and she felt the fine linen of his shirt rub in exquisite abrasion against her tight, tender nipples. Thunder ripped through the sky, mimicking the deep cry of her body.

"We want each other, Maddie."

That low voice against her neck, in her ear, made her shiver. Blindly, she reached for his face and pulled him into a kiss of blistering heat.

"Yes," she moaned against his mouth, needing release from the unbearable pleasure he'd created.

"I want to love you now, so thoroughly, so completely, you won't be able to breathe for a week."

"Yes." The word was more moan than whisper as his fingers worked in her, rubbing her to a tightening desperation. "Yes."

"I want you like this every night."

Gritting her teeth, Maddie couldn't respond to that. She wasn't sure she would survive the next ten seconds if he didn't put an end to this erotic torment.

"Every night," he repeated, flicking a thumb over her breast. "All you have to do is say yes."

She squirmed and writhed, needing something, needing just a little more to send her over the edge, of what she didn't know, but she felt sure she would like it very much.

"I said yes," she protested on a groan.

"You'll be my wife, then?" he whispered against her mouth.

Wife?

Wife!

The truth belted her like a fist, diffusing the sensual fog in which he had surrounded her, degree by degree.

He had seduced her. Completely. She had let him, fool that she was. And he'd been much too good to fight.

Fury penetrated the haze of her pleasure with resolve, though her body still throbbed with ardor. She twisted away from his questing fingers, then scrambled to her feet, ripping the scarf from her face. She glared at Brock in the near darkness.

"No, I cannot marry you."

His jaw tightened, his gaze drilled her, but he gave no other sign that he heard.

As if sensing the battle tonight was over, Brock stepped back, but he looked nowhere ready to concede the war. Instead, he stalked to the far side of the room with a heavy sigh.

"Damn," he muttered.

Maddie stared at the taut expanse of his shoulders as he drew in large draughts of air.

Even now, just looking at Brock, Maddie could not deny she wanted him—his strength, his seductive power. Even his smile.

Suddenly, he turned to face her, his hands on his hips. He met her gaze before his stare trailed down each inch of her naked body. Wide chest heaving, he shook his head. "I must go."

He grabbed his greatcoat off the rack moments later, thrusting his arms in the sleeves, then reached for his gloves.

He could leave so easily? A foolish part of her wanted to deny he could. Yes, her body ached, all but demanding he show her the pleasure she had merely glimpsed. But Maddie also feared her reluctance to see him go wasn't that simple.

She wanted to say something—anything—to call him back. But she dreaded weakening and agreeing to marriage if he came near.

"Be careful, Brock," she said finally. "It—it's raining."

His gaze swerved to hers, eyes pinning her in place. Maddie read a tangle of heat, disappointment, surprise. A carefully blank expression finally erased them all.

"I will." He swallowed. "Do the same."

His rough voice reached inside her and dredged up emotion she did not understand. Tears threatened, pricking her eyes. To hide them, she closed her eyes and nodded.

A moment later, Maddie heard the slam of the door.

Fear, frustration, thwarted need, and some foolish memory of their past roiled within her. She fought to resist the onset of more tears. But fight them she did.

Brock had toyed with her, damn him! And no matter how talented, no matter how much she wanted him, he would never get the better of her again.

EIGHT

Body aching from sleeplessness and unsatisfied desire, Maddie dragged herself from bed a little after sunrise and trudged into the obnoxiously sunny breakfast room. She nearly groaned. England was known for its ever-present rain. Why could the weather not cooperate when she was in a foul mood?

Plopping into a chair beside the table, she sighed. She had no way to earn her own money and rescue herself from debt, nor could she seem to seduce the cad holding her notes, though he clearly wanted her. Nor could she deny that she wanted him, a fact that frustrated her beyond bearing. Brock knew his way around a woman's body, knew exactly how to arouse her. While she . . . She realized she knew next to nothing about making him ache.

Someday, somehow, she would have her revenge for the pain he'd caused her five years ago, and for the tumult on her emotions and her body these past few weeks.

Lowering her head in her hands, Maddie refused to shed another tear over Brock Taylor. She'd given that up five years before and would not start again now.

But at desolate moments like this, resuming the habit seemed tempting, indeed.

"Good morning, love," Aunt Edith called from the front of the room. This morning she was sporting a small hat with a blue bird on her head. Vema stood behind her, looking exotic yet muted, much as she always did.

"Such a lovely day!" Edith exclaimed. "Just look at the sun." She pointed to the white-gold streams of light pouring into the room from the east-facing windows, overlooking the garden that needed tending.

"Lovely," she muttered in a monotone.

"Ah, out of sorts, I see. Was your outing with Mr. Taylor last night not to your liking?"

It was too much to my liking. . . .

"She is unsatisfied," Vema answered before Maddie could.

Surely Vema could not mean—could not know how Brock made her body ache.

Maddie's mouth fell open in shock. She had told the ladies nothing of her wager with Brock, only that he took her out each evening. How did they know she and Brock did so much more than attend the season's social events, yet not nearly enough?

Edith turned to her companion. "Unsatisfied?"

Vema nodded her dark head, strands of gray standing out in her thick mane. "She is tense, yet flushed. Past ready for his plucking."

Maddie worried her bottom lip with her teeth, wondering how Vema managed to see so much.

"I've long wondered why Maddie put herself on the shelf at such a young age," Edith said, as if she weren't there.

"I have no wish to marry again," she reminded them.

"A shame, really. I found the marriage bed to be one of the most enjoyable aspects of my union with Mr. Bickham," Edith twittered.

Maddie felt her mouth drop open again. "Aunt Edith!"

The older woman waved her scandalized expression away. "Pooh. You're a widow with a child, as well as a man seeking your hand. You know what I speak of."

"Yes," Maddie admitted with reluctance.

"If you refuse to wed Mr. Taylor, why not enjoy whatever else the association might offer?"

This time, Maddie's eyes widened as her jaw dropped. "You, a proper woman, are suggesting an improper liaison?" Of course, hadn't she suggested the same herself to Brock?

Aunt Edith flounced into a chair and grabbed a slice of bread from a plate Vema had retrieved from the adjacent sideboard. "You would hardly be the first widow to take a lover, dear. Nor the last, I daresay."

Maddie could hardly believe her ears. Her own aunt condoned her taking a lover, even sounding as if she might have taken one herself in the past.

Drawing in a deep breath, Maddie doctored the cup of tea that Vema set in front of her. Stirring an absent spoon through her brew, she wondered if these two women, richer in life experience, could help her succeed in seducing Brock. Maddie needed to do more than merely interest him. She had to send him to the edge, as he had done to her last night. Could Brock's restraint withstand such sensual torture? And even if it did, he would at least experience her pain. Sipping her tea, Maddie decided she could do no worse with Edith and Vema's advice than without.

"It is common enough for widows to take lovers," she conceded. "But how does one go about such an affair?"

Edith laughed. "Silly girl! You're clever, so I've no doubt you will find just the way to tell him."

Maddie felt heat creeping up her cheeks. "Actually, I have told him. He wishes to wait for marriage. Wants to do the thing properly, and all that."

"And you do not wish to wait. How delicious!" She rubbed her hands together. "Can we not help with that, Vema?"

The two women cast a glance between them rich with history and mischief, with a hint of a smile.

"She needs the *Kama Sutra*," declared Vema quietly.

"The what?" Maddie questioned the uncommon phrase.

"The *Kama Sutra*," Vema repeated. "It is an old Hindu

text, dating back over a thousand years, filled with descriptions to enhance one's *Kama,* or sensual gratification."

Maddie resisted the urge to gape in shock again. Someone had written a book on bed sport over a thousand years ago?

"It is also about achieving harmony in one's soul through balancing the *Dharma,* your religious merit, and your *Artha,* your worldly wealth, with your *Kama.* According to its author, Vatsyayana, if you find that symmetry, you will succeed in everything, including finding a compatible life mate."

Her soul was not lacking balance, thank you, nor did she need a life mate. If marriage to the sullen Colin had been bad, she could only imagine life with the ruthless Brock would be worse. He was likely to reject her wish for autonomy as Colin had, but worse, be able to control her body with his skilled lovemaking. But the rest of the text could prove useful in winning this blasted wager and easing her unsatisfied body.

"And do you have this book?" Maddie asked, hopeful.

Vema glanced at Edith, whose aging cheeks flushed.

"I believe I do, dear," her aunt said. "I shall see if I can find it in the attic."

Though Maddie sensed the book had not been put away in storage at all, she bit her lip on the subject. "Thank you, Aunt Edith. I do believe such a book could prove helpful."

Imagining all the ways she could surprise and arouse Brock into surrender, she slathered butter on a piece of bread, feeling more optimistic than she had in weeks.

Clutching the imperious missive in his hand, Brock read it again.

Mr. Taylor,

> *I have questions regarding our endeavor. Come to my home this afternoon at four. I expect a complete status on every parcel of land.*

Cropthorne

Cursing roundly, Brock crumpled the thick-papered note in his fist. A page bearing the duke's livery had delivered it to his office at ten that morning. Brock had been fighting a dense anxiety ever since.

Cropthorne knew. Somehow, the man had managed to find out about Maddie's land and its tentative status. God forbid Cropthorne had somehow learned about his wager with Maddie. Any hint of a scandal would send him running.

Brock sighed, pressing tight fingertips to his aching forehead. What could he tell Cropthorne? Certainly not that he had kissed Maddie senseless last night—her mouth, her breasts, her feet, the succulent core of her. Kissed her until she had moaned, panted . . . made him sweat and ache to take her on the sofa with her chemise askew and her stockings filming her shapely legs. She had wanted him, had even admitted it. She had been wet, her thighs taut with need, her fingers pressed into clenched fists.

Damn. He should be focused on business. Instead, he kept seeing Maddie in his mind, golden by firelight, head thrown back, hair as fiery as her passion.

With a frustrated grunt, he tossed Cropthorne's missive across the swaying coach and propped a shiny black Hessian on the seat across from him. Why could he fire Maddie's body but not overcome the objections in her mind?

The Maddie of old, that girl in the hay, had been full of spontaneous desire. She had raised no objections to their lovemaking. Indeed, she had encouraged him, seemed eager to take him in, despite her virginity. Her passion had overridden her natural caution. Why could he not achieve the same ends with her reserve about marriage?

Brock did not delude himself; he knew why Maddie refused to wed him. He knew the reason she'd broken faith with him five years ago: because he did not have a drop of blue blood. Despite the fact that she had come to his rescue after Lady Litchfield's slight, Brock knew he embarrassed her, believed him beneath her, and Maddie would continue rejecting him as long as she could.

His coach came to a jarring halt in front of Cropthorne's town house. With all the enthusiasm of a condemned man, Brock climbed out and made his way to the door. Within minutes, a servant showed him into Cropthorne's massive, dark-paneled study.

Behind a huge desk sat the duke, all hue and size of shelved books serving as background. Brock knew by looking at Cropthorne's angular, angry face that the man knew something Brock wished he didn't.

"Sit down, Mr. Taylor, and I'll get right to the point."

Sinking into a George III mahogany library chair, Brock did as the man bid, wishing himself elsewhere. The duke's displeasure increased the rapping of the anxious drum beating in his stomach. Brock tried to shrug off his foreboding.

"I received a letter from Kent Wainwright, Viscount Belwick," Cropthorne spit out quickly. "Apparently, he knows I'm your primary investor for the railroad project."

"Belwick makes it his business to know when someone is pitted against him in a business venture."

Cropthorne leaned forward, his eyes narrowed. Clearly, he had not appreciated Brock's observation. "He's also learned that you are poised to buy every parcel of land necessary, except one in Warwickshire. Is that true?"

Gritting his teeth to hold in a biting curse, Brock drew in a sharp breath. He wondered how much Cropthorne knew and hoped it wasn't all. He decided to take a gamble.

"The parcel isn't legally for sale. A . . . woman inherited it, but not freely. She holds it in retainer. The land may only be owned outright by any future husband she takes."

"What?" Cropthorne nearly came out of his chair. "That old practice died centuries ago. Who the hell would leave land to a woman in such a manner?"

So Cropthorne didn't know the land was his distant cousin Maddie's. Praise be! Brock wasn't about to tell his demanding investor, either. Not only would Cropthorne most likely object to Brock's methods against his kin of the fairer sex, he might well object to the marriage. And this time, nothing, no one, would stand in his way of acquiring not only more wealth, but Maddie as well.

Brock forced himself to relax. "The woman's affections are . . . engaged at the moment, and I feel sure she will wed within a month. Two at most. Her future husband will sell to us."

"You've spoken with him, then?"

"Yes." The half-truth came out in a robust syllable that made Brock's teeth hurt. "I've even arranged clandestine meetings for them, to hurry their courtship along."

With a raised brow and the cocking of his head, Cropthorne conveyed that he was impressed. But his eyes still drilled Brock to his chair. "What if this woman doesn't wed?"

"She will," Brock assured him, hoping like hell he could live up to that promise. He didn't want to explain to Cropthorne that rivers and hills and Belwick's holdings would take the railroad far out of its straight path and drive the construction costs as high as the moon.

Cropthorne banged his fist on the solid desk. "One month, damn it. Those banns had better start posting in one month, or Belwick will beat us to construction and you can find yourself a new partner. Am I making myself clear?"

"Perfectly."

Brock hid his worry and impatience behind an impervious mask. Christ, he had more at risk here than Cropthorne; his entire fortune, his reputation, an aristocratic beauty he'd never forgotten—everything he'd sweated all his life for was tied up in this railroad—and hinged on Maddie succumbing to his seduction, becoming his wife.

His mind raced. Paddington. Yes, he would go there to-night. Use every method, every whispered word, within his power to seduce her. She had to marry him, damn it, and soon.

Cropthorne rose. "I want to hear about your progress in two weeks, Mr. Taylor."

"Consider it done," he said smoothly.

"And from now on, I expect to hear about *everything* that affects my investment."

Brock left with a nod, knowing Cropthorne wouldn't want to know absolutely everything. The truth, unless he convinced Maddie to wed him soon, would only ensure that he lose Cropthorne's backing for the railroad immediately and suffer a shattered reputation forever.

When Brock entered the silent cottage in Paddington later that evening, determination beat an urgent dance in his veins as he removed his gloves. Maddie would marry him. Tonight, she would agree—finally—no matter what he had to do. He'd been so close in seducing her at their last assignation; the rigid writhing of her body told him that.

As he divested himself of his greatcoat, a vision of Maddie stormed his mind, strands of her copper tresses clinging to her damp face, sleek ivory limbs bare for his hungry eyes and hands. Brock grew stiff imagining all the ways he could continue his seduction, awaken every inch of her skin, whisper of his every desire.

The need to possess her—her body, her land, her hand in marriage—plagued him until he could think of little else.

Brock could not remember any woman who had stirred his passion to such levels. Perhaps the game they played provided the extra edge. Certainly the feeling had nothing to do with her. Nothing to do with his heart.

Then why don't you want another woman?

Shoving the irritating question aside, he wandered into the house and concentrated on this evening. He would cajole Maddie into giving her consent to marry him. Then he would make love to her, a lightning fast union with gasping insistence and need. He would follow that with a long, slow melding, designed to enthrall and engage her—a loving that would last half the night.

Maybe then he could purge his need for her. Perhaps he would stop dwelling on her when he should be focused on investments, the railroad, on money—the pulse beat of his life.

Brock frowned when he realized Maddie was nowhere in sight. His gaze skimmed over the velvety pink sofa, a pair of green baize chairs atop a matching Persian carpet resplendent with burgundy accents. The orange-yellow glow of a fire crackling in the hearth told him she was likely here.

A search of the kitchen, study, and garden also proved them empty. Scowling, he trekked back to the entry and started up one of the twin staircases that led to the bedrooms, taking two stairs in a single stride.

"Maddie?" he called.

"In the bedchamber," came her soft reply from behind the door of the master suite at the hall's end.

Was she hurt, unwell? Had she caught a plague, a pox, a wretched fever?

Or did she lie in wait for him?

Sprinting up the stairs, Brock pushed his way to the door. Troubled, he shoved the heavy white door open with an impatient sweep of his arm. He had expected almost anything.

But nothing in his entire life had ever prepared him for this Maddie.

He struggled to find his next breath, a coherent thought, as Maddie stood before him dressed in a sheer golden drape, sari style—and nothing else. The thin gossamer clung to the swells of her breasts, yielded to the curve of her waist, hugged lush thighs, and left little doubt that she was completely bare beneath the exotic garment.

"Dear God." His whispered oath, fervent and hushed, slipped out and hung in the quiet air.

Maddie's only reply was a kittenish smile.

Brock clenched his fists at his sides, wondering how in the hell he would find the strength to resist her now. One thing he remembered well of the younger Maddie was her determination to win, once she'd set her mind to it. Apparently, she had decided to force an end to their game tonight.

Talons of lust clawed like fire through his belly. Staring at the creamy expanse of her shoulders beneath exotically piled curls the color of a dark blaze, the bare arms, plunging neckline, Brock felt the foundation of his self-control shake. *Don't look any lower,* he admonished himself. The visible outline of tight nipples—rouged to dark perfection—made his mouth water. The erotic indention of her navel gave way to the plane of her stomach. *Damn it, no lower.* Reddish curls, hidden in damp shadows, beckoned his gaze to the delta of her femininity. And he remembered her taste, her response to his mouth.

Without a word, she took a sway of a step toward him, then another. Her every move seduced him, devastated him, as the transparent garment alternately billowed and clung to her tempting curves, brushed the tight pebbles of her breasts into hardened beads he hungered to taste. Sweat rolled from his temple when he caught the scent of her vanilla-jasmine skin, taunting him with memory, urging on his desire.

Brock started toward her with all the patience of a bull, forgetting everything but possessing Maddie in that erotic golden drape. . . .

Clasping the folds of her makeshift sari to keep her hands from shaking, Maddie made her way to Brock. Part of her felt jubilant, powerful. Her plan was working! The pure lust in Brock's gaze, coupled with the hardening of his manhood, visible through his tight blue breeches, told her this hazardous plot was succeeding—and beyond her wildest dreams.

But she never expected to feel the weakening of her knees,

the moistening of her secret self, at Brock's rapacious gaze as he charged toward her. Blast it, she was seducing him, not the reverse!

Drawing in a deep breath, Maddie sidled over to him, trying to remember all she'd read in Edith's *Kama Sutra*. Pressing embraces and rubbing embraces. Bent and clasping kisses. Scratches and bites. Even congress of a crow, mutual oral stimulation, the description of which still made her flush. And intercourse in so many different positions . . . Woman on top: the pair of tongs. Man behind the woman: the congress of a cow. Woman on top and man from behind: the mare's position. So many different variations she had never considered. Maddie had read most of the day and found the message shocking, scintillating. Everything she had never imagined—and wanted fiercely tonight.

And Vatsyayana wrote of a man's obligation to satisfy his partner, suggesting different motions for penetration, like piercing her with his member, pressing within her, churning once inside her. She wanted to feel them all, certain Brock would more than meet his responsibility.

He reached her then. He grasped her transparent sari in his firm grip, twisted the fabric, using it to pull her flush against him. He sent a searching green gaze to her face, into her soul. Maddie answered with a wicked smile.

Remembering the clinging embrace described in the book, she twined herself about Brock's heated body like a vine, grabbed his neck and brought his mouth to hers in an instant kiss, a tangle of lips and breathy moans. His own hands rose to her, fingers pressing into her nape with clamoring ardor.

Need rose up from her belly, washing over her senses. His nearness sensitized her to his every touch and breath, to the essence of his need, which he pressed against her belly with demand.

Maddie kissed Brock back with all the aching insistence

he'd created in her over their nights together, losing herself in the flavor of brandy, the scent of spice and man and desire.

Suddenly, Brock tore himself from her embrace. His breath came in short, hard gasps. His stare accused and possessed her at once. Objection and denial formed on the hard angles of his jaw, settled in the furrow beneath his brows.

Panicked, Maddie stared back. He could not control the pace. Vema had stressed that the only way to really seduce a man was to make him forget all else. She latched onto all she had read since this morning and formed a hasty plan.

"Brock," she whispered, sidling closer again. "Darling." She took his cravat in her hands and untied it, fingers lingering about his neck, palms drifting over his chest.

"No, Maddie." He made no move to stop her.

His breathy appeal infused her with triumph. She'd been right to block out Colin's mocking voice in her head, telling her that she was too icy for any man to truly desire. Brock was proving her late husband wrong with every breath.

Tearing the cravat away, she tossed it to the carpet. His pulse pounded furiously at the base of his neck. Then she made quick work of the buttons of his shirt, one at a time, grazing her fingernails across his feverish golden skin, his hard male nipples, as she descended farther, down toward that rigid male part of him. He sucked in a sharp breath and swallowed hard.

"Maddie—"

Before Brock could complete the protest, Maddie melded her mouth to his and guided him with unerring steps to the sumptuous four-poster bed in the corner. When they reached it, she pushed him down with a gentle shove and a determined smile until he sat on the mattress.

Brock sent her a hot, questioning stare. The passion etched onto his face sent her own desires flaring. Arousing him aroused her. Why had she never considered that possibility?

"What are you doing?" he demanded.

Hovering above him, she wrapped her taut fingers around the edge of his shirt and pulled it over his head. Bare to the waist, she watched the hard ridges of his chest rise as he sucked in air.

Reveling in a hedonism she had never felt before, Maddie kissed only his lower lip, dragging it between her own lips, toying with his flesh between her teeth. He moaned. Encouraged and incited, she outlined his lips with her tongue. When he tried to seize her, take control of their lovemaking, she danced away.

"Maddie, you are killing me!"

Smiling, she sauntered to the side of the bed and leaned back toward him to whisper, "I am trying."

Groaning, Brock reached for her again, but she made her way behind him, crawling across the mattress. He turned to her, but she took the warm, rippling steel of his arms in hand and turned him away.

The wide expanse of his powerful brown back lay before her. Blending her newfound knowledge with her urges, she applied her hands to his flesh, her mouth to his neck. He gasped as she nibbled on him, leaving tiny love bites along the way. She underscored his sensitivity to her touch by grazing his back with the length of her nails. Goose pimples broke out all down his arms.

According to the book, they would be compatible lovers. They would form the highest union; her feminine sheath, untouched for three years, would form a tight glove about his large member. The force of their passion seemed equal, for his hungry gaze mirrored her own growing appetite.

Teeth nipping on his earlobe, Maddie draped her arms about his neck and worked her way to his side. Brock hooked an arm about her waist and fastened his mouth to hers as if only she could bestow his next breath. Gladly, she gave of her lips, her passion, as she returned the kiss. With a growl, Brock pulled her across his lap, grasping her hips, fingers digging with need. His unrelenting mouth continued to seduce her as he settled the apex of her thighs against his hardness and pressed.

Maddie cried out, needing him, aching with a mindless desire Brock aroused so easily. With him, she felt secure in her desirability as a woman and craved the chance to explore all that could be between them, to capture the thoughtful Brock who had once invaded her soul and tenaciously stayed.

Without warning, Brock stood, turned, and lowered Maddie to the soft cushion of the bed. His lips never left hers as he followed her there, covering her body with the broad strength of his own. His hand probed between them, twisting, tugging. He cursed, then sighed. Maddie was too lost in the feeling of him, in the force of her desire, to take much note.

With a thrust of his hips, he wedged himself between her legs so tightly, she felt every long, demanding inch of him pressed against her—with only thin gossamer separating them.

He had unfastened his breeches. Yes, the man most equipped to fulfill every secret desire, to help her prove she was not frigid, was finally ready to be her lover. She tried to remember why he'd been resisting the pleasure, but his mouth fastened on her breast, driving away rational thought. His fingers found their way inside her, her need for him escalating to heady new heights.

"Brock, now. No more waiting. Please!"

Her hoarse plea reverberated in the air between them. Of its own will, her body unfurled for him, thighs parting wider. Impatient, she shoved the corner of her sari aside until they touched flesh to flesh.

Breath held, eyes closed, she waited for Brock to fill her, to satisfy her body's urgent demands.

Instead, he thrust himself away and fastened his breeches, issuing a litany of curses he could only have learned in the gutter.

Dazed, aching, she sat up and peered at him.

He ran a tense hand across his face and glanced at her, his stare trailing down her disheveled nudity. He cursed again and tore his gaze away.

"Maddie, damn it!" He fastened his breeches in short, angry yanks of his buttons. "This cannot happen. Not until we've wed."

Every muscle and sensitive nerve in her body cried out: *No!* He couldn't leave her now, couldn't walk away so that she agonized over the colorless void of his absence. So that she thought of nothing but him while she twisted restlessly in her lone bed.

"You don't want me?" she whispered, half-afraid he would affirm her fear. But she had to know the truth.

His cynical laugh grated the air between. "Maddie, if I wanted you any more, I would explode."

Brock's green eyes echoed his sentiment. A quick look at the hard ridge of flesh in his breeches seemed to make a mockery of her fear.

Still, she did not feel reassured. He wanted her, but not enough to take her. Determined to succeed, she crossed the room to him and threw her arms about him.

But the feel of him hot and hard, pressed against her, only revived the aching frustration deep within her.

Why was her body and mind such a tangle of contradictions?

"Make love to me," she whispered. "Say you will. I've never felt this way. Ever. I want—"

"I can't." He swallowed and grabbed his shirt, throwing it on over his head. Lips pursed, he shook his head. "You tempt me so badly, I can scarcely breathe, but I will not give up—" He stopped himself, raking a tense hand through the thick waves of his hair. "I cannot."

His rigid jaw, taut cheeks, and narrowed, pained eyes grabbed at Maddie's heart and tugged. For an instant, she forgot their wager, his demands, her vow of revenge. She remembered the young idealist she had loved, and hated knowing that she caused him distress.

Did he perhaps resist making her his mistress, clearly at great discomfort to himself, because he really did want her as his wife and could not use her like some tart?

Almost as soon as the thought came, Maddie shoved it away. Brock did not love her. He never had. Accepting that had been one of the most bitter lessons of her life. Wondering about his emotions, wishing she could ease his mind— that was dangerous. Brock would not hesitate to use her inexplicable affection against her if he knew of it.

"Go, then. I hardly care if you stay." Her tone sounded petulant; she knew that. Still, she could not keep her yearning, her insecurity, her unfurling feeling from clouding her voice.

Taking her face in his hands, Brock positioned his mouth a mere breath from hers. "Miss me," he demanded softly, then fled into the night.

NINE

Clutching Aimee's little hand in her own, Maddie made her way up the stairs to Brock's office in the heart of London's financial district. She dreaded the coming encounter more with every step.

Since last night's *Kama Sutra* disaster, she had never been more aware of her own deficiencies as a woman. Yes, he'd claimed to want her. She had even seen proof. But he did not want her enough to cast reason—or their wager—aside.

The realization that Brock could walk away from her left Maddie with a sharp, wretched embarrassment. Her cheeks heated with something close to shame.

When she had arrived home after an hour of tears, she'd run up to Aimee's room, as she did each night, only to have the sobs rack her as she stared at the pale innocence of her daughter's sleeping face. She could not risk her baby girl's happiness, ever. True, Brock did not seem like the kind of man who would actually condemn a child to prison or mistreat her under his roof.

But Maddie was painfully aware that she had been wrong about Brock before.

All night, Maddie had paced and cried. She knew that she alone stood between her daughter's childhood contentment and the cruelties of the world. She could not afford to make the wrong choice, could not allow the Fleet to swallow

Aimee in its dank, dismal claws—at Brock's command. Transportation to a workhouse would be worse. Exhaustion and hunger often ended the lives of the tenderly young in those hells.

Yet marriage to Brock could be no less dangerous.

If she wed him, she and Aimee both would become his property legally, to treat as he saw fit. He could beat the girl, if he wished. While Maddie doubted Brock was that cruel, he could well send the girl away to some remote school, where Aimee would be raised by strangers, without the comforting familiarity of home, without love.

Maddie knew she had failed her daughter by marrying Colin, who had regarded the child with contempt. And, despite Brock's tolerance of Aimee so far, she had little reason to believe that he would behave any better, believing her to be Colin's daughter.

Lord, what a terrible irony. Even if she told him the truth of Aimee's parentage, would he believe her? Would he care? Or would he use the girl against her for revenge?

The unanswered questions represented chances she could not afford to take with her daughter's future.

Maddie's last one hundred and fifty pounds weighed heavily in her reticule. Since she could not seduce Brock, he must be made to see reason, to compromise. During last night's tears, she had come up with a new plan, one she prayed he would accept.

"Mama, I can't run anymore," Aimee panted beside her.

Maddie stopped and did her best to smile at her sunny daughter as desolation made her grip her little hand tighter. "We'll slow down, sweeting. Mama is sorry."

At a more sedate pace, Maddie continued with Aimee to the end of a plush, red-carpeted hall, squinting against the late afternoon sun that penetrated the thick windows. Determination fired her exhausted mind to succeed at protecting Aimee and escaping the hellish bonds of matrimony.

Clenching a fist to steady her trembling fingers, Maddie

lifted the latch to the door of Brock's office. Inside, his bespectacled secretary sat, cravat askew, papers strewn everywhere.

He glanced up with a distracted frown. "Lady Wolcott, hello." The thin man rose from his desk. "Mr. Taylor wasn't expecting you."

A truer statement had never been uttered. "I need a moment of his time, if you please."

"I will see if he is available now," the secretary said before he disappeared behind the door that led to Brock's office.

"Mama, can Mr. Taylor joust with me today?"

Resisting the urge to refuse her inquisitive child, Maddie knelt. "Probably not, sweeting, but you may ask him when I finish speaking to him."

Aimee nodded solemnly. "I shall. Then can I wear my new dress?"

She smothered the pang of regret she felt at having sold the luminous pearls Brock had given her to afford her daughter's new dress—and this new plan.

Smoothing the child's golden hair with a tender sweep, she said, "You may, for you need a new dress, my little minx. A pretty blue for a pretty girl."

As Aimee giggled, Brock opened the door, his expression cautious but unreadable, and motioned her inside.

Did he remember the burn of last night's pleasure with anger or regret? Did he remember it at all?

Maddie turned to Brock's secretary. "I'm sorry, I do not know your name."

He puffed up with the pleasure of being asked. "I am Mr. Chiltam, my lady."

"Very good. Will you be here for the next few moments?"

He nodded his dark head. "I should, my lady, yes."

Facing Aimee, she instructed, "Sit right there, close to Mr. Chiltam." She pointed to a Louis XIV chair with lush green upholstery. The sale of that chair alone would feed them all for a month. "Mama will be back in a moment."

Glumly, Aimee nodded, then plodded to the chair, where she sat with a plop.

"Thank you." Maddie squeezed Aimee's warm hand one last time before she disappeared through Brock's door, ever conscious of his watchful eyes upon her.

He shut the door behind her, enclosing them alone in silence.

That piercing green gaze of his traveled over her, seeming to miss nothing. She resisted a shiver, but not of fear. Dear God, were it only that easy. Her body remembered him, the feel of his skin against hers, the taste of his flesh where his neck met those powerful shoulders. She could hardly forget the feel of his mouth on her everywhere . . . everywhere. Maddie closed her eyes, took a deep breath, and forced the memory aside.

"I've come here today to end this farce of a wager."

His watchful gaze pierced her. "So you'll marry me?"

She clenched her fists, pushing down frustration. "No. This whole wager is ludicrous. We live in Eighteen-thirty-four, for goodness sake. In this modern time, must we marry for money? Is my debt so important that you will find yourself in the Fleet without repayment?"

Brock lingered above her, looming. "I told you, Maddie, I don't need your money. I need your connections. We may live in modern times, but your blue-blooded brethren still believe in breeding over brains, just as they did a thousand years ago."

"You've always wanted to change things. So start now. Don't play into their societal trap," she challenged.

He shot her a disparaging glare. "That will get me nowhere. I know which rules I can break and still succeed, Maddie. That is not one of them."

"As you will." She held in a long sigh of disappointment, clutching the reticule that would soon be empty. "Then I've come to give you a monthly installment against my debt. Did you not say one hundred twenty-eight pounds?"

While Maddie fished the funds from the small pouch, she felt Brock's glare upon her.

"Where did you get that much money?" Despite the quiet voice, she could not miss the razor-edged tone.

"Not that my finances are your affair, but my farm land in Warwickshire recently made me a modest profit," she lied. "And if you will compromise with me, I shall give you half of those profits for the next three years, along with the title to the cottage in St. John's Wood. I will agree to escort you to society functions as you see fit until you gain the entrée you need. Do we have an arrangement?"

Brock stared at her for a silent thirty seconds. Beyond the closed door, Aimee hummed to herself. The shuffle of papers came from the anteroom as well. Maddie could read nothing of Brock's reaction in his stern, square face, except perhaps anger. Was he considering her proposal? Her galloping pulse prayed it was so.

In the next heartbeat, Aimee thrust the door open, skipping into the room with swishing skirts and bouncing curls.

"Mama, I want to joust with Mr. Taylor now."

Maddie bit her lip to smother a curse. "Not now, Aimee. Mama and Mr. Taylor are having an adult conversation. When we are done, you may speak with him."

Aimee stomped her feet. "I want to talk now."

"Wait in the next room, Aimee," Maddie demanded, her tone a warning.

"That chair hurts my bum," she said, rubbing her offended posterior.

Beside her, Brock chuckled. Maddie elbowed him in the ribs and shot him a glacial glare.

"A lady does not mention such . . . parts of her body in the presence of gentlemen. You may stand, but you will wait until I am through with Mr. Taylor."

"Let's play 'Ring Around the Rosy,'" Aimee suggested, as if Maddie had not spoken.

The girl grabbed her hand and Brock's before Maddie

could protest. Neither Brock nor Maddie made a move to join hands.

"We are not playing now, Aimee."

"Just once," the girl wheedled. "I want to play."

Maddie debated the wisdom of such capitulation, then gave in. Aimee had been deprived of decent clothing, plentiful food, and a loving father. If "Ring Around the Rosy" would make her happy, that was the least Maddie could provide.

"Once," she agreed, her tone soft.

"Thank you, Mama." She bounced in happiness. " 'Ring around the Rosy. Pocket—' " Aimee stopped her singing. "Mama, you and Mr. Taylor have to hold hands."

With a grin, Brock held out his hand to her. Maddie stared at his outstretched palm, the strong, brown fingers, before winding her gaze up the broad power of his biceps, his shoulder, and his neck. His expression could only be termed a challenge, with a sweep of raised brown brows, the dare lurking in his gaze.

Taking his palm would be like agreeing to bed down with the devil. Refusing it meant admitting she feared him.

Gritting her teeth, Maddie slapped her palm into his.

Brock clasped her hand tightly, until she felt every inch of skin, every callus, and the oven of warmth he radiated. Somehow, in this embrace she felt frighteningly in his possession.

As if their connection attuned her senses to Brock, his manly scent drifted to her. She catalogued it, rather than succumbing to the experience of it—a forest perhaps, but after a rain, filled with rich earth. Yet something of the East, tinged with a hint of a smell she refused to consider pleasing. Sandalwood? Still, the strongest element was simply his essence, something vibrant and dimensional, something impossible to ignore altogether. Something so Brock.

A telltale warmth crept through her belly, down to her legs. Her heart beat conspicuously fast as Aimee sang the child's song. Maddie moved in a circle, her gaze riveted to her old lover and new rival.

What was he thinking? Had he, too, wondered what the previous night could have been like, had he not walked away?

Soon the song ended, and Aimee clasped her hands in glee. Brock maintained a firm hold on Maddie. Discreetly, she tried to pull herself free. Keeping the grip, Brock slid the smooth pad of his thumb over the back of her hand, leaving a trail of tingles in his wake, before he finally released her.

"That was fun!" Aimee shouted into the silence.

The little voice jolted Maddie back to the present, back to the fact she and Brock had been bartering over Aimee's future, her very life.

"Now," she instructed the girl, "you must do as you promised and wait in the next room while Mr. Taylor and I finish talking."

Aimee's little smile fell, and Maddie hated being the cause. But this conversation was too important to put off any longer.

As Aimee cracked open the door to the outer office and disappeared in a trail of faded pink skirts, Maddie repressed her guilt over her harsh tone. She must give Brock her full attention. Everything counted on Brock agreeing to her latest plan.

"Well," she prompted, shutting the door behind Aimee so the child would not hear how dismal their finances really were. "What do you say to my plan?"

Brock walked around her in a nearly silent circle, pausing at her right shoulder. His even breathing sounded in her ear, making her shiver. Blast it all, why could she not forget him as a man and remember him as an adversary?

"What do I say?" he asked rhetorically. "I say I've no desire for modest profits from uncertain farm lands for so little a period as three years. I want compromise even less.

I have no use for your St. John's Wood cottage now that I've purchased a better one of my own in Paddington. I did not ask you to be my eternal escort. I asked you to be my wife. And I expect you to say yes, or suffer the consequences."

Maddie closed her eyes as she felt hope leak ruthlessly from her soul. She'd known deep down that her chances of persuading Brock to accept this proposal had been slim. Until now, she had not wished to admit just how slim. Still, she couldn't give up, give in to his demands. Too much was at stake.

"Please, leave me and my daughter be. She is a child and does not deserve to be punished for Colin's sins and my inability to pay for them. She needs her mother and she needs a chance in life. How often in the past did you say you needed that very thing yourself?"

Brock's expression remained unchanged. He stood close enough to have touched her if he chose. He didn't. At least not yet.

"I cannot leave you be. It is impossible."

"But—"

"Marriage is hardly a punishment for the girl. I'll see her cared for, I told you. She'll be fed and clothed and looked after. I shall even provide her a dowry, if you wish her to have a chance to wed well. The only way she will be punished for Sedgewick's foolishness is if you choose the Fleet as her fate."

Maddie sucked in a painful breath. Aimee's fate? No, her death, most likely. Yet with marriage to Brock, Aimee did not have the complete assurance of physical safety. And emotionally, she might be ignored, perhaps even harmed.

"You have no notion what you demand of me. Why me? Buy yourself another impoverished, well-born wife. Certainly anyone will do, if all you need are connections."

"No. Damn it, Maddie. We've been over this. You will wed me. It is the way things should have been, and the way I insist them to be now."

The arrogant blackguard! Fury erupted in her mind, her heart, racing with her blood to her limbs, blotting out reason or consequence. He had left her, once upon a time, afraid and alone and with child. Whirling on him, Maddie struck out with her palm. It connected with Brock's cheek with a loud clap. "We were *never* meant to be wed, you cad. Never, do you hear me?"

Brock stopped her flailing hands by clenching angry fingers about her wrists. "You've made it perfectly clear in every way possible that you never intended our future to include marriage, *my lady,*" he sneered. "I am even more determined it shall."

"Go to hell, Mr. Taylor." She jerked free and turned away.

Maddie reached for the latch, her hand trembling. She must collect Aimee and leave, find another plan, steal money if she had to. Anything to avoid Brock, to prevent becoming a shivering, pleading mass at his feet, begging for money . . . and pleasure. Anything to prevent succumbing to him, to avoid putting Aimee in his path.

Maddie swung open the door to the anteroom, only to find it empty. Irritation plagued her. Aimee's antics were ruining her escape. She needed to leave now, before Brock found some other way to parry his point home.

"Aimee, we are ready to leave. Where are you?"

Silence greeted her.

With a troubled frown, Maddie looked about the room, conscious of Brock's gaze boring into her back. Why must Aimee choose now to play hide and seek?

"Aimee," she called. "Come out to Mama. Now!"

In the silence that followed, Maddie gazed around the still room, all too aware of Brock standing in the portal, watching her. She was determined to ignore him as she bent to search behind a large leafy plant, under the now vacant secretary's desk, in a corner behind the drapes.

Still, she found no trace of her daughter.

Maddie frowned. Certainly Aimee must be here somewhere. Where else would the girl have gone?

Glancing over her shoulder at Brock, she forced herself to be civil enough to ask, "Can you think of anywhere she might be hiding? Another room? A closet? A cabinet?"

"No."

His words drained Maddie of annoyance and filled her instead with worry. If he could think of no other place Aimee might hide, where could she be? Outside this office? Her mind—and heart—began to race.

"Aimee!"

Silence. Alarm crept into the pit of her belly and Maddie began searching the room again, tearing aside draperies, knocking over Mr. Chiltam's chair. "Aimee!"

More unsettling silence. Alarm became panic.

When Aimee hid, she giggled. The horrible silence in Brock's reception room terrified her.

"Aimee!" she cried, her skin clammy. Her hands shook.

Argument forgotten, she looked to Brock in a panic. "She's gone!"

Brock came quickly to her side with a gentle whisper. "Stay calm. She may be in the hall or outside with Mr. Chiltam. We will find her."

"Yes," she murmured, praying Brock was right.

Brock put his arm about her shoulder. "Let's search about. Where would she most likely go?"

Maddie's mind whirled as she tried to fight down the terror. "She loves to be outside."

With a nod, Brock suggested, "Perhaps Mr. Chiltam took her out for a bit of air. You look in front of the building. I'll check the stairs and halls here."

"Check the water closet as well."

At Brock's nod, Maddie scrambled down the stairs to her task, her heart pounding. She prayed all the while that Aimee had not gone far, that she was safe.

Outside, the bright spring sun assaulted her eyes, momentarily blinding her. Alarm biting her gut, Maddie shielded her eyes from the glare with an unsteady hand at her brow and scanned the massive building's walk, the tiny scrap of grass that served as decoration. She saw her horse and a sidewalk full of busy bankers beginning to leave their jobs for the day.

But she saw nothing of Aimee.

Hoping Brock had had better luck, Maddie turned back to the building, only to find him emerging alone. His grave expression sent Maddie's fear spiraling.

"Any sign of Mr. Chiltam either?" She heard her own voice tremble.

"No," he admitted. "Though I cannot imagine where he would have taken her or even if he would have done such a thing."

Fear clawed deep lesions into her composure. Sweet heaven! Where could Aimee be? Terrible things could happen to an innocent child in a city as big and depraved as London. What if she was not with Brock's secretary? What if they could not find her?

The tears must have revealed her panic. "We will find her, Maddie," Brock assured. "I promise."

"But sh—she's so alone and so vulnerable. Aimee lives in a fairy-tale world. She trusts ev-everyone. She will be so afraid." Fear trickled in a cold, relentless stream through her veins. "I've heard the terrible things that happen to children in this city. Oh. Oh, dear God! They are sold into work-houses, into prostitution—"

"Maddie, don't think of that now. Concentrate on finding her," Brock commanded, his words softened by his firm touch.

"I'm all she has," Maddie sobbed, feeling as if her insides were being torn to shreds. "She's all I have. Please . . ."

Tears overtook her. Fear and despair vied to control her. Each took its own merciless chunk of her composure and peace.

Brock wiped the tears from her face with callused thumbs and cupped her cheeks in his large hands. "I know, but you have to stay calm. It is the only way we can help her."

Maddie gave him a shaky nod, but the sharp edge of panic cut her equanimity again and again. For Aimee's sake, she took a deep breath and tried to think rationally.

"Look around you. Try to guess which way she might have gone."

Shaking, terrified, she shot him a distraught glare. "If I knew, I would be running after her now!"

He caressed her shoulder in soothing strokes. "I know. You're frightened. Just look around you; try to imagine what Aimee might do."

Tears blurring her vision, Maddie looked up and down Prince's Street. *Think! Think of your little girl!*

Directly across the street afforded her only a side view of the huge cavern that was the Bank of England. Aimee would not be interested in that. Behind her lay Cheapside, but that way was dark, with tall buildings and trees. Out of fear alone, she doubted Aimee would go there. But directly across the street, a statue of Wellington stood proudly, adorned with singing, red-breasted birds. Yes, that might have caught her fancy.

But the little girl was nowhere near the monument, just bankers and barristers with starched shirts and indifferent faces heading home.

With dawning horror, Maddie realized the road fanned out into four lanes beyond that. Throgmorton lay in a northeasterly direction that could lead her to the mean streets of Spitalfields. Cornhill stood almost directly east, winding its way to the hellish depths of Whitechapel. Lombard Street wandered southeasterly before heading back to Whitechapel as well. King William Street slashed south, toward London Bridge and the Thames.

No! Sweet Aimee was only four years old, lost in a giant

city with which she was totally unfamiliar. Anything could happen to her. Anything at all!

"Maddie?" Brock prompted at her side.

Knowing she had to be strong, she swiped at her new tears. As she did, she noticed the birds—robins, from the look of them—on Wellington's statues take flight, their soft wings guiding them low to the ground. She watched as they followed an invisible path down Cornhill Lane. Maddie sent a prayer upward that her hunch was right.

"Follow the birds."

"What?" He frowned, his face revealing his confusion. Then he saw them, too, flying in a seemingly fluent ribbon of red breast feathers not far above their heads. "Oh, she would like that."

"Yes." Maddie nodded, hope stirring. Caution made her hesitate. "Do you think there have been others?"

"Indeed," said Mr. Chiltam as he arrived upon the scene from the other side of the street, his brown hair blowing in the wind. "I've seen small groups of birds behave in such a fashion for the past week or two. Is something amiss?"

Brock turned a look of such fury on Mr. Chiltam that the small man took a step back. "Aimee is not with you?"

"No, sir. She is not." Chiltam looked confused.

Maddie's last hope died and another slash of fear tore through her at the secretary's words. Dear God, Aimee was truly alone in the descending London night.

"You left her, damn you! She is missing now."

Chiltam pushed his glasses up on his nose in a clearly nervous gesture. "S—she asked to . . . relieve herself, so I took her down the hall, to the water closet. She said she could find her way back to the office, so I walked across the street to the bank so I might deliver some papers—"

"Imbecile!" Brock's face was the picture of contempt. "Start looking for her. And keep looking."

Brock's secretary mumbled something, then shot a look Maddie's way but could not quite meet her eyes. Chiltam headed off in the direction of the river, down King William Street.

Maddie felt the tears threaten her again. She should have left Aimee at home with Aunt Edith, instead of listening to her daughter's begging to accompany her. She should not have left her alone with a stranger, not even for two minutes. How foolish! But Mr. Chiltam had seemed so intelligent, and her conversation had been all too inappropriate for Aimee's ears.

Excuses, all of them. Not a one would bring Aimee back.

"Come with me," Brock urged. "We will find her."

Her stomach twisted tighter than a sailor's knot, she nodded and followed Brock down Cornhill Lane.

They walked briskly in the descending dusk, brushing past hurrying people. Maddie anxiously scanned the crowd, looking at every face. Brock stopped other bankers who crossed their path to ask if they had seen a wandering girl with swinging blond braids.

Every man's answer was no.

The sky became gray, tinged with the vibrant oranges of dusk. Maddie's panic escalated. She spoke to a hearty butcher, a withered baker, a crone selling flowers. She asked them all if they'd seen Aimee. None had noticed any child more than another today.

Dark would be upon them soon. As they continued east, the alleys in this part of town seemed limitless—and dangerous. Aimee might have wandered down one, into trouble. She would be cold soon, scared and hungry. The thought that her daughter might really be lost to her made her break down. Hot tears burned her cheeks as Maddie shouted Aimee's name. The taste of salt and fear invaded her mouth mercilessly.

Still Maddie trudged forward. The scent of sewage began to assault her nose. As Maddie continued calling for her daughter, a pack of alley cats meowed about her legs for a morsel. Even in the approaching dark, she could see the streets no longer had the shine of prosperity. She stumbled on a man sleeping at the edge of the street, clutching a bottle in a lax fist.

Was Aimee lost *here?*

Brock was at her side instantly, a supporting arm about her shoulders. "Maddie, I know this is hard. Be strong. I promise I won't rest until we find her."

She looked up, into his solemn green eyes, his strong face. Even through her panic, she realized he truly meant that promise.

"I won't give up. I can't," she whispered.

A hack rushed by, horses' hooves resounding like thunder on the dirt street. It barely missed the people hustling about. Another coach followed minutes later, equally heedless of the choking dust it sent flying or of the surrounding humanity. Mercy, they were so careless! What if one of them hit Aimee? She closed her eyes as fear chewed at her stomach.

Suddenly, Brock took her by the hand, led her forward, and called with her for Aimee.

Within minutes, the streets became narrower still. Here in Whitechapel, the stench of hunger and desperation permeated the air. Buildings with little rooms stacked on top of one another seemed to glare with meanness, as did the unwashed people around her. Aimee was at their mercy, and Maddie feared for her baby.

Cutthroats, pickpockets, and pimps prowled the streets. Laughter and drunken singing spilled from seedy pubs. In the alley, a swaying man urinated against an abandoned building.

"A shilling for ye. And the missus can watch," called a painted woman from above.

Shocked, Maddie glanced up at the open window of a brothel, into the face of a very young whore.

Kindness had little value here. She feared a little girl's life had even less. Maddie wanted to believe these people were too engaged to bother hurting a lost child . . . but feared her thinking was wishful.

"You're shaking," Brock commented at her side, concern softening his hard features. "Ignore them."

"I'm terrified," she confessed.

"I know. I'm here." He wound his arm about her as they moved on.

After half an hour, Maddie feared they had taken a wrong path, that Aimee had not followed the birds. But luck finally struck when Brock stopped a young seamstress hurrying home.

"Aye, I saw 'er, not ten minutes ago. She was cryin' and callin' for her mama. Asked her wot was wrong, I did," said the needlewoman. "The lass pure run off."

"Which way did she go?" Maddie pleaded.

The woman pointed a bony finger straight ahead.

Brock pressed a coin into the woman's hand. Maddie thanked her through her tears.

She and Brock began to run, shouting Aimee's name. But Maddie became aware of the small streets and alleys again, any of which Aimee might have turned down. They slowed again, checking every dirty crevice. Holding her breath against the awful stench, ignoring the prostitutes conducting business, she called Aimee's name over and over.

No answer.

The last of the vivid colors left the sky as night fell, blanketing the land in black.

Desperation and denial clawed at Maddie. God, let her baby be safe!

As they wandered into the heart of Whitechapel, a little girl with a grubby face and lank brown hair passed them, a mismatched batch of candle scraps displayed on a tray suspended by a rope about her little neck.

"Guv!" she called excitedly to Brock. "Be ye wantin' more candles?"

More candles?

Brock squinted, then recognition dawned. Maddie could not imagine where on earth he would have met the child.

He knelt at the girl's feet and took her thin shoulders in his hands. "Molly, I've no need for candles tonight, but I need help. Very badly."

The young girl nodded solemnly, as if she understood the urgency.

"We're missing a little girl." Brock cast a glance at Maddie. "She belongs to my friend. Can you help us find her? I'll pay you twenty sovereigns if you bring her back to us."

Molly's eyes threatened to come loose from their sockets. "Cor, twenty—What does she look like?"

Brock gave Molly a brief description of height and hair color, with Maddie interspersing details of her eye color, her voice.

"She's wearing a pink woolen dress and black boots," Maddie added. "Her name is Aimee. She'll be crying and scared."

Molly bowed her head to lift the rope from about her slight neck and dropped her tray of candles in the street. "I'll round up me friends. We'll find 'er right and tight."

As Maddie watched Molly scamper off, she prayed the Whitechapel girl could live up to that promise.

Thinking of the alternative was too frightening.

For the next two terrifying hours, Maddie and Brock searched the grungy streets of London's East End. Up busy Whitechapel Road, polluted with sewage and vice, down less-traveled Leman Street filled with gin houses and thugs who appeared as if they might kill anyone for a coin.

Maddie called for Aimee in raw desperation until her throat ached. When her voice grew weak, Brock took over. Maddie could not help but be grateful.

He stayed at her side without complaint, shouting for the daughter he did not know was his. His voice carried farther, true. But his help meant more. He'd taken control of the situation, enlisting the help of others who knew these dingy streets, children who might think more like Aimee. For once, she even had the twenty sovereigns to pay Molly and her friends should they prove successful, thanks to the sale of the pearls Brock had given her.

The fearful part of Maddie wanted to blame him for this debacle, but she could not. The look on his face, the strain evident in his frown, the tracks of his fingers through the thick strands of his coffee-colored hair, more than demonstrated his worry.

For that alone, she welcomed him at her side.

"How are you?" He turned to her. The very touch of his hands upon her shoulders, gentle, guiding, resonated with concern. He was in this hell with her, beside her every step of the way.

Part of her wanted to tell Brock the truth about Aimee, here and now. But neither were up to the strain of the truth tonight. It would bring questions and confrontation. Finding Aimee was most important at this moment. She could decide the rest tomorrow when—if—they found their daughter.

"Let's get you something to eat. You look as if a stiff wind might blow you over."

Maddie shook her head. Although the hour neared nine o'clock, she had not felt the slightest rumble of hunger.

"Eat if you wish. I must keep looking."

With a shrug, Maddie broke away from his tender grip and took a handful of steps into the foggy, moonlit night.

Brock slipped his hand into hers, staying her. "Maddie, these are not streets you should walk alone."

She looked up, around her, at the rows of rickety shanties, their dark windows like bruises. She heard a shrill scream in the distance. The crack of a pistol punctured the night. Grim silence followed.

Clearly, Brock was right, but she could not worry about her own safety. In fact, Brock's warning made her hysteria rise again. "I must keep searching. Aimee is out there alone!"

"Shhh." He gave her hand a reassuring squeeze. "We are doing all we can. If you wish to keep looking, we will. I meant my offer of food to distract you. I did the thing poorly; I'm sorry."

Touched by his apology, his very sentiment, Maddie lifted a hand to his face. Stubbles of whiskers darkened his jaw now. He'd wrenched his cravat away hours ago. Dirt stained his crisp white shirt, attained by searching through countless dark and dismal alleys. Maddie could not consider him the enemy at that moment. Instead, her heart regarded him as an ally who had come, without hesitation, to her aid.

"I'm sorry to be cross," she whispered. "I'm just so frightened. What if I never see her again? How will I live with the worry that she's hurt or been taken captive by debauched—"

"Do not think that now," Brock broke in, covering her mouth with his hand. "We must think our best thoughts, pray often."

Then Brock enfolded her in his embrace, strong and unflinching, and brought her close. She felt his heartbeat, drew in the scents of ink, leather, dirt, and man. He comforted her, somehow made her believe he understood.

Now she could only hope that all would be well somehow.

TEN

"Guv!" Molly's little voice shouted from down the dark road. "We found 'er!"

Breath catching, Maddie whirled from the warm haven of Brock's embrace and looked toward the voice. Her heart pounded when she caught sight of Molly and four of her ragtag friends. In the middle, Aimee hobbled, holding their hands.

Relief burst inside Maddie in a well of warmth.

"Mama!" Aimee shouted, tears in her voice.

Maddie ran to her baby, eyes hot with salty tears. Joy surged, taking hold of her fear-filled heart and unchaining it. Her feet pounded upon the hard-packed dirt as she drew nearer and nearer to her only sweet child.

As she reached Aimee, Maddie flung herself to her knees and enveloped the girl in a hug. Aimee trembled, cried, as she clasped her little arms about Maddie's neck and squeezed as if nothing else mattered. Nothing else did.

For timeless seconds, no one moved, no one said a word. Maddie felt her happy tears mingle with those of her daughter. Their cries punctuated the night's silence.

"Oh, thank goodness!" Maddie sobbed. "I worried so much. Are you well?"

She grasped Aimee's shoulders and pushed back long enough to look at her daughter's smudged, dirty face. One of the girl's braids had come loose. She had scrapes on both knees, but to Maddie, the child had never been a more welcome sight.

"Mama, I got a hurt ankle and I'm hungry."

Maddie frowned. "Your ankle? Which one, sweeting?"

Aimee held out her left foot. Maddie took the ankle in her hands to examine. It did, indeed, appear swollen. Squeezing it earned her a yelp from the girl.

"We found 'er in an alley, all curled up with a kitten and givin' 'erself a proper cry," said Molly. "Said she's tripped and fell trying to dodge an angry bloke on a horse."

The fear of what might have been made Maddie's heart stop for a moment, but she drew Aimee close again, held her dear baby. She relished the fact that, once the girl's ankle healed, all would be right with her.

"Thank you," she said to Molly, feeling a resurgence of tears. "Thank you so much for finding her."

Molly scratched her head, looking oddly embarrassed. "Me own mum would be worried fer me, too, if I was lost. 'Tweren't nothin' to findin' her."

Maddie disagreed. Finding Aimee had been a miracle.

"You did a great thing," Brock assured Molly. "Far more than nothing."

In silent agreement, Maddie lifted Aimee's little body against her own and stood, holding her tight. "Don't you ever run off again, young lady. You scared me!"

"I'm sorry," the girl muttered, eyes downcast.

While Maddie was still steeped in the need to hold her child close, Brock counted out twenty sovereigns and handed them to Molly. "Thank you. We're very grateful."

The candle girl's brown eyes grew saucer wide. "Cor, me mum won't have to worry 'bout payin' for the roof over our heads for the rest of the year. Thank ye!"

"Where's our share?" asked a lanky boy.

"Aye, where is it?" demanded another of Molly's friends.

As the East End children began debating about how to split their new fortune, Maddie peered at Brock.

"I had twenty sovereigns to give them," she said. "You needn't have put yourself out on that score. Let me reimburse you for that at least."

"No." His tone was completely unyielding.

"But I owe—"

"Maddie, you need the coin far more. Let me help. The money brought back your daughter, so I was happy to give it."

Other words hovered on the tip of her tongue. Maddie couldn't decide if they were another argument designed to salvage her pride or a gracious acceptance intended to soothe his. In the end, she acknowledged his gesture with a small incline of her head and a whispered, "Thank you."

Within moments, Molly handed the other four children one sovereign each. "That's wot I promised, so that's wot ye get."

The poor children muttered a few colorful words but capitulated and accepted the sum. Quickly, they each scattered in a different direction, Maddie presumed toward home.

Only Molly remained beside her, Brock, and Aimee.

"Your mother will be very proud of you for doing such a good deed," Maddie said.

"She'll be happy 'bout the blunt," Molly corrected. "Now maybe I'll be eatin' supper every night."

Molly sounded cheered by the prospect. Maddie was appalled. No matter how destitute she'd known herself to be, she'd never been so poor that she'd had to deny Aimee a meal. And poor Molly stood here, all elbows and knees, joyful about the prospect of supper?

She and Brock exchanged glances. He nodded, then turned his attention to Molly.

"Speaking of which, why don't you let us feed you? You certainly missed supper tonight while you searched for Aimee."

Molly shook her head at Brock. "Thank ye, Guv, but I'm needin' to get home to me mum and show her all this coin. We'll both eat for sure tonight."

With that, Molly skipped off toward the tenement that was undoubtedly her home. As night swallowed the girl up, distress mixed with the exultation inside Maddie.

"That poor child," she murmured.

He shrugged. "It's what East Enders know."

Maddie wondered how Brock knew that.

"We must find a hack," she said, gazing into Brock's stiff profile.

As Maddie began walking, Aimee in her arms, she noted Brock still looking in the direction of Molly's departure. Though remote, something about his expression looked pained, haunted.

"Brock?"

He blinked, glanced about, and frowned. "Let us find a hack."

Maddie nodded, and they began walking toward the busier Whitechapel Road, where they would certainly find some means of transport. She found him looking back toward Molly again.

"Did you grow up here, Brock?" she asked impulsively.

Maddie had long suspected Brock was Whitechapel bred. Five years ago, however, he had refused to tell her of his home, of his past. And she knew she should not have asked now. He would likely be as stubborn and private today as he had been before. After the manner in which he had helped and supported her tonight, she knew it was not fair to barge in on the pain in his childhood, whatever it was.

"I'm sorry," she began. "You don't have to—"

"Yes," Brock cut in. He drew his hands into fists as he walked beside her. "I grew up here."

It seemed odd to Maddie that she should want to thank Brock for his confession, but somehow she did. Before she could respond, Brock shook his head and directed a kind glance at Aimee.

"I'll wager you're cold and hungry, young lady," he said to her daughter, to their daughter, with a manufactured smile.

Aimee did not know the difference. She nodded, then rubbed her little gray eyes with a dirty hand. "I'm hungry. I want gingabread."

"Gingerbread?" Brock murmured above Aimee.

Maddie nodded.

"Sweeting, Mama did not make any gingerbread today. What do you say we go home and grab some quick bits of bread and cheese? We can bake gingerbread tomorrow together, you and I."

"Nnnooo," she wailed and rubbed her eyes again. "I want gingabread."

A pair of prostitutes walked by, smelling of perfume and gin. They eyed Brock, who ignored them. A hulk of a man passed to their left.

Maddie clasped Aimee close, wishing in that moment that she could always protect the girl, give her everything her heart desired, as well as the meal and the bed the girl needed. Both would be hours away, unfortunately.

"I'm sorry, sweeting. Mama doesn't have any now." As she held Aimee against her as they walked the dark, stench-filled streets, Maddie was conscious of how much the girl had grown, and hugged her warm little body. "Put your head on Mama's shoulder. Perhaps Mr. Taylor can help us find a way back to his office, so we can take another adventure on the pony back home."

"Maddie, you can't mean to go home tonight. It's too far."

She peered up at Brock's scowl. Beyond the irritation, the moonlight illuminated his concern—a great deal of it.

"Aimee needs a bed and food. I—"

"I can get her those things."

While Maddie knew Brock was right, she wondered why he would care. Why would he volunteer to help Aimee and seem insistent about doing so? She had no answer for that question and was much too drained by the traumatic evening to ponder the puzzle overlong.

A pack of older children ambled by with hard expressions, passing around a bottle. One of them took a sip and spit it out very near Maddie's feet.

"Wot is this slop?" asked one. "It tastes like piss."

The other boy replied with a curse Maddie had rarely heard.

Brock ignored them. "Hampstead is too far away, Maddie. Aimee's ankle needs rest. And neither of you need to be riding across Hampstead Heath near midnight."

Brock was right, completely. Maddie knew that. She felt her tiny wall of resistance to accepting his help crumble hopelessly. Aimee must come before pride.

With a nod, she murmured, "Thank you."

Brock shrugged, his fine coat hanging a bit askew on his wide shoulders. "I know just the place to take her. It will be close and comfortable. Come morning, I'll have one of my servants retrieve your horse and bring it to you."

As they reached the corner of Whitechapel Road, Brock glanced about. He spotted an approaching hack and stepped up to hail the vehicle. It stopped immediately.

After helping her inside, Brock gave the driver instructions and followed her inside the musty interior, settling into the old, faded seat beside her.

Aimee fell asleep shortly after their journey began.

Neither Maddie nor Brock spoke into the long silence. She didn't know what to say, how to reconcile the Brock who had threatened her daughter with the man who had helped save her. Weariness crept in after her harrowing evening, and such thought became too difficult. She would sort it all out tomorrow.

She watched the London scenery pass by, still troubled,

despite the fact that Aimee was now safe. Whitechapel soon
melted into the City. From the City, they trekked past St.
Paul's Cathedral. Brock stared straight ahead, seemingly lost
in thought. Maddie cast a glance in his direction. As if sensing her eyes upon him, he turned and met her gaze.

Rolling fog obscured the moonlight, making it difficult
to discern his face in the dark, but she caught the familiar
glitter of his eyes, the shadows clinging to his angled cheek-
bones, the blade of his nose. He'd pressed his full mouth
into a hard line, and Maddie felt an overwhelming urge to
touch him.

Resettling Aimee on her lap, Maddie freed her left hand
and reached across the small space separating her from
Brock. She laid her hand over his. Brock's eyes turned sharp,
questioning. She squeezed his hand, even as she felt her
expression soften.

"I don't know how to thank you, Brock. Without your
help, I fear I might never have found Aimee."

"I did very little," he murmured, then cast an absent eye
out the window, presumably to the passing scenery, hazy
with fog. Knowing he had seen these streets many times,
Maddie realized he avoided her more than took in the sights
of London.

Yet he kept hold of her hand.

Maddie felt compelled to whisper, "It meant everything
to me."

Brock greeted the remark with silence, and she wondered
why he seemed reluctant to speak with her. Perhaps he was
tired . . .

With a shrug, she turned her gaze out the window as well.

Up Fleet Street they traveled, slowly through the Strand.
The streets were much quieter at this time of night.

Moments later, after a right turn and a left turn, Maddie
found herself on Maiden Street, a street loosely surrounded
by the Adelphi Theater and Covent Garden. Directly before
them lay a rather seedy-looking pub.

She turned to Brock in question.

He merely opened the door to the hack and stepped out, then turned to pay the driver. As Maddie scooted across the seat with her sleeping daughter in her grasp, Brock bent to retrieve Aimee from her tired arms. He lifted her against his chest with very little effort. Aimee barely stirred.

Without a word, Brock passed the door to the pub's raucous common room and made for a side door. Not without confusion and trepidation, Maddie followed.

"No one here will know who you are," Brock offered finally. "Nor will they question you. If you leave just before first light, no one of consequence will see you, and your reputation will not be harmed."

Numbly, Maddie nodded. He had considered her reputation when fear and weariness had made her quite forget it.

With a glance over his broad shoulder, Brock took in her expression, which she knew must be befuddled. "After all your attempts to disguise yourself during your trips to St. John's Wood and Paddington, I thought it best to be cautious."

He was right.

They entered the pub through a cozy parlor. A warm, spotless kitchen lay visible just beyond. An old man greeted them with a jolly smile, minus most of his teeth. Within moments, Brock had arranged for accommodations at the top of the stairs.

In silence, they trudged up to the room, Brock leading with a sleeping Aimee in his arms. Maddie followed behind tiredly, suddenly very glad she would not have to make the trip to Hampstead tonight.

The room Brock had procured was surprisingly clean, if sparsely furnished. A worn brown sofa sat to the side of an empty grate, just beneath a window that overlooked the alley. Through a door to her right lay a bedroom of simple white and blue.

Gently, Brock lay Aimee on the sofa.

"Put her on the bed," Maddie protested.

He shook his head. "No, you'll need a good night's sleep, and her foot needs elevating. She'll be fine here once she's covered."

With a turn of his shoulder, Brock edged past her, to the bedroom, where he retrieved a soft, well-worn quilt of blue and yellow, along with a pillow. Wordlessly, he placed the blanket over Aimee's exhausted form and lifted her left leg over the sofa's arm. He edged the downy pillow beneath her little head.

Maddie watched in touched silence. "Thank you. I—"

"It's nothing," he murmured once more.

Then he left the room.

Maddie stared at the width of his back as he departed. Did he plan to return? She had no notion.

Lord, she was tired. But more, she felt uncertain. Until tonight, Brock had often behaved as if he hated her and enjoyed toying with her for some perverse reason. She had assumed that his male pride had been stung by her marriage to Colin—or that he was simply a bastard who enjoyed her anguish. Tonight, he had shown unparalleled kindness, and she had nothing to which she could attribute this behavior.

With a shrug, Maddie decided his reasons did not matter. Aimee was warm and safe again. That meant more than anything.

She sank to her knees and stared down at her daughter, sleep granting Aimee complete oblivion from the evening's turmoil. But Maddie lived it over and over in her mind, those dark hours when she thought the most important person in her world had been lost or harmed. With gentle fingers, Maddie brushed the golden hair from Aimee's little face and felt the tears well up once more.

Footsteps at the door alerted Maddie, and she rose.

"Don't ye be mindin' me," whispered a wide middle-aged woman as she waddled into the room with a tray of food. "Yer mister sent a bite up for ye and the girl." The serving-woman smiled at Aimee's sweet sleeping face as she set the tray on the table beside her. "Poor mite; looks like she's had a day of it."

Maddie tried to squeeze out a smile. "Indeed."

A moment later, a boy nearly grown to manhood entered the room and started a fire in the empty grate.

The woman made her way into the bedroom and turned the sheets down somewhat clumsily. Maddie guessed this was not part of their usual service and that Brock had paid for it.

Why? With a frown, Maddie searched for an answer to that question but found none.

"From the looks of ye," said the woman as she shuffled back into the room, "ye should avail yerself of the food afore ye fall asleep."

She was right, Maddie realized with a tired sigh. She turned to wake Aimee, but her daughter's deep breathing and peaceful face made her change her mind.

Placing a soft kiss on Aimee's cheek, Maddie rose to the feel of the spreading warmth from the fire and meandered to the tray. The fare was nothing fancy—bread, cheese, a bit of ale, a mutton pie. But Brock had seen both she and Aimee cared for.

Tears pricked her eyes in a hot rush. Tonight he had been the man she remembered from girlhood—thoughtful, understanding, encouraging. He had stayed by her side, helped to bring Aimee back to her, comforted her during those terrible hours when she feared for her daughter's life.

As the ruthless blackguard who had threatened her with the Fleet, he had been easy to hate. Since he'd come waltzing back into her life, he had showered her with kisses and delicious caresses, as if he delighted in turning her melting body against her strong-willed mind.

But after tonight, she felt as if he had waylaid her defenses and begun encroaching upon her heart.

Again, tears stung her eyes and were fortified by others,

large, heavy tears that refused to be denied. They flooded their way out, down her cheeks in hot, salty paths, to her jaw, to the floor. . . . More came at the thought of Aimee in peril, then suddenly safe and warm—all due to a man she'd sworn to hate.

Brock entered the fire-lit room on silent feet. At a glance, he noted the innkeeper's wife had done all that he'd asked— turned down Maddie's bed, brought food, had a fire started. Seeing to her comfort had distracted him from the foolish confession he'd made in Whitechapel.

He shook his head at his stupidity. Why had he told Maddie the truth of his lowly origins? Why had he given her another reason to disdain him?

He could think of no sensible explanation. Rather, Brock was aware of an odd disturbance in his usual calm. He had been affected—deeply—by Maddie's tears tonight, by her stark terror and pain. For hours, he'd thought of nothing but erasing that panic from her lovely features. Even after the child had been found, Brock had been stirred by the honesty of Maddie's joy and relief. For a moment, he'd envied Aimee for Maddie's caring.

Even so, that did not explain why he had told Maddie something he'd never told anyone.

A catch of breath snagged his attention and brought it to Maddie, to her shaking shoulders. She still cried. Latent fear? Sublime relief?

Without knowing, Brock went to her and, clasping her shoulders, turned her to face him. Tears made silvery tracks down her pale face with even more force than before. That damned something inconvenient stirred inside him again.

"Maddie?" he whispered, looking down into her face, willing her to look back at him.

She did finally, her gray eyes resembling a storm-drenched sky. Where he'd believed peace should reign, he saw tumult. Most of her hair had come down from its chignon, the silken auburn skeins framing her face. Despite being overwrought and red-nosed, her beauty staggered him. Her pain softened him.

"Maddie." He pulled her against his chest, soothing her with a stroke of his hand on her back.

She eased away. "You needn't bother with me anymore. I am much better. Thank you."

The erratic pattern of her breathing told him without words that she struggled to bring her emotions under control. He knew she was not better at all.

"Have you eaten?" he asked.

"A few bites, yes."

Brock poured her a glass of wine, hoping it might relax her. She would need sleep to begin recovering from this evening's ordeal. He pressed the glass into her hand. "Drink."

With a weary bob of her head, Maddie did so, downing every last drop. Then she turned her gaze to the sofa, to the sight of her daughter.

"She's sleeping, Maddie," he murmured. "As you should be."

"I can't." She turned to him with tearful eyes, but this time they seemed to ask for something. Understanding? Comfort?

Brock answered instinctively, wrapping his arms around her again. "Aimee is here with you. She is safe. You will be all right here."

Maddie said nothing; she simply held on, clutching him.

And he was all too glad to hold her, not just to have her near. He liked her proximity, craved the feel of her in his arms. But this . . . this was different. Now she *needed* him in some way he did not fully understand. However, knowing he was vital to Maddie at that moment had a powerful impact on him.

Their silence raged with emotions and unspoken words

Brock didn't comprehend. But he refused to speak for fear of shattering the moment. He did not want to let Maddie go.

As she had five years before, Brock feared she was wrapping herself around his heart.

When she eased back a moment later, Brock ignored the silent protest within him and allowed her to put space between them. But she did not leave his arms. Instead, she gazed up at him with gray eyes that swirled with so many emotions, he could not separate one from the next.

"Thank you for being so wonderful tonight," she murmured.

Before he could reply, she urged his head down, toward hers, with soft fingers at his nape, and opened her mouth below his. She kissed him tenderly. As a way of expressing her gratitude, it was a method he preferred far above all others. Unable to deny her—or himself—he took her mouth gladly.

Immediately, he tasted something new and sweet in her kiss; he savored the heady essence of need on her lips, sweet as pure sugar. When he sank deeper into her mouth, Brock found that same intoxicating flavor on her tongue.

Maddie opened eagerly to him, welcoming him with a delectable invitation that stirred him. She flowed like honey around him, all through him. He kissed her again and again, addicted to this new flavor, to the feel of her.

She responded beyond his dreams, surging forward, pressing against him. Capturing his nape in a firm grasp, she kept his mouth on hers, a willing prisoner. Passion joined the need he savored in her kiss.

Unable to resist this new lure, Brock raised his hands to her hair and removed the rest of the pins, which fell to the ground, forgotten. The silk of her tresses spilled into his palms, through his fingers. He wrapped it around his hands, pulling her closer still.

A low moan escaped Maddie, jolting Brock to his senses.

Maddie needed comfort tonight, not lust. Whatever kind of cad she thought him, he would not take advantage of her after such a harrowing ordeal. Brock brushed her lips once more, twice, then began to ease away.

Maddie's fingers tightened around his neck instantly. "No." Her voice trembled. "No, don't."

Brock looked down at Maddie's face, now flushed, her lips swollen, red. Her look revealed a clamorous pleading that struck Brock square in the chest. The question in her eyes suddenly became clear. Would he stay? Would he comfort her with his touch? His body leapt to answer; his mind resisted her vulnerability.

"Maddie—"

She inched up to stand on the tips of her toes. She spoke against his mouth. "Don't leave me. Please. I'm still afraid."

Maddie kissed him, a gossamer brush of allure. Then again, this time tempting him while conveying both desire and urgency.

With her hair still wrapped about his hand, he pulled gently to tilt her head back. Brock stared down into her eyes once more and found that damned question still lingering. Her expression beseeched him.

Maddie's face told him that she needed him and was fully aware of all she asked for.

Brock couldn't breathe for fully ten seconds. His heart chugged in his chest at the thought of holding Maddie, possessing her. He imagined giving her all she wanted.

Most important, he knew Maddie needed this and could not deny her.

Bowing to the demand raging inside him, he turned to kick the bedroom door shut and surrendered to her request. Hell, he couldn't have left her now for anything.

"I'm here. I will not go," he promised.

Then he layered his mouth over hers with care.

The welcome on her lips exalted him, beckoning him closer. Brock sank deeper into the kiss, and Maddie opened beneath him once more, granting him full access to the honeyed depths of her mouth. He roamed. Hunger surged, mounting recklessly as she met him, breath for breath, sigh for sigh.

Maddie released his nape to slide her hands down his chest. In tight fists, she grasped the edges of his coat and tugged it down, past his shoulders. The garment fell to the floor.

After she freed him from the constriction of the coat, Brock felt a sharp rise of his desire. He must have her. The need that haunted her eyes compelled him to answer her call.

As he ended one kiss, she began another, this time edging a bit to the right. Desperate to stay near her, with her, he followed. She tiptoed another step, then several more. Always Brock kept pace with her, never allowing more than a whisper between her mouth and his own.

Maddie swept her lips over his in a tender grazing that made him ache all the more. Then he felt her smile against him before she turned and presented him with her back.

"Maddie . . ." He heard the raw desperation in his voice—and he didn't give a damn. She knew he wanted her; he had no doubt.

Over her shoulder, Maddie cast him a reassuring glance. Then she lifted her hair into her hands, revealing the graceful arch of her pale neck—and the row of buttons down the back of her dress.

Brock wasn't sure which he wanted first. He stormed both.

Releasing the groan he could not keep in, he trailed his lips across the sweet jasmine skin of her neck, even as his shaking hands found the first of her buttons. Maddie shivered. Her pulse fluttered. Encouraged, he plied the flesh just below her hairline with gentle nips of his teeth as three more of the tiny buttons came undone. To this, she moaned and arched her neck until her head lay against his shoulder, and they rested cheek to cheek. He soothed the sensitive spot between her neck and shoulder with his tongue and his heated breath. The last of her buttons gave way.

Brock grazed the graceful arch of her throat with slow fingertips, then caressed each of her arms in a downward stroke, easing the dress from her. The fabric hung about her hips, at the mercy of her petticoat. At her waist, he found the ties for the voluminous undergarment and quickly saw them freed. He eased the mass of her clothing down her hips until it pooled about her feet.

Maddie, clad only in her corset, stockings, and chemise, stepped away from her clothing and set her small fingers to the buttons of his shirt. With every button she released from its catch, she pressed her sweet mouth against his burning skin. From the top of his chest down, he felt the aphrodisiac of her mouth brushing lower until she kissed his navel. Brock thought he might explode.

When Maddie stood again and gave him a soft smile, she eased the starched cloth of his shirt away. Breathing became bloody difficult with her hands and eyes touching him in ways he had long craved. She did not try to seduce him; tonight she reached out to him in supplication. Brock found that more tempting than anything he'd ever known.

He guided his hands in a slow journey down her back, unlacing her corset and removing it as he went. Then he smoothed his hands down to her hips. Her lashes fluttered closed. His fingers settled there, pressing her in, closer, as close as he could get her. With a moan, she clung to him.

Brock ceased thinking then. Instead, he reveled in sensation and closed his eyes, forgetting everything but the need trembling between them. He kissed Maddie again, a skimming of mouths, followed by a long, sweet sampling. As before, she received his mouth with an honest hunger tempered by entreaty. Thick and insistent, desire curled inside him.

It was a melding as much as it was a kiss. Brock sensed her everywhere, against his flesh, her taste on his tongue, her scent in his nostrils, the smooth ivory of her shoulders and the swells of her breasts available to his hungry gaze. The awareness was even more heady for the way he knew she wanted him, needed him.

Brock removed her chemise and stockings in silence. Finally, Maddie stood before him, flushed and naked and trembling. Her pulse skyrocketed as she waited for his touch, a reaction, anything, to let her know he wanted her and would surrender to her urge to have him near.

Maddie sent a cautious gaze up, deep into Brock's green eyes. She read lust there, definitely. But she also read understanding, as if he realized she needed his touch to believe everything would be all right. Elation swept over her, along with a sense of connection she had felt all night.

No, that wasn't quite true. The connection had grown tonight, but she had felt it from the moment she'd first met Brock five years past.

"You look so beautiful," he whispered, reverent.

Maddie knew he meant each word with a sincerity that brought tears to her eyes once again.

"Touch me," she entreated. "Please."

He reached for her. Their mouths met, and Maddie felt a surge of elation at his acceptance.

The man kissed like the very devil. His lips warmed and possessed her, conveying desire and security in a single sweep. Maddie melted, her body swaying against the hard breadth of his. His tongue conquered her mouth. She could only grasp him tighter as he took her to heights she had scarcely before imagined.

Pressing him closer, Maddie sought relief from the building, tingling ache. The fine dusting of hair on his chest grazed her nipples. The movement shocked her with sensation, and she arched to him, seeking him.

As if her wanton demand were the most natural in the world, Brock cupped her breasts in his large palms, still slightly rough from his years of labor. His thumbs flicked across her tight crests. Fire shot down her breasts and belly. She moved restlessly against him, never questioning how he could both arouse and console her at once.

With Brock, nearly anything was possible.

Eager for more, for him, Maddie reached out. She stroked a hand across his wide chest, delighted by the solid slabs of muscles carved on his chest and abdomen. Wondering if he felt the same sensitivity as she, Maddie brushed his flat nipples with the pads of her thumbs. He rewarded her with a hissed rush of breath. The realization made her pulse soar.

Pressing his mouth to the sensitive curve of her neck, he plied her with kisses. The stubble of his morning beard chafed her skin, adding to the dizzying sensation.

Restless now, Maddie sent her hands roaming down the flat plane of his belly, to his hips. She caressed the curve of his taut thigh. He tensed, and she realized Brock was holding his breath.

Continuing to stroke him slowly, as she might a cat, he arched to her touch, allowing her more access to his flesh, moaning his encouragement. His reaction made her feel strong, desirable, and powerful, for once. Not frigid at all. She gave him pleasure, and he let her know it.

With a nudge of her face to his, he possessed her mouth again. Next, she felt his hands roaming her back and buttocks in deep urgent sweeps. Brock used the embrace to pull her closer until she was flush against him, feeling every inch of his body. Maddie could not miss the male part of him that stood hard. For her. The feel of him sent her blood racing.

Before she could speak or move, Brock banded his arms

around her ribs and lifted her to the bed. The cool coverlet at her back contrasted with Brock's heated body upon her chest and belly.

Not a moment passed before Maddie felt his mouth at her breast. A gasp escaped her. His laving tongue wielded pleasure across the pebbled tip of her breast once, twice, again, until she lost count. Her breathing turned harsh. Pleasure roared down to her belly and her woman's place, drowning her senses. Her flesh felt as if it glowed with need.

"Brock . . ."

Maddie couldn't say any more. Instead, she fisted her hands in his hair and held his mouth to her breast in desperate fervor. She arched into his heated embrace.

In response to her entreaty, Brock lifted her other breast to his waiting mouth. His lips stroked her; his teeth scraped her nipples. He drove her delirious by fondling the sensitized breast he had previously devoured. The pleasure at both her nipples tightened the potent pressure in her belly, her thighs. She writhed beneath him again, seeking relief.

As if he understood her growing need perfectly, Brock slid his hand down her ribs, smoothed his palm across her belly. Then he covered her mound with the whole of his hand. Maddie tensed, even while she ached for his touch.

His fingers pressed inside her while his thumb delved into her folds. An instant later, he found the bud of her pleasure and began to stroke it in a soft rhythm. She gasped and felt herself moisten in earnest.

When he bent his head to take her breast in his mouth again, her excitement mounted to unbearable levels. She found herself parting her legs farther, like a wanton. Soon she was wriggling in search of relief. Her sighs became moans; her moans turned to groans. A tingling insistence built in her belly and thighs and began to center at his touch. The pinnacle of this mounting pleasure felt close in her grasp. She panted out an incoherent moan that sounded, even to her own ears, like the plea that it was.

The explosion she sensed was seconds away. Maddie lifted her hips to Brock, wanting the pleasure so badly she had to restrain herself from crying out.

"Damn, not alone," he muttered, his face stark with tension. "I want to feel you around me."

Maddie wasn't sure what he meant. His hands left her suddenly, and she cried out in protest. She felt him fumbling between them. A bare instant later, his breeches were gone. He gathered her hips in his hands and pressed himself inside her.

Feeling him against her seemed a relief, but Brock moved without haste, easing in—but never completely—before withdrawing once more. Desire screamed inside her. Her need rose to seemingly impossible heights.

Above her, perspiration began to dampen the dark hair about his face. His expression was a study in concentration, his jaw clenched, his gaze fixed on her mouth.

Not content to lay passive, Maddie planted a hard kiss on his mouth and surged her hips up to him. She quickly realized Brock was larger than Colin had been. Discomfort stung her immediately, and she pulled back.

"You're so tight," he panted in her ear. "Relax, Maddie-cake."

She nodded and tried to ease the tension in her limbs and belly, truly. But she wanted him inside her so badly, yearned for him to bring her to the magical place she'd only read about in Aunt Edith's *Kama Sutra*. For she had no doubt he could.

In a languorous sweep, he took her mouth with his. She wanted him to hurry, to impale her. But the delicious kiss added to her tumult. The mating of their mouths seemed to last an eternity. He neither surged farther into her body nor left it.

Patience and skill; he showed both in equal measure.

Maddie soon felt herself sink into his kiss, her taut limbs relax. The heels of her feet relaxed against the mattress. She lowered her hips and spread her thighs wider.

A moment later, Brock eased into her once more.

To the hilt.

The sensation of her body accepting his made her gasp. The tingling joy of it was so strong, and she wanted him so badly . . .

With a tortured moan, Brock withdrew, then pushed into her slowly. Too slowly. And this time when Maddie lifted her hips to him, she encountered no resistance from her body, only unimaginable pleasure mounting at a breathless pace.

As Brock thrust, Maddie met him halfway, eager to feel him inside her again. Their pace increased, and Brock fit a hand between them to touch her woman's place again. The dual sensations of pleasure sent her breath careening out of control. Her heels found the mattress again as the pressure built, sending her soaring to the edge of pleasure.

"Ready, Maddie?" he breathed against her mouth.

She could make little sense of the overwhelming sensations, much less his question. "No."

Immediately, he ceased all movement and remained still within her tight sheath. Her body tensed in protest, ached as if she had a fever. Above her, Brock's breathing grew labored. A rivulet of sweat ran down his neck.

"No!" she cried out. "Don't stop."

Maddie felt him smile that devil's smile against her mouth as he resumed his thrusts, this time quicker, with more force than before. The tingling between her legs surged to life with a vengeance, dominating her flushed body. His fingers on her most sensitive place sent her soaring hard and fast to the edge.

"Ready now?" he asked.

The magic feelings built, tightened, converged, making her sizzle. "Yes. Yes! Oh, yes!"

The pleasure crackled, spreading ecstasy like liquid delight all through her. Brock cried out above her, and she felt a flood of warmth deep inside her. After a moan that bespoke satisfaction, he kissed her mouth and lay atop her, his face in the crook of her neck.

No wonder the *Kama Sutra* had failed to adequately explain the amazing sensation of release. She could hardly describe the enchantment of it herself.

Lethargy began to spread through her body, so intense she'd rarely known its like. Brock stroked her shoulder, his soft touch keeping her attuned to his nearness. Next, he pressed tender kisses onto her neck, her shoulder, as if he worshipped her, as if he had made love with his heart, as she had.

A rush of released emotions barraged her. Maddie curled her hand in the hair at his nape and cuddled into the warmth of his body. A sense of utter tranquillity suffused her. She sighed.

He raised his head and brushed stray curls from her face. "Maddie?"

Concern shone in the glitter of his green eyes. She drew in a deep breath, searching for the words to describe how she felt. "I never expected—never knew . . . I've never felt like that."

She expected a swagger of a smile. Instead, he merely nodded. "We are good together."

Brock closed his eyes and frowned, looking as if he wanted to say more. When he opened them again, his eyes gleamed bright with resolution. *"Very* good together, in many ways."

His gaze became very serious. Maddie found herself holding her breath.

He brushed a gentle thumb along her damp cheek. "Marry me, Maddie. Truly. I know I've lost our wager by making love to you tonight—"

"Tonight had nothing to do with our wager," she refuted instantly. And she meant that.

The thought of sullying the bliss they had shared with thoughts of a bet made her stomach roil. No, tonight had been about the fact she'd needed someone—needed him— and he had been there for her. Maddie refused to think of it in any other way.

Yet she couldn't imagine resuming the terms of their wager. Next time he came to the cottage to seduce her into marriage, she would likely agree to anything, now that she knew the magic of his touch.

How would she resist him?

Or should she?

Maddie exhaled raggedly and realized Brock stared at her intently, awaiting her reply to his unexpected proposal. She had none to give. The man who had held and helped her tonight was not the man who had threatened her with debtor's prison. He was not the same man who delighted in her discomfort and doom. Indeed, he had done all he could tonight to keep her from either. Surely such a man would not treat her or Aimee cruelly.

But could she be certain of that? Was she ready to marry again, to chain herself to a man who seemed to disdain her more often than not? And how much would he hate her if he discovered the truth about Aimee? Perhaps she should tell him of that . . . or perhaps it was already too late.

Maddie bit her lip, conscious of Brock's questioning gaze. "I must have time to think. A few days, please. I am exhausted. I cannot think now."

Brock's mouth tightened, but he nodded. Though he did not like her answer, he accepted it. She reached across the space between them to touch his bare brown shoulder.

"I will truly consider it. I promise. I must be certain before I enter into anything."

Again he merely nodded. But he did not meet her gaze.

Maddie wanted to explain, tell him that she feared for her

independence . . . for her heart. But she knew he would only argue. "I vow I will think of nothing else and give you an answer by week's end. Perhaps I simply need sleep."

"Then sleep," he whispered as he gathered her up in his arms. He held her as slumber overtook her.

ELEVEN

Maddie opened her eyes to a dark, unfamiliar room. She lay alone in a cold, white-sheeted bed.

Something—a noise?—had jolted her from a sound sleep. Dazed, she sat up. The sheet slid down her breasts to fall into a heap in her lap.

To her astonishment, she was naked.

Memories of the previous night came rushing back. Aimee's disappearance, Brock's tender determination and help. And in the aftermath of her ordeal, the blistering warmth of his succor.

Dark and disquieting, desire flooded her stomach in a wild remembrance of shared kisses and sighs, of his skilled touch and the heaven beyond her imagining he had shown her.

How easily he had guided her to that sweet bliss. Even more surprising had been the poignant delight she had felt in sharing the moment with him.

A shocking turn of events, to be sure.

Then he had asked her to marry him.

Despite Brock's naked, disheveled, damp-skinned form, Maddie had seen only his face—and the sincerity in his green-eyed appeal. Inside, her heart had shouted yes. To Brock she had remained mute—barely. But she owed him an answer by week's end.

Lord, what answer would she give?

The noise that awakened her resounded again. The smart rap told her it was a knock.

Someone was here. Brock, perhaps?

Maddie scrambled from the bed and searched the floor for her chemise. Fumbling in the weak moonlit glow filtering in from the next room, she finally found her shift and donned it.

As she headed for the door, she peeked at Aimee, who still slept soundly on the sofa, all tangled in the soft quilt.

Unable to resist, Maddie succumbed to the need to kiss her slumbering daughter, to draw in the powdery scent of her little-girl skin. She felt a moment of peace with the world. Aimee was the most important part of her life. Having her daughter returned and safe meant more than words could express.

And she owed so much of it to Brock.

"Mrs. Smith?" a woman from the other side of the door called out.

Smith? The voice belonged to the innkeeper's wife; she remembered it from the previous night. Did the woman, perhaps, have the wrong room?

Before Maddie could tell her to knock elsewhere, the cheery older woman said, "Yer mister had a horse sent to ye and told me to wake ye before the sun rose."

Brock. Clearly, he had left hours ago and sent her mount so she could return home, as he had said he would. Still, he continued to do his utmost to protect her good name, even misleading the innkeepers to believe they were man and wife.

"Thank you," Maddie called to the woman.

Since the innkeeper's wife did not look as if she'd fallen off the apple cart yesterday, Maddie had to assume the woman found Brock's early morning disappearance and his instructions to his "missus" more than a bit peculiar. However, Maddie would also bet her last few sovereigns that

Brock had paid the woman handsomely to look the other way.

Money did have its advantages, and in the past twenty-four hours, Brock had used it to her benefit.

She could not deny that she found that fact wonderful beyond words. Was it possible the man himself fell into that category?

"Oh, and yer mister had me bake some fresh gingerbread for the little lassie. It'll be waitin' downstairs for ye."

"He remembered," Maddie whispered to herself, heart warmed.

Aimee would love it. Why had he cared enough to have it baked for the girl?

Lost in a moment of stirring surprise, she found herself awestruck by the fact that Brock treated Aimee far better than Colin, who had legally claimed the child.

In fact, from the day Aimee emerged following a trying two-day labor, Colin had despised the girl.

And Brock, having no notion that Aimee was of his own flesh, had nearly behaved like a concerned father last night. Could the man who had done so much to see Aimee safe really see her sent to the Fleet or transported to a work-house?

She began to doubt he could.

Moreover, Maddie had awakened to a rebirth of the heart. For nearly five years, she had believed her emotions toward Brock all but dead, crushed when he had abandoned her without a word. Finding fortune had been more important to him then. Now, he acted as if he found her significant. And, sometime in the past day, those old feelings had resurfaced, shimmering, glowing inside her like a secret.

Maddie bit her lip. Dare she care for him again?

After last night, how could she not?

Aimee moaned, interrupting Maddie's thoughts. She turned to find her daughter lying on the sofa with half-open eyes.

Maddie smiled and went to the girl's side, enveloping her in a giant hug. Aimee laid her soft golden head upon Maddie's breast, breathing soft breaths of comfort and trust. Maddie was relieved to see the child's ankle nearly back to normal.

It wasn't long before Aimee's stomach roused her. Quickly, Maddie dressed and helped the groggy child stand. They descended the stairs to find the innkeeper waiting with the warm gingerbread, courtesy of Brock, and a smile.

Maddie accepted both with thanks, took Aimee's hand, and led her outside.

"Mama, is that gingabread for me?" she asked, her eyes hopeful.

After breaking off a piece, Maddie handed it to her. "Yes, Mr. Taylor had it made especially for you."

Aimee put as much of the bit in her mouth as possible and chewed with a look of bliss on her little face.

Her horse awaited them, freshly brushed and fed, from the look of things. Maddie sent another silent thank-you to Brock. He'd thought of everything, from her comfort to her reputation—and, of course, of Aimee.

The vestiges of night fog swirled around them as she and Aimee traveled northwest. The sun turned the sky a mysterious gray within half an hour. Servants of all shapes and sizes descended from houses to begin daily tasks for their employers. By the time they reached the edge of the city, it teemed with people and activity, a loud display of London's humanity.

Soon, she and Aimee arrived at Ashdown Manor to find Aunt Edith—and thus, the whole house—in an uproar. Quickly, Maddie explained Aimee's disappearance. Her elderly aunt and Vema surrounded the little girl, oohing and cooing, clearly jubilant at her safe return. With no compunction whatsoever, Aimee devoured the attention.

Weary to the bone, Maddie tried to sneak in a quick nap,

but her mind would not rest. One question dominated her every breath: Should she marry Brock?

If she did not, how could she resume their midnight assignations and resist the lure of his lovemaking, now that she knew how wonderful they felt together? How could she resist the man himself, knowing how caring he could be?

Or did his caring have a more devious purpose, as before?

With a sigh, Maddie punched her pillow and gave up the idea of rest.

"My lady," Matheson said as she descended the stairs. "A Lord Belwick wishes to see you. Will you receive him?"

Maddie frowned, more than a bit puzzled. She did not know Lord Belwick personally and scarcely knew of him. What on earth would he want with her?

Curiosity got the better of her. "Show him into the parlor," she told Matheson. "I shall be there directly."

Maddie returned to her room and contemplated her wardrobe with a frown. All her gowns were either suitable for hard work or the most fashionable soiree. Knowing she had nothing truly suitable, she changed into one of her better serviceable dresses, one still somewhat acceptable for a Sunday.

At the parlor door, she stopped. Lord Belwick sat on the edge of the sofa, short fingers fidgeting restlessly. His graying hair made him look a bit pale, yet he projected an impression of incisive knowledge and unquestionable power.

"Lord Belwick, I am pleased to make your acquaintance—"

"Thank you for seeing me." He took her hand and bowed over it. "These are highly unusual circumstances, and I can only apologize for my breech of conduct. Please know that only my genuine desire to help you has led me to your door, despite not having been formally introduced. I came today to give you a bit of information, my lady. Something I suspect you will find quite . . . enlightening."

Help her? Maddie stared at the man in puzzlement. How

could he have any information that would be of interest to her? "I am flattered that you should take so keen an interest in a stranger."

He chuckled, and Maddie frowned. What had the man to laugh about?

"I feel as if we've met. I am well acquainted with your sister-in-law, Lady Dudley. We've spoken of you often."

That Belwick had aligned himself with Roberta made Maddie wary instantly.

"My lord, I lead a simple widow's life. I can hardly imagine what interests you enough to travel all the way to Hampstead."

"I've come to talk to you about Brock Taylor."

A little jolt of surprise ran through her. Though she did her best to hide it, Belwick had her attention now. "I see. I did not know you were acquainted."

"Quite, yes. Through business and financial circles, of course," Belwick said, as if Brock weren't worth knowing otherwise.

Maddie still could not fathom why the man had come here or what he knew that might pique her interest. "Of course."

Belwick hesitated, his pale blue gaze sharp as a freshly stropped razor. He drew in a deep breath, as if reluctant. Maddie knew better. She watched him, quite certain he paused only to make sure he had her undivided attention.

"Lord Belwick?" she prompted, then baited him. "If you are reluctant to share your information with me, I understand."

Belwick's faded mouth twisted up in a smile. "I am not so much reluctant as cautious. I want to be certain I tell you the information that will best serve you."

Another pause, another sigh. Maddie restrained a glare.

Finally, he said, "I believe you are acquainted with Mr. Chiltam, Mr. Taylor's secretary?"

The odious man who had let Aimee roam an unfamiliar building and city by herself. How could she forget him?

"Yes."

"It seems that Mr. Taylor released Mr. Chiltam from his duties this morning."

Maddie stared at Belwick, her mouth agape. Brock had *fired* the man for his negligence yesterday? Startling indeed.

"Understandably, Mr. Chiltam is now seeking employment. He came to me to inquire about a possible position early this morning. I hired him; he is an impeccable secretary. At any rate, he gave me some very interesting information."

"Indeed," she murmured, still not certain what he wanted.

Did Belwick know of her marriage wager with Brock? Did he know she owed Brock huge sums of money? Panic began to gnaw at her gut. It was entirely possible Chiltam had heard her and Brock arguing yesterday afternoon.

"Mr. Chiltam happened to overhear that his employer— um, former employer—has extended an offer of marriage to you. Is that so?"

Maddie met Belwick's clever gaze. He was watching her every move, every reaction. She felt as if he knew everything that had taken place between her and Brock, and it unnerved her. She drew in a shaky breath.

Belwick was like a bored cat with a dazed mouse; it wasn't a matter of whether he would pounce, merely a question of when. Maddie knew she had to speak carefully.

"I think that matter is between Mr. Taylor and myself," she answered in her frostiest tone.

Suddenly Belwick became all consideration. "Indeed. I meant no offense. I did not come here to pry. I merely thought you might wish to know the reason behind Mr. Taylor's proposal."

Did Belwick mean to tell her of her own debt? Or did he imagine that Brock had not yet informed her that he had purchased all her outstanding notes?

Drawing herself to her feet, Maddie stared down at her guest. "Reason? If he had proposed, I should assume his reason is like that of any other suitor."

"Not so. Has he told you about the railroad?"

Railroad? What on earth . . . ?

Belwick gave a shallow laugh. "I thought not. Shall we start over?"

Uneasy now, Maddie nodded and sank to the sofa once more. What did Brock have to do with a railroad?

"I first heard of railroads about two years ago. I felt certain they would be the transportation mode of the future. If one could reach one's destination in a fraction of the time without enduring England's ill-kept roads, certainly one would pay a few pounds for the convenience. The first party to establish such a line in any populated area is sure to make a fortune."

Though Maddie had heard little about railroads, if what she had heard about the speed of the transportation was true, Belwick was indeed correct. She nodded and urged him to continue, though the knot in her stomach clenched tighter.

"Mr. Taylor had the same realization, it seems. We began competing to form the same route, London to Birmingham. I purchased necessary land, as did he. I bought a particularly large chunk in one rural area, bordered by a river on one side and a mountain to the east of that. To the west lay a piece of land not for sale. In doing so, I thought for certain I had Mr. Taylor beat at this game.

"Then, recently, he hired a new engineer and brought on some investors. One of whom is your cousin, I believe. The Duke of Cropthorne, yes?"

Maddie nodded, wondering what she had to do with all this. Did he mean to have her save Cropthorne from a bad investment? Surely not. She had seen little of the man in years.

"Yes," Belwick went on. "Mr. Chiltam informed me this

very morning of the reason for Mr. Taylor's optimism about the railroad he would like to build. That, my dear, is you."

Maddie blinked in surprise. "Me? I know nothing of railroads. I cannot imagine how I might help him in the least."

Belwick smiled, as if he was relishing the moment. "The location of the last piece of land Mr. Taylor needs is in Warwickshire. As I understand from Mr. Chiltam, your father left you such a piece of land, in right of your next husband."

She stared at Belwick with dawning horror. The jolt of his words reverberated in her gut once, again, endlessly. Her thoughts whirled, her heart lurched. Was it true?

Had Brock offered her marriage for her land, rather than social advancement, as he claimed? Though her heart screamed in denial, Maddie released a shaky breath. She had begun to wonder if Brock wanted to bind her to him as some method of revenge, perhaps because she had not pined for him forever. Who knew the man's mind? But for her land . . . ?

"I see I've surprised you," Belwick said, breaking into the rush of her tangled thoughts.

"How would Brock know about my land?"

Belwick merely laughed. "Mr. Taylor may come from less than sterling beginnings, but he is very crafty and very thorough. And he has enough money to find out anything he wishes to know."

Numbly, Maddie nodded, acknowledging Belwick's assessment. Brock *was* both crafty and thorough. And the implications—so many of them—barraged her in the next silent moments. She hardly knew what to think, much less what to say. Once again, he had lied to her. As before, he had schemed to sacrifice her to line his pockets. He had not changed in the least, for sure.

"I believe I've given you plenty to think about," Belwick said, rising. "I'll show myself out. Good day." He bowed his head politely and left with a casual stride, as if he had not completely destroyed her state of mind.

Alone now, she rose to pace. So Brock wanted to marry her for her land. It would explain his insistence that only she, and not another impoverished widow, would be an acceptable bride. It explained why he had never succumbed to the temptation of sexual congress she had offered during their midnight trysts. He had a huge fortune at risk! But last night . . . Was he so manipulative that he would help her find Aimee and make love to her with such tender care in the hope she would agree to marry him? The same man who had taken her virginity one hour, then a thousand pounds from her father in the next to abandon her?

Yes, Brock Taylor was capable of the most dastardly manipulation. She had merely forgotten that fact.

The insidious ache of betrayal crept through her, making her bleed pain. In the past day, Brock had made her believe that he still cared. She had believed him worthy, possessed of an innate goodness beneath his ruthless facade. How else could she have responded to his lovemaking with such candor and abandon? Why had she believed him again?

Tears stung her eyes. Damn him! Some foolish part of her heart had responded to the seeming care in his embrace. And now, Belwick had revealed him as nothing but a liar. . . .

Maddie's anger surged, roared. It rolled over her relentlessly, reminding her that Brock had taken her for a fool again—and she had let him. God, how he was probably laughing, certain that a few kind words and an orgasm would be enough to make her his rattlebrain for life.

A violent heaving of fury fast became an inferno. She was done playing into his schemes. If Mr. Brock Taylor thought to deceive her again for the purpose of making money, Maddie was willing—no, eager—to set him straight.

Three hours later, Maddie tapped her toe impatiently in Cropthorne's parlor and awaited the man's presence. She hadn't seen much of her cousin Gavin since her father and his had suffered a falling out. Maddie was not surprised; her father had done his best to alienate everyone over the years. He'd been cantankerous every day of his life. And her branch of the family had suffered for it, being cast from the other's good graces. The wealth evident in Cropthorne's Aubusson carpets, crystal fixtures, and abounding servants proved that Gavin had been much luckier than she.

"Dear Cousin Madeline," boomed a deep male voice from across the room.

Maddie spun around to find Cropthorne standing in the doorway, wearing an immaculate burgundy coat and biscuit breeches.

Despite her anger, Maddie noticed that Gavin's face looked much the same: wide forehead, dark eyes, slashing nose, firm jaw. Still, she sensed a change. Nothing about the man could be considered warm, despite the hint of a smile he wore.

"Cousin Gavin." She inclined her head in greeting. "How good of you to see me."

"I'm glad you've come. We haven't spoken more than a handful of words since our nursery days."

"Indeed. We have my father to thank for that."

All trace of expression vanished from Gavin's face. "Your father spoke the truth about my esteemed sire's scandals. It was a truth my father simply had not wished to hear. And as a duke, he had the power to ruin your father, so he did."

Taken aback, Maddie stared at her cousin. He painted a black picture of his sire, indeed. But family history did not occupy her today. "That's the past. I've actually come to talk to you about something more recent."

Gavin cocked a brow at her, and she knew she had roused his curiosity. Thankfully. Now she could get on with ruining that manipulative blackguard Brock Taylor. She very much hoped that in less than five minutes, revenge would be hers.

"By all means, you have my attention," Gavin confessed. "Shall we sit?"

Keen to get on to the matter at hand, Maddie sank into a thick cream velvet-covered chair and watched as Gavin did the same with an innate grace few men possessed. He moved in fluid lines, without any hint that his towering height hindered him.

Once they were settled, Gavin peered at her as if dissecting her. "I mean no offense, but you look out of sorts."

Squaring her shoulders, Maddie put on a regal face. "Indeed. I'm given to understand you plan to invest in a London-to-Birmingham railroad with Brock Taylor."

He sat back in his chair and studied her further. "And that distresses you? I'm only doing so because Taylor has proven he's capable of making large sums of money nearly overnight. I know he was once your father's servant, but—"

"Has Brock Taylor told you that every necessary parcel of land for the railroad is secured?"

As if he was quite interested, Gavin leaned forward in his chair and placed his elbows on his knees. "He is due to provide me with an update in a few days, but at last discussion, no. There is one, he said, that was left to a woman by her father. If we could buy it outright we would, but apparently it was left in right of any husband this woman might take."

"That is true. Has he given you the identity of this woman?"

Gavin scowled. "Does it matter? Taylor said a man was courting the woman and that she soon would be wed. Why all this interest in my investments?"

At her cousin's revelation, Maddie felt a scream tear up her throat. How like Brock to arrogantly assume she would succumb to his proposal. He had been so confident of his persuasion and her stupidity, he had even lied to his partner.

Clenching her fists, Maddie reined herself in. She must remain calm. This moment of revenge was too sweet to allow anyone or anything to spoil it.

"The woman's identity matters very much because I am that woman."

Cropthorne bolted to his feet and stared down at her with nothing short of shock on his face. "You? Your father had land in Warwickshire?"

"He bought it before I was born, apparently. He wished to keep it in the family but did not think I was capable of seeing to its upkeep on my own."

A dry humor curled his lips. "Ah, because you're a woman, naturally incapable of intelligent decisions."

More because she had proven irresponsible and uncaring by giving her virginity to a servant and getting with child. But Cropthorne needn't know that. "Exactly."

Gavin's black brows slashed down to meet in a vee above his nose. "And you have no such suitor?"

"Oh, I have one: Mr. Taylor himself." She let the surprise show on Gavin's face before she continued. "He's asked me to marry him—more than once, actually. I only learned today why he's been so eager to get me to the parson."

He paced. "I must say I'm stunned."

"Well, let me assure you now, Brock Taylor is the last man I would *ever* consent to marry. He wants my land and will contrive some affair of the heart to get it. He is both deceitful and despicable. Do yourself a favor and withdraw from this project. Without my land, it cannot happen."

Gavin nodded. "And this affair of the heart—you must have reciprocated the feeling in some fashion, else you would not be quite so angry."

Maddie felt a hot flush charge from her shoulders to her neck, her cheeks. She ignored it with a proud toss of her head. "I do not like being played for a fool."

Anger hardened his expression. "Nor, cousin, do I."

It was early that evening when Brock reached Ashdown Manor. Agitated, he vacillated between panic and fury. He paid scant notice to the orange sunset, the chirping crickets, or the spring air. He felt only the anger roaring in his temples. How in the hell had Maddie learned about his interest in the railroad and his need for her land?

Flinging himself from his mount, Brock stalked toward the door. He wasn't entirely certain what he would say to Maddie. While it was true he must have her land to build the railroad, it wasn't his sole interest in her. No, as much as he hated to admit it, even to himself, Maddie was the fever he could not shake. But after last night, after feeling her slick, silken flesh enclose him, after hearing her jagged sighs and sharp cries of passion, he wanted more. Much more. He wanted her now, regardless of the fact he was furious with her.

Damn, what a sap he was.

Why had she gone to Cropthorne with her newfound knowledge? And why couldn't he get her out of his blood?

Raking his tense hands through his hair, Brock sighed, doing his best to forget both his lust and his last uncomfortable interview with Cropthorne. He'd managed to retain the duke as a partner—barely. Brock had had to talk fast, convince the man that he hadn't purposely omitted the truth so much as keep a personal matter as personal as he could. He'd hinted that he and Maddie had quarreled. Cropthorne had given him one month to persuade Maddie to marry him. Otherwise, he and his money would find another investment.

Damn! In the previous month, he'd made precious little progress in gaining Maddie as his wife. He hoped like hell he could accomplish much more in the next four weeks.

As Brock stood before the solid oak door, he did his best to compose his thoughts. He had to see Maddie, convince her to marry him—somehow—using any means at his disposal.

He knocked. Within moments, her ever-present butler Matheson bowed and greeted him. "Mr. Taylor."

"Hello, Matheson. Is your mistress at home?"

"No, sir. Shall I tell her that you called?"

Double damn! Could this day get any worse? He must find Maddie, talk some sense into her, make her see why a marriage between them would be good financially—and sexually. She had to know that. If she didn't, Brock would be more than happy to demonstrate that fact for her again.

"No," he said to the butler. "I'm sure I shall find her soon."

Matheson bowed his graying head. "As you wish. Good evening, Mr. Taylor."

"Mr. Taylor?" called an older woman's spry voice beyond the portal.

A plump, wrinkled hand grabbed the door and shooed Matheson away. Then she peeked her head around the door to peer at Brock. Graying curls framed a round face. Atop her head, she wore a silly hat topped with angels dancing in a field of flowers.

Despite his anxiety, Brock found he had to repress a smile.

"So, you are *the* Mr. Taylor? My, what a handsome devil you are. Well, don't stand there. Come in. Come in."

The woman opened the door wide and waved him inside. He had no idea who she was, but if she lived with Maddie and could give him information, he would follow.

He trailed her down the familiar, shabby foyer with its fading blue paint and carpets, into the parlor in which Maddie always greeted him. He scanned the comfortable room, disappointed not to find Maddie about. He'd half hoped she'd instructed Matheson to lie about her whereabouts.

"Oh, where are my manners?" quipped the older woman. "You must think me all that is gauche. I am Mrs. Bickham. Maddie's mother was my sister."

When the elderly lady thrust her gloved hand toward him, Brock took it and bowed. "A pleasure, Mrs. Bickham."

"The pleasure is mine, dear boy. This morning when Maddie arrived home, she told us all about the manner in which you helped bring about Aimee's safe return. I cannot tell you how grateful I am, we all are."

"I did very little—"

"You are far too modest. Reuniting a mother and child; that is far more than nothing, I tell you."

Before she even finished speaking, Brock became aware of Mrs. Bickham's shrewd blue gaze sizing him up and down. Clearly, she was a woman with something on her mind. The questions was, what?

"A pity we did not meet sooner," she went on. "I was in India with family when you resided at Ashdown. But we can rectify all that now. Come to dinner Tuesday next. Yes, that will do quite well."

Dinner? Mrs. Bickham invited him to sit with her for a meal? Did she know he had once labored here?

"You look confused, you dear boy. May I be plain?"

Brock found himself all but gaping. "Please do."

"Maddie has been alone too long and needs a good man to care for her. That despicable Sedgewick—oh, the things I would do to that impertinent rogue if he still lived! A nasty tongue and a nasty temper that one had. But Maddie must put all of that behind her now."

Brock stared at the older woman in surprise. So, she had disliked Sedgewick? Excellent. Dare he hope she favored himself as Maddie's next husband? She sounded as if she did. An ally close to Maddie would be most helpful.

"Indeed," he agreed noncommittally.

"She says you have offered her marriage." Again, that shrewd glance took his measure. She smiled as if she liked what she saw.

"More than once."

Mrs. Bickham positively beamed. "Splendid! Wait until I tell Vema," she all but squealed. Then, as if realizing her error, she cleared her throat and tried her best—without success—to look firm. "So you'll come Tuesday next? I'm quite certain that Vema, Matheson, and I will be much too busy after supper to visit for long. Maddie will simply have to entertain you herself."

Brock was certain now that Mrs. Bickham indeed encouraged his suit of Maddie. And if the older woman wanted to offer him an advantage, he would take it. He would see Maddie before then, but another opportunity to persuade, cajole, ramrod, or seduce the lovely redhead to the altar was an opportunity he would never refuse.

He smiled at the older woman. "I would be delighted."

TWELVE

Brock paced the carpeted floors of the Paddington cottage in long, angry strides, alternately cursing and pacing. An hour past, he'd removed his coat and cravat. They lay discarded and wrinkled on the garish pink sofa. His tense fingers had raked a well-used path through his short hair.

He had managed to prevent Cropthorne from withdrawing his support. For now, at least. But his problems were far from over, beginning with the fact that the duke no longer fully trusted him and ending with the knowledge that Maddie was furious and clearly intended to fight him to the altar.

Brock yanked his pocket watch from his waistcoat, but the dark of night pressing through the windows told him the hour grew late indeed. Damn it, Maddie hadn't answered his summons yet. With every moment that passed, he feared she had no intention of replying with anything but silence, forcing him to action.

Even if she appeared in the next few minutes, Brock wasn't entirely certain what he would say. He did need her land—desperately. But worse, she was in his blood now. He ached for her. If he had to possess her to purge her from his system, so be it.

The click of the cottage door sent him skidding to a stop. He whirled about and strode hell-bent for the door. Maddie stood there in her usual disguise. But the shapeless woolen cloak could not hide her lush body from his hungry gaze. He remembered far too well every soft curve and provocative swell. Damn! Concentrating on his explanation would gain him far more than thinking about the feel of her breasts in his hands.

Brock lifted his gaze to Maddie's face to find her removing her widow's hat and veil. With dim firelight at his back, he had no trouble discerning the taut curves of her mouth and the firm line of her jaw—or perhaps it was the chill in her gray gaze—that bespoke her fury with terrible, perfect elegance.

His fingers made the familiar trek through his hair again. "Now that you've come, we must talk."

"That is not so," said Maddie, removing the cloak and draping it across the nearby banister. "I will talk and you will listen."

Apparently she'd come to fight; Brock was ready. "I hold your promissory notes."

"I can ruin your little railroad."

"You damn near have," he snarled.

Maddie approached on silent feet, her smile as cold as her eyes. "No, I merely warned my cousin to steer clear, particularly since that land will never be yours. The *Times*, however, might be most interested in hearing all about your attempts to press a poor widow into marriage by the most dastardly means of seduction."

It was Brock's turn to smile as he approached Maddie and walked around her in a slow circle. "Really? Wouldn't those same readers be interested in your scandalous agreement to meet me at midnight every night? Though it's a long time between now and the year Aimee will want a husband, the *ton* tends to remember such tidbits, don't you agree?"

Maddie's face flared with fury. "You bastard. I have no trouble believing you would do that."

"If you intend to ruin my name without listening to my reasons, then yes, I would."

Maddie's sharp inhalation and the stiff arms she thrust across her chest told Brock she was defiant and angry. It bothered him. He tried to ignore it. He tried hard. This was business, after all.

True, but Maddie had never been just business. . . .

Despite his best resolve, he softened and grasped her shoulders with a sigh. "I do need the land; I cannot deny that. But the other reasons I gave you for wanting you as my wife still stand. Your social status will help my business, open doors for me."

"You might have told me about the land," she bit out.

"I knew you would defy me on principle alone."

Maddie nodded, conceding the point. But her glare didn't disappear. "You think I am the means to an end, your pot of gold?"

He didn't. A confession of something more hovered, but Brock wanted to keep it to himself. It revealed weakness, he knew. Still, if the truth affected Maddie as he hoped, he might turn the admission into a strength.

"I want you far too much for that."

Maddie tensed, her gray eyes hard. "You want money."

Brock leaned in close, until he could smell her jasmine skin, nearly taste the plump moistness of her lips. His concentration blurred in a rise of heat and awareness.

"I want everything. I especially want you—every sweet, flushed, aching inch of you. Every day, every night, in every way imaginable."

Maddie gave a soft gasp of surprise, her eyes widening.

Fingers clasped around her shoulders, Brock brought her closer, against him, until their mouths were a breath apart. Maddie's tense stance didn't change, but her eyes . . . yes, they darkened, her pupils dilated. Her breathing quickened.

Brock bent his head to close the gap between their mouths. With a cry, Maddie wrenched away.

"I want nothing to do with you."

He tried to ignore her words. After all, she spoke in anger.

But the rush of denial and anger her avowal created only fueled his resolve. He would not give up. He would marry her. He would taste her again.

"I can change that, Maddie," he murmured, challenging her.

"No! You have made my life hell for the past month. I will not be your convenient means to fortune. I will not be used." She clenched her fists at her sides. "Get out of my life and leave me be!"

He sauntered closer to her again. "I can't do that, Maddie. I won't."

Maddie heaved a sigh of frustration. "What do you want, my blood? Do you want to own me? Or do you simply enjoy making me miserable?"

Brock felt her anger climbing, and it provoked his own. How could she loathe him so much when he could not muster an ounce of hatred for her in return? Where was all his resentment of her and her marriage to Colin Sedgewick now?

Gone, he feared, in a single night of straining kisses, needy caresses, and honest lovemaking.

Today, he feared he had wanted her for years and had masked his unfulfilled yearning with animosity. It was a terrible twist of fate, one that had him in knots. . . .

Frustration mounted—at her, at himself, at his inability to hate her. "I presented you with a sincere offer of marriage twice. Regardless of whether you like or believe my motives, I require an answer."

Maddie glared at him, fury shimmering from her. "Go to hell."

"I'm there, sweetheart," he shot back. "You went to my chief investor and nearly managed to convince him to withdraw his funding. You've made your contempt for me known at nearly every moment of this last month. As far as I'm concerned, we are even. It also leaves us back at the beginning of our recent association. You owe money to me. So I will ask you once more, do you wish to become a wife or a debtor?"

She glared at him, her full mouth curled in a triumphant smile. "Neither, you blackguard. I have no intention of marrying you, ever. I've more than made myself clear on that score. And though you may be mostly heartless, last night at least proved to me that you will not send Aimee or me to the Fleet. Therefore, I shall pay you as I'm able and ask you to never darken my door again. Good-bye, Mr. Taylor."

Maddie whirled away, her stride purposeful. Her soft scent lingered. Brock caught her by the elbow and pulled her back, until she rested flush against him. She struggled, and he put his other arm across her chest to subdue her. The hammer of her heartbeat knocked against his arm, matching the rhythm of his own.

She had called his bluff. Damn, now what?

Though Brock wanted to deny the truth, Maddie was right—he could not send her and Aimee to the Fleet any more than he could send his own father. He didn't want to see them suffer.

But how to keep her close? How to persuade her that marriage was the best course? She had already turned down the lure of money and security. He had no family name to recommend him, as she well knew. Bloody hell, why did others wed?

Why? Brock paused, feeling the rise of her breathing against him. He had to think of another reason to compel her to the altar. What might that be? It wasn't as if she were with child—or was she?

"I think you should consider another matter, Maddie-cake. What if you conceived last night?"

She laughed, taking Brock aback, and stepped from his embrace. "Highly unlikely."

"Perhaps, but possible."

The smile on her face did little to reassure him that she believed that fact or cared. "I shall take my chances."

"And what will you do, bear a bastard? That would set the *ton*'s tongues wagging about you—and Aimee. There is a legacy for your daughter to be proud of."

Her eyes were full of disdain. *"If* I were to conceive, perhaps I might be persuaded to marry. For now, I simply choose to believe the odds are in my favor."

Her words gave Brock both hope—and an idea. "We still have the pesky matter of that money between us. You do not wish to marry me, and I admit I have no wish to see you put into the Fleet."

A bright smile matched Maddie's triumphant glare.

"However," he continued, "neither do I think it fair to have you pay me 'when you are able.' You won't find any creditor to agree to those terms. So we must come to a solution. I believe you once offered your services as my mistress as a way to alleviate your debt. I find that offer acceptable today."

Her smile crumbled into a mask of shock. "You cannot!"

"I can, Maddie-cake, and I do."

"I made that bargain with you under duress."

Brock shrugged. "As I recall, you *offered* your . . . services to me. How is that duress?"

She gaped, "You were threatening me, pressing me—"

"That's irrelevant, really. The question is, do you truly mean to do the dishonorable thing and go back on your word? Tsk, Maddie. I expected more from one of your breeding."

Maddie flinched, then shot him a defiant stare. "You intend to hold me to this bargain?"

"For each and every night of the next six months."

Already he relished the idea of possessing her again, her damp skin and heated sighs belonging to him. He felt challenged to make her crave him, as he did her. He wanted to consume her, urge her to accept him, take her on a sensual exploration that would lead to mind-numbing satisfaction.

And if she happened to conceive along the way, all the better.

Cropthorne had given Brock a mere month to persuade Maddie into marriage. Brock wasn't sure she would conceive that quickly, much less be able to confirm that fact. Instead, he would do his utmost to use their time in his bed to bind her to him in every way possible.

In the end, he would have her as his wife.

"I will hate you every time you touch me," she vowed.

But she had given in. She would become his mistress.

Still, her barb hit its mark, gouging his belly with pain. He refused to let her know it. "Hate me if you wish. It's your pleasure—and mine, of course—that concerns me."

He paused to send her a hot, searching stare, one that mentally disrobed her and liked the view. Then he crooked a finger at her, wearing a wicked smile. "Come here."

Defiance and panic gripped her face at once. "No."

"That isn't the answer a good mistress gives, Maddie. That word should be removed from your vocabulary where I am concerned. If I ask you to disrobe slowly for my pleasure, the answer is yes. If I say my plan is to arouse you until you explode, you agree. If I ask you to look into my eyes as I thrust my—"

"That is hardly asking; that is demanding I behave like—like some cross between your trained puppy and a whore."

"Semantics." He shrugged. "With a good mistress, the answer is always yes."

Maddie looked ready to protest again. Brock could think of far more productive activities than arguing.

"You offered yourself to me," he reminded her. "I am merely accepting."

She clenched her teeth so hard, Brock thought she might grind them into powder. Her lips pursed, her skin flushed. He'd seen her more beautiful before, but there was nothing like Maddie with her passionate spirit roused.

With an angry toss of her head, Maddie spat, "As you

wish. I will return tomorrow so we may begin this degrading exchange."

She turned away, toward the foyer. Brock grabbed her around the waist and pulled her back. Her shoulders encountered his chest. He splayed his fingers at her waist and caressed the flat of her belly.

"I prefer right now," he murmured in her ear.

Brock grasped her arm and turned her to face him. Before she could protest, he captured her face in his hands and took her mouth in a sweeping kiss.

In that kiss, he promised her pleasure. Maddie swallowed, already losing some of the stiffness in her spine. As his fingers curled into the silken strands of her auburn hair and removed the pins, he vowed to be gentle. Slowly, she opened her mouth to him. As he brushed his thumbs across the tips of her nipples, he told her wordlessly that he would tempt her as never before. They hardened at his touch.

It was a sweet victory for Brock, not because he wished to conquer her. No, that would bring him no gratification. Rather the knowledge that she might soon be mewling and demanding made his pulse leap like a man running into a fire.

Brock planted a trail of biting kisses down her neck as he began unfastening the hooks of her dress, one by one. Through it all, he could tell Maddie tried her damndest not to respond. But by degrees, she yielded. He licked at the hammering pulse at her throat and smiled against her erotically fragrant skin.

He unfastened the final hook low on her back, then grabbed the edges of the dress and pushed. The garment began to slide down her arms, exposing the swells of her breasts above her simple chemise. When her arms were free, the dress spilled toward the floor. He divested her of her corset and petticoats. Then Brock helped her step away from the garments, back toward the cottage's little parlor and its firelit warmth. She refused to look at him.

Not content with the scant inches of distance between them, Brock took hold of her arms and urged her closer. She resisted, as he'd suspected she would. Maddie was a challenge, no doubt, but one he was ready for. He wanted to give her pleasure like she'd never had. Before she left this cottage, she would know how powerful was the lure between them.

"I'm going to learn every inch of your body," he whispered against her mouth. He was gratified when her eyes widened.

Maddie shook her head. "There is nothing to learn. I am willing to yield myself, so hurry and be done with it."

She wanted him to hurry, take her blindly? Did she hope she would feel nothing if he did?

Brock almost laughed. If Maddie believed he'd allow that, she was sadly mistaken. No, she affected him, arousing him beyond bearing, damn it; now he would return the favor.

"Rushing is not my preference," he whispered. "I plan to take my time, until I know you're wild with wanting."

Even as a rosy flush spread across her shoulders and cheeks, rebuttal gathered in her expression. Brock spun her around to face the wall, stunning her into silence. She stood a few inches from its surface, tense. In one quick motion, he grabbed her wrists, thrust her hands above her head, then placed them flat against the wall.

Her feet were shoulder's width apart. She tried to bring them together, whether to close her intimate self from his touch or out of misplaced modesty, he did not know. Nor did he care.

Brock leaned in to whisper, "Don't move."

"But—"

"Shhh. The time for protests is over. The time for enjoying is now."

"Brock, wait! I—"

Brock did not wait. Instead, he nibbled at the back of

her neck in soft, pressing kisses, little warm breaths that killed her protest and made her shiver. He lifted the edges of her chemise and slid his hands beneath. The silk of her bare skin sent a bolt of hunger through him. He hardened, wanted.

His touch roved from her thighs up to her hips. In slow sweeps, he caressed his way to the low plane of her belly, barely skirting her feminine mound with the tips of his fingers.

Maddie wriggled her hips restlessly.

Pleased with his progress, Brock trailed a finger up the center of her belly, then slowly explored the downy valley between her breasts.

Teasing her teased him as well. His blood simmered.

He drew a thin line across the swell of her breast with his thumb, coming dangerously close to her nipple. He felt her flesh draw up in arousal.

"That's it," he coaxed as he repeated the process with her other breast.

Maddie exhaled raggedly.

"Yes. I love to hear your sighs when I touch you," he murmured.

Moments passed in a flash of tantalizing possibilities, one after the other. Maddie scarcely took a breath. Brock smiled at her attempts to disguise her reaction. Certainly she must realize her body would tell the truth.

Brock skimmed his palms down the curve of her waist. His fingertips brushed their way up her abdomen in the next moment—then continued over her breasts.

Maddie drew in a shuddering breath when he stroked oh so near to her hard nipples and moved away. He returned an instant later, scraping his thumbs across the tips of her breasts until they engorged completely.

She sighed once more, then struggled to silence herself. Brock dragged his thumbs across her nipples again. And again. Maddie moaned, then bit her lip as if to keep further sounds in.

A fine sheen of sweat broke out across his back, and Brock summoned every ounce of his strength to stop himself from lowering her to the floor and burying himself inside her.

"Your breasts are sensitive," he whispered in her ear. "I'll be certain to give them plenty of attention."

He lived up to his promise, rolling her nipples between his thumb and fingers, pinching lightly, sliding his thumbs over their sensitive tops.

She gasped. Her breathing turned fast, hard. She pressed her backside into his straining erection, and he was elated. She was likely as aroused as he was.

But there was one way to know for sure.

Using a pair of his fingers, he glided his way down her stomach until he reached the soft, tight curls covering her feminine mound.

Maddie inhaled sharply when he skimmed the top of her most intimate flesh, then let his fingers delve into the warmth beneath. She was more than slick; she was completely wet, ready. And without a doubt, he was ready to give her anything, everything . . .

Lust pounded at him, a constant, driving pressure inside him. He wanted her. On the floor, against the wall—he didn't care as long as he had her.

"I feel how wet you are, Maddie-cake. It excites me. *You* excite me."

She moaned in response. Her body seemed to heat under his touch. Exultation and need slammed into him, urging him on.

Fingers moist from her arousal, Brock toyed with her until he found her hardening bud. He circled, teased, captured, caressed, and stiffened it completely. Maddie released a sob. Her thighs trembled. He had her on the brink, he knew. She knew it too. Hell, he felt close himself.

Her body all but offered itself to him as she flushed and moaned, spread her thighs wider apart and pressed herself against him. With his free hand, he nipped and caressed the peaked pebbles of her breasts.

His mind reeled with the feel of her. His blood roared. Greedily, he devoured the soft, soft skin of her neck with his voracious mouth.

The tangled mass of her hair streamed down her back, caught between them. He wanted to feel it on his bare body. He could not remember ever wanting anyone—or anything—the way he wanted to be inside Maddie right now. Desire spiraled into a tight, thick coil. He prayed he could last long enough to send her over the edge while buried inside her.

For now, he forced himself to concentrate on her unraveling, courtesy of his hands.

Maddie arched and mewled against him as his fingers plundered her. She was intoxicating to feel as her pleasure mounted, climbed, teetered above the precipice. The air felt primitive and charged. Brock swirled his fingers around her once more, then again.

Then she gave a low, keening cry and pulsed around him.

She sighed, shuddered against him, then fell still. Silent, Brock ran a palm lightly up her hip to her waist. Her body bespoke both repletion and anxiety.

Finally, she turned to him. Her eyes were languid, heavy. If he didn't step in soon, she would begin to feel awkward and shy. That was the last thing he wanted between them.

"Help me out of my clothes, Maddie. I'm dying to feel your bare body against mine."

He started by removing his coat, then his boots. Breathing hard, Maddie hesitated for a long moment. Then she raised her trembling hands to the buttons of his shirt, her gray eyes heated, her face flushed from pleasure. Her willingness enflamed Brock, and he unfastened his breeches.

Soon, he stood naked. Beyond ready, he yanked her chemise over her head and murmured, "I can't wait. I must have you."

"Yes," she whispered. "Now."

Brock looked about. The sofa was too small. The bedroom was too far away.

With a curse, he urged her to the ground and covered her body with his.

Without a hint of hesitation, she parted her thighs and lifted her hips in his direction. He entered her in one solid thrust.

He groaned aloud, deep in his chest. Maddie's flesh around him was so swollen. She gripped him so tightly. He wanted her so badly . . .

Brock captured her mouth in a blistering kiss, then surged into her again. He set the pace and she matched it as he hammered into her willing body. She moved beneath him, lush curves in perfect rhythm. The heat between them smoldered. Desire ripped him, lancing him like a hot blade. He'd known how badly he ached for her, but even he was unprepared for the force of this union.

Beneath him, she writhed. She clutched at his hair, his back. She was noisy in her pleasure, and he liked that. It drove him higher, until need clawed at him. But Maddie's breathing told him that she was damn close to ecstasy.

With a catch of breath and a long cry, Maddie's pleasure burst, and Brock felt her grip his shaft, milk him. Pleasure rushed over him, exploded. He saw black spots, felt nothing but Maddie's soft jasmine flesh, her cry in his ears.

Lord, he'd never known pleasure so perfect.

When Brock caught his breath, he peered down at her. She lay limp, her eyes closed, replete. He'd never seen her look so damp or rosy . . . or beautiful.

Finding paradise with her twice in the past week hadn't been enough. He began to wonder if twice a night would be.

Damn! He needed to move. Yes, leave the heat of her body

and leave this cottage. He'd proven his point. She was his
mistress, to do with as he wished. And she had responded
to his touch—beyond his every expectation, in fact. Staying
now and making love to her again would only prove him
weak.

Gritting his teeth, Brock rose to his feet. He soon realized
leaving her would be more difficult than he'd ever imagined.

In silence, he donned his clothes. Quickly, Maddie scrambled about to find her chemise and her dress, refusing to
look his way. She wore no expression at all when he offered
to assist her with her hooks. She merely presented him with
her back, while attempting to restore some semblance of
order to her auburn curls.

The air was thick, awkward, with an undercurrent of her
anger hanging about them. One look at her face confirmed
his suspicion. Now that Maddie was dressed as properly as
any well-born widow, she cloaked herself in haughtiness.

"Were you pleased enough?"

She spat the words at him, as if he'd done her some terrible disservice. Brock lashed back.

"Almost as pleased as you, but not quite."

Maddie blushed a deep red and drew herself up higher.
Her face was tense with anger. "You enjoy doing your utmost to reduce my pride."

"You hate that I'm forcing you to be honest," he countered. "I won't let you hide from me—not your body, not
your response. I expect complete candor in that area for the
next one hundred seventy-nine days because your pleasure
is my pleasure. I'll want to see it wildly and often."

Maddie marched past him and donned her cloak. When
she whirled to face him, fury spit from her eyes. "You are
the worst cad I've ever had the misfortune to meet."

Shrugging, Brock hid the fact that her words, her very
lack of warmth, hurt him. "So long as you're here tomorrow night, naked and eager, I don't give a damn about
your opinion."

* * *

The next afternoon, Maddie sat in the parlor of the one person she knew could help her: her sister-in-law, Roberta. What were her chances that Roberta would rally round her? Assuredly slim, but Maddie had to try. She was desperate.

Blast it all, she would rather ask Gavin for help than the snappish Roberta. And she would have gone to her cousin if she believed for a moment he would grant her wish. Brock had made it clear, however, that, despite her warning, Gavin had chosen to remain in league with her odious tormentor. Clearly, money meant more than blood. Maddie wasn't surprised.

Over the preceding sleepless night, she had debated the wisdom of coming to Roberta, pride swallowed. Eventually she had decided she must sacrifice her dignity for an hour to ask a favor, albeit a large one, of a woman she had once called family. It seemed better than surrendering her pride every night for the next six months to a scoundrel who sought only to use her.

"You've come to *me* for money? That's nearly a fortune!" Roberta looked both displeased and smug at once. "How have you so sorely mismanaged what Colin left you?"

"As I've told you before, he left me nothing but debts. Since his death, I've been struggling to pay his creditors. I've sold nearly everything that belonged to my father and used the money to pay your brother's gentleman's club, his tailor, his—"

"Are you still insisting Colin left you destitute? He was the heir to an earldom. He had money." Roberta sent her an accusatory glare. "Are you certain you didn't spend it?"

"Quite certain, yes." She gritted her teeth.

"Colin was always excellent with his money."

Maddie bit the inside of her lip to keep in the details she knew Roberta would neither believe in nor care about.

With this avenue closed to her, what would she do?

She rose to her feet, giving Roberta a cool smile. "I can see this was a mistake. Forgive my intrusion."

As she made her way to the door, Roberta raced to the portal and blocked her path. "After insulting my brother's memory, you think you can just leave as if it never happened? I'll have your apology."

Maddie glared at Roberta, feeling every minute of her sleepless night. The sore muscles of her inner thighs reminded her of last night—and all the nights that lay ahead of her as Brock's mistress. He could melt her body, empty her mind, almost instantly. He had more than proven that.

If she wasn't careful, he'd snatch her very soul from her.

Anger and hopelessness rose up inside Maddie. Roberta had always been silly and vain. Now she could add deluded as well.

"You never saw your brother as he was. He enjoyed more than his share of gaming. And he spent a great deal on other women. The only things he left me were a mountain of debts and the cottage in which he kept his mistresses."

"Colin would not have needed solace elsewhere if you had been warmer to him," Roberta shot out.

Maddie reared back. Colin had told his sister that he found her frigid? A wave of humiliation swelled inside her. How much longer would she encounter the repercussions of involving Colin in her life?

She pushed past Roberta. "Forget I came here."

Before she could make her way out, Roberta's birdlike hands found Maddie's wrist and stopped her short. "Do not insult my brother again. And do not darken my door until you can admit that you did not deserve such a wonderful man."

Maddie wanted to shout that the "wonderful man" she worshiped as a sibling had beaten her nearly senseless one night in a fit of rage—after verbally degrading her for years. But she knew Roberta would never believe that either.

"Then we shall not be seeing one another again," Maddie replied crisply, yanking her wrist free. "Good-bye."

THIRTEEN

Across Ashdown Manor's candlelit burgundy- and brown-shaded dining room, Maddie stared at the brightness of Brock's smile, which he directed at Aunt Edith. Its brilliance dazzled and infuriated her at once.

"What is India like, Mrs. Bickham?" Brock asked the older woman, seeming enthralled by her every word.

"Hot!" Edith laughed, the little posies on her yellow and green hat bobbing about a collection of flowers. "And dusty. Oh, my word! But the wilds are lovely, and I adored . . ."

Maddie ceased listening to her aunt and tried to focus on her current problem: the man sitting across her table.

The remnants of dinner lay between them, and still Maddie had spoken no more than two words to the blackguard who wanted her for her land. She still could hardly believe Aunt Edith had invited him to dinner, and without her knowledge.

But Maddie was also ashamedly aware that she'd hardly taken her eyes off him all evening.

Since she had become his mistress and they had shared that first stunning evening naked in the cottage's parlor, Maddie had spent another two nights in his arms. Each time she wanted to resist him, Brock reminded her of her obligation—just before he melted her with his touch. Heat suffused her skin just thinking about those sensual hours.

The first night, Brock had carried her silently to the little bed and undressed her. He had instructed her to undress him. Her heart had been beating rapidly, her limbs trembling. Remembered desire had brought forth a rush of fresh wanting, and she had sighed when he kissed her. She'd moaned when he suckled her breasts to stiff peaks. She had perspired and heated when he brought her hand around his shaft and showed her how to stroke him. She had felt as if she died when he brought her to orgasm with his mouth, then again as they joined. And again closer to dawn.

Come morning, she'd been angry with him for his seduction—but more furious with herself for succumbing and forgetting her anger during those pleasure-filled dark hours.

Last night had been no less consuming. He hadn't bothered to remove her stockings. He had been too impatient to find the little bed. Rather, Brock had led her to the sofa, then taken her on it after he'd urged her to straddle his lap. At his instruction, she had fed him her breasts—and he had feasted slowly, lapping, nipping, making her completely wanton. She grew hot thinking about that—and what came next.

Brock had driven her wild as he had impaled her with his thick member. The Milk and Water Embrace—she remembered that from the *Kama Sutra*. The description alone had made her blush. The reality had been a thousand times more staggering.

He had let her set the pace. The freedom and power had been heady, and as with everything else, Brock used that to his advantage. After her first orgasm, when she was beyond protest, he took control again and drove her to a second bone-melting explosion.

When he finally took his release, Maddie could not deny that she had screamed his name in ecstasy once more—to her shame. As before, his seduction had burned away her anger.

Despite the chasm between them, the intimacy with Brock left her dizzy and limp—and, to her shock, complete.

Now she wondered what tonight would bring. Desire lanced her belly, pressing and demanding. She wanted him, even knowing her desire was both foolish and dangerous. Not that she would tell him, but to herself, she could not lie; she yearned to be alone with him, to feel his strong body filling her, driving her—

"Maddie?" Aunt Edith called, seemingly annoyed. "You agree, do you not?"

All eyes were upon her, waiting expectantly. They suspected she had been woolgathering, but only Brock was likely to know why—and she wasn't about to give him the satisfaction.

"Of course. Splendid," she said, smiling directly at him.

Aunt Edith clapped. "How perfect! The three of you on a picnic. Won't that be delightful?"

Maddie's smile fell. The *three* of them? She and Brock . . . and Aimee? Was that the plan she had unwittingly agreed to?

"Yes! Yes! I like picnics," cried Aimee.

Startled, her blinking eyes fell on her golden-haired daughter—dressed in her new frock and a pair of Maddie's old dancing slippers. She stared in stunned silence. Had she actually—foolishly—agreed to bring Aimee along on a picnic with Brock?

No. It would be a disaster of the first order to allow a man as clever as Brock that much access to the daughter he did not know was his. Sooner or later, he would discern the truth. How, she didn't know, but she did know it wasn't wise to underestimate him. And he could use that knowledge to force her to the altar.

"Oh, Aimee as well?" Maddie pasted an awkward smile on her face. "Goodness, I'm not certain that is a good idea. It always rains this time of year—"

"I won't let her get wet or cold, my lady."

Brock's voice was all charm. Maddie glared at him.

"I wanna go! I wanna go!" cried Aimee.

"You cannot agree to take her, then change your mind, Maddie," her aunt Edith chided. "Let the girl enjoy herself. What harm can come of it?"

What harm indeed? Would Aunt Edith say that after Brock realized Aimee was his daughter and perhaps took the girl from her out of spite? Even if he didn't, Aimee should not have any opportunity to grow too close to Brock. He would only be in her life for six months—if he didn't walk away first, as he had done before.

"Mama, you said I could go," Aimee protested.

"You did say that," Brock chimed in.

"Let Aimee go. A picnic this time of year will be lovely." Aunt Edith smiled, but Maddie wasn't fooled. The older woman was matchmaking, and trying to form a bond between father and daughter in the process.

Maddie wanted to scream, at her aunt for meddling, at Brock for manipulating the situation—at herself for succumbing to the lure of remembering the pleasure he had given her, rather than shutting him out of her thoughts and listening to the conversation.

But there was no hope for it now. If she appeared too reluctant, she might arouse Brock's suspicions about Aimee.

Sighing, Maddie hissed, "She can go this once. If it rains, we will leave immediately."

"Thank you, Mama! Thank you." Aimee jumped around Brock's feet, wearing a huge grin.

"I shall pick you up Friday afternoon at about one," he said to Maddie, wearing a triumphant grin.

Scowling, Maddie turned away.

"See my pretty dress?" asked Aimee.

Maddie feared her daughter had asked Brock that question. Before she could intervene, he proved her suspicions correct.

"Indeed. And such lovely shoes as well." He glanced

down at the too-big slippers with a smile that turned Maddie's heart, despite her wishes. "Most becoming."

"They're Mama's."

"Really?" he murmured. "I would never have guessed."

Aimee giggled, and Brock ruffled her hair with an indulgent grin. Maddie watched. When would he begin to wonder, to guess, about Aimee? And Brock would; she feared it was merely a matter of time.

"Aren't those dancing slippers?" he asked the girl.

Aimee hesitated, as if uncertain.

"Of course they are," Aunt Edith answered.

"Dancing slippers are pretty." Aimee dimpled.

"And made for dancing," Brock added. "Shall we dance?"

"Yes!" Aimee cried with joy.

Brock stood and lifted her. "Why, thank you, Lady Aimee."

Aimee curled a trusting hand around Brock's neck. He flashed a brilliant smile at the girl, looking as if he was having almost as much fun as Aimee.

The sight of Brock holding Aimee, father and daughter together, albeit unknowingly, staggered her. Their shared amusement and closeness roused her emotions until they pressed in on her, making her throat tight. Brock and Aimee genuinely liked each other; that much was clear.

Maddie wanted to hate Brock for that, truly. But the wink he threw at Aimee, the way he engaged her laughter, made that impossible.

Guilt joined the roiling mix of anxiety and tenderness churning in her belly. If only she trusted Brock not to destroy her life, perhaps she could tell him the truth. . . .

But she didn't trust him. He was out for himself and for money. His interest in her and Aimee was temporary at best. Only she could protect her daughter from being hurt when Brock withdrew his attention in favor of his latest quest for wealth.

"Aimee should go to bed now." Maddie stood and reached out to take the girl from Brock.

"No!" Aimee cried. "I don't wanna go to bed. I wanna dance."

"Aimee—" she warned.

"Let the girl dance," her aunt scolded.

Brock shot Maddie a quick grin and then, holding his young daughter, turned about the room. He hummed a familiar tune in his strong, even voice. Through it all, Aimee giggled and squealed, clearly loving every moment. As if her enthusiasm were infectious, Brock tickled the girl and laughed with her.

They looked natural together. Maddie's heart ached.

Again, she doubted herself. Should she tell Brock the truth? Maddie scowled, wondering how she could willingly give Brock that much power over her. Did she owe the truth to a man who had done little but deceive her?

No. But did she owe Brock the truth for Aimee's sake, so she might know her father? Perhaps, but what if he abandoned them again?

Equally horrifying, what if Brock realized her deception? His rage would be boundless, along with his desire for revenge.

Blast it all, she didn't know what to do.

Deep down, she feared she wasn't being fair to either Brock or Aimee, but fear and indecision strangled her courage. And all of these passionate, sleepless nights weren't helping her ability to decide.

A moment later, the dance ended. Brock set Aimee on her feet, then took her hand and bowed over it gallantly. "A smashing dance, Lady Aimee."

The girl giggled. "Thank you."

Aunt Edith clapped beside Maddie. "Lovely, just lovely."

Suddenly, her aunt stretched and faked a yawn. "Well, I am exhausted and must retire for the evening." She turned to Brock. "Forgive my abruptness, young man, but when a body gets old, it needs plenty of rest. And this one is getting quite old! Come along, Aimee, and I will read you a story."

"A story, yes! G'night, Mama. G'night, Mr. Taylor."

"Wait—" Maddie called to her aunt.

But with a wink and a smile, Edith was gone, with Aimee in tow. Vema had long ago pleaded ill. Matheson had disappeared shortly after dinner.

She and Brock were alone.

Silence ensued and lingered. As they stared at one another, a thousand thoughts ran through Maddie's mind—resentment, remembrances, uncertainty.

"Why invite us on a picnic?" she asked finally. "What purpose does it serve?"

"Enjoyment." He shrugged. "Just as I enjoyed myself tonight," he said. "Your aunt is quite a character. And your daughter is wonderful. You have every right to be proud."

"Thank you," she said stiffly.

"Thank your aunt for inviting me."

"I will."

They spoke to one another like polite strangers. It felt awkward . . . and somehow painful.

He withdrew his pocket watch from his waistcoat and glanced at its face. Was he considering the fact that they had but two hours before they were due to meet in Paddington for another night of lovemaking? Desire and dread gripped her at the thought.

Brock pocketed the watch. "I shall see you on Friday at one o'clock."

Friday? Maddie frowned in confusion. "Not before?"

"You look as if you could use the rest," he said with a soft smile, trailing a gentle thumb across her mouth.

Stunned, she peered at him. Had he genuinely put her needs above his desires? Or did he simply not want her?

Then, without another word, Brock brushed past her and showed himself to the door. He shut it behind himself with a quiet click. Silently, Maddie stared after him.

The man constantly surprised her. Why had he released her from their bargain for the next three nights? If he'd grown weary of her already, she should be glad. But she wasn't. She should loathe him, but she couldn't.

Even more perplexing, why did she fear she would miss him?

Breezy sunshine, in contrast to Maddie's mood, ruled the cloudless sky when Friday afternoon and their picnic arrived. Though Maddie tried to calm herself, she found it impossible. Yes, Brock had seen Aimee before—more than once. But now he would have the opportunity to focus on her for hours. What if he started asking questions . . . or drawing conclusions?

"Mama, why are you frowning?" Aimee asked. "This is fun!"

"She didn't like the food," Brock whispered knowingly to Aimee, smiling all the while.

"The food was lovely," Maddie corrected him.

She stared at their empty plates, as well as bits of half-eaten fish and pastries, fruit, cheese, and bread. He'd brought a mountain of food, wonderful wine, and tea. Clearly, he had gone to great effort for this picnic.

Brock had even sent she and Aimee smart new dresses for the occasion. Her own was a confection of yellow muslin with a matching silk pelisse with a perfectly respectable high bodice. And Aimee's dress, in charming little-girl pink and lace, fit her beautifully. He had picked a lovely, if unfashionable spot, in Green Park. They were virtually alone.

Still, she couldn't relax. Maddie couldn't decide what to do about Brock . . . and Aimee.

"Let's play hide and seek!" Aimee suggested.

"A splendid idea." Brock leapt to his feet. "Shall I count while you hide?"

"Yes. Mama, cover your eyes and count."

Maddie nodded, determined not to spoil this bit of fun for Aimee. "Don't go far, sweeting."

While she and Brock counted together, Maddie pretended to cover her eyes so she could keep an eye on Aimee. A glance over at Brock showed he'd had the same idea.

The act surprised Maddie. Was he concerned about the girl? Did he actually care? Until recently, she had imagined that he saw Aimee only as a means to work his way into her own life. As for that night in Whitechapel, perhaps it had been a fluke. But Maddie was uncertain.

Blast it all, she hated the constant uncertainty of not knowing Brock's mind.

". . . eight, nine, ten. Here we come!" Brock shouted.

Aimee giggled from behind a tree a few paces away.

Maddie rose to her feet, and Brock came to her side. He took hold of her hand and enfolded it in his warm grasp.

Stunned, she tried to pull away. Why would he pretend to care for her? Brock held firm.

"No one is here to see our shocking display of ardor," he teased before his face turned serious. "Besides, I miss touching you."

He'd said many sexual things to her, but never tender things. Then he caressed her mouth with his thumb, taking her back five years and a handful of days, when she had believed they could share happiness.

With that gesture and a few simple words, her tense mood shifted. She felt stirred up. Restless. So many emotions rose to the surface, Maddie could hardly name them. They confused her.

He confused her.

Though she wanted to, Maddie couldn't deny she had missed touching him, too.

Lord, what was the matter with her, that she should miss such wanton conduct with a man not her husband, a man who had done his best to swindle her out of her land, her very heart?

He could be your husband, if you wished it, a pesky voice reminded her. It was a ridiculous thought, of course. No one married simply for satisfying sexual congress, especially not a man who had done his best to deceive her.

But she missed more about him than what they did alone at the cottage. As much as she hated to admit that fact, Maddie acknowledged that she missed his smile. She missed the way he teased and challenged her, even when it infuriated her. While Brock was doing his utmost to persuade her to the altar and change her life to his liking, Maddie admired his tenacity. The man simply didn't give up.

Hand in hand, they moved around their picnic, pretending to conduct a great search for Aimee.

"I know she must be near." Brock mocked a baffled tone.

Aimee laughed from her hiding spot. He pretended not to hear.

"Where can she be?" he asked, as if stumped.

Maddie couldn't help but smile at him. His play with Aimee was so effortless. Somehow he understood her four-year-old mind, where Maddie sometimes struggled.

He returned her smile with a warm one of his own, green eyes twinkling with mischief.

"Have we tried the trees over there?" he asked, pointing.

"No."

A quick glance behind the fat trunks revealed nothing, which came as no surprise. Brock scratched his chin and pretended confusion.

"She is quite good at this," he said loudly, so Aimee could hear.

Maddie couldn't resist smiling. "Indeed. Lots of practice."

"I see. Well, we shall simply have to look harder."

Aimee tittered again, no doubt enjoying the game.

Together, they searched around the picnic, behind a few more bushes, pretending to peer within a wild garden of white daisies and pouting yellow cowslips. Absently, he picked a few of each. Through it all, Maddie could see Brock doing his best to act perplexed, and Aimee gleefully enjoying the diversion.

When Maddie and Brock searched behind yet another cluster of bushes, a pair of rabbits came bounding out from the undergrowth. Aimee jaunted after them with a squeal, elated with the new company.

"There she is!" Brock sounded as if one of life's great mysteries had been solved. "Let's chase her!"

Aimee soon lost the foot race with the rabbits and darted away from Brock with a chuckle, stopping at Maddie's side, behind her skirts.

Brock knelt to Aimee's level and handed her the flowers he had picked. "You are excellent at hide and seek. I admit defeat."

Aimee hesitated only an instant before grabbing the makeshift bouquet and launching herself into Brock's arms. He caught the girl with his left arm and gripped Maddie's hand in his right.

"Yes! I won!" Aimee cheered, throwing her arms around Brock's neck, flowers brushing his back.

The three of them stood close, so close—almost like a family. Emotion—both sad and wistful—clogged her throat. Aimee had never experienced this sort of responsive play with Colin. She'd never known the love of a fatherlike figure. That fact tore at Maddie's insides, but she did not fight the feeling. For just this moment, she leaned a bit closer to Brock and savored the idea that this domestic scene could have been theirs, that it could still be theirs . . . if she could believe every day as Brock's wife would be this sweet.

That midnight, Maddie crept into the cottage a quarter hour late, half-hoping Brock had not come. She had been confused, restless, since the picnic.

How could she enjoy the time she spent with Brock when

she did not trust him? Why did her body respond to him so eagerly when she knew he used seduction as a means to bend her to his will and lure her into marriage strictly for her land? And Brock's rapport with Aimee—why did the sight of them together fill her with a wistful remorse she could not shake?

Everything in her head was a jumble, tangled images of past, present, what could be . . . what was likely to be.

She couldn't dwell on that now. She had to survive tonight first. But every night grew more challenging. Every time Brock made love to her, she felt a bit more reluctant to let him go. It was mad, truly, but she could not stop. Nor could he know of her feelings. Brock was like any adept hunter; if he discovered her weakness, he would only exploit it until she surrendered to his every demand.

Maddie drew in a deep breath and straightened her shoulders for the encounter to come.

Shaken by her scrambled thoughts, she divested herself of her cloak and veiled hat and hung them on the peg near the door. When she turned, Brock stood disheveled, watchful and unsmiling, in the entrance to the parlor.

"Hello, Maddie."

She swallowed nervously. "Brock."

What would he want of her tonight? Trepidation assailed her even as her heart increased its rhythm.

"I'm glad you've arrived safely. When you were late, I began to worry."

A glance at his strong, square face told her that Brock's speech was more than mere words. He had been concerned, and it warmed a place within her against her will.

Damn it, if he wanted her for her land, why was he trying to steal her heart? He hadn't wanted it before, not to hold forever. Certainly that hadn't changed.

But he wasn't immune to her either. The realization frightened her, yes. It also secretly pleased her.

Gads, she was a fool, dallying with emotions for a man who would never return them with the same fervor.

"I am perfectly safe," she assured him softly as she made her way to the parlor.

Once there, the settee of pink velvet awaited them, perched before a fire that echoed the heat between them.

He followed her into the room and stopped close to her, so close her heart beat an erratic rhythm. Every inch of her skin tingled with awareness.

With his coat and cravat gone and his shirt open, exposing the bronzed column of his throat, Brock looked dangerous— but touchable. Lord knew, she wanted to touch him so much . . .

"And perfectly beautiful," he murmured. "Since I leave in the morning for three weeks in Birmingham, I am eager to touch you." He bent to kiss her neck.

"Three weeks?" Maddie did her best to concentrate on his comment and respond appropriately. "Why?"

Brock breathed across her skin, alerting her to his scent, his sensuality. The answer to her question no longer mattered.

A shiver assailed her, and Maddie closed her eyes. Her will to resist him was gone. As his mouth moved to the sensitive curve of her shoulder, Maddie knew she ought to refuse him—to save her sanity, if nothing else. But she could not turn him away without violating the terms of their agreement.

Worse yet, she didn't think she had the strength to resist him, even if their wager had given her that freedom. What was it about Brock that made him impossible for her to forget?

He drew in a deep breath, as if taking her in with his senses. "You are as close to perfect as God intended. You're a little stubborn, perhaps—"

Maddie paused at his tone. Was he teasing her? "That's ironic, coming from you."

The low rumble of his chuckle reverberated across her skin. "But you are definitely beautiful."

Before Maddie could absorb his compliment, he lifted his head to look down at her. Every hint of playfulness had gone. Now he stared, deep, green gaze piercing and reassuring at once as he framed her face with his hands.

A charged moment of silence passed. Maddie's heart thumped. She was more than ready for his kiss. Inside, she ached, but the desire went beyond the satisfaction she knew he would give her. She wanted *him*—all of him. The realization that they had never spent an entire night in one another's arms disturbed her.

She closed her eyes against the dangerous emotion. He was the enemy, blast it. Why couldn't she remember that anymore? She couldn't even recall how she had lived without him these past five bleak years.

Slowly, Brock lowered his mouth to hers. Maddie sank into his kiss, giving herself over to the moment.

Threading her fingers through the silk of his hair, she breathed in his spicy scent. It compelled her nearer, along with his slow exploration of the inside of her mouth.

Eager for more, she nipped at his bottom lip with her teeth. He answered her call by brushing his fingers down her spine in a slow glide that made her shiver. She felt his every touch with her senses—deep inside, where her heart beat.

Without waiting, Maddie lay her mouth against his for the next kiss, clasping his larger body against her. Brock met her, his mouth somehow gentle and demanding at once. She coveted the taste of him, yearned for more.

He gave it to her, fusing his mouth with hers in a slow, melting kiss without end. Maddie let the kiss sweep away her fears, her inhibitions, her sanity—until only the desire remained.

Brock brushed his fingers across her collarbones, to the swells of her breasts. Her nipples tightened in anticipation;

her breasts tingled. When he caressed the rigid tips a moment later—so softly her knees nearly buckled—she moaned.

"Tell me you want this half as badly as I do," he panted, his gaze searching, never leaving her face. He wore a frown, the crease between his brows conveying pain.

She could not lie. "I want you more than I thought possible."

"Thank God. All I can think about now is touching every soft inch of your skin and filling you up until you moan."

His words made her stomach pulse with desire. In the past, Brock had been able to rouse her—she could hardly deny that. But this was different, deeper. It was more than strictly seduction.

And dangerous or not, she wanted it more than anything.

Maddie kissed the side of his jaw, moving inward toward his full mouth. "I wouldn't want you to think of anything else."

Then she ran her tongue across his bottom lip. He groaned and grabbed a handful of her hair, pulling her mouth beneath his. A mere heartbeat passed before he crushed her lips with his own. Impatiently, he probed his way inside, tasting, taking, demanding, igniting temptation within her.

Maddie answered every thrust of his tongue, softly persuading him to give her more. As she pulled at the buttons of his shirt, they came undone beneath her impatient fingers, one falling with a clatter to the floor. She didn't care, nor did he.

When she pushed the shirt aside to reveal the smooth steel of his golden skin, Maddie set her greedy hands to his shoulders, the wide expanse of his chest. With a savage jerk, Brock yanked the shirt over his head and flung it across the room, exposing his torso to her hungry eyes.

Then he set to work on the buttons at the back of her dress with an equal lack of care. Hers were more delicate than those on his shirt—and more difficult. Impatience for the feel of his skin against hers danced in her belly.

Maddie raised her mouth to him. Brock met her. Their lips collided. Tension coiled; desire mounted.

They exchanged breaths, expelled sighs, as the storm of need swelled between them. Brock abandoned any pretense of finesse in unfastening her buttons. Urgency reigned as he put both hands to the task. Maddie was heartily glad. The few buttons that clattered to the floor hardly mattered.

But when he parted the back of her dress and, with a heated stroke of his hands, swept it down her shoulders, her breasts, exposing her thin chemise and the tingling breasts beneath . . . that made the damage to her dress irrelevant. That felt more significant than drawing her next breath.

"Damn it all," he swore, "I've got to touch you."

He pressed his lips to the column of her throat. She arched to him in offering as he wrestled the dress past her hips and to a puddle at her feet.

"Yes, quickly," she urged.

His teeth nipped at her lobe; his hot breath fanned out across the sensitive skin of her neck. Maddie moaned, clutching him tighter. Brock set to work on her corset.

Craving more of him, Maddie reached between them and gripped the hard ridge of his erection.

Brock paused in the unlacing. A groan tore from his throat. Head thrown back, jaw tight, wide shoulders taut, he was the picture of masculine beauty.

"Hurry," she whispered, stroking the thick mass of his shaft through the barrier of his breeches.

"You make it difficult for a man to think, let alone move," he groaned.

Maddie took advantage of his momentary ecstasy and bent to flick her tongue across his flat male nipple. Brock drew in a hissing breath between his teeth and cursed. Nothing thrilled her like pleasing him. For good measure, she unfastened his breeches and swept them, along with his drawers, down his legs.

Galvanized into action, Brock's hands moved twice as fast. Almost the moment Maddie was aware of his ministrations, her corset tumbled to the rich carpet beneath the settee.

Her breasts spilled from the whalebone restraint into his waiting hands. He cupped them, dragging his thumbs across her aching nipples. Then once more. That quickly, her breasts became taut. Her whole body thrummed with pleasure.

Brock knew how to touch her. When they had been adversaries, he had taken the time to learn her body, understand what made her mewl. Now that she was his mistress to bed in any way he pleased, he no longer had to exert the effort to see to her pleasure. But he did. Always. Though Maddie knew it was foolish—dangerous, even—she hoped he did so because he cared for her.

She feared she cared for him all too much.

As she stroked his erection, she could not keep that sentiment from her touch, from the touch of her fingers around his bare flesh.

"I swear, Maddie, you're nearly killing me."

She smiled at his oath—until he grasped her wrists and pushed them to her sides, disentangling himself from her touch. He immobilized her arms with a strong grip.

Then he smiled at her with all the pleasantness of a brigand. Clearly, Brock had a plan.

Trepidation and an aching eagerness tumbled over one another in her belly. "Brock—"

He ended her ability to speak when he cupped her buttocks and lifted her legs about his waist. The bump of his hard shaft against her belly and the soft abrasion of the hair on his chest against her taut breasts made her grip his shoulders tight. He nuzzled her neck, nipping at sensitive spots near her shoulder, behind her ear.

Pleasure wasn't a sea she could float on, but a rushing river threatening to drown her. Maddie took his mouth in an artless kiss.

Then Brock sat on the settee and turned to spread his legs out toward the end. He arranged her on his lap so that she straddled him, before settling against the settee's back, still wearing that challenging grin.

"Brock?"

Rather than answer, he lifted one hand from her hip and ran a finger in the cleft between her thighs. His touch was like fire, and he slid through the moist flesh, pausing to tease her at the very spot she needed him most.

Her thighs tightened around his hips. Desire surged. If he made love to her now, it wouldn't be too soon.

Instead, he shocked her by removing his finger and sliding her juices across her nipple. Then, wearing that ever-widening grin, he leaned toward her. Their eyes met and locked. Disbelief and excitement charged her stomach like a battle-field full of steeds. Maddie held her breath.

Brock took her damp nipple in his mouth and sucked strongly.

Maddie gasped. But no sooner had her brain registered the pleasure, than she felt the blunt tip of his erection probe and penetrate her.

In one smooth stroke, he brought her down to the hilt. His flicking tongue drove her to insanity all the while.

She cried out, awash in the consuming desire only he could create in her, the wonder of the depth of their pleasure. Coupled with that, Maddie experienced a gladness that it was Brock who possessed her body.

He dragged his thumb between her legs, across her most sensitive spot. Breath hitching, need spiraling, Maddie could do nothing more than feel the rhythm of their lovemaking and moan.

Beneath her, he thrust, filling her. Her thighs tightened as the pleasure he gave mounted inside her, radiating out from her middle like a bubble, expanding, expanding—before it burst.

The climax began as a tremor, a sharp peak. It overtook her entire body, robbing her of breath, of words.

As she pulsed around him, his shaft swelled, hardened. With a cry, he came, gripping her hips and calling her name.

Maddie opened her eyes at the sound. As Brock slid into her one last time, he looked right at her. His green eyes behind the blackness of his spiked lashes blinded her with a tenderness she'd never expected.

That easily, he erased the last of her resistance to him.

Joy came, followed by uncertainty. As if sensing her confusion, Brock reached up for her shoulders and brought her against his damp chest, where she could feel his racing heart beginning to slow.

The gesture should have alarmed her. Instead, it only made her feel safer and cared for.

He wanted her land, not her. That fact should not be difficult to remember. But around Brock, it was.

"Maddie, you exhaust me," Brock moaned beneath her. "I cannot move."

Despite her uncertainties, she smiled and pushed a stray lock of hair from his forehead. "You must, at least eventually."

Brock laughed and eased her to his side until they crowded together on the sofa. He clasped her hand, locking their fingers together and propping his head up on his palm. "We are very good together."

"Yes." That was the irony of it, really. They were wonderful lovers, but could they be happily married?

Would he still want her after their vows gave him her land?

He paused, looking as if he wanted to say something, and from his expression that something was important. Maddie watched expectantly. With a small shake of his head, he looked down and began placing soft kisses on her shoulder.

Maddie found herself too curious to let the moment pass. "What did you wish to say?"

His head popped up; his gaze met hers again. Surprise molded his features.

"I—I could see from your expression that . . ." she trailed off awkwardly. He hadn't told her what was on his mind because he hadn't wished to. Blast it all, now she had spoiled the moment between them. "It's not important."

"No," he corrected. "I fear it is important."

FOURTEEN

Brock took a deep breath. Then another. He did not want to have this conversation. He couldn't bear to hear Maddie tell him how far beneath her she thought him.

But in order to wed her, he must overcome her prejudice against him and the class to which he'd been born. Besides, with his wealth, he'd moved from the serving class firmly into the wealthiest fraction of the middle class. Women of blue blood were beginning to marry men of his station. Why couldn't Maddie accept him as a husband as eagerly as she accepted him as a lover?

Why did it grind his gut to think she never would?

Donning his shirt, Brock put space between them, gritting his teeth. "I know why you've resisted marrying me. I cannot change my birth. Isn't the money enough for you? Or must you have a titled husband?"

Maddie sat up, hair spilling about her shoulders. When she looked in his direction once more, surprise, confusion even, colored the frown on her face. "You make me sound . . . ambitious. Your lack of title has nothing to do with my refusal."

If all Maddie's lies were like sweet honey, that one would have given him a toothache. Why else would she refuse a match that was advantageous in every other respect? When she needed the money so badly?

"I see," he said slowly. "If my lack of blue blood is not the cause of your refusal, then what?"

Maddie hesitated, the glow of passion fading by the moment to reveal her apprehension. "Marriage for a woman requires trust. By speaking vows, we lose all control of our property, our children, our very beings." She paused, frowning, clearly groping for words. "You've all but demanded I give you complete power over my life—and my daughter's—when I know you regard me as some sort of adversary and merely want me for my land. How am I to know the manner in which you will treat us after marriage, after you have the scrap of earth that will ensure your fortune? You say you will see Aimee and me cared for, but words are pretty and cheap."

She had valid points, and he had never considered the matter from such a frame of reference. "I want your land, yes. But do not doubt I will make certain you and Aimee want for nothing."

With a shrug, Maddie raised her brows and slid her gaze across the room. Brock knew that evasive look well. He had not allayed her fear but did not wish to argue the point further.

"Maddie, what else can I say? I promise Aimee fine tutors to teach her every accomplishment of a young lady and a sufficient dowry to attract the right sort of buck. I will repair Ashdown Manor, see to your aunt in her dotage—"

"I desire all of that." She scowled, shaking her head. "But your money cannot suddenly create trust. The quality of Aimee's life—and mine—depends upon more than dancing masters and a new sofa. Besides, how can I know you would have mine and my daughter's interests at heart, after the vows have been spoken and you no longer have a reason to care?"

Brock stared at her, uncomprehending. "Do you think me some melodrama villain who would lock you in your rooms with nothing but bread and water?" When she did not answer, Brock heaved an irritated sigh. "Good God, woman, I have no intention to seize control of your life or direct your behavior. The property your father left you was never yours outright, so I can hardly see where that is an issue. So what else can you possibly object to?"

Anger dashed across her face. It was quickly fortified by a bolt of steely determination and defiance. Brock hadn't seen that look often on Maddie's face, but he had seen it enough to know it portended nothing good.

"What else can I object to? Plenty, I promise you!"

She looked at him as if he were the stupidest beast she'd ever set eyes on. He loathed the expression and all it implied. Still, she thought him uneducated and lacking in refinement. He counted the country's top engineers and even the Lord Mayor of London among his friends, damn it. Why did she still see him as the ignorant stable hand he'd been five years ago?

Schooling the irritation from his features, he took her hands in his. "Help me to understand, Maddie. What else do you object to?"

At his soft inquiry, her mouth lost its combative set. Silent seconds passed. She tapped an absent finger to her chin. Her eyes told him that her mind was far, far away in contemplation.

Finally, Maddie cleared her throat, the uncertainty gone from her lovely honey-skinned face. "We've never spoken of my marriage to Colin."

Of all the things she might have said, that surprised Brock most. Why would she want to speak of her marriage now?

Before he could run through the possibilities in his mind, Maddie drew her legs up to her chest and placed her chin on her knees, as if defending herself. From what—or whom—did she think she needed protection?

"No, we never have spoken of it." A curiosity he did not want to feel resounded in his voice.

"It was not a—a love match," she began haltingly. "He

kept mistresses and was gone more than he was home. Which suited me. Soon enough, I had Aimee to keep me busy. But there were times he wanted . . . that he seemed to want my devotion, though he had none for me."

Her lack of contentment in the marriage pleased him; Brock would be lying if he said otherwise. But what did the abysmal Sedgewick have to do with him? "I'm not certain I understand."

"Colin came to hate me because I could not be the wife he wished. We had terrible rows." Maddie sighed and bit her lip. "He resented you deeply."

That Maddie had even told Sedgewick about him shocked Brock. "For taking your innocence, I presume?"

She hesitated, then nodded. "I don't think he ever forgave me for coming to him unchaste. But before he died, the fighting grew worse." She swallowed again, her hands now fidgeting, rubbing her arms as if she were cold. She would not meet his gaze.

"What—"

"Brock, men are allowed to display their anger toward their wives in a . . . physical manner. The law accepts such behavior, as does society. *I* cannot accept it, not for myself or Aimee."

Physical? Brock's mind whirled, spun. What the hell did she mean? He examined the possibilities until her words became clear. And the implications of her confession staggered him.

He surged to his feet. "He *hit* you?"

Maddie directed a wary gaze up at him, gray eyes seemingly frozen. From her grave expression, Brock knew he was right.

Fury bolted through him. Sedgewick was lucky to be dead; if he weren't, Brock would have hunted him down and killed the bastard himself—slowly, painfully.

He sank down beside her, taking her shoulders in a loose grip. "Maddie-cake . . . Damnation, I had no idea."

Tears filled her eyes. Maddie thrust her gaze to the cottage's modest white ceiling and sniffed, clearly trying hard not to let her tears fall.

She had always been so brave—beginning an affair of the heart with a servant, surviving a violent husband, enduring years of poverty while raising a carefree child. Even when he had threatened her and her freedom himself, she had refused to give in to his demands. Brock could not help but be amazed at her strength.

Cautiously, he leaned toward her, extending his reach, until he caught her in an embrace. As he held her silent form, Brock realized Maddie was more amazing as a woman than she'd been as a girl. Little wonder he was so caught up in her now.

After a long moment, Maddie leaned away. "I should explain. Mostly Colin belittled me. I—I did not . . . respond to him as he expected."

Brock frowned, mulling over those words. Did Maddie mean to imply that she had not enjoyed her marriage bed?

Brock pushed aside his elation and focused on his deepening confusion. Maddie found sex pleasurable—that he knew. They had proven so again tonight. In fact, she was the most arousing, responsive woman he'd ever taken to his bed. So she must have been cold for Sedgewick in particular.

Even so, the cad's battering response was unforgivable.

"He hit you because you did not enjoy sharing his bed?"

Maddie bit her lip again. When she looked at him, her eyes were haunted yet challenging. "I think he was an unhappy man, and preferred to blame me. I was fortunate that he lashed out physically just once, toward the end of our union."

Brow wrinkled in concentration, Maddie stared at the far wall, seeming to see nothing of the soft pink and cream tones. Brock simply waited to see what she might say or do next.

"It was odd, really. During the incident, Colin's anger

only seemed to increase. After he had gone, I worried day and night that he would return and unleash his fury on Aimee."

Thank God the bastard hadn't. But Brock wasn't prepared to let the matter be.

He touched Maddie's hand in solace, only to realize she trembled. He took hold of her arms. They were cold and covered in chill bumps as he pulled her closer. "Tell me everything that happened."

"It isn't important," she demurred. "I merely wanted you to understand—"

"I want to hear all of it," he insisted. His need for the truth clashed with the knowledge that she needed his gentleness. He softened his voice. "What happened?"

Maddie swallowed and glanced down at her feet again. "A week before Colin died, he came to my room. It was very late. He had imbibed much too many spirits. He smelled of another woman's perfume."

"And he wanted to exercise his conjugal rights?"

"No. He wanted to tell me about his mistress and all the sexual acts she enjoyed performing on him and with him. He pointed out that since other women could respond to him, it was clearly my fault that I did not want him." She hesitated. "He called me frigid, which he had done for nearly two years. But this time he became angry and . . . he struck me until I begged him to stop."

Releasing a trembling sigh, she looked into the distance again, as if she were seeing into the past. Again, her stormy gray eyes clouded over with tears she refused to let fall. Brock's fury warred with his need to hold her.

"Colin left that night and did not return," she murmured. "I went to my father for help." She laughed bitterly. "He asked me what I had done to earn Colin's displeasure and suggested I be a better wife if I wished to avoid such incidents in the future."

Maddie's emotionless voice made Brock even more enraged. He'd always thought Lord Avesbury a bitter, righteous excuse for a man. Maddie's account of her father's reaction proved that. How could any man think his own daughter deserved such callous treatment at her husband's hands?

"After that, I hid in my rooms until the worst of the bruises were gone," Maddie continued. "The morning I emerged, it was to the news that Colin had somehow drowned in the Thames. I donned widow's weeds, but I felt more relief than sorrow."

Brock didn't have to ask if she felt guilt because she hadn't mourned Sedgewick's passing; the cad had hurt her too badly to engender any such devotion.

Somehow, that made Brock feel better . . . and worse. With memories of nothing but enmity, violence, and distrust in marriage, he understood her reluctance to wed again. He searched for his resentment of her refusal to marry him. He found the familiar, harsh sentiment, as he took in the tangled skeins of Maddie's auburn hair and her tender red mouth. But it had faded like a much-washed shirt.

It was possible she did not disdain him as much as she loathed the institution of marriage. He hardly blamed her.

Even if that was the case, however, Maddie must know he would never hit her. Or perhaps she did not . . .

Heaving a sigh, Brock could not take his gaze from the woman who had haunted him for five years. Somehow he would overcome her fears and objections. For Maddie had never encountered a man as determined to wed a woman as he was to marry her.

Brock took her hand in his. "I'm sorry, Maddie. When I began buying Sedgewick's markers, I knew within hours that he was a cad of the first order. I had no idea he had mistreated you."

Maddie shook her head, tangled tresses kissing her bare shoulders. "You couldn't have known."

"Why did you marry him?"

Brock had been thinking the question. He certainly hadn't

meant to blurt it aloud. Indeed, Maddie looked frozen by the inquiry. Impatience for the answer burned his gut.

She hesitated, hugging her knees closer. Her eyes turned wide, skittish. "It's hardly worth speaking of now—"

"I'd like to know." *Patience,* he told himself, gritting his teeth. "Please."

The reluctance did not leave her tense face. Uncertainty shuttered her gray eyes. The beautiful blush that had colored her skin during lovemaking had vanished, leaving her pale cheeks gleaming waxy in the dim light.

"Maddie?" He touched her cheek.

"My father . . . encouraged the match." She paused, took a deep breath, cast a cautious glance his way. "At the time, the notion of marrying Colin seemed a sensible one."

At the time. He mulled over her words, sorting through what he now knew of her marriage to Sedgewick. It was not a love match. She had never responded to her husband's touch. The match had seemed merely sensible, in the manner of most *ton* marriages. Brock wondered why the union seemed so sensible after she had agreed to marry him.

After he'd left for London, Maddie had apparently decided marrying someone of his class was ludicrous. Brock wasn't surprised. Nor was he happy.

But perhaps Maddie had been the one to suffer most. . . .

"I will never hurt you. Never," he vowed. "But nothing has changed. I still want you for my wife." *I always have.*

Brock swallowed, wondering if Maddie could hear the scream of the unspoken words between them as loudly as he could. What would she think of that truth?

"You want my land," she said dully. "You want wealth."

Suddenly, she speared him with a direct gaze other men might have found disconcerting. "Can you say you love me?"

He hesitated, then dared to give the truth. "Yes."

Maddie's face spilled over with bitterness. "That is an

easy word to utter when a fortune is at stake. Would you give up this grand railroad you have planned to prove it?"

The question caught him off guard. He searched for a blithe answer that would appease her while maintaining a shred of honesty—and came up empty.

"As I thought," she sneered.

To his shock, Maddie rose as naked as the day God had sent her to the world. Unaware of her shapely allure, she dressed herself as best she could, moving away when he tried to assist.

"Damnation!" he cursed. "Cropthorne and the others are depending upon me. There is an ungodly fortune to be made! And—and it will be of great value to our economy and our nation."

"Well, then, God save the king," she tossed back with a glare.

Brock let out a sigh of frustration. "Maddie, I cannot stop this railroad now. I fought for the Royal assent and each investor. Every farthing I've ever earned is tied up in this. If I bow out now, I will have nothing, not even my reputation. We're laying the first of the track in less than a week."

That news clearly took her aback. Blast if he hadn't said the wrong thing again.

"Laying track already? You're awfully certain of my ultimate surrender to your . . . charm."

Brock sighed. He was handling this all wrong, he knew. But what else could he say? "I am. I must be."

She made for the door and threw a derisive glance over her shoulder. "Hell will freeze over first."

FIFTEEN

"Mr. Taylor's coach is here for you," said Aunt Edith.

Sitting up slowly from her reclining position on the sofa, Maddie set aside the book she had tried all evening to read. Though she had been unaccountably weary all day, the mention of Brock brought her senses alert.

She peered up to find the older woman hovering over her, her expression both speculative and uncommonly serious.

Maddie's heart stopped, then began beating all too quickly. Brock had returned from Birmingham? Finally—after three long weeks. And he'd sent his coach, making his expectations clear.

His assumption should have bothered her. It did not.

Mixed with the giddy anticipation she chastised herself for was alarm. Aunt Edith knew of her frequent sojourns in Brock's coach? Certainly her aunt did not know what took place between she and Brock. But perhaps she guessed . . .

Maddie cast a cautious glance at the older woman, uncertain how to respond.

Edith spoke into her hesitant silence. "His coach had not come in over a fortnight, so I assumed you had found some way to convince him that you did not wish to be his bride."

Though phrased as a statement, her aunt sought answers as surely as the sun would rise tomorrow.

"Unfortunately, no. He's merely been attending to business elsewhere."

"And now he's returned for you," said Edith. "Will you go?"

"Yes." She had little choice.

Maddie rose to her feet.

She wished she could refuse Brock, wished she did not yearn for him. But such a refusal was neither practical nor possible. She had given him the right to her body. In turn, he had awakened her passions, enslaved her with them.

Why else would she have difficulty in thinking of anything other than him?

"Vema and I observed some time ago that you succeeded in seducing the man. She said you had the look of a well-satisfied woman. I observed that when he dined here with us some weeks ago. The air between you all but sizzled."

Though Maddie knew her aunt was not blind or naïve, the reality that Edith and Vema knew she had been intimate with Brock made her redden. If they could guess even half of the exquisite pleasures Brock had introduced her to, Maddie feared she would perish from mortification.

"I shall take that pink color in your pretty cheeks as a yes." Edith smiled and pushed a stray ribbon from her blue lace bonnet away from her face. "Are you aware that you look at the man as if he's both heaven and hell?"

Startled, Maddie's gaze rose to her aunt's face. "I often think he is. I'm certain he is more one than the other. At the moment, I cannot say which."

"My guess is that you have missed him these past weeks." No hint of a question rang in her voice.

"For some reason, yes," she admitted softly.

Edith could not be more right. These past three weeks had been a trial to her sensibilities. She should hate Brock— or at least be able to disdain the man. He wanted to use her for money again. Yet, when Brock held her, he made the harsh truth disappear, made her remember only the caring in his touch . . .

Even in his absence he haunted her. Since their last parting, Maddie had spent countless hours wondering if he actually loved her, as he'd claimed. When he'd uttered the word, Maddie had known a desperate wish for it to be true. Then she remembered all the reasons such a lie would profit him.

What did the fact she wanted his love say about her?

"I understand why you have missed him. Those green eyes are adoring . . . and quite lustful." The older woman smiled, a combination of something both secretive and wistful.

"Aunt Edith!"

"At my age, lust is a treat." She laughed, her expression self-deprecating.

"Lust is fleeting and a foolish reason to enter into marriage," she disparaged.

"Yes," Edith conceded. "But he loves you, I believe."

Did he, truly? Maddie feared she would never know for certain. In less than five months, they would part ways. Brock would rise in fortune, contrary to his fears, while she . . . would somehow find enough money to see Aimee to womanhood and herself to her old age.

Maddie frowned at the picture. It seemed bare . . . lonely.

"You certainly care for Mr. Taylor far more than you did the odious Lord Wolcott," Edith pointed out.

Truer words had never been spoken. She cared for Brock very much, unfortunately. Perhaps too much. . . .

"He is Aimee's father," her aunt pointed out.

Maddie rolled her eyes. "I am aware of that."

Edith placed a placating hand on her shoulder. "Madeline, your mother left you at such a young age. And I don't imagine your father was any help in matters of the heart."

No, Lord Avesbury had always been imminently practical and wanted the same of her. And always, she had been unable to ignore the pullings of sentiment. Why was she so weak?

"Why not marry Mr. Taylor?" Edith suggested with the same gravity she might have suggested attending a garden party.

"The matter is hardly that simple."

"Of course it is. He loves you. You more than admire him. And you share a daughter. Put aside your pride, your anger, your fear—whatever stands between you. Life gives one few opportunities to truly know love. Why waste yours?"

Before Maddie could respond, Aunt Edith turned and quit the room, gray head—silly hat and all—held regally high. In that moment, she seemed neither old nor doddering.

And Maddie found herself more confused than ever.

Within minutes, Maddie had retrieved her cloak and veiled bonnet and emerged from Ashdown Manor to a brisk, starry country night. Frogs croaked and crickets chirped as she made her way to Brock's coach and the silent coachman, an older gentleman, who greeted her with a nod before he helped her into the vehicle.

Maddie endured the hour-long ride through clandestine darkness, her mind a-tumble with all Aunt Edith had said.

Without a doubt, Maddie had missed the man. And against her better judgment, she cared for him. Some foolish part of her thrilled to the idea that he might truly love her.

But marriage? A death-do-us-part union with an ambitious businessman who would gain what he wanted most the instant they spoke vows? What if he wanted nothing else of her for the next forty years?

The coach halted, and the coachman came round to help her down. After another silent nod, the older man adjusted his powered wig, climbed back up, and drove away.

In three hours, he would return for her. She knew that. Until then, she had to deal with the man inside the cottage.

Maddie gazed heavenward, as if the sight of twinkling

stars in the soft midnight sky might impart wisdom. Only the warm wind of the coming summer blew.

Sighing, Maddie looked about. Shin-high grass swayed with the breeze all about her—except directly before her, where the isolated cottage sat, awaiting her.

Brock was not likely to become easier, she told herself. Then she walked to the little house, where the dim light of a lamp or two illuminated only the front window.

When Maddie pushed open the door, she found Brock in the foyer inches away. Waiting. His expression said little, but he looked both lost and determined—unlike the businessman who had first stepped into her parlor two and a half months before. Tonight was personal, his solemn expression told her. Did he, too, feel emotions that confused him? How could she resist if he touched her with the hint of affection on his face?

Slowly, Brock tread a silent path to her and cradled her cheek with his warm palm, brushing her mouth with his thumb. Maddie resisted the urge to nuzzle into his touch.

"It seems like a year since I last touched you," he whispered. His eyes held an aching expression that swayed her.

While her mind knew they had shared passion frequently since she had become his mistress, her body agreed with his observation.

She stepped closer. "It does."

His green eyes were soft for once, lacking anger. Maddie felt as if she were falling deep into his gaze. The air hung thick with unspoken sentiment. Something inside her—a part that had long wanted to be loved—responded to the silent whisper between them.

Lord, she felt dangerously close to caring for him again.

"You look troubled. Whatever it is, forget it tonight."

The idea tempted her. She could lose herself in the magic of his touch and cease worrying about her vulnerable heart until tomorrow. She knew, however, that a night in his arms would only increase her tumult—and her need.

Maddie tried to pull away from him. He placed his free
hand on her other cheek and let his gaze delve into her
eyes—her soul. His stare asked for her nearness, soothed
her confusion, made her want to melt into him and forget
the world.

With eyes so gentle, he was impossible to resist.

Her surrender must have shown on her face, for he leaned
toward her, into her, and placed a soft kiss on her mouth.
They exchanged a brush of lips, a rush of breath. He feath-
ered his fingers into her hair, and she leaned into his touch,
silently asking for more.

He covered her mouth with his again. Still, she felt no
demand, only a honey-sweet call that enveloped her senses.

Maddie tangled her fingers in his hair and drew him
closer. Her senses reeled. Her mind emptied of everything
but his heat, his touch, his taste. As he pressed soft kisses
on her lips, she swayed closer, until she was fully against
him.

The moment felt perfect, their mute communication more
expressive than a thousand words.

Slanting his lips across hers, he kissed her once more,
feasting on the inside of her mouth. Heat crept up her chest.
Need rose steadily in her belly. He felt . . . necessary to her,
as if some too-trusting part of her never wanted to let him
go.

Brock's hands moved to the buttons at the back of her
dress and eased them from their fastenings, one by one. As
he slid the dress from her shoulders, his mouth was there,
warming, reassuring. Maddie melted into the seductive
stroke of his lips. Brock made her feel worshipped and
wanted, heaven knew. He made her believe she was both
desirable and responsive. Maddie found that knowledge as
heady as his touch.

When her dress hung about her waist, she reached out
with damp palms to remove his cravat and coat. His mouth
returned to hers, as if thanking her. He lingered over her

lips, sampling her as if he had all the time in the world—as if nothing would ever come between them.

Tears stung Maddie's eyes as she removed his coat and shirt. He divested her of petticoats and corset in gentle strokes, touching each inch of skin he exposed along the way.

As she gazed at the bare, hard flesh of his arms and torso, her mind felt slow and heavy. Her chemise clung to her skin, pressing back against her swelling, sensitive breasts. When his fingers traced a slow path down a taut mound, Maddie felt as if he reached inside her, driving her arousal higher.

"When you look at me like that, I want nothing more than to drown in you for hours," he murmured.

A rosy color crept up her skin. But, God help her, not from embarrassment. When he spoke like that, in that voice, she wanted the same. She wanted to feel them joined in passion.

Eager to touch him, Maddie lay her palm across his chest, over his heart, gratified by its strong, quick beat.

What would she do without this, without him, when he had again gone from her life?

"You want me," she whispered.

"I'll never deny that."

His confession sent her soaring. That he wanted her, that she affected him, all but made her glow.

Her hand slipped lower, onto his hard abdomen. He tensed at her touch, his gaze delving into her. She read his anxiety and need, knew those emotions were likely mirrored on her face.

Maddie drew her hand lower, her fingers drawing a teasing circle around the buttons of his breeches. Brock drew in a sharp breath as she unfastened the garment and slid them from his hips, along with his boots, drawers, and hose.

Naked he stood before her, his thick shaft straining toward her. Maddie couldn't deny that he was magnificent, his body strong and well carved—and eager to make love to her.

Brock wasn't content to stand still. He reached out to her, his fingers settling on the hem of her chemise and lifting it slowly. His greedy palms warmed her bared skin, tantalizing, arousing, reminding her of all that was to come.

When she was as naked as Eve, Brock took her by the hand and led her to the small, candlelit bedroom at the back of the house. The bed itself was lavish and large, leaving only enough room for a small washstand and an armoire in the corner.

His eyes never left hers as they sank together to the mattress, Maddie on top. He skimmed gentle fingers down her shoulders, her back. She shivered as he fanned the flames of her arousal. Long and slow, he took her mouth in a kiss that drugged her senses with pleasure. It was endless, bone-melting. It left little doubt he intended to devour her body in the same manner.

His palms whispered over her, sensitizing her to his touch. She curled into him, closer, and he claimed her with relentless hands. Maddie wondered if he, too, felt the deepening bond, as if they understood each other without words.

Brock rolled her onto her back and kissed a warm path down her neck to her breasts. Her nipples ached with wanting before he even touched them. When his tongue swirled around each of the swollen buds, they drew up hard and tight. She sighed. His exploration continued, unhurried and mind-dissolving. Brock's hands soon joined the journey across her belly, hips, and thighs. He touched her everywhere, except where she needed him most.

Her sighs turned to moans. She felt dazed and damp and about to come undone.

"I need . . ." She stopped, unable to do anything more than ache. "Please—"

To lend credence to her words, she reached between them and drew a long path down his belly to his rigid erection. She took it full in her palm and began to stroke him. He groaned, seeming to grow harder in her hand with each moment.

"Maddie——" His voice was half warning, half praise.

"Brock," she moaned in return and spread her thighs beneath him, inviting him in.

He accepted the invitation, settling his hips in the cradle of her thighs and sinking into her slowly, smoothly. She closed her eyes, savoring the moment as he stretched her. Fluid desire filled her veins, and pleasure gathered quickly where they joined.

He entered her with long strokes, one after the other. He did not hurry. Instead, he seemed to take pleasure in each lingering thrust he indulged in.

"Maddie," he groaned. "I can feel the desire in your body. Look at me so I can see it in your eyes."

She opened her eyes, lashes fluttering. The intense green of his gaze consumed her, and she drowned in the pool of desire and tenderness she saw shimmering there.

The truth hit her at that moment. Though she had denied it all she could, she loved him again.

Perhaps she had never stopped.

At the urging of his hands, Maddie arched up to Brock, needing to meet him, match him, still reeling from her insight into her own heart. Caught up in the sweetness of the moment, her love colored every touch, every kiss.

And he responded, bringing her closer, curling his body around her. His shoulders grew taut, his face tense. His fingers sank into her thighs, spreading them wider, telling her silently that he did not merely want to be within her, but rather a part of her. Maddie swore she could feel him in every inch of her body.

She soared toward ecstasy, breath coming hard and fast. Perspiration broke out across her chest, as it dotted Brock's hairline and temples. And still he plunged into her insistently, until the edge of satisfaction teased her, seized her——

overtook her. Brock followed her to orgasm with a hoarse cry.

Maddie felt the force of her peak singe her every nerve. She clung to Brock, fingers clasped to his shoulders. She spread kisses along his mouth, his jaw, unraveling the tension that had held her in thrall.

The glow of fulfillment followed, and she wallowed in it, languorous and sated. What they had shared tonight had been so tender, so honest. They had bonded without words. They had crossed some bridge together—and there was no going back.

With a sigh, Maddie lay her head on the slick flesh of his hard chest and wondered what lay on this side of their path.

A giggle and a squeal brought Maddie out of a deep sleep three mornings later.

"Mama!" was all the warning she received before Aimee launched herself onto Maddie's bed with a thump. Prying her eyes open to slits, Maddie peered at her daughter, blond hair askew about her face.

"You asleeped too long," Aimee teased.

"Slept," Maddie corrected, closing her eyes again.

Though Aimee said she had slept too long, Maddie felt as if she hadn't slept long enough. What was wrong with her? She had been feeling bone-tired for days. Probably influenza.

"Is it time for breakfast yet?" she croaked. "I'll fix some if you're hungry."

"No, silly. I already ate."

Maddie nodded, making a mental note to thank Aunt Edith or Vema, whoever was the saint responsible for the good deed.

"Giddy up!" Aimee shouted, then giggled.

"No—"

The protest came too late. Aimee straddled her mother's

torso, bouncing her thin little backside on Maddie's stomach. The experience was not a pleasant one. Nausea rose, seeming to climb up into her throat.

The feeling only worsened when Aimee slapped her hands down on Maddie's chest, a bit too close to her tender breasts.

"Ouch!" Maddie grabbed Aimee's wrists and moved them.

Sore breasts were a common symptom of her monthly flow, but blast, she wished her menses would hurry up. Her breasts and her back had hurt all day yesterday.

Wonderful; her monthly flow and influenza at once. Sometimes life frowned on people. Apparently it was her turn.

It was a blessing Brock hadn't sent his carriage for her last night. Besides the nausea, she'd apparently needed the extra sleep.

Her daughter bucked on Maddie's tummy again. The nausea swelled once more.

"Aimee, no. Sweeting, Mama is feeling unwell."

"You're ill, Mama?"

"Ill?" She recognized Aunt Edith's voice from across the room.

Maddie opened her eyes in time to see Edith lift the rambunctious child from her stomach and set her nearby on the mattress. Reaching out to the girl, Maddie curled her arm around her little waist. Aimee laid her head on Maddie's shoulder.

Smiling, she assured, "I will recover, I'm certain."

Aimee nodded, her little face looking concerned.

Edith frowned. "You will recover, but not today, it appears. A pity, really. There is a lovely summer festival planned in the village, Mrs. Goddard told me yesterday."

Maddie gave a moan of regret. But she simply wasn't up to celebrating the start of summer—or any season at the moment. She groaned.

June had arrived already? Goodness, how time flew.

"Enjoy the festivities without me. I shall join you later if I can," she promised.

The older woman nodded, then held out her hand to her great-niece. "Come along, Aimee. Let Mama rest while you and I go have fun."

"Yeah!" Aimee cheered as she scrambled off the bed and took Edith's hand. "I see you later, Mama."

"Have a good time, sweeting."

Moments later they had gone, leaving Maddie blessedly alone. Cautiously, she sat up. Thankfully, her back had ceased its pain, but her breasts were worse than ever. No doubt from Aimee's beating this morning. At least the girl would have the summer festival to divert her young energy.

Maddie swung her feet to the floor and froze. Summer festival? Was it already June first?

Frowning, Maddie thought back over the past few months. Her menses normally came at the middle of the month, not the beginning. Her frown became a scowl.

Her menses were two weeks late.

The only time she had ever failed to have her menses in a timely manner was when—

No. Such an event was not possible now. The midwife had told her she could bear no more children. She had never conceived with Colin, despite the regularity with which she had reluctantly shared his bed.

An ominous mantle enveloped her.

Surely her ill feelings were nothing more serious than a sudden influenza.

Except . . . influenza never made her breasts ache or her back hurt. Why would it make her tired days before the nausea?

The only time she had ever experienced all of these symptoms together was when—

No, that simply could not be. Though she had wanted more children someday, the midwife had assured her that such an event would never come to pass. Had the woman been wrong?

Could she be with child?

Maddie rose, suddenly very alert. She paced, her mind racing to the summer she had discovered herself pregnant with Aimee. All the indications were the same.

Shock doused her with ice. Suddenly, she felt cold, numb. Confusion tugged at elation in a battle of wills that neither won.

"With child?" she murmured.

How? Well, she knew how—at least in theory. She and Brock had made love countless times in the past weeks. But how had she conceived with all the scarring the midwife had sworn birthing Aimee had produced?

Had time healed her?

Maddie stared at the peeling plaster of her white ceiling, blinked, stared some more. A haze of shock whirled in her. Only a staggering litany penetrated the mist in her mind: *a baby, a baby, a baby.*

She raised an unsteady hand to her stomach and lay her fingers over the slight curve there, one of the reminders of her last pregnancy.

A baby.

Was she excited? Nervous? In disbelief? Yes. Yes to all. But what should she do?

Her mind raced so fast, she could hardly discern one thought from another.

Tell Brock? Yes, she would have to, and probably confess the truth about Aimee, as well. Her pregnancy was not something she could hide from the man who touched every inch of her bare skin almost nightly. He was a bright man—brilliant, really. Brock would soon realize what her body told her now.

And what of society? She could not hide in Ashdown Manor's walls for months and then lie about the baby's parentage to cover its bastardy. It was not fair to the child. Or to Aimee.

Or even to Brock.

Sighing, Maddie sat up on the bed. Perhaps she should have told him the truth long ago. Fear that he would want Aimee to himself, that he wouldn't want Aimee at all, that he would hate Maddie for her years of silence—all strangled her courage.

Now Fate had decided. She must tell him soon. Somehow, she would find the courage to agree to marriage—if he would still have her. Then she would pray that he would come to truly love her someday, as she loved him.

But once he realized how long she'd kept Aimee a secret from him, Maddie feared her prayer would be too much for even God to grant.

Later that afternoon, Maddie sat tensely in the drawing room, doing her utmost to concentrate on mending her stockings—and failing miserably.

Hearing a caller at the door, Maddie stood and froze, half-hoping, half-fearing Brock was her visitor.

Matheson opened the door and said something most unexpected. "Are you at home for Lord Belwick, my lady?"

Belwick? Brock's competitor in building the railroad?

Confused—and curious—Maddie nodded and rushed to tuck the stockings beneath the sofa cushions. In her faded gown, she looked bedraggled enough; best not to show the man her unmentionables as well.

Pushing away a coil of hair that had strayed into her face, Maddie turned as Matheson announced her guest.

Belwick strolled in, wearing every trapping of a gentleman and a pleasant grin.

"My lord," she greeted cautiously.

His gaze flew to her, and he rose to his feet. "Lady Wolcott, thank you for receiving me. You are gracious, indeed."

"I am at home today, merely overseeing a few household chores, nothing that would interest you fancy Londoners."

Belwick smiled at her gentle jibe.

"Would you care for tea?" Maddie asked, impatient to complete her hostessing duties so she might learn the reason for this odd visit. His last had been enlightening. What did he have to share with her now—and did she want to hear it?

"No, but I am much obliged for the kind invitation." Without further pause, he said, "I know you and Lady Dudley have had some disagreements in the past, but I was greatly disturbed when she shared with me just last evening the fact that you find yourself in need of money."

Shame rushed over Maddie, and she felt her cheeks heat with anger. Blast Roberta! She had made a mistake in asking the woman for help. Even at the time, she had known it. Now, she was more certain than ever.

"My financial state is really none of your concern, my lord."

His smile was sharp. "I have offended where I had no intent to do so. Give me the opportunity to rephrase my reason for calling."

Sighing, Maddie made her way back to the sofa and sat, where she stared at Lord Belwick in expectation. He did not disappoint her.

"Perhaps we may help each other," Belwick began anew.

Maddie had no notion why he imagined thus, but she had agreed to listen, and she would.

"Lady Dudley indicated last night that you had requested a loan from her; I began to ask myself why. I also wondered why such a lovely lady would consort openly with rabble like Taylor."

Though she'd known most of the *ton* thought Brock beneath them, to hear Belwick so openly disparaging him incensed her. "Perhaps, my lord, I find him interesting."

Belwick hesitated, apparently deciding to change tactics.

"You claim your late husband left you deeply in debt, as I understand it, Lady Wolcott. And Mr. Taylor bought up your markers, according to one Mr. Hockelspeck, your husband's tailor."

Maddie stared at her guest in horror, her mouth widening in shock.

He went on. "You owe Mr. Taylor money, and he is pressing you to marry him because of it, is he not?"

Belwick knew. And Maddie feared that if he kept digging, he might learn more—about her trysts with Brock. They had done their best to be discreet, but perhaps there was a witness somewhere. What then?

"That is none of your affair, Lord Belwick. Please go."

"I shall give you every farthing necessary to pay Taylor, plus an additional ten percent, if you refuse to marry him."

There it was; the reason for this odd call. Maddie sucked in a breath and stared at Belwick in mute shock.

He offered her everything she had wished for since the moment Brock had strolled back into her life on that cold March night.

But he offered it too late.

The money would not save her from marriage now, not with a child on the way. Nor would it save her heart from Brock's grip. For better or worse, she loved him.

"I am both stunned and insulted by your offer, my lord. And therefore, I must decline."

Belwick shot to his feet, his round face tightening with anger. "Are you certain that's wise? Let me explain the ramifications—"

"There's no need. I have made my choice."

Maddie stood and walked to the door.

Belwick glared at her, venom darkening his eyes as he made his way across her threadbare carpet. Clearly, he disliked the fact that Brock could now compete fully in the race to open the London-to-Birmingham route.

"You will be sorry," Belwick vowed as he reached the portal.

Maddie merely opened the door, hoping the odious man wasn't right—that she would not regret her marriage to Brock.

With a final glare, he muttered, "I'll ruin you both."

SIXTEEN

"A toast," said Cropthorne the following evening to the crowd of investors gathered at his home. "To the T & S Railroad. May she open on time and always be prosperous."

"Here, here," Brock shouted, standing beside the duke.

All the men present raised their glasses of champagne to celebrate the successful laying of the first mile of track. With luck and good weather, the rest of the route would be finished in two years—well ahead of the schedule Lord Belwick had proposed for his competing line.

Brock smiled. The taste of success was like a fine brandy—purely delectable.

But the moment was imperfect. He turned to Maddie, only to find a distant, nervous expression on her face. What had added the turmoil to her gray eyes? She had said earlier that they must speak tonight after the party. Whatever disturbed her, he would surely learn then.

Beside him, Maddie frowned at her champagne glass before setting it aside, untouched. Brock wanted to stroke her face, smooth away the worry lines between her brows. Too many people, including the snobby Lady Litchfield, who stood at Cropthorne's side, watched them.

"Maddie?" he whispered, peering at her with concern.

She raised her gaze to his and froze under his stare. She hesitated, blinked, then pasted on a false smile.

Did she think that expression would make him believe all was well?

"I'm simply tired," she murmured.

He did not believe a word she said. Being tired would not put lines of worry between her brows.

Maddie would not want to celebrate the railroad, true. After all, in order to successfully complete the project, he and Maddie must marry. He had constantly reassured Cropthorne during their three weeks in Birmingham that Maddie would soon assent to the union. He had been supremely confident of that the night they had last made love.

Now he was not certain at all. If only the matter of marriage weighed upon her mind, Maddie would be angry at his presumption in having this celebration, not sad, as if her world was crumbling. And certainly not frightened.

Brock knew all the reasons Maddie feared marriage, but he did not believe she was actually frightened of *him*. He ached for her, for all she'd endured, but he was not Sedgewick and would not pay for the man's utter stupidity. Brock would marry Maddie, treat her like a queen. But he would *marry* her.

"Is this little . . . party finished?" Brock heard Lady Litchfield drawl to Cropthorne.

The duke wrapped his hand about her arm to stay her. "Already eager to leave, Cordelia?"

"I've done as you asked in attending and lent credence to this little venture of yours."

Brock took the words as a challenge, and turned to excuse himself from Maddie's side. Lady Litchfield apparently needed a bit of his charm. It would either thaw or irritate her, and he very nearly did not care which.

Maddie stayed him with a hand about his elbow. "She has a poison tongue if you make an enemy of her."

"She has a poison tongue, regardless," he murmured.

"Not always. Let her relax. Gavin will help her to come about on this issue. If she becomes your ally, she can smooth your way through the *ton*. If you ruffle her feathers now, you will make an enemy."

Brock paused, weighing Maddie's words. A little amusement at the stuffy lady's expense or an ally who could help pave his way to the future?

Rolling his eyes, Brock whispered, "Blast, and I so looked forward to toying with her small mind."

"You are incorrigible."

At Maddie's scold, Brock grinned. "You like me that way."

Maddie peered at him once more, the haunted expression back in her gaze.

Concern niggled him.

"Maddie, what—"

"Good evening, Lady Wolcott."

Brock turned to find Lady Litchfield regarding him. Scarcely disguised curiosity governed her expression.

"Good evening," Maddie murmured at his side.

Brock wanted to say something to Cropthorne's haughty lady friend. However, he knew that a man always waited for a lady to acknowledge him. And a person of lesser birth always waited for the one of greater rank to recognize him.

The social stricture gave Lady Litchfield the perfect opportunity to cut him again, if she chose.

Brock waited for her snub as he stared into her pale alabaster face and impersonal blue eyes not three feet away.

"Mr. Taylor," Lady Litchfield said finally, regarding him with a stiff smile.

To his surprise, she offered him her hand.

"My lady," he murmured, bowing over her hand.

"Cropthorne tells me you are brilliant with money."

"He is all kindness," Brock evaded.

She sent him a cynical smile. "He is never kind without cause."

Brock merely nodded. "As you say."

Where was Lady Litchfield's conversation headed?

"Would you be partial to the idea of more subscribers in your venture?"

"Naturally." He paused, then added, "More capital means an accelerated production schedule. The sooner we are operational, the sooner we beat our competition in providing rail service from Birmingham to London."

"Indeed. Can you guarantee every subscriber a return on his investment?" she asked archly.

Was this her trick? To back him into a verbal corner?

"I cannot guarantee any investment. That is not the nature of things monetary, my lady. Anyone who makes such a guarantee speaks falsely."

"Of course." The lady's blue eyes regarded him with interest. "Such honesty can be to your detriment, Mr. Taylor."

Nodding, Brock conceded the point. "Perhaps, but I insist upon being a gentleman of honor." *Whatever you may think.*

The unspoken words hung in the air. Brock had no doubt everyone could hear them. Even Maddie's hand tightened on his elbow.

"How noble." Lady Litchfield smiled, as if greatly amused. "Good evening."

Mutely, Brock bowed his head and watched the steel-tongued woman go.

At least she spoke civilly to him. The fact that the rest of the party, including several important members of the *ton* contemplating investment, had seen the exchange would be to his benefit.

"I did not understand the point of her conversation," Maddie whispered.

"Nor did I. She did not *seem* to possess ill intent . . ." Brock shrugged.

Maddie did the same.

Then the press of questions came from the others in the room. How soon would they be operational? What sort of reasonable return could they expect the first year after opening? Would they likely turn a profit in the first three years?

Could competition beat them to opening and completely
ruin their plans?

Cropthorne stood silently beside Brock, arms crossed
over his chest. Brock assumed his grace might field a question or two, but Cropthorne merely glanced at him, then
gestured to the crowd.

In his element, Brock smiled and took questions one by
one.

Two hours—and eighty thousand pounds later—the railroad was funded beyond his dreams. Had Lady Litchfield
intentionally opened that door for him? It seemed unlikely,
but . . . who knew?

Not long after, guests began leaving in a steady stream.
The clock chimed one in the morning when Brock, Maddie,
and Cropthorne all sat in his study. The duke's satisfied
smile matched his own. Maddie, on the other hand, looked
exhausted and pale.

"You look ready to fall over," he murmured to her. "I
shall take you home."

She nodded, apparently too tired to say a word.

Brock turned to Cropthorne. "I think we can say the party
was a success. Thank you for having it."

The duke waved his words away. "Take care of my cousin.
That is more important—"

The plump old butler opened the door to the study, halting
conversation. "Your grace, I am sorry to interrupt. You have
a visitor, Lord Belwick, who says he wishes most urgently
to see you."

"A visit from the competition?" Cropthorne surmised.

"A merger in the making?" Brock laughed.

At his side, Maddie stiffened, her eyes alert. She watched
Cropthorne, apprehension making her red mouth taut.

"Gavin, no," she said. "He—he is unpleasant."

"But harmless, I am sure," answered her cousin. "Let us
find out what he wants, eh?"

Brock nodded cautiously.

"Very good, your grace," the butler said, then disappeared.

While Brock agreed that Belwick was unpleasant, Maddie seemed beyond annoyed with the man's rude demand to see Cropthorne. In fact, she seemed . . . fearful. Why? She had been behaving oddly all evening.

A minute later, the round little butler announced Belwick, who entered the room. The well-groomed snake looked surprised to see Brock and Maddie there. But most pleased by the unexpected development.

A moment later, he turned a malevolent smile on Maddie. Brock glared at his competitor as a furious instinct to protect Maddie arose. The man merely turned the same terrible smile on him, tenfold.

What the hell was going on?

Even more oddly, Lady Dudley entered just behind him, looking decidedly smug.

They both sat on a sofa at Cropthorne's left elbow, and the air thickened around them.

Why had this damned miserable pair come here?

Cropthorne dispensed with the formalities. "A drink, my lord? My lady?"

Impatiently, Belwick waved a refusal. "We apologize, your grace, for our untimely visit. But Lady Dudley and I have only just realized something of terrible import we think you should know."

"Seeing as how you abhor scandal, your grace," Roberta added.

Cropthorne's face shuttered at Lady Dudley's words.

The only thing the duke hated more than scandal was his deceased father, but the two ran a close race.

"Indeed." Belwick stood and puffed out his chest. "I cannot believe you wish to do business with a man who is no gentleman."

Some of the tension left Cropthorne. Indeed, the duke swiped at a lock of black hair on his forehead and murmured,

"I am aware that Mr. Taylor's birth is somewhat less exalted than my own. I hardly fault him for something in which he had no hand."

Brock checked both an urge to cheer and to laugh. He had not truly considered Cropthorne a friend. Perhaps he should reconsider.

"No! We refer to Mr. Taylor's indecent conduct," Roberta declared.

"And with your very own cousin!" Belwick did his best to sound scandalized.

Again, Cropthorne sent the uninvited duo a condescending glare. "I am aware that Mr. Taylor is courting my cousin. She is well past her mourning, and the match will be financially advantageous. Again, his birth has no bearing here."

"Your grace, it is hardly the courting behavior we refer to. The information we have is of a far more lascivious nature."

Brock tensed. Could Roberta or Belwick have learned about his trysting with Maddie? Cropthorne would condone courting, yes. Brock doubted his grace would approve of the myriad ways in which he'd recently taken Maddie to his bed.

"They have been lovers," Belwick announced.

Dread slammed into Brock. Beside him, Maddie tensed. He forced himself to calm. They were guessing, surely. Belwick could have no real proof of that, could he?

Cropthorne paused, flicking a censorious glance in Brock's direction. "Then so much the better for them to wed, wouldn't you say?"

"Your grace!" Roberta chastised, sounding scandalized. "They have been lovers for five years."

Brock jumped to his feet and growled, "If you were a man, I would call you out."

As if Brock had said nothing, Roberta turned a hateful

glare on Maddie. "Why don't you tell them who fathered Aimee?"

"Y—your brother," Maddie stammered.

Brock stared at her in shock. Why wasn't Maddie insulted by Lady Dudley's ugly accusation?

"The truth, damn you!" Belwick demanded.

Roberta glared at her. "That child is no niece of mine."

Maddie bit her lip, all too silent.

Brock stared at her. Shock roared in his head. His mind raced.

"Maddie?" he prompted.

She only looked to her hands, now folded tightly in her lap and swallowed. "Brock."

He was aware that she did not answer him. And his heart beat with the ferocity of a careening steam engine.

"Are you insinuating that Mr. Taylor is Aimee's father?" Cropthorne demanded.

"It's not possible," Brock said.

But it was more a question than a statement.

Brock pressed on. "Aimee's birthday is a full eleven months after I left Ashdown Manor. I inquired years ago."

"You ruined my cousin when you worked for Lord Avesbury?" Cropthorne thundered, slicing a sharp gaze in his direction.

Brock ignored him, his gaze focused on Maddie. Certainly it wasn't possible. Aimee was not his daughter. Maddie would have told him. She would have sent for him in London when she first realized—

A tear splashed down Maddie's pale cheek, splattered onto her clenched hands below. Alarm staggered him. Was it possible? Was it true?

"My brother could not father children—a terrible childhood fever, my parents were told," Roberta told Cropthorne.

The woman had to be lying. Lady Dudley hated Maddie. Surely this was a poison arrow designed to maim her former sister-in-law. Wasn't it? With questions tumbling over one another in his head, Brock turned to Maddie. She had shock and horror written across her waxen face.

Was there a chance—even a small one—that Roberta had told the truth?

Gaping, he whispered, "Maddie? What—How . . ." He sighed, trying to bring order to his racing mind. "Is she telling the truth?"

Lady Dudley scoffed. "Why else would Colin marry a woman he knew to be with child?"

Brock ignored the self-centered shrew and stared at Maddie. She didn't speak, didn't move. She only gazed at him with watery gray eyes. They swam with guilt.

Brock's world shifted, tilted crazily, fell out beneath him.

Aimee *was* his daughter.

Dear God. Elation, fury, joy, and betrayal all rushed through Brock at once. He struggled for a breath, then another. Comprehension eluded him. He was a father?

Brock had felt a real fondness for the clever little Aimee the first time he met her. She'd made him laugh more than once.

And Maddie had deprived him of knowing her for four years.

He drilled her with a stony gaze, demanding she answer him now.

She refused to meet his eyes.

Instead, Maddie frowned at Roberta. "Colin never wanted Aimee. He hated her."

"Of course. He prayed every day you carried that little bastard girl that she would be a boy, but you disappointed him even in that," Roberta sneered.

"He hated me for *that?*"

"Stupid girl." Roberta sighed in impatience. "You came to him pregnant and in need of a husband. Colin wed you, even as you refused to name Aimee's father. He needed you to grant him a son! How else was he to have an heir?"

"Oh, dear God," Maddie sobbed, her shoulders shaking.

Belwick speared Brock with a glance. "We only realized you must have been the one to compromise Lady Wolcott when I remembered the gossip that Lord Avesbury dismissed you without reference shortly before she married Sedgewick."

"You're certain Aimee is my daughter?" Brock asked Maddie directly. Somehow, he managed to keep his voice steady.

Shocking, considering how desperately he wanted to rail at her for stealing the joy of his daughter from him.

Maddie cast him a discomfited glance. Then she nodded.

Brock stared down at Maddie, feeling as if his chest would split open from the pain. He cursed long and loud in earthy streetwise oaths. "Why the hell didn't you tell me?"

"So you *did* ruin my innocent cousin." Cropthorne's voice boomed with outrage. "Clearly, you're not the gentleman I once thought."

Brock did not answer Cropthorne's accusation. He could not. He could only stare at Maddie, her auburn hair brushing her slender neck as her back moved with the tears she shed.

Tears that had come far too late as far as he was concerned.

Lady Dudley screwed up her face in a moue of disgust.

"What about Aimee's birthday?" Brock snapped.

"Colin paid the vicar to change Aimee's birthday by six weeks." Maddie's voice trembled as she faced him. "I'm sorry. I had reasons—"

"You always do." Brock spat the words at her as he rose and crossed the room. "Just as you had *reasons* for not wedding me the first four times I asked. I think I understand perfectly now."

His low birth. Why did everything in his life always come back to that?

Maddie's eyes pleaded with him before she uttered a word. "No—"

"And Colin paid the midwife to tell you that you would

be unable to have more children," Roberta chimed in. "Were you gullible enough to believe her?"

If anything, Maddie turned whiter. She reached out to steady herself on the arm of the sofa.

Reluctant concern tugged at Brock. She might have shattered his every illusion about her, his every hope that she could love him someday, but he'd be damned if he would let a bitch like Lady Dudley kick Maddie.

"Enough!" he roared.

"My dear." Belwick's voice sounded as a pond iced over by winter. "Mr. Taylor is right. We are not here to bring harm to Lady Wolcott, but rather to save his grace from doing business with a man who possesses the kind of conscience that allows him to defile innocent girls."

Roberta lapsed into silence, but her expression refuted Belwick. She cared nothing for the railroad, but she hated Maddie.

"Consider, your grace, that my railroad proposal is far more—"

"Get out," Cropthorne demanded in low, lethal tones. "And take Lady Dudley with you."

"But your grace, you can't mean to continue doing business with a man of Taylor's ilk. He—"

"That does not mean I am in any hurry to do business with you. Good-bye."

Knowing he had been well and truly dismissed, Belwick crossed the room and took hold of Lady Dudley's arm. Wearing a cloak of pride, despite his anger, Brock's competitor left. Lady Dudley shot her sister-in-law a sneer as she exited.

Maddie blanched, looking devastated by the evening's events.

And why not? Her cousin knew her shame, that Aimee had been conceived out of wedlock, sired by her own servant.

If she did not know it now, she would soon realize that Brock had no intention of wasting another moment of his life on her, deceitful little wretch that she was. Of course, she probably would not care.

"Madeline, is all this true?" Cropthorne demanded.

"Yes." She looked ready to break, but she managed to keep her voice steady.

Why not? Hell, now that the truth was out, maybe she would be relieved. Surely she'd found it difficult to remember to tell the father of her child each time she saw him that he was not the father of her child. Yes, that must have been confusing. Now that the truth was out, she need not bother.

"Mr. Taylor," Cropthorne snapped, "you took advantage of a young girl who clearly trusted you."

"We had plans to marry."

Cropthorne raised a black brow in disbelief. "Surely Avesbury did not condone the match."

Brock worked his jaw. Lord, he hated defending himself to everyone who thought they were his better. He had done it his whole life. He would not do it tonight.

"I had good intentions where Maddie was concerned, but I doubt I can convince you of that. I daresay no one cares that she's played me false for years. It seems clear that you've decided I'm no gentleman—and, in fact, am one of the most nefarious cads you've ever had the misfortune to do business with."

"Whatever else I might say about you, Mr. Taylor, I always knew you were bright. Consider my capital withdrawn from the railroad."

Withdrawn? Dismay ploughed him flat. Brock had feared Cropthorne's defection was coming, that Belwick had managed to kill the T & S Railroad, the one project that would make his financial goals a reality. But the duke's withdrawal still stunned him speechless. Without Cropthorne's money, Brock's dream of this railroad would die. His fortune and credibility both would be destroyed. Damn Belwick and the vengeful Lady Dudley.

Damn Maddie!

"And know this." Cropthorne leaned over his desk with a warning and a glare. "It is only my concern for Madeline's reputation that keeps me from truly exposing you for the blackguard you are to the other investors. But I expect you to go quietly and never see my cousin again."

Maddie gasped. "Gavin, no."

Brock wondered why Maddie would bother to protest their separation. Or had she seen all along how lovesick he had been and enjoyed the power she had over him? Did she assume that, with a flash of her gray eyes and an intimate whisper, he would fall to his knees for her?

Fat bloody chance. And she need never know how much like torture it would be to refrain from touching her for the rest of their lives.

"With pleasure," he mocked, saluting Cropthorne.

He couldn't bring himself to look at Maddie, to know that the woman he loved—had never stopped loving in five hellish years—had betrayed him so deeply, so cruelly. And because she thought him too lowly to be worthy of sharing their child.

As Brock left, he closed his eyes against the rush of rage, of pain, he feared would never leave him.

The following morning dawned crisp and overcast. People traveled the streets in their Sunday finest as they made their way to worship services.

Maddie skipped church. She'd likely need prayer after talking to Brock.

He would marry her once she told him the news; there was no question of that. Her predicament meant he could legally build his precious railroad. But what sort of marriage would they have?

Last night, he had branded her with an accusing glare, as if he'd been terribly wronged. While she had not told him about Aimee and perhaps should have, Brock was not without fault. Last night, she had been too exhausted, too shocked and afraid to defend herself from that cold stare. Worse, she actually feared losing his recent tenderness and affection.

Lord, she was an idiot.

Today, she remembered the error had been his. Today, she felt more than ready to face Mr. Taylor.

When the hackney stopped before Brock's town house, Maddie lowered the concealing veil on her mourning hat and paid the driver as she exited the vehicle. With a gray-toothed smile, he promised to await her return.

Maddie doubted her conversation with Brock would be long.

After a perfunctory knock, Brock's butler, a stoic, brooding sort of man with bushy black brows, answered the door, revealing a lavish foyer of dark woods and fine china accents. Of course Brock would live well. He'd sacrificed everything—including her—for the privilege.

The butler took her name and quickly returned. Within moments, he escorted her to a plush study, where Brock sat behind a massive cherry-wood desk, fingers steepled in front of him, his expression nothing less than adversarial.

As Maddie entered the room, she lifted her veil. Their gazes clashed.

His eyes still held blazing censure. Maddie straightened her spine against his expression, hoping hers held an equal measure of the contempt she felt for him.

"Why are you here?" he demanded.

That he did not want to see her was obvious. Anger shimmering beneath a cool exterior, Maddie sent him a frosty glare. Who cared what he wanted? Certainly, not her.

"I've come to accept your proposal of marriage."

"Have you?" Brock laughed bitterly, wearing a superior gaze that made her teeth gnash. "Is that how you mean to atone for keeping Aimee a secret?"

Atone, indeed. The man was demented. For once, Maddie was glad she had the news to rattle him.

"I am with child."

The smirk slid off his face as his mouth dropped open. Dark brows slashed down as he stood, shoulders tense, gaze unwavering. "You're pregnant?"

Generally, Brock wasn't obtuse. Why should she have to repeat herself now? "I believe I just mentioned that, yes."

With that remark, he scowled at her. Maddie surmised he didn't like her flippant tone. Too bad for him.

"You are certain?"

"I can think of no other ailment that would cause me to miss my menses and send my stomach into general turmoil."

Brock banged his fist on his desk. With a curse, he raised his gaze to the ceiling and shook his head. Finally, he drilled his irate gaze to her again. "So you decided to tell me this time, rather than wait until a few weeks before the child's fifth birthday? That's an improvement, I suppose."

Did he imagine *he* had been wronged here? He, who had promised her marriage, took her innocence, and her father's money, before disappearing for five years? He, who had reentered her life with a brash attitude and a threat? Perhaps she should have told him sooner, but what had he truly done to *deserve* to be Aimee's father?

The anger Maddie had collected into an icy pool of reserve before coming melted. Despite her wishes, she felt her temper heat, then boil over.

"You can bloody well go tup yourself!" she shouted and whirled to leave.

Brock surged to his feet and caught her arm before turning her to face him again. His green eyes spit fire. "Too late for that. Clearly, we are having this conversation because it was you I tupped instead."

How kind of him to remind her.

Feeling his words like a verbal slap, Maddie clenched her teeth to keep in a scream. The crude, insensitive cad. Given his response to the news of her pregnancy, it hardly signified that she hadn't known how to reach Brock in London five years ago. It appeared he would not have cared that she'd been with child.

Gathering her reserve around her once more, she spat, "Are we to be married, yes or no?"

He hesitated, glaring, reluctant. "Yes."

Maddie resisted the keen desire to rant and rail at Brock—barely. How could he blame her for their current state when he had left her pregnant five years ago? And to ask him that now would only be admitting she had needed him, had cared.

Instead, she gave him a crisp nod. "Can you procure a special license by Wednesday or Thursday?"

A muscle worked in his jaw. "I will have it, and a minister, here by Tuesday morning."

"Shall I be here at ten o'clock, then?"

"Yes, and bring Aimee," he barked.

His tone chafed her, but Maddie merely shrugged. "Until then."

As she poised to make her exit once more, Brock again grasped her arm and pulled her back to him, this time closer, so close, she felt the angry heat pulsing off him in waves.

"Now that our marital matter is settled, you can explain why the hell you kept Aimee a secret from me. I deserved to know!"

"Did you?" She jerked her arm free of his hold. "What makes you so deserving? You did nothing more than impregnate me before abandoning me. You accepted money from my father to leave me minutes after you took my innocence. Then you came back into my life, only to threaten me and *your* daughter with the Fleet. Do you really imagine I want such a father for Aimee?"

He cursed. "My, how righteous you are, Lady Wolcott," he sneered. "Did you ever consider that Aimee is my flesh and blood and that I should have known of her existence? No, you deigned to tell me nothing of her. Had you planned on ever telling me, I wonder?" he challenged her. "If Belwick and Lady Dudley hadn't spilled your secret, I'll wager you would have married me for the sake of the coming child and taken the truth to your grave." He leaned in, aggressive, furious, his voice rising. "You might have mentioned Aimee's parentage to me recently, you know, say at the Paddington cottage. Somewhere between 'good evening' and the moments I had my cock buried deep inside you—any of those moments—would have sufficed."

Maddie refused to give him the satisfaction of flinching or flushing at his crudity. "And tell you so that you could use your money to take Aimee from me? So you could use her to force me to the altar sooner?" She shook her head. "Believe me, if I hadn't foolishly believed Colin's midwife when she swore I would bear no more children, I would not be marrying you now. I would not have let your cock within five feet of me." She leaned toward him, too furious to care that they were nearly chin to chin. "You did not deserve to know about Aimee. You don't deserve a bloody thing from me."

SEVENTEEN

At one o'clock on Monday afternoon, Brock made his way to Cropthorne's town house. It was imposing, formal, stately. It matched the man.

While he did not imagine Cropthorne would approve of the fact he had taken Maddie's innocence five years ago, Brock had never imagined the duke would so thoroughly denounce him. Clearly, the reserve Cropthorne exhibited went deep to his traditional core.

Perhaps the duke would be pacified by the fact he and Maddie would be married tomorrow. But Brock did not feel assured of that by any means. Hell, his own father, who had known his past with Maddie, had been completely stunned by the news of Aimee's parentage.

Taking a deep breath, he knocked on the solid door and gave his name to the butler. Cropthorne likely wouldn't see him. Still, Brock knew he must try. Though he might be able to acquire adequate funding to begin the T & S without the man, it seemed unlikely. People would ask questions about the duke's sudden departure from the project. Besides, Cropthorne was one of the last bits of family Maddie had left; she would want him at the wedding.

Any reconciliation he could affect would benefit everyone.

If Cropthorne would receive him.

To Brock's surprise, the butler returned, stoic as ever, and led him directly to the duke's study.

By the far window Cropthorne stood, sunlight at his back. The disapproving scowl he had worn Saturday night had not left his face. Brock braced himself to take the blame for Maddie's fall from innocence in the barn years ago. He deserved it, really. He'd been twenty-one, Maddie a mere eighteen. But the day Aimee had been conceived, he had only thought to seal the special bond he'd believed he and Maddie shared. Yes, he'd understood the possibilities. He simply had not believed they would come to fruition.

He was furious with Maddie for all the years he had lost with Aimee, for choosing Sedgewick over him.

Brock sighed as Cropthorne glared at him across the room. "Your grace."

"I should have refused to see you," Cropthorne said. "I will not tolerate any hint of scandal. If the truth makes its way to the *ton,* you'll both be ruined. And Aimee will be forever tainted."

"I want to avoid that at all costs." Brock pulled on the lapels of his coat and straightened his shoulders. "Maddie and I will marry tomorrow morning at ten o'clock. I think it would please her, as well as lend credence, if you attended."

Cropthorne hesitated, mulling over his options. "It will be a quiet wedding?"

Though the duke's reply came as a question, Brock understood he meant it as a command. He agreed his marriage to Maddie would raise less notice if they wed with few witnesses and an even smaller party. Perhaps only a handful of people would make note of the event. Doubtful, but he could hope. . . .

"Only her aunt, Mrs. Bickham's companion, and my father will attend."

"I will be there," Cropthorne said finally. "You understand I'm hardly eager to welcome you into the family. I do not regard you as trustworthy, Mr. Taylor."

How should he answer that? He hated like hell having to explain himself to "his betters," to always justify his actions, his very existence. But the railroad was too important. Any chance—no matter how remote—of Cropthorne returning as his partner was too valuable to lose because of anger and pride.

"I did not intend to ruin Maddie before her come-out."

Cropthorne raised a black brow in contempt. "You were older, ostensibly wiser."

Brock gave a nod of concession. "But I had never been in love."

"Do you imagine that will excuse your behavior?"

From the duke's tone, Brock knew it would not.

"Have you ever been in love, your grace?"

"Thankfully, no. If it impairs one's judgment, as you imply, I hope never to find myself in such a wretched state."

Despite the gravity of the situation, Brock had to suppress a smile. "Love will drive a man to reckless acts, all in the name of claiming his lady."

Brock knew his words sounded terribly romantical . . . but they were true.

Cropthorne's black brows slashed down in a scowl. "Marrying her, even eloping, would have been a far more proper way to go about that."

Brock paced. How much should he say? How much of his soul should he have to bare to a man he did not know well?

How badly did he want the wealth and prestige that would be his if the railroad was completed and successful?

Far, far too badly to remain silent.

"I wanted to marry her but had nothing to offer her. No money, no land, no home. Hell, I worked for her father."

"If you had nothing, you should have done the honorable thing and walked away, man! Why take her innocence—"

"It wasn't as if I bloody planned it!" Brock pinched the bridge of his nose and sighed. "I went to say good-bye, to assure her that I would make enough money in London to return for her soon so we could marry, even if her father disapproved. She held me so tight, I could not let go."

"A man of integrity would have let go long before he breeched her maidenhead."

Cropthorne's insult tore through the charged air, hitting Brock square in the chest. Still, he had never really regretted the fact he'd made love to Maddie in the barn on that sunny day.

At least not until he'd learned he'd lost more than four years of sharing his daughter's life.

"Perhaps," Brock conceded. "I can only say, to that moment, Maddie was the best part of my life. I knew I could not take her with me to London to live in poverty, yet I did not want to be parted from her, particularly knowing her father sought to marry her off to some blue-blooded sop she would likely despise. Maddie was . . . sweet and earnest, her heart so pure."

Or so he'd thought. Last night, after Belwick's announcement, he'd wondered if he'd ever known Maddie at all. Perhaps the girl he'd fallen in love with had been a myth, like fairies and sprites, elusive like the mist. That girl would *never* have kept such a secret from him or implied he did not deserve his own daughter.

It was his misfortune that girl had disappeared, and tomorrow, Brock would wed the deceitful, complex, seductive woman who had replaced her.

"So you took her?" Disapproval still ruled Cropthorne's visage.

Actually, Maddie had offered, but the semantics hardly mattered now. "Yes."

The disapproving line of Cropthorne's mouth cracked into a small smile. "You don't lack temerity, do you?"

"My brashness earned me a way out of the slums. My

audacity allowed me to make a fortune and look titled men in the eye. I understand you dislike the thought of your young cousin being ruined by her stable hand—"

Cropthorne waved his words away. "You're past your serving days now. To me, that is no longer of primary interest. The sooner you cease resenting your past, the sooner everyone will forget it."

Spoken like someone who had always known superiority and wore it like a fine coat, Brock thought cynically.

The duke went on. "Financially, you will be able to care for Maddie better than she can care for herself, I daresay. It is your lack of restraint and morals that give me pause. Men of power should possess self-control, Mr. Taylor."

Clearly impulse did not rule Cropthorne's life—ever. Brock doubted his grace would understand the urgency that had driven him that rainy afternoon to have Maddie beneath him, to claim her in the most elemental way as a silent declaration of his intention to have her forever—physically, emotionally, legally. Trying to make Cropthorne understand was, no doubt, a waste of breath and time.

Brock smiled bitterly. "I only seem to lack restraint and morals where Maddie is concerned. The woman drives me to distraction. But if you prefer to believe that I am false in my business dealings, I doubt I can change your mind."

Cropthorne hesitated. "For some months, you failed to inform me that you were the one wooing Maddie for that necessary piece of Warwickshire land."

Nodding in concession, Brock regarded Cropthorne with a grim gaze. "It seemed foolish to discuss marrying Maddie when the matter was not yet settled. You may allow I've been most persistent in bringing Maddie to the altar."

"Quite," drawled Cropthorne.

The man sounded almost . . . amused. Brock smiled. "Indeed. I confess to keeping silent because I had no notion how you would receive the idea of a former servant marrying your cousin."

Cropthorne shrugged. "The very first duke of Cropthorne received his title from Charles the Second for saving the king's mistress from drowning in the Thames. My illustrious ancestor tended gardens for his wage. I hardly have room to cast aspersions on your birth."

A wry smile broke across Brock's face. Cropthorne had always had a way of making them feel equal. He appreciated that most particularly today. He also hoped it would work in his favor now.

"Granted, the notion of you marrying an earl's daughter will raise some brows, but I care far more about the measure of a man than the lines of his blood." Cropthorne paused, crossing his arms over his wide chest. "Why do you think I should trust you?"

Brock paced closer, quickly gathering his words. Cropthorne had given him a chance—likely his only chance—to redeem himself. He'd best use it wisely.

"I must work harder, be more honest than someone like Belwick, to succeed because of my birth. While you may not put a great deal of stock in my pedigree, most do."

Cropthorne nodded, conceding the point.

"All I have is my reputation as a man of business. I cannot call upon wealthy friends of my father who've known me since I wore swaddling clothes. No idle lords at my club will listen to me over cards and brandy; none of the clubs will have me. I've made a fortune by being the best and most reliable investment broker. Anything I withheld from you regarded my relationship with your cousin, which I hope you will allow is personal. I never lied about the railroad itself."

The duke raised a brow, clearly unmoved.

Brock sighed, his frustration swelling like a well after a hard rain. What else could he say to the man? Most likely nothing. Still, he must try. . . .

"In the end, you can trust me to do whatever necessary to keep any scandal about Maddie and me quiet while making you a fortune on the railroad—if you choose to return to the project."

Cropthorne gave no comment, only a long stare, before he turned away, presenting his back. It was all Brock could do to hold in a curse.

"I make it a point to do business only with men of ethics, Mr. Taylor. But I also make it a point to avoid scandal in my family—at all costs."

So where did that leave him? Cropthorne paused, paced. The man had to know the tension was killing Brock.

"I will, therefore, return my backing to the railroad, as withdrawing would likely cause people to ask questions that would drag my cousin's name—and my own—into a scandal. If it weren't for that, I hope you understand I would never speak to you again. Now you may go."

By Tuesday morning at ten-fifteen, Brock stood beside Maddie, sliding a heavy gold band on her finger. The minister pronounced them man and wife. Other than speaking her vows, his new wife had yet to say a single word to him.

The fury, fear, and defiance tangled on her face told him today—and the next forty years—were likely to be long and unhappy. The thought depressed him.

At Maddie's left, Cropthorne stood stiffly, his face without expression. By his side stood Lady Litchfield, assessing everything with cool blue eyes. Brock understood well why Cropthorne had brought her. The duke might not approve of him as Maddie's husband, but he would give the appearance of approval for his cousin's sake. Brock was thankful for that.

At the back of the room, his father bounced Aimee on his knee. Mrs. Bickham cast them both a doting look. They wore the only smiles in the room.

Finally, he had everything he wanted—Maddie as his

wife, the *ton*'s most revered hostess to lend credence to his marriage, enough money to see the railroad—his dream—completed, a glittering fortune on the horizon, even a beautiful daughter as a bonus.

Why, then, was he so damned miserable?

The minister closed his book, then gave them an expectant look. "Well, don't you mean to kiss her?"

For the first time today, Brock turned his stare to Maddie. She'd bought a new gown at his behest, a muted blue dress of quiet flounces that displayed the elegant slope of her shoulders. Her lush auburn hair had been swept atop her head, leaving only a few curls to frame her face and brush the soft skin at her neck. A wreath of orange blossoms lay atop her hair.

Her eyes, though . . . He could find nothing soft in them. Against her pale skin, the gray orbs seemed to swirl and darken like storm clouds. He read the anger and trepidation her stance displayed. She glared at him, as if she thought him beneath her.

Anger surged like a geyser, close to spewing to the surface. Maddie thought him beneath her, did she? She had concealed the fact that Aimee was his daughter for years! He had held the woman for months, admitted he loved her even, like some pining swain. And still, she had not seen fit to gift him with the truth.

At the moment, she seemed like the unworthy one to him.

Aware that every eye in the room watched him, Brock leaned over, palmed Maddie's nape, and took possession of her mouth in a quick, fierce kiss designed to intimidate.

When he leaned away, he was gratified to see her face transformed by wariness—and awareness. She knew he was angry. She also knew he intended that they would consummate this marriage today. No one would question his right to her land.

Into the tense moment, the minister congratulated them and urged them to sign the register. Once done, Mrs. Bickham rushed to their side with a hug for each of them. Vema bowed her head thoughtfully, her yellow sari flowing about her with grace.

"You will scare Maddie if you don't stop scowling, my boy," Aunt Edith whispered.

He mocked a smile for Maddie's aunt, but at the moment, he was too furious to care about his wife's delicate sensibilities. Let her be afraid. She deserved worse.

Aimee scampered to his side and held up her arms. Brock lifted her against him and held the girl tight. Soon she would know the truth; Maddie had agreed they would tell her together before the month was out. As soon as the girl had settled into her new life in London with a man in the midst, she would know. Despite the turmoil and the lies, he was thankful for Aimee.

The little girl wrapped her arms about Brock's neck and placed a dainty kiss on his cheek. The fury holding his heart receded for the moment as he held tight to his daughter.

"Mr. Jack says I can call him grandpapa," Aimee offered.

"Of course." Brock smiled at the girl's simple happiness in the occasion. Clearly, she felt none of the tension in the room, only noted that her family had expanded.

How he wished he could view the matter as simply.

"Should I call you papa?"

Brock sucked in a breath. Could Aimee's acceptance be that easy? Perhaps. Children tended to be resilient and accepting.

Before he could reply, Brock spotted Maddie and her warning stare. Now was not the time for the truth, he agreed. But Brock wanted to disregard Maddie's wishes. Certainly she had never thought of his when she had failed to tell him the truth about Aimee. But as of today, Aimee's whole life would change through no doing of her own. Brock wanted her wishes met. Maddie would have to overcome her own fears.

"Would that please you?" Brock asked the child.

"Yes!" Aimee squealed, oblivious to her mother's anxiety.

The girl gave him a quick hug, then shimmied down from his grasp, over to her mother. Maddie picked Aimee up and held the little girl against her chest, her palm splayed protectively over her little golden head.

"If you upset her or abandon her," Maddie whispered, "I will tell everyone subscribed in this railroad every objectionable facet I know about your character. I will tell the *ton* the manner in which you coerced me."

Brock reared back, appalled. But Maddie's face was all seriousness. She meant what she said.

"Upset her? Abandon her?" he drilled at her in low-voiced disbelief. "Why would I? I've just found her."

Her gray eyes flashed in warning. "Remember what I said."

Maddie turned away, and he glared at her back, uncomprehending. She must think him low and callous indeed to want to upset the child. And abandon her? That would mean abandoning Maddie. Not bloody likely after chasing the woman for years. Not after discovering he had a daughter. A bomb could not pry him loose from them now.

"Mr. Taylor?"

Brock turned to find Lady Litchfield wearing a cool smile and offering her hand. Automatically, he took her gloved fingers and bowed over them. "My lady."

The woman's smile widened, and Brock knew she enjoyed her social power over him. Normally, people like Lady Litchfield grated on him. Today, he found her a mere irritation.

"Felicitations on your marriage." She paused, gathering the strings of her reticule about her wrist. "It's a good match, for she is beautiful and you are rich."

Brock began to believe it was a terrible match. Maddie was deceitful, and he was determined to succeed in spite of her. But he merely nodded. "Thank you."

"In two weeks, I will have my annual ball. You and Lady Madeline will be there, I hope."

An invitation to the widow's ball was the most coveted one of the season. And marriage to someone of Maddie's ilk had opened that door, for Brock knew well that the invitation would not have come his way without her at his side.

He wanted this—had wanted this sort of acceptance for years. Again, the fruition of his hard work tasted worse than the most bitter brine. But he could not afford to refuse her.

"Naturally, my lady. We would be honored."

She pulled something from her reticule and handed it to Brock. To his astonishment, it was a bank draft for ten thousand pounds. "My lady?"

"Gavin may be put off with you, but consider me one of your subscribers."

How much did the lady know of his row with Cropthorne?

He pocketed the draft. "Thank you."

"A little more fortune would be most welcome, Mr. Taylor. And unlike Gavin, I enjoy a little scandal every now and then."

With that cryptic smile, she turned away. A moment later, she and Cropthorne left, the duke not having said a single word to him.

Brock sighed. He had more meddlesome problems to worry about now. Turning, he sought out his wife, only to find her by the window, staring out into the street.

Yes, he would have to deal with her very shortly. And he knew it would not be pretty.

At a sudden slap on his back, Brock turned to find his father, who wore a wide smile.

"You look miserable."

And Jack didn't look very distressed by that fact.

"I'm elated," Brock intoned. "Doesn't it show?"

"You're going to have to forgive Maddie, son. She made a mistake."

Brock felt his jaw drop. His own father was siding with Maddie?

"No. A mistake is misplacing your gloves. It's dribbling food down your coat in a roomful of people. It isn't neglecting to tell a man that he's become a father."

"She was young," Jack soothed. "More than likely scared witless. And after she married, she would likely have found it difficult to leave her husband to seek you out. That would not have pleased Sedgewick."

"Perhaps not," Brock snapped. "But better his temporary displeasure than completely withholding the truth from me."

Jack shrugged, clearly unwilling to debate the point further. Instead, he patted Brock on the shoulder and cast his gaze across the room to Aimee as she tugged on Maddie's skirts.

"Too bad I didn't see the child sooner," Jack said. "I could have told you immediately that she was your daughter."

Brock turned in surprise to his father. "How?"

Something wistful overtook Jack's lined face. He gazed into the distance, as if seeing the past, rather than the present. "She looks so much like your mother. Same hair, same face, same sunny disposition. Your mother, rest her soul, would have been so thrilled to see you blessed with Aimee. Enjoy her."

Stunned, Brock stared at his daughter. He had never seen a likeness of his mother; his father had been too poor to afford such a thing. Looking at Aimee gave him some idea how wonderful his mother must have been.

It also made him all the more angry that Maddie had deprived him of the girl.

"I intend to enjoy Aimee," he vowed to his father.

"Start by making peace with her mother," Jack offered sagely.

Why did everyone behave as if this breach between them was his fault? "Not bloody likely."

Jack shrugged, his face clearly stating that Brock was making a mistake. Then he retreated and made his way to Aimee again.

Within minutes, the family settled in for a celebration breakfast. Brock had never seen more somber merriment in his life. But he felt little like rejoicing, despite the fact he should. He had everything he wanted.

Except that his faith in Maddie had been shattered.

Merely looking at her hurt. Somewhere in his chest, he ached. Like a fool, he still wanted her, naked, writhing, moaning, taking him deep inside her. No, he wanted more than that. He wanted . . . that fleeting bond he had felt with her to last forever. But she disdained him, and he distrusted her.

Brock stared absently at the fruit and eggs on his plate. What the hell could he do? Everything inside him was a tangle. In some dim corner of his mind, however, he realized he still loved Maddie.

While that made him a stupid sap, he doubted he could forgive her.

Breakfast ended mercifully soon. Mrs. Bickham and Vema kissed Maddie and Aimee, then set off for Hampstead once more. Jack and Aimee disappeared to the new rooms Brock had prepared for the girl, hopefully to play with the mountain of toys he had bought.

That left he and Maddie alone.

She fiddled with the ribbon that had tied her bridal flowers, wrapping and unwrapping the satin length about her finger. He straightened his blue frock coat.

Abruptly, she stood. "I should like to unpack my belongings."

"I imagine the servants have already done so."

Maddie shrugged. "I'm sure you'll agree it's been a trying morning. I think I shall rest."

"Why are you avoiding me?"

She shot him an incredulous stare. "What can we possibly have to say to each other? You've acquired the land you need to finish the railroad. You have Aimee and I under your roof. No doubt, you're feeling smug in the knowledge that your bullying and conniving won you everything you wished. I would rather not be witness to your glee."

With that, she made her way out the door and started toward the stairs. Brock watched her go, his anger rising. Bullying and conniving? He had made her a wager. She had agreed to it, by God. Later, she had come to him wanting marriage for the baby that would come. Why did she blame him?

You didn't deserve to know about Aimee. You don't deserve a bloody thing from me. Brock heard those words in his head over and over.

Brock rose and stalked after her. "We aren't finished yet, my dear wife."

Maddie, standing two stairs above him, turned to him with contempt in her eyes. "We've done our duty to one another for the day. We can have nothing left to say."

"It is our wedding day," he said silkily.

"Yes, and you have already enjoyed all the benefits our marriage bed will afford."

With a frosty glare, Maddie turned and began climbing the stairs again. He stared at her retreating back, her hips swinging, his fury mounting. Hadn't she enjoyed the nights they had spent locked in one another's arms? Did she mean to imply that only he had found pleasure?

Brock darted after her, taking the stairs two at a time. He reached her at the top of the landing and grasped her arm.

When he spun her around, her gray eyes sizzled enough to spit fire. She jerked from his grip. "Leave me be."

"What are you bloody angry about?" he demanded. "It isn't as if I hid anything from you for nearly five years."

Maddie clenched her fists at her sides. "No, you've merely ruined the rest of my life."

"By marrying you?"

"By forcing your way back into my life. You made yourself clear when you left me for London that wealth, not a wife, was your priority. Oh, but when you realized I held that land you needed, suddenly I was important again. And no matter how I refused you, you turned my life—and Aimee's—upside down. You cornered me until I agreed to your ridiculous wager. Even then you weren't satisfied until you had reduced my pride and made me your mewling wanton. I have yielded to you time and again, and I am done with it."

Once more, Maddie turned her back on him. Brock found himself stomping after her.

How could she understand so little? She had always been important, even when he'd fooled himself into believing their wager was about the land. Even then he had known he wanted her again. Nothing had changed.

When Maddie entered the room that adjoined his, he barreled his way in behind her and shut the door, locking the world out.

"We have a marriage to consummate."

"So you want a willing wife because the law commands it? Regardless of my wishes," she said sharply.

"It is my right."

She laughed bitterly. "You're not so unlike Colin after all."

Brock stared at her, his eyes widening with fury. She had delivered him the ultimate insult, as far as he was concerned. Her contempt for him could not have been more plain.

"Damn you! I would never raise a hand to you, no matter what. And I adored Aimee even when I believed her to be Sedgewick's daughter. And the other difference? I know I can make you melt, but I won't force you to share a marriage bed."

Hell, after her slur, he wouldn't even take her if she begged him.

Brock cast a glare at Maddie in the wake of her surprise before he turned to the door connecting their rooms and slammed it shut between them.

EIGHTEEN

A week passed in silence. Other than Aimee's happy laughter, the town house was quieter than a gravesite after a funeral. The icy civility between he and Maddie disturbed Brock. By comparison, his office seemed relaxing.

Since the wedding, he'd spent each day, as well as half the night, there. Now that the railroad was in production, he had dozens of details to oversee. Additionally, since the announcement of his marriage in the *Times* Friday last, he had received new calls from titled clients, inquiring about his financial services. Every memory of childhood hunger and cold drove Brock to cultivate them all. He nearly had more appointments than he could keep.

He didn't spend eighteen hours a day at his office to avoid Maddie. No; his every professional dreams lay within his grasp, and he had every intent to fulfill each one.

Brock pushed away the dissatisfaction that pressed in on him and searched for the triumph he had expected. So far, he'd had no luck finding it.

"You've arrived early," his father said, strolling into Brock's office with a cup of tea. "Again."

"I'm busy."

"You removed the majority of the papers off my desk and saw to those matters yourself. For some purpose?"

Leave it to Jack to be perceptive when Brock least needed it. "I thought you might require my help."

Jack snorted. "You thought you might avoid your wife."

His father took pride in being right, the bloody wretch. What else could he do? Brock wondered. Maddie had thought his birth low enough to shun marriage, to refuse to tell him of his child for nearly five years. Now she thought his character as low as a wife beater's. Why should he stay to hear more of her insults?

Why did her contempt hurt so bloody much?

He'd wanted so much from this marriage, beyond his business aspirations. A caring mother for his children, to start. Maddie would care for children—it was in her nature. But she would not care for him. Never him. Always he would be beneath her, the servant of common blood. Brock cursed silently.

Foolishly, he'd wanted a confidante and lover in a wife as well. Instead, Maddie had become his coldly silent enemy, rarely deigning to speak to him in the days since their marriage. In fact, she did her utmost to evade him.

Looking at Jack's pitying expression, Brock nearly choked on the ashes of what might have been . . . if Maddie had loved him half as much as he foolishly loved her.

Brock stood and tossed a stack of papers on his desk with a slap. "If I did, she's my wife to avoid."

Jack scratched his chin, wearing a thoughtful frown. Brock held in a sigh. Fatherly wisdom would follow, along with advice he did not want.

"You've loved this woman for years and she's finally yours. Why behave as if you hate her?"

"I don't hate her. Does that please you?"

His father said nothing, merely sent him an annoyed glance.

Brock understood his sentiment. "Must we talk about this now?"

"Apparently. You're behaving like an ass. Aimee asked after you this morning."

Regret sliced through Brock. He'd seen his daughter every morning but this one. Today, however, he simply hadn't wanted to deal with Maddie. Guilt came next. Whatever stood between he and Maddie, he never wanted Aimee to worry or suffer.

"I'll make a point to leave the office early today to see her."

"Aimee would like that. She is a rambunctious girl, and I fear she's worn out this old man."

Despite the graying at Jack's temples, Brock knew better. He speared his father with a dubious glance. "If anything, you've tired her with all the attention."

"At my age, grandchildren mean everything," Jack defended himself.

"Well, come January you'll have another to keep you occupied." Brock picked up a new stack of papers and rifled through them, hoping his father would take the hint and leave.

Naturally, he did no such thing.

"You don't sound very pleased by the prospect of another child."

Brock raised his gaze back to his sire, resigned to the fact Jack wasn't going to leave—or stop talking—until he was good and ready. "At least Maddie told me this time before the child was half grown."

"Ah, so that's the reason for your anger."

Jack hadn't been able to guess? As if keeping a child a secret for nearly five years wasn't reason enough to be furious? As if such proof that she thought him too baseborn for her didn't enrage him?

"Bloody right!" Brock shot back. "She deceived me for months. Hell, years."

"Have you considered this matter from her point of view?"

Brock tossed the papers aside. "What other point of view can there be? Maddie did not tell me of Aimee when the girl was conceived. She had no intention of telling me until recently. Truly, she had more than enough opportunity."

His father frowned at him as if he'd taken complete leave of his senses. "She had no reason to believe you wanted to know of Aimee. Five years ago, you left her mere minutes after ruining her."

There was that accusation again, even from his own father. Brock had had good intentions, honorable ones, but had made the mistake of letting his love eradicate his good sense for a few bittersweet minutes. "Damn it, I intended to come back as soon as I could support her. You knew that."

"Yes," he conceded. "But did she?"

Brock gaped at his father. Did Jack imagine that, as wildly in love with Maddie as Brock had been, he'd intended to let her go? "I told Maddie repeatedly that night I would return as soon as may be."

With a shrug, Jack conceded that point—before he jumped in with another. "How long did you work before you felt you had adequate means to take a wife like Maddie?"

It hadn't taken long, Brock remembered, mulling the past. Shortly after arriving in London five years ago, he'd worked hard for weeks, finding odd jobs at first, before Mr. Jordan at C. Hoare and Company, bank of the elite, had believed in Brock's instinct and hired him. Mr. Jordan had tutored him endlessly for months. Brock had truly mourned when the old man had died. But before that, he'd made enough money to support himself and Maddie. He'd enjoyed phenomenal success by any standard.

"It took me eight months to carve out the first of my fortune, but Maddie simply could not wait." Brock pounded his fist on his desk, everything in his gut churning, chugging faster than a steam engine. "It *infuriates* me to know she wed that blackguard Sedgewick because I wasn't well-born enough for her. I live with that fact every damn day, and it eats at me."

Jack scowled with disapproval. "Son, you have more pity for yourself than for Maddie."

Brock leapt to his feet. "I never deceived her! I did not break her heart or crush her every illusion. She reserved that special pleasure for me." He hissed a ripe curse. "I could have seen to her care in a mere eight months. You can bet she would have waited had I been a titled man."

"Waited while pregnant?"

At that, Brock froze. Pregnant? Yes, Maddie *had* been pregnant while he'd been away in London. He knew that now, but . . . His thoughts spun, tumbled over one another, careened through his racing mind.

"Why did she not contact me? I would have returned—" Brock pressed his fingers into his suddenly throbbing forehead. "Hell, I would have raced back with a single word from her." He sighed. "I would have loved her every day, worked to build her a future she could have been proud of."

"All Maddie knew was that you left her unwed and pregnant without a single word of your whereabouts or when you might return," Jack pointed out. "Her father told her you had accepted money to leave her forever. What was she to think?"

"I—I . . ." Had Maddie truly believed he had simply turned his back on her after taking her innocence? "I loved her. I never meant to hurt her, but she married that bloody sap Sedgewick—"

"She took a man she did not love as a husband so your daughter would not be branded a bastard." Jack slanted a mocking stare to Brock. "Don't imagine she devised that perfect scheme to hurt you simply because she believed you beneath her."

Brock froze. Was Jack right? Had he, confined in a strait-jacket of his own rage, grossly overlooked what Maddie had endured all those years ago?

"Use that thick skull of yours and tell me what you would have done differently in your wife's place?" his father challenged.

In her place, alone, unwed, and pregnant? Maddie would have been forced to take action while he'd been toiling in London, and during the last of those eight months, her pregnancy would have been far too obvious to conceal. Far too obvious to avoid marriage . . . to someone.

Stunned by the thought, Brock exhaled raggedly.

But why not marriage to him? Why hadn't she dispatched a note to London? That was the obvious question, of course.

But where would she have sent such a note? a pesky voice in his head asked. He hadn't written to Maddie of his lodgings when he had first reached London. He'd had a well-born lady awaiting him to return and sweep her off her feet with a fortune in his pocket. Given that, he could hardly confess to Maddie that he was renting a room in St. Giles above a gin house. His pride hadn't allowed it.

He had been both arrogant and afraid, determined to be better than his serving-class birth. Had he lost years with Maddie because of it? Had she truly believed he had trifled with her, then abandoned her? Apparently, yes. The thought hurt like a dull, rusty knife slicing through his gut. Dear God, had he blamed her for their parting when the deed had been his own doing?

Brock exhaled. Paced. His heart thudded, twisting his stomach with every beat. True, he had labored in London for his fortune. After Maddie had married Sedgewick, Brock had refined his every social skill. He had eventually purchased a town house worthy of an earl's daughter. He had nursed a broken, bitter heart, blaming her—all with the vague idea of someday extracting his pound of flesh.

All that time, Maddie had been shamed and mistreated—while believing herself abandoned by the very man who had taken her innocence and professed to love her. And his first contact with her after five years apart? He had bullied and threatened her, after treating her to his anger and contempt.

What the hell had he done?

He felt low and unworthy, and for once, not because of his birth. Cropthorne was right; character made the man. And Brock feared he hadn't measured up.

Desolation spread before him, dark and deep like a chasm. Now that he understood the truth, how could he ever begin to apologize? Why would Maddie ever forgive him?

"You haven't said as much," Jack cut into his thoughts, "but I assume Maddie endured a dreadful marriage. Why else would she be so against the institution?"

Colin Sedgewick had struck Maddie—after using his words to assault her for years. She'd had a difficult time in her first marriage. Brock wished he could have saved her from Sedgewick's brutalization. He wished that like hell. The blame for her misfortune lay squarely at his feet. He'd been bloody blind.

He had no idea how—or even if—he could atone.

"Maddie did not wish to marry again."

"So you forced the issue."

Again, Jack's words were direct and unerring. They made Brock's heart sink.

He had hoped Maddie would conceive so that she would have no choice but to surrender her freedom—her very future—to him. He had kept her in his bed until the deed was done, without ever wondering how she felt. An icy wave of nausea curled his stomach, and he closed his eyes against the ugly truth.

"Yes," Brock murmured. "I am an idiot."

An idiot with no notion how to right his error.

How could he atone for something so terrible? He couldn't, he feared. Did he have the means to please her in any way? What did *she* want?

Brock tore through his memories until he found an answer that chilled him.

The only wish Maddie had ever expressed was to be left in peace. Brock swallowed. Giving Maddie up—again— would be the most difficult thing he had ever done. But he should not interfere in Maddie's life anymore. Instead, he should become her husband in name only, give her the funds to renovate her Hampstead country house and live quietly with no more worries of creditors screaming for payments or cads scheming a seduction. Hopefully, he could persuade her to allow him to visit Aimee and the coming babe. Perhaps she would even speak to him again someday.

But perhaps not.

Jack nodded, quiet for once. But his sudden discretion came too late. He had opened the Pandora's box of the past, and inside Brock had found denial, regret, loathing, fury.

Determined, he made for the door. "I think I know a way to make Maddie happy."

Becoming an invisible husband wasn't what Brock wanted; everything inside him screamed against the idea. But he had ignored her wishes for too long. If she could find happiness in his sacrifice, well . . . he owed her nothing less.

Jack nodded, looking uncharacteristically fatherly. "I hope you can do that."

Afternoon sun streamed through his town house when Brock arrived. It was a hot day, even for July. But he knew it wasn't the heat making him sweat; it was the thought of facing Maddie, possibly for the final time.

Brock shoved aside the stab of pain that fact provoked.

In the dark foyer he'd designed to impress one and all, his butler remained professional and silent. But the curious eyes under those dark bushy brows, questioning his master's presence here at such an early hour, was unmistakable.

"Where is my wife?" Brock asked.

Damned if he couldn't hear his heart thudding, feel his palms sweating.

"I believe she mentioned a desire for a nap after luncheon, Mr. Taylor."

Disappointment that he must wait to make Maddie happy and relief that she would remain under his roof a bit longer warred. "And Aimee?"

"Pretending to nap, I am certain."

At that, Brock had to crack a smile. According to his staff, Aimee's antics to avoid her afternoon nap had become so creative, they were nearly legendary.

Brock nodded to his butler and began climbing the red-carpeted stairs in search of his daughter. He found her quite easily on the third floor by following her shrieking laughter.

Inside the shadowed nursery, Miss Edmunds, the nanny he'd hired only last week, stood near the window, gaping outside. The white-faced woman wrung her hands.

"Miss Aimee, come inside this minute!"

"But I almost got it," she answered from somewhere. Beyond the window?

"What is going on here?" he demanded.

Miss Edmunds started and turned, jumping guiltily. "Mr. Taylor, I—I put the child down for her nap. I believed her to be asleep . . . but—help us!"

"Aimee is *outside?*"

The nanny opened her mouth. She raised her hands, but no words came forth, only sighs and grunts. Obviously, the woman didn't know what to say.

Brock took her lack of coherent response to mean yes.

The fact Aimee was outside the window scared the hell out of him. There was only a small balcony there, intended more for show than use—with a three-story drop to the ground below.

Urgency twisting in his gut, Brock charged to the window and peered out. There, his daughter leaned precariously over the railing, doing her best to reach a tree some feet away.

"Almost . . ." the child grunted, leaning to the nearest branch.

Brock's heart surged, slamming into his chest. He scarcely saw her throw one leg over the railing before she lost her balance. Aimee screamed as she teetered, but she managed to hang on by one hand and the crook of her knee. Most of her body dangled above the dangerous drop.

Brock lunged out the window and caught her by the wrist. With a curse, he wrapped an arm around her waist and lifted her into his arms. As he ducked back into the nursery, he held Aimee tight. His heart skipped when she squeezed him in return, her little breaths coming fast.

He'd known Aimee was his daughter for a mere week, but already he loved her as if he had known her forever.

And she had scared him witless. "What are you doing?"

"I wanna climb the tree."

"It's too dangerous, Aimee. You nearly fell."

"But I wanna!" she said mutinously.

"No." And he made a mental note to have the branches trimmed far back and the window locked shut.

"Please . . . Papa."

The little imp was intentionally pulling his heartstrings. And it worked. Brock didn't think he would ever tire of hearing Aimee acknowledging him, even if she didn't fully understand yet.

Still, he had to be firm. "I said no. I meant no."

Brock turned to Miss Edmunds. "Why didn't you pluck Aimee off that balcony? Why did you allow her to climb out there at all?"

To her credit, the little dark-haired woman looked shamefaced. "I tried to bring her inside, Mr. Taylor. Truly. But I am terribly afraid of heights. When I went near the ledge, I became dizzy."

Brock sighed, making a mental note to have some manner of lock put on the window at once. Miss Edmunds, who was in every other way most acceptable, could not be trusted with an open window. "Put Aimee back in bed and be certain she sleeps."

The woman looked uncommonly pale as she gave him a nervous nod. "Of course, Mr. Taylor. Right away. I will not fail."

As the nanny took Aimee's hand, Brock cast another stern glance at the girl, which he hoped looked parental. "No more climbing of trees."

Her little bowed mouth formed a scowl. "But my mama—"

"I'm certain your mother would agree," Brock said, knowing Maddie would not allow Aimee such a dangerous activity, as the child had been about to claim.

"I do agree," Maddie said from behind him.

Brock spun to find her framed in the nursery door, the afternoon sun lighting her sleek auburn hair, kissing her beautiful red mouth.

His chest felt suddenly tight.

Aimee squirmed out of the nanny's grasp and ran to her mother. Maddie bent to hug the child. Brock couldn't read her expression, but he was so ridiculously pleased to be standing in the same room with Maddie, he could hardly breathe.

The first time he'd come to love Maddie, he had learned the sentiment could twist a man's gut in two. This time, he'd learned love could melt even the fiercest heart—and bring him to his knees.

"I'd feared she would try that soon. Thank you for saving her."

"You don't have to thank me. I care for her." *She is my daughter, too.* The words hung unspoken between them.

"I know," she said softly.

Brock knew she meant the words honestly.

The yearning inside his chest expanded. He wanted to share his love with her, but he had imposed his wants on

Maddie long enough. She desired to be alone. Brock would grant her wish, even if it killed him.

Finally, after another scold from Maddie, Miss Edmunds took Aimee back to her bed.

Alone now, Brock paused, wondering how to approach Maddie about the future. He sent her a cautious stare. "I would like to talk. Are you occupied now?"

Maddie looked wary and curious at once, her gray eyes shining with wary speculation. "No. We can talk."

Brock led Maddie down the hall, to the stairs, his hand at her back all the while, warming her. She was excruciatingly aware of the fact that he was her husband and could make her want him with just the slightest kiss. She should hate him. She should! But her defiant heart simply disagreed. . . .

He took her to his study and shut the door behind them. The click of the latch seemed too loud to Maddie's frayed nerves. What did Brock want? To talk about Aimee? Their tense marriage? Did he want to touch her? Merely be with her?

Warmth flooded her at the thought.

Maddie drew in a deep breath, willing the warmth away. She was a fool for wishing he wanted her or her company, she thought as she paced to the sofa and sat. He had *blamed* her for not telling him about Aimee, when he'd been the one to break faith and abandon her. She'd married Colin and endured her father's wrath because of him. And still he blamed her.

As if he'd deserved the truth after lying to her about his love and leaving her with child.

Still, he was Aimee's father. Perhaps she should have told him. She'd had opportunity; Brock had been right in that. Fear, anger—resentment, even—had held her tongue.

Maddie lifted her chin and sent Brock a calm stare. But in her mind she kept seeing visions of him saving Aimee, holding her so tightly. As he had said, he cared for the child.

He simply did not care for *her*.

Perhaps Brock had deserved the truth, and her own anger—along with her hurt—had obscured that fact. And now, nothing could change the fact he'd learned about Aimee in the worst way possible.

Trying not to wince, Maddie said, "You wished to speak to me?"

"Yes. It's quite urgent."

She nodded. Brock had spoken four complete words to her at once. Since their wedding night, she doubted he had spoken more than a dozen. She couldn't decide if she was ridiculously pleased by this new turn of events or merely angry.

The reality of their marriage matched her expectations: Brock had merely wanted her for her land. He wanted to build that damned railroad, make yet another fortune at her expense. Why else would he ignore her so thoroughly?

And why did it hurt so much?

Brock braced his elbows on the arms of his large leather chair and steepled his hands at his chest. "I've done you a great disservice in forcing you to marry me. I see that now."

Maddie went cold at his words. "Really?"

"You asked me repeatedly to leave you be, and I ignored your wishes. I realize it's too late now to change the fact we are married. We"—he sighed—"we have the coming child to consider."

"Indeed," she murmured, trying to keep the confusion from her face. Did he want to change the fact they were wed?

"I've sent workmen to Ashdown Manor, to refurbish and repair the house. I've set up an account for you as well."

He pulled a slip of paper from his waistcoat and slid it across the table. Dread vibrating within her, Maddie picked up the thick white paper and unfolded it with numb fingers. It was confirmation of a bank deposit made today, in her name.

"Five thousand pounds?" she muttered, zinging her confused glance to him.

"To start. Once the railroad gets further underway, I will deposit more. It should see the house repaired, however. Select new furnishings. Set up a grand nursery for the new baby. Buy yourself a new wardrobe. Whatever you like."

Brock's words painted a picture Maddie neither understood completely nor appreciated. "Are you telling me you would like me to return to Hampstead?"

He sent her a smile so strained, it looked painful. "Indeed."

Shock sent Maddie reeling. She felt rooted to her chair, yet as faint as if she'd turned in too many circles.

He was leaving her alone and breeding—again. Now that he had legal possession of that unfruitful farm property of hers and could fully exploit it, he was through exploiting her.

Pain lanced her heart. Looking away, Maddie chastised herself for allowing him to hurt her, for the hot flow of pain. She should have learned by now! But when Brock had held her, she'd wanted to believe he cared . . . His caring had been nothing more than a rainbow-bright illusion her idealistic mind had painted.

Brock did not care for her at all. He never had.

This time he would abandon her without leaving her penniless. He wasn't such a complete cad as to let his children live in poverty.

But oh, how she longed to throw his money in his face, every last insulting farthing of it. But she had two elderly women and two children to consider. Her pride could have no place in this discussion.

"You're pleased, aren't you?" he asked.

Brock's confident expression had faltered. Shocking; Maddie had thought nothing could wipe that assured mien from his strong brown face. Then again, life was full of surprises, few of them pleasant.

To her horror, Maddie felt tears at the back of her eyes. She cast her gaze down to the thick burgundy and blue carpet beneath her feet to hide them.

"Of course," she said. "We'll leave come morning."

Maddie rose. Brock shot to his feet and blocked her path. "I only ask that you allow me to see the children."

Another offer Maddie longed to refuse him. But it was unfair to the children. Brock might not love her, and he might well be a master manipulator, but the children deserved the opportunity to know him for themselves. Besides, he would likely stop coming to see them when he became too busy. Then she would not have to worry about seeing him even infrequently, about the pain of having him near but untouchable. Wondering who his mistress was, how much pleasure he gave her, or if he cared for her. Then Maddie would no longer have to look into the face of the only man she had ever loved and know with every breath that he did not love her in return.

"You may see the children," she said.

"Thank you."

He looked relieved, and Maddie wondered if the expression was real, or merely another mirage created by her pining heart.

"Had you planned to live at Ashdown, or merely visit?"

Brock hesitated. Usually he was quick with a decision. Today he looked torn. "Visit, I should think. Does that please you?"

Did he think it would? Or was that what he wished to hear? "Immensely."

Frowning, Brock leaned closer. He reached out to touch her. Need crept up in Maddie, and she braced herself for the contact. Instead, Brock paused, then dropped his hand to his side.

"I will only be in your way at Ashdown. Besides, with the railroad underway, I'll need to be in my offices often to see to business matters. I've some new opportunities as well, so . . ." He shrugged.

He was discarding her in favor of business and money—again. It should not surprise her; nor should it hurt. But it did, so very, very much.

This time, she wanted him to hurt as well—every bit as much as she did.

"Ah, yes. Your precious fortune," Maddie spat in anger. "You do realize that money will never buy you respect, I hope. You will always be a servant to everyone who matters."

Maddie waited just long enough to see the shock trip across the hard-edged lines of Brock's face before she lifted her skirts, brushed past him, and quit the room.

With the slam of his study door, she left his life. Running up the stairs to her room, she leaned against the door, put her head in her hands, and began to cry.

NINETEEN

Dark fell on Finch Street in Whitechapel, enveloping the eternal midnight of grueling poverty. Brock stood at the edge of the road, looking at the dim filth of the shanty houses stacked on top of one another, at the gray faces of hunger passing him by in the dusk.

Brock had traveled here on purpose, or at least he thought he had. He wasn't certain why. One minute he'd been giving the wife he loved the separation she wanted, although he would rather slit his throat. The next minute, she had sneered at his offer to cut his heart out for her benefit. He simply did not understand her.

And choking on a new dose of her contempt for his serving-class origin had hurt worst of all.

Not that he was proud of his Whitechapel upbringing. On the contrary. He loathed it—but damn it all, he could not change it.

Even as a young boy, he'd run to the City, to listen to bankers and powerful men discuss fortunes won and lost. He had paid attention when they spoke, to the manner in which they had talked, vowing someday to walk in their shoes.

And he had, eventually.

At sixteen, Brock had vowed he would make something of his life. Until then, the only skill he had acquired had been as a pickpocket. But when he donned his church clothes and applied for job after job in the City, he had slowly learned that no one would accept—or believe—that an uneducated, lower-class boy could excel in their world. Dejected, he had left his father and London behind.

He'd wandered for four years, taking odd jobs with folks of quality. The elderly had been eager for someone to talk to, and they had unwittingly taught him a great deal about society, manners, proper modes of speech. Those with children always had tutors and various instructors he'd befriended and learned from.

This time, he'd vowed when he had returned to the City, no one would be able to detect a trace of his baseborn origins.

On his way to London, hunger had drawn him to Ashdown Manor, where he'd learned they were in need of a stable hand. It had been menial work, not something he intended to do for more than a few weeks.

Then he'd met Maddie. He had fallen in love with her. And his determination to do more with his life—be more—so that he might claim her became not just a fire in his belly but a compulsion.

Today, he had succeeded in business but lost Maddie.

Shoulders slumped, Brock made his way across the dusty lane, over to the worn brown door of the mean dwelling he and Jack had called home ten years earlier, and he stared, seeing not the past but the present.

Maybe Maddie had never truly been his. She was still repelled by his lowborn blood. That fact was unavoidable. And still, he could hear her voice: *You do realize that money will never buy you respect, I hope. You will always be a servant to everyone who matters.* Brock knew she included herself in that description. He voice had all but shouted that fact.

He cursed. Damn it, he could no more help where and to whom he had been born than anyone else. He had no way to escape his past. Why must she—and everyone else—punish him for it?

" 'Ello, Guv. 'Aven't see ye in a bit. Are ye well?"

Brock blinked, focused on the present, and looked down. Molly stood before him with her candle tray draped around her neck and her gaunt little cheeks smudged with dirt. She looked hungry and tired. Very hungry. But she still wore a smile for him.

"Hello, Molly. How have you been?"

"Fair, I s'pose. Me ma took sick a while back. She was dismissed."

Brock knew what that meant. Her mother hadn't been able to work and had lost her job. If she didn't get well and find a new post soon, they would starve. Chances were Molly had never known her father. Now only the money Molly made selling candle scraps kept food in their mouths. A terrible burden for a girl of six.

He did his best to keep the pity off his face, but Brock hurt just thinking about the plight this little girl had endured.

She lifted her tray over her head and set it at her feet in the foul-smelling dirt. "But Ma will get better. When she starts workin' again, I'll teach meself to read."

"That's an admirable goal. I taught myself as well."

Molly nodded solemnly. "Someday, I'll 'ave a job workin' in a fancy house."

Someday, he hoped she would be mistress of that fancy house. "You may have more," he said, "if you want it enough. Dream big, Molly. Never let anyone make you feel badly for what you want."

"More, Guv? Ye think I can?"

Brock smiled. "If you want it—"

"I surely do!"

"Then you will find a way."

Molly sighed, contented by the thought. Brock realized then that he could help her, as no one had helped him. He wouldn't give her charity; likely she would not accept it. But he could give her a start.

"What does your mother do, Molly?"

"She's a kitchen maid, Guv."

A kitchen maid. A meaningless post to him, really. He didn't even know if his household needed an extra one. "I would be pleased to hire your mother."

Molly's brown eyes rounded. "Ye would?" Then she frowned. "Where?"

Ah, removing the skeptic from the Whitechapel-bred was nearly impossible. He hoped that innate caution would serve Molly half as well as it had served him over the years.

He gave her a card with his office address. "When your mother is well enough, tell her to come to this office. You come as well. If you'll accept it, I have a very important job for you, too."

If possible, Molly's eyes widened. "Ye do?"

"Certainly. The girl you helped me find was my daughter. She is a bit younger than you, but she's lonely and needs a companion. She'll be learning to read soon, as well. Would you consider attending her classroom and helping her?"

Molly's little face fell. "Me, help 'er to read? Cor, I don't know how."

"Neither does she, but you can help each other. I will pay you as well. Fifty pounds annually. Is that acceptable?"

Her dark eyes widened to impossible widths. "Fifty pounds! That's more than I made in me bloomin' life! Aye!"

A shining grin illuminated Molly's little face. Her expression lightened his mood. In fact, he was pleased with this day's work.

Brock said good-bye and reminded Molly to bring her mother to his office as soon as may be. Molly assured him she would do just that, whistling as she walked away.

The thought of leaving this baseborn life, of being more, clearly made the girl happy. As it had made him all his life.

Whitechapel had done that to him; it had carved ambition in his gut. Every night Brock had gone to bed hungry or cold, he had wanted more. Every day he'd spent fleecing the pockets of rich folk to stay alive, he had vowed life would be better someday. Well, that day had come. And why? Because memories of the dank hopelessness that Whitechapel bred had driven him, shaped him.

Sighing, Brock looked around at the darkened streets of squalor. For once, the sting of resentment did not curl his belly. When he considered the past, he actually felt curiously . . . grateful.

Why should he be ashamed when he'd done so well for himself?

All these years, he'd been railing against his serving-class birth, bemoaning the one thing he damn well could not change. But poverty had given him the guts and the heart to achieve his dream. Yes, being disadvantaged at birth created obstacles. But he had overcome them through determination and sweat. Overcoming those hurdles had taught him far more than a life of privilege ever could.

Brock laughed aloud, not caring who heard him. Had he ever imagined he would think that? Never. But he sensed that a burden had been lifted from his shoulders, and the relief of it filled him with gladness.

In fact, he was almost pleased with his background. Proud even, for with the burgeoning railroad, he would soon accomplish everything he had dreamed of.

Well, nearly everything.

For five years, he had craved Maddie by his side, in his bed, as his wife. He had achieved the last goal—at the destruction of the first two.

Puzzled, Brock turned away from Finch Street and the past. On Whitechapel Road, he found a hack and climbed inside the musty vehicle. Though he focused his gaze on the world passing by his window, he saw nothing.

Why had Maddie not been more pleased when he'd given

her her freedom? For months she had sought nothing else. Hell, Brock thought, he had even granted her complete financial freedom, as well as autonomy. She should have been ecstatic.

Instead, her face had seemed so cold and unmoving, she might have been carved from alabaster.

Why? Why wouldn't she be happy with her independence?

She bloody well should be. Instead, she'd behaved unexpectedly, as if . . . well, as if she did not want her freedom.

The thought staggered Brock. Was that possible, or just wishful thinking?

He considered the conundrum from every angle. Again and again, he came back to the theory that Maddie did not desire his departure from her life anymore.

But why? Perhaps because she cared?

He found that thought seductive, alluring as hell, just like Maddie herself. Still, if she wanted him to stay, why did she not say so?

The drone of activity on the street resounded like a buzzing in Brock's head. He blocked it out, certain the truth lay just out of his grasp.

Why would a woman not tell a man she cared? Most obviously because she thought him beneath her. But if she cared nothing for him, wouldn't she have been elated with her freedom? One would think so.

If she wanted to be by his side but did not tell him she loved him . . . why would she keep her sentiment to herself? Certainly not because she believed he did not reciprocate her feelings. Remembering the hurt swirling in her gray eyes when he'd given her her freedom, he paused. Could she believe exactly that? Brock frowned. Was it possible Maddie thought—even for an instant—that he did not love her?

She had made the same assumption five years ago. Why not now?

Brock tried to imagine their earlier conversation from Maddie's perspective. Immediately, the truth hit him, hard as a thunderbolt from the night sky.

She viewed his gift of freedom as another abandonment on his part. Maddie believed he would leave her alone and pregnant again.

Foolish, stubborn woman!

Brock dared to smile. Maddie didn't hate him. She cared! And, with a little luck—and a great deal of devotion—perhaps she could trust him again. Even love him.

But she would have to believe he had not married her for any reason other than love.

The thought rocketed through his head. Brock tried to push it away, duck it. Once there, however, the notion took root and expanded.

What proof did he have to give Maddie of his love, beyond his words? None. None at all. Repeatedly, she had accused him of pursuing her for her land, marrying her for the money the railroad would bring him. Maddie believed he had put money above her once and would do so again.

And suddenly, he knew exactly the means by which he could prove her wrong.

Brock hesitated. Such a step would change his fate—his entire life—forever. He sighed, wishing he could pace. A glance out the window proved he was still miles from home.

Still, the choice was clear: continue to live a life filled with pounds and pence or seize the opportunity to claim Maddie once and for all.

Peace settled over Brock instantly. There was no choice, not really. Fortunes could be acquired; he'd proven he had the determination and wits to amass one already. Maddie, however, was irreplaceable.

Smiling, Brock stopped the hack driver and directed the man to his office. He had a few letters to write. . . .

* * *

The following afternoon, Maddie sat upon the sofa in her worn parlor in Hampstead. Misery had never felt so terrible, never seeped into every joint, roiled her stomach, caused such heartache.

Despite the fact she knew it was abject stupidity, she loved Brock. She had loved him as an idealistic girl who believed love could conquer all. She loved him as a jaded woman who knew love was imperfect and sometimes caused pain.

But he did not love her. That fact hurt, just as badly as the realization that she could not make him love her in return.

Back in her own home and after the hot journey to the country, Aimee had been hiding her yawns behind her little hands. Though Maddie would have appreciated the diversion her daughter always provided, she put Aimee down for a nap. Amazingly, the girl had fallen asleep immediately.

Vema was outside, communing with her garden, as was her wont. And Aunt Edith, upon hearing of the generous account Brock had established for the refurbishment of Ashdown Manor, had immediately left for London to visit friends and look at all the latest fashions in furniture.

While Maddie knew the house needed a great deal of work, she could not muster the energy. The resulting sadness of Brock's abandonment sapped too much of her energy to spend elsewhere.

Maddie rose, intending to stare aimlessly out the window once more, when she heard a shuffle from the foyer. A raised voice—a man's voice—followed.

Brock?

Stomach tightening with anticipation, Maddie ran to the parlor door. She opened it only to find her cousin Gavin filling the portal, wearing a thunderous scowl. Disappointment stung Maddie, and she hoped the surprise rolling through her would crush her uncharitable sentiment.

"What in the hell is happening here?" Gavin barked.

Maddie faltered, shrugging. "Well . . . I was merely spending a quiet afternoon at home and—"

"You can spend a quiet year at home, if you like," Gavin interrupted. "What I am trying to determine is the meaning of this?"

Her cousin held up a missive written in a scrawl of black ink on thick vellum. Instantly, she recognized Brock's penmanship. She frowned, feeling the absurd need to hold her breath.

"While I see it is from Brock, I know nothing of that letter."

"You have no notion what it says?" To say that Gavin's expression held disbelief was an understatement.

"Should I?"

"He did not tell you?" Before she could answer, Gavin held up both his hands. "He must have said *something*. You are his wife."

Yes, she was his wife, but in name only. And the fact Brock had told Cropthorne of some great news or event, rather than her, told Maddie she would never be anything but a wife in name only. Yet more proof he did not love her.

Hiding her embarrassment, forcing down her hurt, she returned to the sofa and sat, gesturing to Gavin to join her. "I'm afraid Brock has told me nothing. Perhaps if you spoke with him yourself . . ."

"I've tried. He is nowhere, apparently." Gavin leaned forward and peered at her as if in examination. "He told you nothing?"

Maddie wished he would cease asking the same question that would only result in the same discomforting answer.

"Nothing, Gavin. Truly."

"Do you love him?" her cousin asked suddenly.

The question took Maddie aback. How could she answer something so personal? How could she bare her heart to her cousin, particularly when he must know Brock did not love her in return?

"It's really of no concern."

Gavin held up a protesting finger. "Oh, but it is. If Brock is going to sacrifice the fortune we all could make on the railroad because he loves you, I think it's fair to know if his love is misplaced."

The man might as well have been speaking Greek. *Because he loves you . . .* Hope began to bloom in her tightening stomach. Shaking her head, she quickly squelched the sentiment. Likely, her cousin was mistaken.

Maddie peered at Gavin, beyond confused. Had he gone mad?

"I—I'm sorry, but I do not understand. Brock will never sacrifice anything with regard to the railroad. The land is his now, through marriage, so he may complete the track. He . . . The project has already broken ground. His entire fortune is involved in this—"

"Apparently he is willing to lose it." Gavin regarded her with a very vexed expression.

Impossible! Still, Maddie's stomach jolted with shock.

Gavin went on. "He wrote me yesterday to inform me that he is ceasing production of the T & S Railroad. He returned my investment money."

Maddie sat up, more confused now than ever. "You're certain?" At Gavin's precise nod, she asked, "Did he say why?"

"He said that, because the Warwickshire land was yours, you should be allowed to decide how it would be used."

Maddie leaned forward, mouth agape. "He wrote that?"

Hope curled in her belly.

Gavin nodded. "He also wrote that he loved you more than his fortune. What the hell does that mean?"

It sounded as if he was willing to prove in the most expensive way possible that he valued her more than all the money he had once left her for.

Stunned and joyful, Maddie leapt to her feet. Tears wet

her eyes, stung her nose, tightened her throat. She covered her face with her hands, ecstatic.

"He loves me!" she whispered.

"Yes, he wrote that," Gavin said impatiently. "What does that have to do with giving up the railroad?"

"Everything!" Her voice shook as happiness multiplied.

He loved her, more than his ambition. More than money. And he'd proven it beyond a doubt.

Why, then, had he abandoned her just yesterday? If he loved her, how could he want this civilized separation?

Perhaps he did not want it, but rather thought that *she* did.

Had she not been trying to break free of him for months?

Yes. Oh, she had to find Brock now. Sooner than now.

Maddie rose and raced for the door.

"Wait!"

She turned back to her tense-shouldered cousin.

"Madeline, you both are speaking in riddles!" Gavin sighed in frustration. "Why should he imagine that giving up a bloody fortune would have any impact on whether he loved you?"

Maddie found she could not wipe the wide smile off her face. "Perhaps someday you will understand that love does not always make sense."

With Gavin's snort of disbelief in her ears, Maddie ran out of the parlor, making plans all the while.

TWENTY

Come midnight, I will lay in Paddington and wait for you.

Madeline

Brock read the missive again, doing his best to ignore the drumbeat of his heart. He glanced up at the young messenger. "Is she awaiting a reply?"

"No, sir. She said you would understand."

Indeed, he believed he did—or at least he hoped he did. Maddie, upon learning that he valued her more than money, had freed her heart to love him. Could it be true?

He smiled, jubilation infusing him.

After pressing a groat into the youth's hand, Brock withdrew his pocket watch. Eleven o'clock. Just enough time.

He raced toward his town house's front door just as Jack walked in. "In a hurry?"

Brock grinned. "Now that we no longer have a railroad to build, I'm going to woo my wife. I have plenty of time."

Rolling his eyes, Jack stepped inside. "Did you hear from the investors?"

"Indeed. Most are angry as hell." Brock shrugged. "They will recover, I'm certain. Some have asked to purchase my Royal assent . . . and Maddie's land."

"Are you selling?"

"That's up to Maddie. But I'd say, not a chance." He smiled. "She is too important to me to ever risk losing again."

In one of the few fatherly actions of his life, Jack hugged his son. Brock was grateful for his sire's understanding.

"Go claim her. And hold on tight. I lost your mother so soon, before I learned the importance of living every day for such love. Now that you know—"

"Now that I know"—Brock clapped his father on the shoulder—"I'll be sure to hold her forever."

If she would truly have him.

The next hour was a blur of night, stars, wind, and wishes. They all passed his consciousness, danced along his senses, along with utter impatience. He could scarcely wait to see Maddie, to hold her. It had been weeks since he'd made love to her. . . .

Forcing his mind down another path, Brock was relieved when he and his winded mount finally arrived in front of the darkened Paddington cottage. He withdrew his pocket watch. Two minutes past midnight. God willing, Maddie would still be lying here, waiting for him.

Brock bolted to the door and thrust his way inside, shoving the door out of his path. A look down the foyer into the breakfast nook proved it empty. Charging across the empty space, Brock sprinted around the corner, into the parlor.

And there lay Maddie, draped on the plush rose settee, wearing her wedding ring, her stockings—and nothing else.

Brock felt his mouth go dry and his body spring to attention.

"I see you received my missive," Maddie all but purred.

"Indeed," he choked. "I have a hundred things to say to you, but I can hardly think when you look so enticing."

Maddie smiled. "Must we talk now?"

The seductive note in Maddie's voice nearly undid Brock's good intentions. He sighed. "Unfortunately, yes."

Vowing he would soon deal with the disappointment on

Maddie's face, Brock scanned the room and found a woolen lap blanket. He grabbed the blue coverlet and shook it flat, then handed it to Maddie, concealing the vanilla-and-jasmine-scented nudity that was quickly driving rational thought from his brain.

His lovely wife merely pouted. "And here I thought, perhaps, that you wanted me."

He groaned. "Without a doubt, I do."

Nodding, Maddie sat up, her face serious now. "I also thought, perhaps, that you . . . loved me."

Erasing the empty space between them with two steps, Brock sank to the settee and swept his arms about Maddie. "You should have no doubts on that score, my darling wife. I love you more than . . . anything. More than I thought possible." He squeezed her shoulders. "More than I ever realized."

Maddie smiled, the expression so beautiful, so luminous with happiness, Brock's breath caught in his throat. He wanted to see her this happy each and every day. The fact that his love made her happy . . . He swelled with pride and need—and more love.

"And I love you," she murmured.

The happiness he had hoped for, had been saving forever it seemed, burst within Brock. He grinned so widely, he felt sure his smile matched hers. "Yes, but have you always loved me?"

Slowly, Maddie nodded. "Even when I wished I didn't."

He brought his palm up to cradle her cheek. "I've loved you from the day I met you."

At his simple words, Maddie's face fell into a mass of tears. "Why did we waste so many years apart?"

Brock hugged her, doing his best to soothe her with a soft hand at her nape. "I *never* should have left you after making love to you that first time. I should have insisted we marry and brought you to London with me."

Brock could see the questions hovering in her eyes, but

she did not give them voice. She trusted him now and wanted to put the past behind them! God, he felt like the luckiest man alive.

But he also wanted to explain.

"It was me, Maddie. I left you with your father because I had nothing. I knew I was going to live in squalor. I couldn't take you with me. I was ashamed, and I'm so damned sorry," he whispered. "My pride came between us. I believed I wasn't good enough for you as I was."

Maddie gasped, and more tears fell. She curled her arms around his neck and squeezed him. "I never cared where you were born, or to whom. It did not matter where you lived. I only wanted the wonderful man I fell in love with to love me in return."

"Instead, I made you believe I'd betrayed you by accepting your father's money, and I'm sorry. I bloody wish I had refused his insulting offer. I wanted to. But I wanted the money so badly. With it, I knew I could soon amass a fortune you could be proud of."

"And you did." Her eyes were a soft gray, full of pride.

"At a terrible cost. I spent five years without you, without Aimee—"

At his words, Maddie sobbed harder, gray eyes like rain clouds, intense and vivid. "I should have told you about her long ago. I did you both a terrible injustice—"

"When you conceived, you did not know where to find me in London. I realize that now," he assured her, his voice soft.

"But later, when we became . . . lovers."

"I threatened you."

"Yes, but even after I knew you would not send us to the Fleet, I kept my secret. I—I"—Maddie shook her head, as if searching for words—"I feared you had the same contempt for me as Colin. I was angry with you, as well, for not realizing that I married Colin only because I had no choice." She sighed. "That seems foolish, I realize—"

"No, you only asked me to see my own daughter. I was too blinded by jealousy and greed to do so."

"Brock, please, let me apologize. Aimee is your daughter, and you had the right to know. I denied you that right. For that, I am sorry." She peered up at him, her gray eyes drenched with new tears, no longer a siren, but a woman— with a woman's heart. "But I was afraid. Of your wealth, of your anger. I feared you would take Aimee from me or use her against me—"

"Shhh." He held her close, soothing her. "We both made poor choices. Can you forgive me?"

"Of course. I only hope you find it within you to do the same for me."

"It's done," he vowed. "And we have nothing but the future ahead of us."

Maddie frowned. "Yes, a future without a railroad, if I'm to understand Gavin correctly."

Brock shrugged. "I no longer need to build it. I realize that building it might make me wealthier, but it will never change who I am or where I came from. The only respect I need in business is that I give myself." He grimaced sheepishly. "That is something I have never done."

"Oh." She held him tighter. "How clever you are!"

"No. It took me far too long to realize that I could not force the *ton* to accept me. Now, I no longer care if they do. I know my ability to make money. And wherever there is a nobleman desperate for new funds, I will be there. I shall make us a new fortune doing it."

"Your money is truly gone?"

"Most of it, yes." He cocked a teasing brow at her. "Are you disturbed by that fact?"

"Indeed!" She sat up, clutching the blanket above her breasts. "Have we not both had enough of poverty?"

Suddenly, Brock was reminded of her nakedness. His concentration strayed. "If you say so." He leaned down to plant a string of kisses on her neck, her shoulders.

Maddie softened under his ministration. "This is serious," she protested weakly. "You should build the railroad."

"There will always be opportunities to make money. It would be a crime, however"—he brushed a kiss over her waiting mouth—"to allow an opportunity to make love to my wife slip away."

"Perhaps what we need is a wager."

Brock paused, assessing her sultry smile. "Are you challenging me again?"

"Indeed." She smiled wickedly. Then she dropped one corner of the blanket to reveal a perfect breast.

His mouth went dry.

She laughed. "Here are my terms: If you can resist me"—she dropped the other corner of her blanket to reveal her other pink-tipped breast—"you may return us to poverty as you see fit. We will always have one another, is that not so?"

Brock could do nothing more than nod dumbly and reach for the perfection of Maddie's creamy skin.

"If you cannot resist me, however," she purred, throwing the blanket to the ground, leaving the long length of her legs and everything between breath-stoppingly visible, "then you will build this railroad, continue your dream, and be happy by my side."

Before Brock could respond, Maddie reached for his shirt and pulled it from his breeches, over his head. She placed a series of soft kisses upon his neck and chest. Her tongue flicked across a suddenly sensitive nipple. He could not hold back his groan.

"What do you say, Mr. Taylor?" She writhed deliciously beneath him. Brock felt desire claw at his belly.

Using his last shred of coherency, he muttered, "You're certain you won't mind the railroad?"

Maddie slanted her mouth across his, opening beneath him like a flower to the morning sun. Brock could not resist her invitation and took complete possession of her mouth.

Long moments later, Maddie broke the kiss. "I won't mind. Your gesture was noble. That you were willing to give it up at all proves you love me."

"I do," he murmured and took her mouth again. "I love you very much."

With a hand between them, Brock did his best to remove his uncomfortably tight breeches. Laughing, Maddie helped him.

"I love you, too," she whispered. "Does it make you ache to know I want to take every inch of you inside me and make love with you until you can no longer see straight?"

"Definitely," he groaned, tugging his breeches down past his knees, his ankles.

Maddie grabbed them and tossed them across the room. "So, do I win the wager? Or can you resist me?"

Brock slid inside her, a slow, slick homecoming. Maddie gasped as she held him tight. Nothing had ever felt more perfect as having Maddie as his wife, his friend, his lover . . . his everything. He had never felt this close to forever. He intended to hold on to it always.

"Resist you?" he murmured as he eased a gentle kiss on her mouth. "I won't even try."

If you enjoyed STRICTLY SEDUCTION, be sure to watch for
Shelley Bradley's next fabulous romance,
STRICTLY FORBIDDEN,
available in bookstores everywhere,
September 2002.

A PASSION MORE POWERFUL THAN PROPRIETY

Miss Kira Melbourne is anything but a proper English rose. Her exotic beauty, courtesy of her foreign mother, has marked her as an outsider, and her ghastly reputation as a woman of loose virtue has only added to that status. The victim of a devious viscount's horrible lies, Kira has the chance to redeem herself and become a member of polite society as the fiancée of a respected country clergyman. She'll finally have a place to belong . . . even if it's in the tepid arms of a man she doesn't love.

Gavin Daggett, Duke of Cropthorne, isn't about to let his naïve country cousin marry a scandalous woman like Kira Melbourne. The solution is a simple one: Gavin will seduce the vixen and prove her unworthiness, thereby releasing his cousin from any obligation. But spending time with Kira is like awakening to a world of color and beauty, and it stirs the fiery desires Gavin has fought to suppress his entire life. Caught in his own dangerous game, sharing forbidden pleasure with Kira, Gavin knows that the price for loving her is high—and yet it is one that he will willingly pay . . . with every beat of his heart.

ABOUT THE AUTHOR

Originally from Southern California, Shelley Bradley is now a transplanted Texan, living in the Dallas area with her husband and preschool-age daughter. Shortly after reading her first romance in college, she became determined to write her own stories, tales designed to touch readers' hearts. Her March 2001 release, HIS REBEL BRIDE, received a KISS hero award from Romantic Times. To date, Shelley has won or placed in over a dozen writing contests, including Romance Writers of America's prestigious Golden Heart. Besides enjoying a good romance novel, she hates ironing, and loves traveling, dancing, football (go Cowboys!), and anything chocolate.

Visit Shelley on the Web at www.shelleybradley.com, or write to her at: P.O. Box 270126, Flower Mound, TX 75057.

<u>BOOK YOUR PLACE ON OUR WEBSITE</u> AND MAKE THE <u>READING CONNECTION!</u>

We've created a customized website just for our very special readers, where you can get the inside scoop on everything that's going on with Zebra, Pinnacle and Kensington books.

When you come online, you'll have the exciting opportunity to:

- View covers of upcoming books
- Read sample chapters
- Learn about our future publishing schedule (listed by publication month *and author*)
- Find out when your favorite authors will be visiting a city near you
- Search for and order backlist books from our online catalog
- Check out author bios and background information
- Send e-mail to your favorite authors
- Meet the Kensington staff online
- Join us in weekly chats with authors, readers and other guests
- Get writing guidelines
- AND MUCH MORE!

Visit our website at
http://www.kensingtonbooks.com

DO YOU HAVE THE
HOHL COLLECTION?

The Queen of
Romance

Cassie Edwards

__Desire's Blossom 0-8217-6405-5	$5.99US/$7.99CAN
__Exclusive Ecstasy 0-8217-6597-3	$5.99US/$7.99CAN
__Passion's Web 0-8217-5726-1	$5.99US/$7.50CAN
__Portrait of Desire 0-8217-5862-4	$5.99US/$7.50CAN
__Savage Obsession 0-8217-5554-4	$5.99US/$7.50CAN
__Silken Rapture 0-8217-5999-X	$5.99US/$7.50CAN
__Rapture's Rendezvous 0-8217-6115-3	$5.99US/$7.50CAN

Call toll free **1-888-345-BOOK** to order by phone or use this coupon to order by mail.

Name_____

Address_____

City_____ State _____ Zip _____

Please send me the books that I have checked above.

I am enclosing $_____

Plus postage and handling* $_____

Sales tax (in New York and Tennessee) $_____

Total amount enclosed $_____

*Add $2.50 for the first book and $.50 for each additional book. Send check or money order (no cash or CODs) to:

Kensington Publishing Corp., 850 Third Avenue, New York, NY 10022

Prices and numbers subject to change without notice.

All orders subject to availability.

Check out our website at **www.kensingtonbooks.com**.